PRIMAL
DECEPTION

JACK SILKSTONE

BOOKS

By Jack Silkstone

The PRIMAL Series

PRIMAL Origin
PRIMAL Unleashed
PRIMAL Vengeance
PRIMAL Fury
PRIMAL Reckoning
PRIMAL Nemesis
PRIMAL Redemption
PRIMAL Renegade
PRIMAL Deception
PRIMAL Exodus

PRIMAL books are dedicated to those who have fought for a just cause.

Vinci Books

vinci-books.com

Published by Vinci Books Ltd in 2025

1

Copyright © Jack Silkstone 2016

The author has asserted their moral right to be identified as the author of this work in accordance with the Copyright, Designs and Patents Act 1988. This work is a work of fiction. Names, characters, places and incidents are the product of the author's imagination or are used fictitiously. Any resemblance to actual persons, living or dead, places and incidents is entirely coincidental.

All rights reserved. No part of this publication may be copied, reproduced, distributed, stored in any retrieval system, or transmitted in any form or by any means, including photocopying, recording, or other electronic or mechanical methods, nor used as a source for any form of machine learning including AI datasets, without the prior written permission of the publisher.

The publisher and the author have made every effort to obtain permissions for any third party material used in this book and to comply with copyright law. Any queries in this respect should be brought to the attention of the publisher and any omissions will be corrected in future editions.

A CIP catalogue record for this book is available from the British Library.

Paperback ISBN: 9781036701970

Printed and bound in Great Britain by Clays Ltd, Elcograf S.p.A.

Prologue

JARJANAZ, SYRIA

THE RAMP of the Hercules LM-100J dropped with a whine and Aden Bishop shielded his eyes from the sand that whipped inside the cargo hold. The tall dark-haired Australian pulled on a pair of goggles and lifted his shemagh to cover his nose and mouth as he peered out of the aircraft.

"Bish, chock the wheels. This wind is trying to push us back to the Emirates," transmitted the pilot through his cordless headset.

"Roger." Bishop unhooked the blocks of plastic joined by rope and strode down the ramp to the dirt airstrip.

He glanced around. There wasn't much to see. Thick red dust hung in the air and in the distance a massive wall of sand crept toward them. He quickly shoved the blocks against the aircraft's wheels before returning inside.

"No sign of our reception party yet," he transmitted.

Deep within war-torn Syria, the aid delivery was a typical mission for Priority Movements Airlift, a specialized wing of Lascar Logistics.

"What do you think, Mirza?" the captain asked his copilot, Mirza Mansoor, over the intercom.

"We'll give them ten minutes. If they don't turn up we should takeoff, get clear of this sandstorm, and head across to Baghdad."

"Sounds like a plan."

Bishop stood on the ramp peering into the gloom. Dark shapes grew until they were recognizable as vehicles. "We've got company."

A convoy of four-wheel drives materialized from the sandstorm and parked in a line facing the aircraft's ramp. "Five vehicles, Red Crescent markings," he reported as figures appeared. "At least eight guys."

"Acknowledged, I'm coming back now," replied Mirza.

The men strode forward unarmed with their faces wrapped in keffiyehs, traditional Arabic scarves. One of them stopped at the ramp and lifted his hand in greeting. "*As-salaam alaykum*," he offered in a soft voice, dropping the scarf to reveal a narrow face with a protruding chin and scraggly facial hair. "My name is Salim."

Mirza, a bearded dark-skinned Indian, appeared from behind the crates of supplies secured in the cargo hold. His hard Asiatic features softened with a welcoming smile. "*Wa alaykum salaam*, Salim, it's a pleasure to meet you. My name is Mirza and this is Aden."

"The pleasure is mine." Salim gestured to the crates. "Are all of these for us?" The aircraft was stacked with wooden boxes stamped with World Health Organization markings.

Bishop nodded. "Yes and we need them offloaded as quickly as we can."

"Of course, you wish to beat the storm. We will hurry." He turned and snapped an order to his men. They formed a line as Bishop released the cargo straps.

The first pair of men lifted one of the wooden crates and struggled down the ramp with it. They were immediately replaced by two more, who lifted the next box clear.

He watched as they rapidly unloaded the stores from the back of the four-engine transporter and piled them on the sand-covered runway. Once all the boxes were stacked in front of the vehicles Bishop recovered the chocks and ducked back inside.

Mirza shook hands with Salim and the Syrian strode out of the cargo hold and down the ramp.

Bishop looked beyond him at the looming sandstorm as Mirza headed back to the cockpit. "Pedal to the metal, guys, we need to get the hell out of here."

"On it," replied the pilot.

The Hercules' engines roared at full thrust adding more sand and wind to the mix. Bishop hit the ramp button as he watched the workers struggle to keep the stack of supplies upright. One crate toppled over and splintered, tossing its contents across the sand. He caught a glimpse of dark green tubing among the broken wood.

When the ramp thumped shut he removed his goggles and scarf and secured himself in the loadmaster's seat. He felt the aircraft gather speed, bounce and lurch into the sky. It shuddered as the storm hit.

"Hold on, this is going to be rough," transmitted Mirza in a tense voice.

"That's what she said," managed Bishop as he braced

himself. The turbulence tossed him violently in his seat as they tried to outrun the storm.

After five minutes of turmoil they leveled out and he unclipped his safety belt. As he walked toward the cockpit a glance out the side window revealed clear blue skies.

Bishop climbed the short ladder to the cockpit and opened the door. "Mirza, can I have a quick word?"

"What was in the boxes?" he asked once they were back in the cargo hold.

"You know, medical supplies."

He shook his head. "That's not what I saw."

"What did you see?"

"Goddamn TOW missiles."

Mirza frowned. "You sure?"

"I know what a bloody TOW looks like. Tariq has some explaining to do." Bishop referred to the CEO of Lascar Logistics, the parent company responsible for delivery of the humanitarian aid contract.

"He might not know this is happening, the UAE government organized the payload."

"Then someone's using him, or he's using us. We have no idea where those missiles will end up."

Mirza nodded. "There's another shipment due out in two days."

"We need to find out exactly what's going on."

Mirza returned to the cockpit leaving Bishop alone in the empty cargo hold. He walked across to the aircraft's side door and peered through the window at the desert landscape below. His thoughts turned to his former lover, Saneh. She was probably in South East Asia by now, or so he hoped, turning to meditation and yoga to come to terms with the loss of their child. She had her way of dealing with loss and he had his. He would find out who was using

Priority Movements Airlift to smuggle sophisticated weapons into a civil war rife with rogue militias and religious extremists. He had a new mission, one close to his heart. Poachers may have taken his child but it was an arms dealer who had cost him his parents.

Chapter One

MOSUL, IRAQ

THICK, acrid smoke billowed up from behind the wall of sand-filled wire cages that fortified an Iraqi Army outpost. A flash lit the early morning sky, and the earth shuddered as a massive fireball rose above the base. A smile spread across Mohammed 'Al-Bab' Yassin's face as he watched the destruction through a pair of binoculars. There was a cheer from the men gathered around him as a second explosion followed the first.

The battle was part of a coordinated ISIS offensive against Mosul. Taking the Iraqi Army by surprise, they were on the verge of capturing the city. Mohammed, an Islamic State warlord, had left the primary offensive for his Sunni brothers. His target was the Iraqi Army compound and the weapons and munitions within.

From over a mile away he supervised the engagement, sitting on the hood of his captured armored Humvee. A suicide bomber had initiated the attack followed by a barrage of 120mm mortar bombs. Now, his fighters lay concealed in an irrigation ditch ready to make the final assault. A grin parted his cracked lips revealing yellowed teeth through a thick beard. In a matter of moments the outpost would fall, and he would have his spoils.

The snap and hiss of high-velocity rounds sent him diving behind his Humvee. One of his men was a fraction slower. The fighter's head exploded, splattering Mohammed with blood and gore.

Using the tail of his black keffiyeh, he wiped his face then raised his radio. "What the hell was that?"

The radio crackled as one of his men reported, "A tank, they're trying to escape in a tank."

Mohammed ignored the rounds snapping overhead and rose to a knee. In the distance he could see an Iraqi Army armored vehicle, one of the American-supplied Strykers, leaving the burning outpost. The remote-controlled turret on top of the eight-wheeled beast spat rounds at them.

Mohammed clenched his jaw. "Kill it."

A moment later a detonation sounded from one of his technicals, a Toyota pickup fitted with a TOW missile launcher. He caught a glimpse of the missile as it streaked across the desert and slammed into the Stryker. There was a flash, and the machine gun turret flipped a dozen feet into the air.

Screams of *Allahu Akbar!* filled the air as he yelled into his radio, "Send the warriors forward!" He lifted his binoculars and squinted. Through the thick haze of battle he could make out figures running and firing AKs, leapfrogging each other toward the outpost. The destroyed Stryker burnt fiercely a dozen yards from the entrance.

Climbing to his feet, he glanced down the line of technicals he commanded. Pointing at the Toyota with the TOW launcher, he called out, "The man who killed the tank will have a slave tonight."

A grinning face appeared from behind the launcher. "Thank you, Al-Bab."

Hearing a cough from his left he turned to face his second-in-command, Abu Malik.

The squat Syrian shook his head. "We're running out of women. If you promise them, and we do not have them, they will not fight."

His lip curled. "If they don't fight they will die. I don't have money to waste on whores." He gestured to their vehicles where bedraggled children, old men and women were collared and chained. "Give him one of them."

The radio in Mohammed's hand crackled, and he held it to his ear.

"The fortress is ours!" reported one of his squad leaders.

"The fortress is ours!" he screamed manically.

More cheers of *Allahu Akbar* overwhelmed the distant sound of gunfire as Mohammed climbed into the passenger seat of his Humvee. Malik joined him in the cabin as he waited for their human shields to clamber aboard. The armored vehicle rattled to life and Malik steered them behind another truck, toward the captured Iraqi outpost.

When they entered the compound they were greeted with cheers from fighters dressed in camouflage coats and waving assault rifles. A line of captured Iraqi soldiers knelt facing the perimeter wall. The bodies of their comrades sprawled in the sand.

As Mohammed alighted from his Humvee one of his men approached, grinning broadly.

"You must see what we have found."

He led Mohammed past a row of burning vehicles to a

concrete pillbox. He ducked inside, and Mohammed followed him down a flight of dusty stairs. Below, lit by flickering fluorescent lights, was a bunker stacked to the roof with green military crates. He checked the markings on them: 120mm mortars, M72 rocket launchers and crate after crate of ammunition.

"Excellent," he whispered.

"There's more." The fighter directed him past a dead Iraqi officer to a smaller room.

Inside, black plastic equipment cases were stacked waist high. One lay open, revealing its contents, bundles of crisp US hundred dollar bills.

"How many have money?"

"All the ones we opened."

"Post a guard and check the rest." Mohammed climbed the stairs back out into the smoke-filled compound. As he strode past Malik, the compact Syrian fired him a question.

"What do you want done with the prisoners?"

"Burn them." Mohammed reached his vehicle and pulled a satchel from the cabin. Removing a phone, he tossed the bag back inside, pulled a notebook from his assault vest and flicked it open. The number he wanted was scribbled on the first page. He made the call and as the phone rang, he watched one of his men approach with a gas can.

The call connected. "Salim, is that you?" he asked over the terrified cries of the prisoners.

There was a pause before a soft voice answered. "Yes, who is this?"

"Mohammed!"

"Ah, my old friend. How are you?"

"Good, I have the means to order more of your wares."

"You haven't settled your last debt."

"I have the money and more. Cash. US dollars."

"Then I can get whatever you need."

Mohammed watched as the man with the gas can doused the prisoners with fuel. "I want more TOWs. As many as you can supply." The powerful anti-tank missiles were the key to defeating both Iraqi and Kurdish armor. An unlimited supply would make Al-Bab even more influential among his extremist peers.

"I'll do my best."

"And get me more brides for my men, good Islamic girls. In a week I will return to Al-Bab. You can deliver them then."

"They will be ready."

"Good, I will send someone with the money I owe." He ended the call and fished a packet of cigarettes from his vest. Lighting one he strolled across to the fuel-soaked prisoners. There were six Iraqi soldiers in the line, all begging for their lives and crying for Allah. The man with the gas can locked eyes with him, and Mohammed gestured for him to leave. Sucking back on the cigarette he stood behind the prisoners and relished in their fear.

Then, when he grew tired of their wailing, he flicked the cigarette into the fuel-drenched sand. A faint roar filled the air and flame flashed over the men. It took a split second for them to realize they were alight and then they screamed. The blaze gained intensity as their clothes and hair ignited. Mohammed took another cigarette from his vest, lit it, and stepped back from the heat and stench. One by one the burning prisoners toppled over, writhing in agony. He watched impassively until the screams died and they were smoldering blackened corpses. Turning he waved to Malik. "Bring up the trucks and have the men load the equipment."

"We could have used the prisoners as human shields."

He flicked his cigarette and shrugged. "Go to the town and get more." He returned to his Humvee and the civilians shackled to it. Grinning, he glanced skyward. Somewhere high above one of the American Predator drones could be watching. But, as long as he had his shields, they wouldn't dare strike for fear of civilian deaths. Ultimately, that was why they would not defeat the Islamic State.

COVENTRY, ENGLAND

The two brothers sat in a high performance Ford Fiesta parked on a bustling street in Coventry. Recent converts to Islam, they watched the lunchtime crowds of unbelievers through a rain-flecked windshield. Mubarez was the older of the two. Tall, Caucasian, with a lean build, he drummed the fingers of one hand on the steering wheel as he rubbed his freshly shaved face with the other. Alongside, his brother Saifan sat clutching a camera with white-knuckled hands. Both youths were dressed to blend with the passing foot traffic. They wore jeans, hoodies, gloves and baseball caps pulled low to hide their faces.

His brother squinted through the windshield. "Look, there."

Mubarez activated the wipers, clearing the drops from the glass. Thirty yards away, between pedestrians, he spotted the fluorescent yellow vests worn by the police. Their domed black helmets bobbed through the crowds as they approached. Turning to his brother, he managed a faint smile. "For the glory of Allah."

"For the glory of Allah," Saifan repeated.

He slipped a hand up his sleeve and touched a razor-sharp hunting knife strapped to his arm. A second check identified the Taser in each pocket. Glancing through the windshield, he confirmed the two police officers were approaching. They were now less than fifteen yards away and closing.

"Are you ready?"

"Yes."

"Then, let's do this." Mubarez climbed from the hatchback and shut his door. Reaching into his pockets he grasped the Tasers, flicking off the safety bail on each. Saifan appeared on the opposite side of the car and shot him a grave look. Heart pounding, he strode onto the wet pavement. A glance over his shoulder confirmed his brother was following.

The fluorescent vests of the two male police officers shone like beacons as they strode along the sidewalk. His mind raced. How easy it would be to walk past them and continue down the street. No, that was not his destiny. Allah had plans for him, Imam Rahman had told him so.

He passed the officers and turned, breathing hard. Clutching both Tasers he pulled them from his hoodie and lunged forward, jamming the prongs against their vests.

One of the officers arched his back with a moan and fell face down on the asphalt. His partner staggered forward, recovered and spun clutching at his belt.

Mubarez's heart skipped a beat as the officer extended his baton with a snap of his wrist.

"Drop the weapons!" the man ordered raising the baton.

Adrenaline coursed through his veins and he contemplated running. Then, two gunshots sounded. Pedestrians screamed and scattered as Mubarez watched the face of the police officer. The man's eyes went wide and blood bubbled from his mouth. He pitched forward and hit the asphalt with a wet slap. Behind him stood Saifan, a pistol clutched in one hand, the camera in the other.

The shriek of a bystander jolted Mubarez into action and he drew the knife from his sleeve. Kneeling, he pulled the helmet from the stunned police officer. The man convulsed on the pavement, his eyes wide with terror. Grabbing a fistful of hair, he plunged the knife into his throat. Crimson blood sprayed from the mortal wound, jetting across the sidewalk.

Bloodlust overcame Mubarez and he wrenched his victim's head up by the hair and hacked at his neck. The officer managed a gurgle as the jihadist screamed with rage. The blade sliced cleanly through flesh until it ground against the spine. The body spasmed and Mubarez pressed his knees against the man's chest as he sawed with the knife. Finally, after what seemed like minutes, he managed to sever the bone, beheading the policeman. Climbing to his feet he held the head high and screamed at the top of his lungs, "For the glory of Allah! For my brothers in Syria!"

"For Allah!" his brother joined the chant.

The wail of sirens interrupted their celebration.

Mubarez spun towards the sound. He had no intention of becoming a martyr. The Imam had told him he would travel to Syria to wage jihad. "We need to go."

He sprinted back to the car with the head swinging in his grip. He caught a glimpse of his reflection in a window. His face was splattered with blood, a mask of rage and adrenaline. Finally, he was a warrior.

Saifan was already waiting inside the hatchback. The younger brother had tears flowing from his eyes. "I killed him. I killed the copper."

He tossed the severed head into the back and started the engine. "Yes, you did, my brother. Today we both killed. Today we became lions of Allah."

Spinning the wheel he pulled out and accelerated along the busy street. Glancing in the mirror, he spotted the flashing lights of a police car.

Saifan dropped the pistol and camera into the footwell. "I'm scared, Michael," he said, using his brother's birth name.

"My name is Mubarez," he snapped.

Saifan wept as they swerved around a garbage truck.

"You are a warrior, my brother. Stay brave, for Allah, for the Imam and for me." He sent the turbocharged Ford screeching around a corner. Grinning, he stomped on the gas; there was no way the police could catch them before they reached the safety of Birmingham.

BIRMINGHAM, ENGLAND

The Audi A6 Estate roared as Senior Constable Peters downshifted, sending the unmarked police vehicle screaming past a patrol car. As they flashed past, siren blaring, the cop behind the wheel shot he and his partner a nod.

Peters and his partner Constable Reynolds were Firearms Officers of the West Midlands police force. Clad in black tactical rigs, their Armed Response Vehicle was laden with weapons and equipment. They'd been on the other side of Coventry when 'officers down' had hit the airways. An avid motorhead and weekend racer, Peters had gotten them across town and onto the A45 in a matter of minutes.

"Eyes on," reported Reynolds. The former Royal Marine had an MP5 submachine gun across his knees.

Peters spotted the Ford Fiesta a hundred yards ahead. The hot hatch weaved haphazardly through traffic.

His partner clung to the grab handle. "These murdering assholes reach Birmingham, and they're gone, mate."

"Yeah, got it."

Peters closed the gap with the Fiesta to a car length as they flashed past the sign indicating the turnoff to one of England's largest Islamic communities.

"I'm going in for the PIT." The Pursuit Immobilization Technique was a maneuver that enabled a skilled driver to disable a fleeing vehicle.

"Go for it. You've got a hundred yards till the exit."

Peters accelerated the Audi in behind the hatchback. Ahead he could see the off-ramp. If he timed it right, he could use the median strip to his advantage.

"Fifty yards," announced Reynolds.

Peters moved the car to one side, ready to touch bumpers. The Fiesta suddenly swerved around a taxi. Flicking the steering wheel, the officer narrowly avoided a collision at ninety miles an hour. "Shit!"

The Fiesta sped off the highway and down an access road as Peters fought to keep the Audi from spinning out of control. Tires squealed as he skidded onto the off-ramp before recovering and accelerating after the suspects.

Reynolds lowered his window and raised his submachine gun as trees flashed past on either side of the car. "I can go for the tires."

Ahead the Fiesta barreled through an intersection.

"Too risky." Peters turned a knob, increasing the intensity of their siren.

"We've got to stop them before someone else gets killed."

Buildings replaced trees as they roared through Birmingham's outer suburbs. The Fiesta filled the windshield as Peters brought them bumper-to-bumper. The smaller car skidded around a corner, and he held the Audi in a slide, bumpers touching. As they raced across an intersection, he turned a little harder and pumped the accelerator.

The Fiesta swerved to one side, and Peter slowed as the driver overcorrected. The hatchback rose onto two wheels and teetered for a second. Then, as it slammed back down, it spun and smashed through a row of parked cars into a light pole.

Peters brought the Audi to a smooth halt and leaped out, drawing his pistol. Reynolds was already approaching the crumpled Fiesta, his MP5 held ready. Scanning the street Peters spotted bearded men and burka-clad women emerging from the houses on either side.

One of the doors on the Fiesta popped open and a young Caucasian in a hoodie and baseball cap staggered out.

"Police, let me see your hands!" screamed Peters.

The man turned toward them. He had a gash on his face; the car door hid his hands.

"Show me your hands!"

Peters saw the pistol appear from behind the door. He registered the two shots fired by Reynolds and saw the youth fall backward as the rounds struck his chest.

A flash of movement caught his eye, and Peters ducked as a brick smashed into the roof of the Audi. A group of men had gathered further along the road. They were joined by women and children as more people emerged from their homes.

"Police get out!" screamed a woman as she broke from the group and threw a rock.

"We've got a second guy," bellowed Reynolds.

Another youth emerged from the Fiesta and stumbled down the street. He looked to be wounded and unarmed.

Reynolds shifted his aim. "Stop or I will shoot!"

Before either of them could react the crowd swept forward, shielding the perpetrator.

Peters grabbed his radio. "Base this is Trojan Two-Four we're in Bordesley Green. Request immediate backup and crowd control."

No sooner had he spoken than a bottle sailed over the crowd and smashed into the car.

"Cops get out!" chanted the horde. "Cops get out!"

"Fuck, boss, what do we do?" Reynolds had his MP5 trained on the crowd.

"Do not fucking shoot. You fire and they'll tear this town apart."

"We don't shoot, and they'll fucking kill us."

A youth ran forward from the crowd and tossed half a brick at the car. It smashed into the windshield splintering the glass. In the distance, sirens wailed. Backup was minutes away.

Peters locked eyes with his partner. "We got one of them. Let's get the hell out of here."

He got no objection from Reynolds as they climbed into the car and he dropped it into reverse. The crowd surged forward as he glanced over his shoulder and accelerated. At the end of the street he yanked on the wheel, skidded the car around, and threw it into gear.

Reynolds punched the dashboard. "We just let that cop-killing prick go."

"We'll go in once the riot boys arrive," he said as they sped away from the enraged mob.

Ahead of them, two police cars were stopped either side of the street, their lights flashing. Peters slowed the Audi between them and lowered his window. "How long till the riot squad arrives?" he asked the constable inside.

"The OSU won't be here for twenty minutes but that won't change anything. We can't go in there. Count yourselves lucky you got out alive."

Peters frowned. "What do you mean, you can't go in there?"

"Imam Rahman. Evil fucker's got the whole community under his thumb. We can't enter without his authority."

Reynolds shook his head. "We can't get in to apprehend a cop-killing terrorist? What the hell is England coming to?"

Chapter Two

BIRMINGHAM, ENGLAND

ESHITA SAT cross-legged at the front of the group of youths and listened intently to the words of the Imam. Born in India, the fifteen-year-old had immigrated with her father only six months earlier. Culturally and emotionally the move had been an upheaval. She'd left all of her friends to come to a strange country whose language she barely understood.

The first few months were lonely. Her father worked long hours and was rarely around. She spent most of her time on the web chatting to friends in India. But then she met Vashti and everything changed. Now she had a friend who spoke her language. A girl her age who understood what it was like to be a young Muslim girl in the western world. It was Vashti who had invited her to Imam Rahman's youth groups.

She drank in every word that spilled from the long-bearded Imam's mouth. He spoke with such conviction, such passion, and on topics that mattered to her and her new friend. He was a light, shining into the dark corners of the community, revealing the oppression and segregation of Sunni Muslims.

The Imam sat in a comfortable chair, dressed in white robes and matching kufi cap. His dozen students, all teenage girls, sat before him. He cleared his throat and continued the lecture. "Yesterday an atrocity occurred in our community."

Eshita swallowed and fought back tears.

"A son of Allah, a warrior in our battle against oppression, was martyred by the Crusaders." He paused, his face stern. "Saifan and his brother Mubarez struck down two of the enemy. But then they invaded our community and murdered him before his friends and family."

Eshita felt Vashti take her hand, and she turned to her friend as tears welled in her eyes. They both knew the softly spoken Steven from before he had adopted his Islamic name. An English convert, he and his brother had been accepted into their community as one of their own.

"It may seem helpless," Imam Rahman continued, "but Saifan did not die in vain. He struck at our oppressors, and he has inspired others. His brother and other warriors will leave soon for the Caliphate. There they will fight like lions to free our lands from the oppressors..."

Eshita's grip on her friend's hand tightened.

"But, the fight is not only for the brothers. They need sisters to stand with them in their struggle. They need women to tend the wounded, to prepare food and to bring them bullets."

The Imam continued to lecture, but Eshita did not hear him. In her mind, she was now in Syria standing alongside Mubarez as he fought back against the oppressors of her faith. She felt pride and something else, something she had never felt before in England, a sense of belonging.

A squeeze of her hand snapped her back to reality. "Eshita, the sermon is over. It's time to go."

As the girls walked home, they passed a group of young men patrolling the streets. With their hijabs on and in each other's company, the girls had nothing to fear from the Sharia patrol. In fact, it gave Eshita confidence to know that the young men were keeping crime at bay. "I want to go to Syria," she announced as they waited at an intersection.

Vashti grasped her shoulder. "Really?"

"Yes!"

Her friend smiled. "I want to do the same thing. I think the Imam is right. It is our duty and the will of Allah."

Eshita hugged her friend. "Then we will go together."

"It is important not to tell your father. He will never let you go."

She released her friend and smiled grimly. "He won't even know I am gone. When will we leave?"

"As soon as we can. I will ask the Imam. Pack a bag and wait for my call."

As Eshita walked the last block to her house, she felt a sense of hope. Finally, she was going to be a part of something special. Together, she and Vashti would embrace adventure and help her brothers throw off the shackles of Western oppression.

ESHITA LAY awake staring at the ceiling. She had bid her father goodnight hours ago. He'd barely acknowledged her presence from his study where he worked late every night. He wouldn't miss her, she told herself.

Turning her head she checked the glowing numbers on her alarm clock. They read, 0115. Vashti's message had said to meet her at the bus stop outside at 0130.

She checked the clock again, 0117. Unable to wait any longer she pushed back the duvet and swung out of bed. She was already fully clothed in jeans, a T-shirt and a sweater. Glancing out of the window, she confirmed it was still raining and shrugged on a jacket. She slipped on a pair of boots and took her backpack from the wardrobe. Wrapping her hijab, she gave her room one last scan. The picture on her dresser caught her eye. It was a memory from better times: a beautiful young woman held by her handsome husband as she cradled a happy toddler, Eshita. A tear ran down her cheek, and she took the frame, removed the photo and slid it into the pocket on the front of her backpack.

Creeping downstairs, she spotted a sliver of light under the door to her father's study. Treading softly she made her way to the front door and unlocked it. Pausing, she turned back and stared at the study door. Then, with a sigh, she stepped outside into the cold and closed the door gently behind her. Walking along the rain-soaked pavement, she made for the bus shelter.

When she arrived, Vashti was waiting. The pair embraced and then her friend led her down the street. "The Imam gave me an address. It's not far from here."

As they walked in the rain, Eshita glanced back over her shoulder. She gave her street one last look before they turned a corner.

Their destination was a two-story Victorian-era townhouse on the outskirts of Bordesley Green. Eshita noticed a removal van parked in a narrow lane alongside the building. The home was run down with boards over the lower level windows. It looked creepy.

"Vashti, are you sure about this?"

Her friend nodded. "Imam Rahman said it wouldn't look like much. The police are trying to stop people from going to help. They have to move the safe places all the time. Do you want to go home?"

Eshita shook her head. "No, this is our duty."

"For the glory of Allah." Vashti knocked on the door.

A moment later it was opened by an elderly man dressed in sweat pants and a tunic. "Hello, what do you want?"

"Imam Rahman sent us."

The man nodded. "Oh, please come in."

He ushered them into a living room and directed them to a couch. "Wait here."

They sat quietly and a moment later a younger man entered dressed in traditional white robes.

"Give us your phones," he demanded.

Reluctantly, the girls handed over their phones, which disappeared beneath his robe. He emptied the backpacks onto a table and went through their belongings. Eshita sat quietly as her makeup was placed into a plastic bag and confiscated.

"The rest of your things, you can keep." He handed over two folded black robes. "You will wear these burkas. Soon, someone will come and show you to your room." He made to leave.

Vashti frowned. "When do we leave for Syria?"

He shot her a stern look. "When the time is right."

Eshita quietly gathered her clothes and stuffed them back into her bag. Then she unzipped the front pocket and checked that the photo of her family was still there. "I'm sorry, daddy," she whispered as reached out and clutched Vashti's hand.

AL-BAB, SYRIA

Translated into English the words Al-Bab literally means 'the door'. A concise description of the Syrian township located between the cities of Aleppo and Buza'ah. In former years it served as a gateway between the two population centers that offered travelers a place of worship, markets to purchase food, and baths in which to relax. In time it had grown into a bustling city of nearly fifty thousand residents. However, with the onset of the Syrian civil war came bloodshed and violence and soon the city fell to the Islamic State.

A brigade led by Mohammed 'Al-Bab' Yassin had toppled local Free Syrian Army forces, bringing the city and its inhabitants under his iron rule. On the outskirts of town, a former grain warehouse had been converted into a hospital and aid distribution facility. It was from behind razor wire topped brick walls that Mohammed ran his headquarters, safe from the Americans and their drone strikes.

Mohammed stood smoking a cigarette as he watched a team of locals sweating in the heat of the midday sun. They were erecting a framework to extend his headquarters. His victories in Iraq had delivered more vehicles, weapons and equipment that needed to be hidden under the Red Crescent marked roof. His army now occupied most of the warehouse. A medical clinic still operated in one of the buildings to the rear of the compound, below his residence and office. A steady stream of civilians helped keep up the illusion of a functioning hospital.

The growl of a powerful diesel engine caught his ear,

and he turned to face the compound gates. A new four-wheel drive and a large truck, both white with UN markings, pulled to a halt. Mohammed whistled, catching the attention of his guards at the checkpoint. He had been tracking the convoy's progress ever since it reached his first outpost on the edge of the city. "Let them in."

The two vehicles swerved around the new construction and entered the warehouse. A slender figure, dressed in cargo pants and a shirt, stepped from the four-wheel drive and approached Mohammed.

Salim Wayeed was the man who had introduced him to the art of deception. A representative of the UN's World Health Organization, the narrow-faced Syrian was also a prolific smuggler and arms trafficker. He sold weapons, women and supplies to the highest bidder regardless of their ideology or loyalties.

Mohammed opened his hands in greeting. "*As-salaam Alaykum.*"

Salim wore a grin above his protruding chin and scraggly beard. "*Wa Alaykum Salaam*, my brother. It is good to see you again. I hear your adventures in Iraq were very successful."

Mohammed nodded. "Word spreads fast."

"Oh yes, they have been singing the praises of Mohammed Al-Bab from Aleppo to Mosul."

He strode toward the truck. "You flatter me. Now, was the cash I sent you sufficient? Have you got what I ordered?"

Salim's men stood waiting at the rear of the UN marked truck. He gestured for them to drop the tailgate.

Three sets of scared eyes stared out from inside. European teenage girls, shackled at the wrists and clad in rags, sat huddled in the tiny space behind the truck's cargo.

Mohammed shook his head. "Only three."

"There is a shortage. I brought extra weapons to compensate you."

The ISIS warlord stared at the girls. "What I need are jihad brides, Salim. My best men need good Islamic wives, not more of these *kafir* whores."

Salim nodded. "I have a contact who can provide. I will make inquiries."

"Do more than that." He spat in the sand. "When will my next batch of missiles arrive?"

"Soon, I have another shipment due today."

"I will need them as soon as possible."

Salim grinned. "Planning a new offensive?"

Mohammed fixed him with a glare before signaling a group of his men to unload the truck. "You must be tired from your journey. Come, let us break bread." He led Salim across the dusty compound to the two-story cinder block building that housed the medical facility. A long line of civilians waited alongside the building, under the watchful eye of one of his fighters. Wounded children, bloodied and bandaged, were carried by burka-wearing women and old men. There were no young men left in Al-Bab. They had either fled when ISIS took control of the city or joined the ranks of Mohammed's brigade.

Women and the elderly called out to the warlord as he passed. Reaching out they touched his long camouflaged coat and praised him. In a city devastated by war, his army provided the only medical care and food distribution available.

"You passed through the FSA's lines?" he asked Salim as they climbed the bare concrete stairs to the next level. A soldier dressed in black, wearing body armor and carrying a G36 assault rifle, guarded his home. The man, one of his personal bodyguards, opened the door and Mohammed gestured for his guest to enter.

Salim moved inside. "Yes, they have positions just outside of Aleppo. The Russians have been bombing the city."

The living room in Mohammed's apartment was lavishly decorated with thick Persian rugs and tasseled cushions. A burka-clad figure appeared from behind a curtain. The warlord lowered himself onto cushions in the corner of the room. "Bring food and coffee." Another woman appeared and knelt to remove Mohammed's boots.

"What is the condition of their forces?" he asked gesturing for Salim to sit.

"Battle-worn. Assad's offensive has ground them down, and they're low on cash."

"Not buying as many of your missiles?"

Salim shook his head. "No. But, the Americans are still supplying them through Turkey."

"Do you think they can hold off Assad and his dogs?"

A woman arrived with a tray. The earthy smell of black coffee wafted up from a silver pot and mugs.

Salim took the cup offered to him. "For now. In the coming months, who knows?"

The warlord nodded as he sipped. "I have heard rumors that the Jews have been supplying weapons to the FSA."

Salim frowned. "This is the first I have heard of it." He shrugged. "But, it would make sense. Hezbollah fight for Assad. Every bullet they give the FSA is potentially killing their enemies."

Mohammed's eye twitched as he scowled. "Eventually we will have to fight them. Israel is our mortal enemy. If you find me intelligence on which of the FSA brigades is taking their aid, I will pay you well."

Salim stared at him over his coffee. "It would seem that fighting for the Caliphate is lucrative."

Another of the warlord's wives arrived with a plate of flat bread, dips and roasted meat.

"Allah favors the bold," declared Mohammed as he took a piece of bread and stuffed it with meat.

Salim nodded in agreement. "Yes he does, my friend. Well, I must return to Jarjanaz. I am expecting a shipment later today."

Mohammed gestured to the food. "You will not eat?"

"Of course, of course."

"Then eat. We will have you on your way in no time. The quicker you return to Jarjanaz the quicker you can bring me my jihad brides and my missiles."

Another woman entered the room and poured glasses of cold water.

Salim shot the warlord a wry smile. "It would seem you already have many wives."

Mohammed laughed spraying crumbs across the floor. "Too many. I am beginning to think that from now on I will stick to the whores, they come with less nagging."

Chapter Three

AMMAN, JORDAN TO JARJANAZ, SYRIA

A GUST of hot desert wind blasted across the tarmac at Queen Alia International Airport, buffeting the gray LM-100J Hercules transporter that sat in front of the freight terminal. One of its four propellers spun lazily drawing the attention of a tall, dark-haired man dressed in a flight suit. Aden Bishop, the loadmaster, watched the six-bladed prop turn in the wind as he conducted a walk around. A recent addition to the Priority Movements Airlift fleet, the J-model had logged less than a hundred hours of flying time. That made it a baby compared to the Russian-built Ilyushin it had replaced. Content that the outside showed no signs of damage or wear he made his way back to the ramp.

As he arrived, he spotted their cargo trundling across the tarmac on a freight loader. Standing in the back of the Hercules, he directed the machine's operator to line up with the ramp. Then, when the flat-deck was aligned, he gave the man thumbs-up. With a whirr the rollers under the cargo pallets spun, shunting the pallet onto the rollers attached to the floor of the Hercules. The three heavily loaded pallets moved slowly inside until they reached the bulkhead that separated the cargo hold from the cockpit.

Happy that they were in place Bishop stepped off the ramp and met the driver at his loader. The dark-skinned Jordanian flashed him a smile over his clipboard.

"Three pallets of medical supplies bound for Jarjanaz, Syria, yes?"

Bishop returned the smile revealing dimples underneath a crooked nose and warm brown eyes. "That's correct."

The man nodded. "Your crew is very brave. Flying into a war zone to deliver supplies for those poor people."

He took the clipboard and signed the paperwork. "It's what we get paid to do."

"Yes, Priority Movements Airlift. Very brave."

Bishop winked as he handed the man the document. "Thanks, mate."

If only the dispatcher knew the full extent of what Priority Movements Airlift really did, Bishop thought as he locked down the cargo.

Nicknamed PRIMAL, the tight-knit team were running humanitarian aid missions instead of their usual clandestine operations. Elements of the CIA had come close to revealing PRIMAL's secret; that it was in fact a vigilante organization targeting the world's worst perpetrators of injustice. No one fell outside their remit, not even those protected by politics and government institutions.

Independently funded, manned by elite operatives and equipped with the latest technology, they were a lethal force. Bishop was one of PRIMAL's veteran operatives, a man driven by the need to fight for the oppressed.

Confident that the load was secure he raised the ramp

and made his way to the cockpit. Pushing open the door he stepped inside and tapped the copilot, Mirza Mansoor, on the shoulder. The lean, bearded former Indian Special Forces soldier was a fellow operative and close friend. "Cargo is secure. We're all set when you guys are ready."

The aircraft's Captain, Mike Winter, had recently been promoted to being a full-time PRIMAL pilot. He turned and gave Bishop thumbs-up. "You mind taking your buddy back into the cargo hold? She keeps trying to chew the headset cables."

A four-year-old brown Border Collie dog currently occupied the spare seat. Hired from a company that supplied working dogs to the airport, she was onboard for a very specific reason. Bishop grabbed the dog's vest and gently lifted her clear of the seat. "Come on Daisy, we've got work to do." He carried the dog from the cockpit, down the short ladder and placed her on the floor in the cargo hold. The aircraft started moving, and he tightened his seatbelt and clipped a retention lanyard to the dog. The collie looked up at him with her tongue lolling from her mouth. "Nothing fazes you does it, girl?"

He felt the jet turn sharply onto the runway. Then, with a roar, it pitched forward and gained speed. Seconds later the transporter lurched off the ground and climbed skyward.

Once they leveled off at cruising height Bishop unlatched the seatbelt and released the dog. The cockpit door opened, and he glanced up to see Mirza entering.

"You think they're in this load?" the Indian operative asked.

He nodded. "We'll see." He gestured to the dog. "Daisy, come."

She walked across and sat next to a long black case. He opened the lid and gestured to the tube inside. "Daisy, find."

She leaned forward and snuffled, then raised her nose into the air and sniffed. Then, she took off, tail wagging furiously as she worked around the pallets of cargo in the hold. She completed two loops, both times stopping at the bag to sniff again. Mirza and Bishop stood watching.

"Not looking good," said Mirza.

"Give her a little time."

On her third inspection of the stacked pallets she gave an excited bark and sat alongside one of them.

"Bingo." Bishop moved forward and unfastened the cargo net that secured the wooden crates. Then, grasping the handle on Daisy's vest, he hoisted her up onto the boxes.

The dog sniffed again before pawing excitedly.

Mirza helped Bishop lift two of the boxes off the pile.

Daisy jumped into the new space and pawed at a layer of long crates, barking.

"Good girl." Bishop reached into the pocket of his flight suit and produced a rubber ball. It squeaked as he squeezed it. Daisy grabbed the toy and disappeared toward the front of the aircraft.

Each crate was four feet long and heavy. It took both Bishop and Mirza a minute to manhandle one of the boxes clear of the pallet. Bishop inspected the box carefully for any measures designed to warn someone if it had been opened. Using a cordless driver, he removed the retaining screws and popped the lid. Inside were two green fiberglass tubes. They were the launch containers for BGM-71 TOW missiles.

"You were right," said Mirza.

Bishop shot him a concerned look. "We've been smuggling arms into Syria."

"That's less than desirable."

"Proper cluster fuck."

They pried one tubular launch container from the crate and examined it. Bishop noted that the lot numbers were ground off and the identification decal removed. "Someone wants deniability."

"In case Daesh gets them."

"Exactly."

They laid the tube on the floor of the aircraft and Bishop dragged across his black case. The tube inside was a replica of the missile container. They switched the tubes then Bishop took a phone from his pocket, unlocked it and accessed a hidden menu.

The phone was actually called an iPRIMAL, a sophisticated communications, tracking, intelligence and hacking device that allowed the organization's operatives to link back to their headquarters in Abu Dhabi from anywhere on the globe. Bishop synched with the replica missile and activated a tracking system.

"Now, we'll be able to find this sucker wherever it goes."

Mirza frowned. "And what if the missile is fired?"

"Mitch said it'll function normally until impact. He's disabled the warhead." Mitch was PRIMAL's resident tech head. The former British Ministry of Defence scientist was currently in the US on a quest for the latest science and technology.

Mirza grimaced. "A hit is still going to hurt."

Bishop nodded in agreement. "Let's hope they shoot it at a tank. Right, let's deal with the others."

They found two more crates, six missiles in total. It took them thirty minutes to sabotage the weapons and repack them into the pallet of supplies. As they finished lashing the netting in place, the aircraft conducted a sweeping turn.

That was Mirza's cue to return to the cockpit, and Bishop's to prepare for landing.

Bishop secured Daisy's leash to the crash-netting seat then strapped himself in. The dog laid her head on his thigh and licked his hand. He ruffled her ears and braced for touchdown. As he waited, he found himself thinking how much Saneh would adore the lively hound. The love of his life had a soft spot for animals, especially dogs. A hard lump formed in his throat. She'd disappeared after losing their unborn child following an attack by poachers in Africa. It was two months since he had last seen her and there'd been no contact.

The sudden thump of the transporter landing snapped his mind back to the present. He placed a hand on Daisy as the engines roared and they decelerated. Once they'd slowed, he moved to the ramp controls. As he passed the side door, he glanced out through the window. Blue sky could be seen over the barren desert. It wasn't a familiar sight. On his previous trips to Jarjanaz, the airfield had been shrouded in dust.

He felt the aircraft brake at the end of the strip and turn, readying for a quick takeoff. When the engines throttled back, he hit the controls for the ramp. It lowered with a soft whine, revealing a line of four-wheel drives marked with red crescents and a truck painted in the white livery of the UN. A gaggle of men loitered around the vehicles. One of them broke away from the group and made a beeline to the back of the aircraft.

"Here comes Salim," said Mirza as he joined Bishop on the ramp.

"The one and only."

As the slender Syrian approached the aircraft, a broad

grin split his narrow face. "Ah, my friends Mirza and Aden. Welcome back to Jarjanaz."

Bishop shook his hand. "It's good to see you, Salim." He gestured over his shoulder to the cargo pallets inside the aircraft. "We've got a big load today. You might need more trucks."

The Syrian nodded enthusiastically, taking his phone from his pocket. "Good, good. I'll make a call. I can have another truck here in five minutes. In the meantime, my people will unload." He waved his men forward as he held the phone to his ear.

Bishop glanced at Mirza. "Would have been good to have Mitch along." The PRIMAL technician could have intercepted the transmission from the suspected arms dealer's phone. Then, in no time, the team at their headquarters would pull apart Salim's network of contacts giving them a better idea of exactly who he was.

"Once we know where the merchandise is going we'll have a better idea of where best to use his skills."

"True."

The PRIMAL operatives unhooked the netting that secured the cargo pallets and piled it on the side seating. Then Mirza returned to the cockpit while Bishop supervised the unloading of the boxes. In a matter of minutes, the first pallet of crates was piled behind the aircraft.

Salim finished his call and joined Bishop at the side of the ramp. "It is good that so many people are so generous. Without them, the people of Syria would suffer even more."

Bishop fought the urge to punch him in the face. Instead, he nodded. "It must be difficult getting the aid to those most in need. Where do you take the stores?"

"I have a warehouse near the town. From there we deliver it by truck."

"You don't have any problems with ISIS or the rebels?"

"I try to avoid ISIS. The Free Syrian Army is not a problem, they are susceptible to bribes of medical supplies. Everyone has a shortage. I find that the UN trucks help us move with limited interference."

Bishop turned his attention back to the men unloading. They'd reached the bottom of the second pallet. He watched as two men hefted the box containing the modified TOW missile and shuffled with it across the cargo bay. As they reached the ramp, one of them stepped on a roller and slipped. The box hit the ramp with a crunch and teetered on the edge. Bishop lunged forward and stopped it. With a grunt, he hefted it back onto the ramp. "Guys, careful with the merchandise."

Salim issued a harsh sounding rebuke in his own tongue.

The rest of the unloading progressed without incident. Bishop shook hands with Salim, raised the ramp and fastened himself in next to Daisy, who lay fast asleep. "Hard life," he murmured as he slipped on his headset. "Guys, we're good to go back here."

"Roger," replied Mike. "It's clear skies from here to Abu Dhabi. We should be on the ground and sipping cocktails at the yacht club by 1900."

"Sounds good to me," replied Bishop as he settled back into his seat and closed his eyes. A moment later he felt Daisy move across and place her head on his leg. He ruffled her ears as his thoughts returned to Saneh. Hopefully, when he got back to the Sandpit, the PRIMAL team would have news from her.

LOS ANGELES, USA

Mitch Freeman took a magazine from the coffee table and examined the cover. Robotics Monthly was exactly the type of publication he expected to find at the University of Southern California's Robotics Research Laboratory. He flicked through the pages, skimming articles that piqued his interest.

"Mr. Sampson?"

Mitch glanced up and caught the questioning expression on the silver-haired academic's face. Maybe he didn't meet the man's expectations as to what a head of procurements for a logistics company should look like. Rising, he straightened his jacket and reached for the man's hand. "Doctor Hammer?"

At six foot, two hundred and ten pounds of lean muscle, and sporting a lumberjack beard, Mitch looked more 'operator' than management. PRIMAL's head of technology and Chief Pilot wasn't afraid of a gunfight, it just wasn't where his expertise lay. His forte was technology, more specifically, integrated spec ops related technology. Sourcing a bionic hand for a wounded PRIMAL operative had initially led him to the research lab. Impressed by the institute's robotics program he'd arranged a significant grant for the development of a specific capability.

The University's Head of Robotics flashed a broad grin. "It's good to finally meet you." He pumped Mitch's hand with vigor. "You're going to be amazed at what we've achieved with your funding."

The man's words flew from his mouth like rounds from a Gatling gun. His energy was infectious, and Mitch found himself caught up in the enthusiasm as he was led through the administration building down a corridor to a set of doors.

Dr. Hammer swiped an ID card and held the door open. "The demonstrators are ready, and I think you're going to be impressed. We've surpassed all of your specifications."

"How many units in total?" asked Mitch as they entered a large workshop with a high ceiling and bright lights. Workbenches lined a wall with computer terminals and racks of tools. Industrial 3D printers and CNC milling machines occupied part of the floor space. On the far side, rows of shelving were stacked high with components, cabling and half-finished projects. In the center of the room, surrounded by half a dozen students, was a human-sized shape draped with a gray cloth.

"We have three. This prototype and two more, complete and ready for shipment. But now, let us show you what we have created." He gestured for one of his students to pull back the sheet.

When Mitch had proposed that PRIMAL, through a cover company, sponsor a technology build, both Vance and Chua had been skeptical. It had been the vigilante organization's third, and mostly silent, director who had approved the line of funding. As Mitch watched the sheet drop he grinned. The robotic prototype standing before him was almost exactly as he envisioned it: robust looking hydraulic and electric powered limbs attached to a central command module.

One of the students stepped forward and activated a button on the side of the bright yellow exoskeleton. The student turned, stepped into the feet, and tightened the straps on the lower limbs. A waist belt and shoulder straps were next. Finally the robotic arms automatically latched onto his wrists. The student raised them into the air and manipulated a pair of articulated claws.

Dr. Hammer turned to face him. "We call it RALF, the Robotic Assisted Logistics Facilitator. It enables the average person to lift over eight hundred pounds and move it with ease."

"Exactly what Lascar Logistics needs," Mitch observed.

With a whirr of motors, the exoskeleton-enabled student strode across to a rusted engine block and hefted it effortlessly off the ground.

Mitch clapped his hands. "Outstanding. What's the power source? How long does it last?"

Dr. Hammer wobbled his head as he smirked. "The suit has two hours of endurance if operating continuously unloading cargo. Or, if it is only providing assisted mobility, double that. Power is provided by a hydrogen fuel cell built into the backpack unit."

The student turned around so Mitch could see. "The hydrogen gas tank sits below it. The only output is water. It's stored in a bladder that the operator can drink."

With a whirr, the student lowered the engine block and turned to face them.

"Is it hard to use?"

Dr. Hammer shook his head. "No, very simple functionality. You move as normal, and the suit detects and augments your actions. It has controls inside the grips that can be connected to a range of accessories and tools. I think you will find it highly suitable for your line of work."

The requirements guidance that Mitch had initially provided called for an exoskeleton that would enhance human performance, allowing freight to be unloaded from aircraft in underdeveloped countries.

Mitch shot him a sideways glance. "So, can I try it?"

"Certainly."

As the student stepped clear of the exoskeleton, Mitch shrugged off his jacket and removed his tie. He stepped into the padded confines of the robotic limbs and strapped in.

"You'll find the toggles inside the right gauntlet," Dr. Hammer continued.

He found the button and the robotic arms latched on to his own. Then, tentatively, he raised one hand. Effortlessly the suit replicated the move, exactly as if it was part of him. Stepping forward he clunked around in a circle and approached the engine block. The metal claws responded to his movements allowing him to grip the steel. He hefted it effortlessly from the ground and hoisted it over his head. "This is the duck's nuts. Team, you've outdone yourself."

The group of students broke into a round of applause as Mitch squatted with the engine block above his head and jumped. Hydraulics launched him two feet into the air then cushioned his landing. He grinned; this was going to blow the PRIMAL team away.

Chapter Four

LONDON, ENGLAND

SONIA JAYARAM PLACED the file she was reading on her desk, removed her glasses and rubbed the bridge of her nose. She'd been working on the case for over a week and seemed no closer to finishing. For six years now the elegant Indian lawyer had been working as an immigration litigator. Unmarried and dedicated to her job she was more often than not behind her desk with a case file in hand.

She glanced at the clock on the wall of her tiny office and saw that it was half past eight in the evening. Time to grab something to eat, she thought, possibly even call it a night and head home. Sighing, she redirected her attention back to her work. There was simply too much to do before her case went to court.

Her desk phone startled her as it rang. She glanced at the caller ID bar, saw that it was a former client and answered. "Padak, is that you?" Padak Mozaz and his daughter Eshita were Indian Muslim immigrants whose case she had successfully represented. Despite being born a Hindu, Sonia respected all religions and many of her clients were Muslims.

"Yes, Sonia, I apologize for calling you so late. I did not know who else to turn to," Padak said with a hint of stress. An engineer, he was usually logical and calm.

"No, it's fine. What can I help you with?"

"It's Eshita, she's gone."

Sonia grabbed a pen and notepad. "What do you mean gone? Did someone take her?"

"No. I mean yes. Look, I don't know. She spent a lot of time with another girl called Vashti, who is also missing."

"And you've spoken to the police?"

"Yes. There's nothing…" His voice wavered. "There's nothing they can do. The girls were attending a youth group in Birmingham run by an Imam. Imam Rahman I think. The police believe that they could have been convinced to…" This time, he sobbed.

The anguish in his voice tore at Sonia's soul. She had a good idea what he was going to say. "Padak, I've worked with some of the people in the Imam's congregation. I can try and get a meeting with him to discuss the girls."

"You would do that?"

"Of course."

"You are an angel."

"If there is anything you need please don't be afraid to ask. I'll let you know if I can get a meeting and call as soon as I hear anything."

"Thank you."

Sonia hung up the phone and flicked open the diary on her desk. She'd worked on the immigration case of a close associate of Imam Rahman. Finding her notes, she confirmed the name and number of her contact and grabbed the phone. She needed to move fast. From what she understood of people smuggling they didn't stay in one place for long.

ABU DHABI, UAE

Bishop ran his jet ski up onto the white sandy beach in front of a luxury villa and killed the engine. Climbing off the high-powered watercraft, he pulled a dry-bag from the seat compartment then crossed the beach toward the residence.

Known as 'The Sandpit', PRIMAL's headquarters looked out onto lush green grass surrounding a crystal blue swimming pool. The pool looked tempting. Abu Dhabi was stifling in the summer time especially with the sun directly overhead. For a second Bishop fought the urge to dive into the water. Then he relented, dumped his bag, stripped off his T-shirt and launched himself in. Ice-cold water drove the air from his lungs as he swam underwater, touched the far wall and broke the surface.

"Pretty good, huh."

The voice belonged to PRIMAL's longest serving operative, James Castle, nickname Ice.

He grinned at the hulking former CIA paramilitary officer. "How the hell is it so cold?"

Ice reached down and offered him a robotic prosthetic hand with a rubberized outer skin. "Mitch set up a refrigeration unit in the wine cellar."

Bishop grabbed the mechanical hand and was hauled effortlessly from the water. "You guys are really doing it tough."

"I'm not the one who commutes on a jet ski from his

penthouse apartment." He threw Bishop a towel. "C'mon, the team's waiting."

As he dried himself, he watched Ice walk toward the sliding glass doors of the luxury villa. Despite having an artificial arm and lower leg Ice moved with lethal grace that belied his size. If it weren't for the scarring on his face it would be hard to believe he had been severely injured, almost killed in fact, on a PRIMAL mission in Afghanistan five years earlier.

He threw on his T-shirt, grabbed his bag, and followed Ice into the villa. "Big man, has Vance given you the green light for field ops?"

"Not yet. I've got to pass a few tests then I should be good to go."

"Sweet. How's the rest of the team doing?" He yanked open the refrigerator and found a can of energy drink.

The organization they called PRIMAL had previously been based on an island in the South West Pacific. However, a near compromise by the CIA had resulted in that facility shutting down, and now they ran a much leaner presence in the UAE.

"Yeah, they're keeping busy monitoring intelligence channels."

Bishop cracked the can and took a swig. "Anything from Saneh?"

Ice shook his head. "Not that I've heard. Stop worrying, Bish, she'll be OK. She loves you, you just need to give her time."

"Yeah, I know." Bishop finished the can, crushed it and tossed it in the recycling container. "Let's head upstairs, yeah."

They walked up the white tiled staircase to where the rest of the team was working. Two of the luxurious bedrooms had been converted to an operations center and an intelligence facility.

"You'll want to touch base with Chua. I'll let Vance know you're here." Ice disappeared into the ops center.

Bishop gave the door to the intelligence room a soft rap then pushed it open.

Inside two men were sitting in front of computer terminals perched on a counter. Chen Chua, a slightly built Asian American and PRIMAL's chief of intelligence, glanced up at him. "Hey, Bish. Good job on the TOW infil. We've got a fix on the missile as of an hour ago."

Dropping into a chair, Bishop checked the screens on the wall. "Where is it?"

"A warehouse on the outskirts of Jarjanaz. The tracker will alert us if it moves."

The other man glanced up from his computer. Dressed in a baggy T-shirt and a flat brim cap, 'Flash' Gordon was PRIMAL's electronic intelligence expert. "Bro, good to see you."

Bishop leaned forward and they bumped knuckles. "Up to no good?"

"You know it. Hey, check this out." Flash gestured to another of the wall-mounted screens.

A video recording played of a TOW missile slamming into an Iraqi main battle tank. It quickly cut to a scene where another missile smashed into a bunker. Black-clad ISIS fighters could be seen clustered around a TOW launcher, cheering with their weapons held high.

"There's more on the web, bro. ISIS has got their hands on more than a few missiles. Our boy Salim has been busy."

Bishop stared at the screen. "We need to find out who he's supplying. We need to follow the source in Jordan."

"Not yet, hotshot."

Bishop turned to see PRIMAL's Director of Operations, Vance Durant, standing in the door. The bald-headed, barrel-chested, African American wore a stern expression. "We're still laying low, remember. I need to talk to Tariq before we hit out on a new mission."

Tariq Ahmed was PRIMAL's third director and financial benefactor. He, along with Vance and Chua, decided on the missions that their operatives executed. Currently they were ultra conservative in their approach to dealing out justice; a change in tempo that did not sit well with Bishop.

Vance tilted his head toward the stairs. "Walk with me."

Bishop followed him back down to the kitchen. "Have you heard anything from Saneh?"

"No. She'll reach out when she's ready." Vance opened the fridge and took out a beer. "I know you want to go after the arms smugglers supplying ISIS. We just need to be real careful. There's been a change of CIA station chief here in the Emirates. I need to get a read on who he is and where he's come from before we start smacking Daeshbags in our backyard." He passed a cold Coopers to Bishop and took a Coors from the fridge.

"Yeah, I get it. But doesn't Tariq feel responsible? I mean we could have delivered a dozen TOWs, maybe more."

Vance took a swig from his beer. "He certainly does. But, if we're compromised, then who's going to deal with these scumbags? You need to sit tight until we're ready to make a move. Take some time off and enjoy yourself."

Bishop sighed. Time off meant time to think, and that was the last thing he needed.

PORTSMOUTH, ENGLAND

Mubarez's sneakers slapped on the wet concrete as he made his way along the dock toward a waiting boat. Rain fell from the dark skies above Portsmouth hitting his anorak with a soft patter.

As he walked his thoughts turned to his brother. Anger coursed through his veins as he replayed Saifan's death, over and over. The police had shot his brother in cold blood, gunning him down in front of their community. His only solace was that he had the opportunity to avenge his brother's death. In Syria, he would slay hundreds of the *kafir*.

Through the gloom he spotted a figure standing alongside a fishing boat. As he got closer, he could see the man was dressed from head to toe in waterproof clothing.

"Mubarez?" the fisherman asked.

"Yes."

The man waved him toward the gangplank.

He stopped at the edge of the wharf, fixated on the fishing boat pitching against its moorings.

The fisherman clasped a hand on his shoulder. "Hurry up, we need to go."

"I can't swim."

The man shoved him onto the gangplank. "Then stay in the boat."

He stumbled across the walkway onto the deck of the vessel where two sailors were struggling with a bulky object wrapped in plastic. As he passed, a bloodied arm slipped out from under the sheeting.

"Who is that?" Mubarez asked as he followed the fisherman downstairs.

"Someone who stuck his nose in someone else's business."

The mess room of the trawler was battered and worn. It smelled like a sardine tin. Mubarez's host gestured to a bench seat. "You can sit here. Once the others arrive we will get underway."

"What others?" he asked as he sat.

The man ignored him, heading back upstairs.

Alone, Mubarez gave the inside of the boat a detailed inspection. There was a small galley on one side of the space and two doors to the stern that he assumed were cabins.

He heard female voices as the door above him opened and the fisherman reappeared. He stomped down the stairs with two burka-clad figures behind him.

One of the girls turned to face him as the man unlocked a cabin. He could see the fear in her eyes as they stared at each other. Then, the girls were bundled into the room, and the door locked behind them.

"Who are they?" he asked.

The fisherman grinned. "Brides for the Jihad. We'll be heading off now. In a few hours, you will be in France." He climbed the stairs, leaving Mubarez alone.

It took him a moment to realize where he had seen the girl. She attended Imam Rahman's spiritual guidance classes. He smiled; it was good that, like him, she had chosen to serve her faith. Perhaps, if Allah willed it, they would become husband and wife.

The boat shuddered as the engines started. Mubarez slumped against the bulkhead. Finally, he was on his way to Syria to continue the Jihad that he and his brother had begun.

Chapter Five

BIRMINGHAM, ENGLAND

SONIA CHECKED her phone as she stepped from her Mercedes coupe. Her contact had yet to reply with a time to meet Imam Rahman. Grabbing her coffee and bag, she hurried across the street and through the doors of Birmingham central police station. The counter was empty so she pressed the buzzer.

"Sonia Jayaram to see Detective Smithson," she said when the female desk clerk arrived.

"Please, take a seat."

She sat in a cheap plastic chair and checked her phone; still no message.

"Miss Jayaram?"

She glanced up. The overweight man standing at the station's security door wore an ill-fitting suit and an exhausted expression. "Yes."

Rising she straightened her jacket and walked toward

the man with her hand extended. "You must be Detective Smithson?"

"Correct. This way please."

He led her down a musty corridor and into an office with his name on the door.

Gesturing to a chair, he sat at his desk. "Look, as you are probably aware, we're very busy here at the moment."

"Yes, my condolences for the loss of your colleagues."

He stared at her with sad eyes that reminded her of a Basset hound. "Thank you. Now, I've looked into the missing person's case filed by Mr. Moziz."

"Mozaz," she corrected. "Padak Mozaz."

He checked the file in front of him. "Ah yes, so it is. Well, I've looked into it, and I note that it's only been twenty-four hours. It's possible that his daughter will return home. We require someone to be missing seventy-two hours before we start a full investigation."

"Except she hasn't run away from home. We think she's been recruited by Jihadists who will smuggle her out of the country."

Nodding he closed the file. "That may well be the case, but if she chooses to run off with these people there's not much we can do about it."

Sonia shook her head. "She's fourteen, she's been coerced. The least you can do is question Imam Rahman."

He snorted. "You don't seem to understand, Miss. We can't bring him in for questioning. One of his people killed a police officer yesterday, and we can't enter the damn suburb without causing a full-blown riot. You've got more hope of finding this kid than we do. I mean they're your people."

Sonia fixed him with a glare, a harsh rebuke at the tip

of her tongue. Then, she reconsidered. Clearly, the detective was under a tremendous amount of pressure following the killings. She rose from the chair and extended her hand. "Thank you, detective."

"I'm sorry I couldn't be more helpful."

She smiled grimly. "Good luck with your investigations."

On her way out Sonia's phone buzzed. She glanced at the screen. Her heart skipped a beat. It was her contact. He'd managed to arrange a sit down with Imam Rahman for later that day. Scrolling through her phone she found Padak's number and sent him a text. She didn't want to raise his hopes but she had promised to let him know if she arranged a meeting.

Outside, she glanced up and down the street searching for a café. She needed somewhere to plan exactly what she would say to the Imam. Thankfully she had a hijab in the glove compartment of her car.

ABU DHABI, UAE

Lascar Towers soared fifty-five floors above street level in the business district of Abu Dhabi. It wasn't the tallest building in the city, but it was one of the most energy efficient. Its sleek facade of black glass reflected the intense Middle Eastern sun and heat while at the same time converting the sun's rays into electricity. Huge tubes encased in the center of the tower took hot air from ground level and channeled it skyward where turbines turned it into more power. So efficient was the structure that on the hottest days it actually added electricity back into Abu Dhabi's grid.

Vance drove a nondescript sedan down a ramp into the underground parking levels. Chen Chua sat in the passenger seat. They parked, walked across to the high-speed elevators and entered the first one available. There were fifty-four floors marked on the touch screen panel. Vance hit eight of them in sequence before pressing his palm against the touch screen. A series of beeps emitted and the elevator took off with a faint hum.

"What if Tariq knows about the weapons?" asked Chua as they climbed.

Vance shook his head. "There's no way he does."

The elevator reached the fifty-fourth floor and paused. Then it rose a few more yards and stopped.

Chua turned to him. "You feel that?"

Glancing at his arm, Vance saw the hairs were standing on end. "What the hell is it?"

"Some kind of magnetic scanner."

Vance chuckled and pointed as Chua's thin hair lifted from his scalp.

"Laugh it up, baldy," said Chua. "At least I've got hair."

A moment later the doors opened and they walked into a marble-floored foyer. Tariq's assistant greeted them with a bright smile. "Good morning, gentlemen. Mr. Ahmed is in his office. Go right through."

Vance nodded, knowing that the bookish-looking secretary had a submachine gun behind her desk. "Thanks, Emily," he said as a pair of bulletproof glass doors parted, revealing a spacious modern office. The faint smell of paint hung in the air as they entered.

Tariq Ahmed, the CEO of Lascar Logistics and PRIMAL's benefactor, sat behind a white desk working on a silver laptop. He glanced up and shot the two men a broad smile. "Vance, Chen, welcome." He rose from behind the desk and strode toward them. Dressed in a sharp pinstripe shirt, tie, navy blue suit pants and brown brogues the Arab businessman could have stepped from the pages of Gentlemen's Quarterly magazine.

Vance shook his hand. "What's with the renovations? You've gone all modern."

"It was time for a change." He shook Chua's hand and directed them to a glass table surrounded by curved white leather chairs.

Vance frowned as the one he chose groaned under his weight. "This safe?"

"Yes, ergonomically designed," said Tariq as he poured them each a glass of water from a jug. "So, how is the team faring?"

"Still working hard," replied Vance. "Chua and Flash have been busy monitoring intelligence feeds."

Tariq nodded. "Any indicators of a compromise?"

Chua shook his head. "Not at this stage."

"Good. How is Bishop doing?"

Vance shrugged. "As well as can be expected. He and Mirza have thrown themselves into your Priority Movements shipments into Syria."

"And we've heard nothing more from Saneh?"

"No, she's dropped off the grid."

"Have we considered using Ivan to locate her?" asked Tariq.

Ivan was one of PRIMAL's deep-cover operatives, a former Russian spy who specialized in moving unseen, gaining access to information and recruiting intelligence assets.

Chua leaned forward in his chair. "We could—"

"We could leave her to deal with her issues and return

to us when she feels she's good and ready," interrupted Vance. "Like Bishop, she's handling her emotions in her own way. We need to respect that."

"Of course," said Tariq. "I only thought it might make sense to know where she is."

"If we need her then Chua can find her."

Tariq stroked his manicured beard. "What about the rest of the team? The last time we spoke you mentioned that Kruger was still in Africa."

"Yes, he's working with an anti-poaching foundation. He's under strict instructions to keep his activities low key and non-kinetic. Technically, he is on leave."

"And what he chooses to do in his own time is up to him," said Tariq.

"Exactly."

There was a moment of silence as Tariq pondered the information. He sipped from a glass of water then locked eyes with Vance. "So, are we going to discuss whatever it is that has brought you here?"

Vance had known Tariq for over a decade. The Arab businessman began his career as an intelligence officer in the Emirates military. Following that he'd commanded Abu Dhabi Police's Special Tasks Branch. From there his career had deviated from government service. With Vance's assistance he'd taken over his father's empire and raised PRIMAL. In all this time Vance never had reason to question Tariq's intentions or motives. This was the first time he'd ever had to confront him with information that cast doubt on both.

"Tariq, Bishop and Mirza found weapons in two of the shipments they delivered to Syria."

The regal Arab's brow furrowed. "Weapons? I was

under the impression the shipments were humanitarian aid. Specifically, medical supplies."

Vance sighed. "Smuggled among the medical supplies were crates of TOW missiles."

"To the Free Syrian Army?"

Chua shook his head. "We've got evidence that TOW missiles are being used by ISIS."

Vance watched Tariq carefully. He spotted the bulge of the man's jaw as he clenched his teeth.

Tariq turned to Chua. "Do we have any idea how many weapons?"

"We estimate somewhere between ten and twenty live missiles. Bishop and Mirza sabotaged the most recent shipment and swapped in a replica containing a tracker. We followed it from the airfield to a WHO logistics facility on the outskirts of Jarjanaz, where it has remained."

"We need to find and destroy as many missiles as possible," said Vance. "I want to investigate the source in Jordan and the holding location outside of Jarjanaz."

Tariq paused before replying. "We need to tread carefully. There are those within the UAE who are sympathetic to the extremists. I will make discreet inquiries to find out who is funding the shipments."

Vance nodded. "Discretion is the key. Once we've established the facts we can decide on a course of action."

"Agreed, Priority Movements will continue with the scheduled deliveries. We don't want to arouse suspicion at either end. Can we ensure the missiles remain ineffective?"

"Yes, all the missiles we transport will be inoperable."

Tariq sighed. "Until we know who is responsible I guess that's the best we can do. Now, gentlemen, please excuse me as I have a board meeting that I anticipate will consume the rest of my day. I'll see you out."

They shook hands and a minute later Vance and Chua were alone and descending in the elevator. They waited until they were back in their car before Vance spoke.

"What do you think?"

Chua shrugged. "My gut feeling is he's as angry as we are."

"Yeah, that was my read too. Now, we just need to find out who's been using PRIMAL to do their dirty work."

BIRMINGHAM, ENGLAND

Sonia sat on an uncomfortable chair studying the peeling wallpaper in a musty living room. An hour had passed since she'd arrived at the townhouse for her meeting with Imam Rahman. She adjusted the hijab that framed her face and smoothed her calf length skirt. A Hindu, she didn't normally wear the headscarf; she had donned it out of respect.

Tired hinges creaked, and the door opened revealing the face of the man who'd shown her to the waiting room an hour earlier. One of the Imam's fanatical followers, the teen sported a patchy beard and a full-length white robe.

"Come with me," he said, attempting an authoritative tone.

She followed him along a dark corridor into another room. The smell of floor cleaner assaulted her nose as her eyes adjusted to the bright lighting.

The Imam sat on a couch at the back of the room. Overweight, with beady eyes that peered out over a long unkempt beard, he wore what she could only assume was a permanent scowl.

The youth directed her to the moth-eaten Persian rug that covered the freshly mopped tiles.

Sonia shook her head. "Can you please find a chair?"

He turned to the Imam who shrugged.

She stepped aside to let him leave the room.

The Imam cleared his throat. "What do you want, Miss Jayaram?"

The assistant returned with a chair, and Sonia sat. "I'm here on behalf of one of my clients. His daughter has been attending your sermons."

"Who is your client? Why does he not attend my teachings?" His English was crisp with a trace of a Pakistani accent.

"His daughter is missing. Her name is Eshita Mozaz."

The Imam's brow furrowed. "I know Eshita. She attends many of my classes, a troubled girl whose father did not provide the teachings and discipline a Muslim girl needs. It does not surprise me that she has run away from home."

She swallowed. "Her father loves her dearly. Do you know where she has gone?"

The Imam folded his arms. "Where a young Muslim girl runs is not my business. Nor is it the business of an outsider. I am sure Eshita will return home when she is ready."

She clasped her hands in her lap. "Imam Rahman, if you know where she is I implore you to tell me. Her father is distraught; she needs to be with her family."

"What would you know of family? You dress like a man and pretend you are of great importance. Do you have a child of your own or a husband to guide your actions? No, in fact, you are no better than a common whore."

The hatred that burned in his eyes startled Sonia and she was lost for words.

"I agreed to see you because you have represented some of my family. However, you have made a mistake coming here and putting your nose in matters that do not concern you. It is best that you leave this community and not return." The Imam dismissed her with a wave of his hand.

Sonia's eyes narrowed and she saw herself out. As she left the Imam's residence her phone vibrated in her bag, and she checked the screen. It was Padak. She let it ring out as she rushed down the street to where her car was parked.

"Hey, woman!"

The voice rang clear in the crisp air. Sonia glanced back over her shoulder as she walked. Her pulse quickened as she spotted the group of four men. They were dressed in tracksuits with dark hoodies pulled forward to hide their faces.

"We want to talk to you!"

Sonia walked faster.

"Hey, stop you stupid bitch."

Her Mercedes was only a dozen yards ahead. She fished the keys from her bag and pressed the unlock button.

"Fucking stop!"

As she yanked open the car door, she glimpsed the men running toward her. Slipping inside she slammed the door, her heart racing. Fumbling with the controls on the armrest, she managed to activate the central locking. Fists pounded on the glass, and one of the men jumped onto the hood.

"Open the door you *kafir* whore!"

As she fumbled to start the car, one of the men pressed his face against the driver's window. Sonia refused to look at his contorted features as he screamed through the glass.

"Keep your nose out of our business, bitch. Come here again and you're fucking dead."

The car started with a roar and she swerved out onto the road. The assailant on the hood slid off and something smashed into the rear window, cracking the glass. Sonia's knuckles were white as she gripped the steering wheel. Tears welled in her eyes and her heart felt like it was going to burst through her ribs as she left the suburb and accelerated along the motorway to London.

FRANCE

Mubarez's head bounced against the side of the truck and his eyes snapped open. In a panic, he scrambled to stand.

"It's OK. You're safe here," a soft and feminine voice reassured him.

Memories of the last few hours flooded back. He remembered leaving the fishing boat and climbing into the grocery truck.

A warm hand touched his. "You were dreaming. Everything is OK."

As his eyes grew accustomed to the gloom, he could make out the dark shapes that were the two girls, the jihad brides. "Where are we?"

"I don't know. We've been driving for hours."

He fumbled with his watch, lighting the screen. It was a few minutes after midday. His stomach grumbled loudly; they hadn't eaten since leaving the boat that morning. "Here, you can have this." The girl who had spoken pressed a granola bar into his hand.

"Thanks."

As he chewed the snack, he struggled to remember the girl's name. His brother would remember. He was always better with faces and names. Pain welled up inside him as his thoughts turned to Steven. No, his name was Saifan, and he had died a martyr.

"You're very brave," said the girl.

"What makes you say that?" he snapped.

"Because you have given up everything for your faith. That takes real courage."

He nodded. "So have you and your friend. What are your names?"

"I am Eshita, and this is Vashti."

He caught a glimpse of the other girl raising her hand.

"I remember you from the Imam's lectures. You were friends with my brother."

"Yes, he was a kind boy," said Eshita.

Once again he choked back grief. Kind was exactly what his brother had been. He remembered the softly spoken boy who had volunteered to run errands for elderly members of the community. Saifan had always claimed that Islam was ultimately a religion of peace. The Imam, with Mubarez's encouragement, had convinced him of their duty to wage jihad.

"Do you know where we are heading?" Eshita asked.

"Across France, to the coast. From there we will go by boat to Libya where I will train for the jihad."

"And us?"

"I don't know. Perhaps you will go immediately to the caliphate. I hear a great many of the young lions are without wives. You do them a great justice by volunteering."

"Yes. Do you suppose they will let me call my father when I am there?"

She sounded scared. Mubarez fought the urge to take her hand and reassure her. "I don't see why not. Is he proud that his daughter has chosen to serve her faith?"

"I miss him," her voice cracked, and she sobbed.

He reached out and grasped her hand. "We need to be strong. No matter what happens, we need to be strong."

ABU DHABI, UAE

Tariq Ahmed excused himself from the executives gathered in the Lascar Logistics boardroom and escaped to the elevator. The security system automatically detected his presence and sent him rocketing to his secure floor. When the doors opened his assistant, Emily, looked up from behind her desk.

"Sir, you've got thirty-five messages and seventy-three emails," she said in her crisp London accent. "I've arranged them according to priority. Most importantly, Prince Azahir called and wanted to know if you would be joining him at the Equestrian Club tomorrow?"

Tariq paused before entering his office. "Tell the Prince I will see him at the club. Hold all calls, meetings and interruptions," he glanced at his watch, "until six."

Safely inside his office, Tariq removed his jacket and took a seat at his desk. Pressing his thumb to the touchpad of his laptop, he unlocked the operating system.

Lascar Logistics used sophisticated software to track everything from aircraft maintenance to expenditure on tea and coffee. As CEO and owner of the company, Tariq was intimately familiar with the program. He quickly found the menu for live aviation contracts. Scrolling through the list, he stopped when he found the document regarding the delivery of aid into Syria.

It took him a minute to scan the fifteen-page contract. It made no mention of lethal aid. In fact, it explicitly detailed the types of medical supplies that would be shipped. He checked the list, no mention of TOW anti-tank missiles.

The contract was clean. It had been issued by the newly formed Ministry of International Cooperation and Development, commonly referred to as MICAD. As its name suggested, MICAD was responsible for the delivery of both aid and development funding to countries in need.

Tariq stroked his beard as he leaned back in his chair and contemplated the facts. Someone was using MICAD as a tool to smuggle weapons to ISIS. That someone would have to be well connected, well funded and harbor extremist views. Unfortunately, there were plenty of men who met those criteria in the Emirates. His own father had been an advocate of Wahhabi ideals and had gone so far as to directly plan and sponsor terrorist attacks. Tariq had made it his life's work to make amends for the pain and suffering men like Hussein Ahmed brought to the world. It was the very reason that PRIMAL existed.

Staring at the computer screen, he reflected on the fact that someone was using his company to transport weapons to the very people he'd sworn to destroy. There was no doubt that the man responsible was powerful and could pose a serious threat. He reached for his phone. "Emily, who do I know in the MICAD?"

"Give me a second, sir, and I'll find out."

He could hear her fingers racing across the keyboard.

"I've got a Mr. Kashif Totah on file. Would you like me to arrange a meeting?"

"Yes, as soon as possible." He turned back to his laptop and opened the MICAD website. "Inform Mr. Totah that I wish to make a significant contribution to one of their programs."

"Splendid sir, I'll enter the meeting in your diary."

"Thank you, Emily. Once you've done that feel free to finish for the day." Tariq replaced the handset, turned and gazed through the floor-to-ceiling windows at the Arabian Gulf. The sun was setting behind the city casting long shadows across the water. He loved Abu Dhabi, but it had a dark underbelly. It was his duty to expose the darkness and bring it to justice. Because, if he didn't, who would?

Chapter Six

ABU DHABI, UAE

BISHOP TWISTED the throttle on his Zero MMX electric motorcycle and aimed it at a steep dune. Propelled by a fifty-four horsepower motor, the black stealth bike made short work of the slope. He crested the rise, slid the bike sideways and raced along the spine of the dune.

Behind the tinted visor of a full-face helmet, he grinned. Silent, light and responsive the bike was as close to flying you could get on two wheels. Launching off the dune, he landed, sliding through the sand before hitting the bottom and gunning the throttle again.

Bishop had spotted the bike in the corner of PRIMAL's covert hangar at Abu Dhabi International Airport. With Mitch Freeman out finding new toys and Vance telling him to take some downtime, it made sense to give it a spin. As he sped the bike up another dune, he laughed out loud. Finally, he was living in the moment, any thoughts of Saneh pushed from his mind.

A vibration in his pocket caught his attention as he flew off the top of the dune and whipped the bike sideways. Landing hard on the down slope he skidded to a halt, flipped up his visor, and pulled his iPRIMAL from his pants. The phone was unremarkable, a ruggedized Android device. However, in the hands of a PRIMAL operative, it was far more. Accessing a hidden menu he established a secure communications link to Vance, in the Sandpit. "Boss, what's up?"

"What the hell are you doing out in the desert?" Vance asked gruffly.

Bishop glanced around at the dunes before realizing he hadn't disabled the tracker on his phone. "You told me to take some time off."

"Yeah, I meant bars and broads, not some kind of outback walkabout."

Bishop smirked at the Australian reference.

"Look, I've got some good news," Vance said.

"Saneh?"

"No, bud. You've got a green light on the TOW mission. I want you and the team to backtrack the source in Jordan."

"The team?"

"Mirza, Ice and when he arrives, Mitch."

"Ice is on board?"

"Yeah, I've cleared him to return to duty."

"The A team's back together."

There was a moment of silence before Vance continued, "No more rogue ops. No more fuck ups. You're the team lead, but if you screw this up, you're on the bench, permanently."

"Got it."

"Be aware, Tariq is running his own investigation. He's

going to try and find out who hired Lascar to deliver humanitarian aid to Syria."

Bishop's stared into the distance. "I thought it was a government contract?"

"Allegedly, things aren't that simple. Tariq's playing his cards close to his chest."

"And that doesn't bother you?"

The pause at the other end of the line told him it did. "Chua and I will provide him with assistance where we can. Mirza's already at the hangar with Ice. Mitch will arrive in a few hours. The next shipment is set for pickup in Jordan, this time, tomorrow. Let's keep this very low-key. Find out how the missiles got in the shipment, sabotage them and we'll go from there."

"Roger."

"Chua will brief you when you get back to the hangar, Vance out."

The call terminated. Bishop slipped the phone back into his jacket. He glanced at the bike's charge indicator. It read half-full. Lowering his visor he twisted the throttle, sending a rooster tail of sand into the air.

LONDON, ENGLAND

Sonia glanced at the clock on the wall of her office and sighed. Once again she'd worked past midnight without a break or meal since lunchtime. She shut her laptop and stretched her neck. All day she'd been trying to convince a judge to issue a search warrant. Her only hope of finding Eshita Mozaz was to have the police raid Imam Rahman's properties.

It hadn't been difficult to requisition the Imam's holdings. It turned out he was quite the real-estate baron with eleven properties registered to his name, or variations of. Once she had that list, she'd lobbied all of the judges she knew. So far the responses had been less than positive. Without the direct support of the Birmingham police, she was flogging a dead horse.

Calling it a day, she locked her office and rode the elevator down to the basement level. As she walked through the underground parking lot, the clack of her heels echoed off the bare concrete walls.

She noted the absence of all but two other cars, the night owls. A fluorescent light flickered off as she approached her Mercedes coupe. She fumbled in her bag for the keys. As she searched, she heard the soft tap of footsteps. Finding the keys, she glanced around. The footsteps stopped.

"Hello?" She swallowed. "Is anyone there?"

Behind her something hit the ground with a clang. She nearly leaped out of her skin and shuffled as fast as she could toward her vehicle. The lights flashed as she thumbed the keyless entry. She wrenched open the door, climbed inside, slammed it shut and hit the central locking. Breathing hard she thumbed the ignition button, and the engine rumbled to life. In the glow of the headlights, she noticed a note stuck to the outside of her windshield. Squinting, she leaned forward to examine it.

On the paper, written in blood red ink were the words:

Mind your own business bitch or you will end up with your throat cut.

Sonia gasped, flicked the wipers on and dropped the car into reverse as the blades knocked the message away. The

Mercedes shot back with a squeal of tires. Slamming the car into gear she raced out of the basement before stomping on the brakes, almost colliding with a garbage truck. As she waited for it to pass, she glanced down the street.

A few feet from the car a figure in a hoodie stared directly into her window. He wore a thick beard and a gaze laced with malice. He ran a finger across his throat.

Sonia's blood ran cold as their eyes locked. Then she turned onto the street and accelerated away. Her heart pounded as she sped through the empty London streets. It took fifteen minutes for her to calm down and by then her fear had evolved into rage. How dare these people threaten her. Tomorrow she would go to Birmingham central police station and demand that they take action. She wasn't going to run, she wasn't going to hide. Long ago she had fled India because of men like these. There was no way she was going to let them chase her from the city she called home and the clients who depended on her.

ABU DHABI, UAE

Bishop keyed his pin into the security door on the side of the Priority Movements Airlift hangar and pushed it open. A clanging sound reached his ears as he wheeled the electric bike under the wing of a business jet and made his way to the transportable buildings and shipping containers nestled in the corner of the cavernous space. Leaning the bike against a wall, he used another combination to access the container from which the noise emanated.

The inside of the forty-foot shipping container was brightly lit and had a workbench running down it lengthways. The space was cluttered with tools, weapons, laptops and various machines that Bishop struggled to identify. At the rear, he spotted the broad shoulders and bald head of PRIMAL's tech head and pilot, Mitch Freeman. "Hey, wingnut."

Mitch turned and flashed a smile. "If it isn't the convict. I hear you stole one of my new toys."

Bishop raised his hands. "Hey, if it's not bolted down it's fair game. How was your trip?"

"Very productive. Check this out."

He dodged around an arc welder and an air compressor, to join the Brit.

Mitch stood in front of some kind of exoskeleton. "Don't tell me you've been off playing Tony Stark?" Bishop inspected one of the claws attached to the bright yellow colored robot. "This for unloading cargo?"

Mitch nodded. "That's what it was designed for. They call it RALF, Robotic Assisted Logistics Facilitator. I'm going to jazz it right up. Gear it for fire support or assault. You'll be able to run around with a hundred pounds worth of kit, heavy weapons, the whole box and dice."

Bishop lifted one of the arms and let it drop with a clang. "This thing?"

"Wait and see, champ. It's going to change the way we wage war."

He gave a wink. "I'm sure it will. In the meantime, we've got a briefing with Chua."

As they left the engineering container and made for transportable buildings, Mitch inspected the e-bike. "What did you think?"

"Brilliant; plenty of power, great endurance and real quiet. Perfect for long distance covert insertion and extraction."

"My thoughts exactly."

They entered the planning room where Mirza and Ice were packing equipment into four drag bags. Handshakes and greetings were exchanged before they gathered around a video conferencing unit perched on a desk. Mitch used a remote to dial in, and a moment later Chua's face appeared on the screen. The intel chief had a can of energy drink pressed to his lips. He gulped the drink down before speaking. "Sorry guys, wasn't expecting you online for a few more minutes."

Bishop gave him a wave. "All good. We're super keen. So, what have you got?"

Chua wiped his mouth. "Gentlemen, as you already know the aid we've been delivering originates in Amman. The not-for-profit organization supplying the aid is called Global Aid Initiative. I've had Flash do a deep dive on them. So far he's turned up nothing suspicious. They've been around for a few years and seem legitimate."

"Apart from the fact they're hiding TOW missiles in their aid consignments," said Bishop.

"It's possible someone may be using GAI as a middle man."

"The same way they're using us," added Bishop.

"Exactly. However, GAI is the only lead we have, and subsequently, it's your target. They have a warehouse and head office located a short distance from the airfield in Amman. Your next shipment is due out tomorrow. Perfect cover for an infiltration."

"Security measures?"

"Flash has hacked their systems and will facilitate entry to both locations. I'm uploading the target package to each of your iPRIMALs."

On cue, Bishop felt his device vibrate in his pocket.

"The intel is light, I apologize for that."

Bishop shook his head. "No need. That's why we need to get out on the ground."

"True, if Flash digs up anything else, I'll send it straight through. Good luck team."

"Thanks, mate."

The connection ended, and Mitch killed the screen. "OK, Bish. What's the game plan?"

"We play this one by the book. Low profile and low risk."

"Not your usual playbook then," added Mirza.

He shook his head. "No, but that doesn't mean we won't be prepared for the worst."

MARSEILLE, FRANCE

Mubarez felt the truck come to a halt. When he pressed his ear against the wall, he could hear men talking.

"Are we there?" asked Eshita.

"I think so."

The cargo doors swung open revealing a figure silhouetted by lights. "Quickly, get out."

Mubarez helped Eshita and Vashti climb down from the back of the truck and glanced around. It was early evening and the air smelled heavily of the ocean. They were standing on a concrete wharf lit by dim floodlights from a nearby warehouse.

"This way." The man who had ordered them out of the truck beckoned them to follow as he stepped onto a gangplank.

This vessel was at least three times the size of the

fishing boat that had transported them across the English Channel. Modern with a wide equipment-covered stern deck, it looked like some kind of dive boat. He waited for the girls to follow the man then stepped onto the gangplank behind them. They were led across the ship to the opposite side.

"Down the ladder."

The girls froze and Mubarez moved to the railing and glanced over the side. Below the ladder a small fishing trawler bobbed in the water. "How far will that take us?"

The man grinned. "All the way. Now, get down the ladder."

Eshita shook her head and stepped away from the man. "No. I'm not going in that. We'll drown."

"Get in the boat," the man insisted.

Eshita started crying. "I can't."

The man raised his hand to strike her. Mubarez reached out and grabbed his wrist. "You hit her, and I'll kill you," he snarled.

They locked eyes, and the man looked as if he would resist. Then he sneered, "Tell your whore to get on the boat." He snatched his wrist from Mubarez's hand and strode away.

"It's OK, Eshita, I won't let anything happen to you."

She turned to him, her eyes wide. "I don't think I can."

Vashti turned and climbed down the ladder.

"Look, your friend can do it. So can you." He grasped her shoulder. "Do it for me. Do it for Saifan."

She moved toward the steel ladder and then slowly she turned and took her first tentative step.

"That's it."

Rung by rung she descended until she reached the boat. Another man, with ebony skin and a black kufi cap, helped her aboard and directed her inside the cabin. Mubarez scrambled down the ladder and joined him on the deck.

"Where are we going?" he asked as the man untied the craft from the side of the larger ship.

"Tunis, and then Benghazi."

"How long?"

The man smiled revealing a set of perfect white teeth. "A long time. I hope you don't get seasick."

Chapter Seven

BIRMINGHAM, ENGLAND

SONIA COMPLETED the police report and slid it across the counter. A stern-faced constable took the document and dropped it in a basket.

She frowned. "That's it?"

The constable nodded. "Yes miss, you file the report and then we investigate it."

"Right, in that case, I would also like to talk to Detective Smithson."

"Is it concerning a standing case?"

"Yes, a missing person case."

"I'll check to see if he's available. You can wait in one of the interview rooms. I'll buzz you through."

"Thank you."

The constable showed Sonia through a door and into a room containing a table and two chairs. She took a seat and waited. A moment later Smithson appeared dressed in a beige suit. His basset hound eyes had dark circles under them, and he clutched a coffee mug.

He took the seat opposite her. "Miss Jayaram, I hear you lodged an incident report." He wore an expression of genuine concern.

"I was threatened by Imam Raman."

"Go on."

"I met with him, and he threatened me. Then, last night I found a note on my car."

His brow rose. "You met with the Imam?"

"Yes, I met with him to discuss Eshita Mozaz."

"The missing girl. Did he know anything?"

"Not that he admitted. He did tell me to keep my nose out of his business."

"Ah huh." The detective scribbled in a notebook.

"I take it your own investigation has not revealed anything."

He swallowed. "That's not something I can discuss with you."

"I'm Mr. Mozaz's legal representative. Feel free to keep me updated."

Smithson sighed. "Miss Jayaram, dealing with the Islamic population of Birmingham is complex."

"I'm aware of this. Does that mean they're above the law?"

"No, but it does mean we need to be delicate in how we enforce it."

Sonia shook her head. "I came to this country because it offered me sanctuary from men who thought they were above the law. It would seem that I escaped nothing."

Ten frustrating minutes later Sonia left the police station and marched back to her car. Sunshine had finally penetrated the gray clouds that seemed to perpetually blanket

England. She didn't feel its warmth. Suspicion and fear clouded her thoughts as she checked over her shoulder to make sure she wasn't being followed.

She didn't notice the black-hooded youth who watched her from a bus shelter across the road. He used a phone to take a photo as she climbed into her car. Then as she pulled away from the curb, he posted the photo to an encrypted chat he shared with a dozen of his 'brothers'.

As Sonia pulled onto the highway that led back to London, she made the decision to drive directly to her apartment. Rahman's people would know where to find her office, and the apartment had additional security that included a guard. She would work from home for the next few days while she came up with a plan.

AMMAN, JORDAN

The Priority Movements Airlift LM-100J touched down in Amman with a thud and a puff of smoke from the wheels. The pilot, Mike, guided the aircraft off the airstrip and onto a taxiway as Mirza, his copilot, contacted the tower. In the back of the Hercules, Ice and Bishop sat with Daisy the explosives detection dog. Across from them Mitch had his head bowed, focused on a tablet.

They came to a complete halt and one by one the turboprops powered down. Bishop left Daisy tethered to the seat as he unclasped his belt. He pressed the button to lower the ramp, flooding the cargo hold with morning sunlight and the stench of aviation fumes.

He strode down the ramp and glanced at the other aircraft parked in the freight zone of Queen Alia

International Airport. To their right, a blue-tailed Kuwait Airlines Boeing 777 was being loaded with cargo containers. On the other side, an Embraer 195 in the livery of the Royal Jordanian Airlines was refueling from a tanker.

Bishop donned sunglasses as he checked to see if their cargo was on time. He spotted a flat-topped carrier leaving a row of warehouses. Yawning he considered ducking into the galley for a cup of coffee. The team had been up all night working through the details of their plan. They'd wargamed every possible outcome and had contingencies for each. He was quietly confident that they were as prepared as they could be.

The freight carrier with its pallets of humanitarian aid trundled across the tarmac toward them. He wondered how many missiles were hidden inside.

As the carrier lined up with the ramp, he recognized the driver and gave him a wave. This was Bishop's fifth time to the airport, and this guy had been on duty for all but one.

Ten minutes later, with cargo loaded and paperwork cleared, Bishop raised the ramp and took his seat next to Ice. The big man was staring at the pallet-load of boxes strapped under webbing nets. "Pretty smart little setup."

Bishop secured the belt across his lap and patted Daisy. "Yeah, if it hadn't been for a gust of wind they might have gotten away with it."

The roar of engines filled the cabin as the pilots ran through the startup sequence. Across from Bishop, Mitch stood peering expectantly out a round window. With a shudder, the transporter lurched forward and taxied away from the freight terminal.

Mirza's voice came over Bishop's headset, "Guys, engine three is running a little rough. Can you see if it's blowing smoke?"

"Yeah, I'll check it out." He shook his head, unclasping his sash belt. "And so the theatrics begin."

Mitch glanced back from the window and gave him a wink. Bishop joined him and peered out. Sure enough, thick smoke was trailing from the engine. He had to hand it to Mitch, the faked emergency looked real. He jumped as the turboprop backfired, spitting flames from the exhaust manifold. "Holy shit, it's on fire."

"Keep your allens on, Bish. It's all for show," replied Mitch.

He watched as the engine throttled back and the smoke and flame disappeared.

"Tower this is Papa Mike Alpha Three Three, we've got an engine out. Aborting takeoff. Please advise," broadcast Mirza over the radio.

Five minutes later the LM-100J was parked in an exclusion zone at the opposite end of the runway with a fire truck watching over it.

Mirza appeared from the cabin. Mitch gave him a slap on the shoulder. "Pretty convincing, hey."

Mirza looked skeptical. "Are you sure you can fix it?"

Bishop glanced out the window at the fire truck and its flashing lights. "Definitely got the locals wound up. OK, the plan from here is to check the engine out and then organize accommodation for the night. Mitch, how long do you need?"

"An hour, maybe less. It should be fine but I'll order some parts to make it look legit."

"Right, we'll use the time to check the cargo for TOW missiles." He gave Daisy a pat. "Then I'll contact customs and sort visas. Mirza, can you book cheap accommodation for the four of us?"

Mirza nodded. "And Mike?"

"He'll stay here and look after the Herc and Daisy. The rest of us will dine together to keep up appearances and then head out as briefed. I'll hire a car for each pair. Ice and Mitch are on the office. Mirza and I will hit the warehouse. Right, have we forgotten anything?" He locked eyes with each man. "Nope, good, let's do this."

LONDON, ENGLAND

Sonia was reviewing a case file when Padak called. The frantic father had uncovered something that he wanted to discuss with her, in person. She'd contemplated staying at home, but her sense of duty to the man and his missing daughter was too strong.

It was late afternoon when she met him in a country town, at the Cottage Café halfway between Birmingham and London. The engineer looked exhausted, his face gaunt and listless. Tears filled her eyes as she embraced him. "I'm so sorry."

"You tried your best, Sonia. That is all I can ask."

"It's not over yet."

They sat at a table for two, and Sonia ordered a pot of tea from the homely lady who owned the café.

Padak shook his head. "It is."

"No, there is more we can do."

"Sonia, you don't understand. I hired a private investigator to find her."

"And?"

"And I cannot reach him. He's disappeared off the face of the earth." He leaned in, his red eyes wide. "These people are fanatics. I think they killed him."

"No, no they wouldn't go that far."

Padak's eyes brimmed with tears. "You need to let it go, Sonia. If you don't, they could hurt you, or worse."

"We can't give up."

"I won't. But, I can't be responsible for something happening to you."

Her hands trembled as she poured tea into a cup and pushed it across to the devastated father.

"Padak, I know someone who may be able to help. He's a good man who knows people, people who are not scared of animals like these."

"Can he keep you safe?"

She nodded.

"Tell me, what will it cost? I do not have much, but what I have you can give to them."

"No, there is no price. If he can help it will be because he wants to."

"As long as you are not in danger."

Sonia managed a half smile. It had been a long time since the man she'd mentioned had saved her life in New Delhi. Over a decade since a handsome stranger had snatched her from certain death. Now he worked as a contractor, helping protect aid workers in Africa. "No, he'd never put me in danger. Just promise me that you won't do anything else before I can make arrangements."

He nodded as he sipped his tea.

She farewelled Padak and walked back to her car in the dark. As she approached the vehicle, her pulse quickened.

The two-door Mercedes was trashed. The windows had been smashed, and all four tires were flat. She peered in through a shattered window. Blank eyes stared back at her from a bloody goat's head.

Her scream echoed off the stone walls as she stumbled

backward, slipped and fell. Panic turned to pure terror as a dark figure stood over her.

"Sonia, it's me, it's Padak." He pulled her from the ground. "They did this. We need to get you somewhere safe." He led her up the road to his own car and held the door for her.

Soon they were racing along the country roads. Her breathing subsided, and she managed to speak. "My family has a summer house in Poole. We'll be safe there."

Padak nodded. "I can drive you." He leaned across and opened the glove box, revealing a black pistol. "Have you ever fired a gun before?"

Sonia nodded.

"Good, I haven't. I want you to take this. If they come for you, then use it. I'm going to search for my daughter."

She glanced out the window as they merged onto the highway. It was happening again. Power-hungry men were preying on the weak, and no one would do anything to stop them. Pulling her phone from her jacket she thumbed through her contacts until she found a particular email address. Then she started writing. If anyone was going to be able to help it was the man who had saved her in New Delhi, Mirza Mansoor.

JARJANAZ, SYRIA

Salim leaned against a white Land Cruiser as he sucked on a cheap unfiltered cigarette. Smoking it all the way to his fingers, he stubbed it out on the red crescent stenciled on the hood of the four-wheel drive and flicked it into the sand. His eyes narrowed behind aviator sunglasses as he scanned the sky above the bleak desert landscape. The horizon was clear of aircraft.

"Salim, they're not coming. We're wasting our time."

He turned to face Joran, his assistant. A former policeman, he trusted Joran to run his operations when he was absent.

Salim nodded and opened the door of his vehicle. The cabin was littered with soda cans and plastic wrappers. He searched through the garbage until he found his satellite phone. He stared at it for a moment before building up the courage to call. Then he punched in a number and held it to his ear. It took a moment for the phone to locate a satellite and connect.

The voice that answered was authoritarian with a hint of arrogance. "I take it you're calling about the cargo?"

"It hasn't arrived."

"I am aware. It would seem there was a technical issue in Jordan. It is being investigated."

"The Islamic State is planning another offensive. They need a resupply of missiles to defeat the FSA."

"I am aware of this. I will call you once I know more regarding the shipment." Salim's contact terminated the call, and he slid the phone into his pocket.

Joran approached from the front of the four-wheel drive. "Well?"

"There has been a delay of some kind."

"How long?"

Salim shrugged. "Who knows? Let's go."

"Mohammed will be furious," Joran said as he got in the driver's seat and started the engine.

He shivered involuntarily as he imagined facing the rage of the ISIS warlord.

"Perhaps we should look at supply from Libya?" Joran

suggested as he drove back to the WHO compound. "Huron can get us what we need."

"Huron is a thief. He charges more than is fair."

"When the Sheik is paying the price is irrelevant."

"True, the problem will be transportation. Smuggling by sea takes too long."

"I am sure the Sheik can arrange aircraft."

Salim nodded. "I will make the necessary inquiries."

Chapter Eight

AMMAN, JORDAN

BISHOP WATCHED the warehouse through a hand-held night vision scope from the front seat of their hire car. Mirza sat behind the wheel, his eyes firmly fixed on the screen of his iPRIMAL.

He lowered the night vision device. "No sign of any guards. They're either pretty confident no one's going to touch their gear, or there are no missiles here."

"Flash has shut down their alarm system," Mirza said still looking at the device.

"What type of alarm?"

"Nothing special. Sensors on the doors and PIRs inside."

"Responders?"

"A local security company. They're at least fifteen minutes away. I've got their patrol schedule. Not due here for at least an hour."

Bishop shook his head. "You remember the time we had

to watch a place for days to get that info. Now, Flash just remotes in from his laptop and boom, we're all over it."

Mirza chuckled. "I prefer this way."

"Hey, I wasn't complaining, merely reminiscing. OK, shall we do this?"

They left the car parked by the side of the road a hundred yards from the target location. The gargantuan warehouse was surrounded by a chain fence topped with razor wire and illuminated with security lights.

Both operatives wore dark clothing that would blend in with the shadows but wouldn't draw suspicion if they were seen. Neither carried a weapon. In a country like Jordan, the ramifications of being found with a firearm were dire.

Bishop checked his iPRIMAL was synched with his Bluetooth earpiece. "Sandpit, this is Mobile One, confirm you have us online."

The earpiece's built in bone-microphone picked up Bishop's voice, which was transmitted to their HQ in Abu Dhabi. It was Chua who replied. "We've got you, One. Mobile Two is also online."

"Roger. Over to you for access."

As they strolled toward the warehouse the streetlights flickered and a dozen paces later the street was plunged into darkness. He glanced around; the entire block was blacked out.

"Well done, lads."

They moved quickly to the door alongside the main gates. As they approached, a card-reader flashed green, and the lock clicked. Mirza pushed the gate open and they slipped inside.

"Cameras are down along with all sensors," reported Chua over their earpieces. "Mobile Two is standing by. Once you've gained entry, I will give them the go ahead."

They reached a door at the warehouse and once again the lock flashed green, allowing them to enter.

"I could get used to this," whispered Bishop as they stepped into the pitch black air-conditioned warehouse.

They paused near the door and listened.

"Team, we've been watching the camera feeds for the last few hours. There's no one inside," reported Chua.

"Better safe than sorry," whispered Mirza.

Bishop took a flashlight from his pocket and switched it on, illuminating rows of shelves. "It's a pity we couldn't bring Daisy." He'd left the explosives detection dog at the Hercules, silence and stealth not being the dog's strong suit.

"Her nose is incredible," said Mirza as he activated his own light and they made their way between shelves that stretched to the roof."

"Saneh always wanted a dog," Bishop mused as they made their way along the aisle, searching for missile-sized crates.

"You still haven't heard from her?"

"No. I need to give her the space she needs. If I try to find her, she'll run."

"You know Saneh better than anyone."

As they progressed down the aisle, Bishop's mind wandered back to the last time he had seen his lover. She'd awoken from a coma only to learn they'd lost their unborn child. A lump formed in his throat as he remembered the grief etched on her face. Instead of being there for her, he had sought vengeance. When he returned, she had run. Run from her friends, run from PRIMAL, and most painfully, run from him.

"Bish, check this out." Mirza's voice dragged him back to the mission.

The powerful flashlight illuminated a stack of wooden crates loaded on the bottom level of the shelves.

"About the right size."

Pushing Saneh from his thoughts, Bishop knelt and inspected the crates. "They're similar."

The screech of poorly lubricated bearings hit his ear, and he turned to see Mirza pushing a trolley cart. Bishop helped him drag one of the boxes clear and pried the lid off with a multi-tool. Underneath the packing material lay a machine that resembled an air-conditioning unit.

Mirza sighed. "That's not a TOW missile."

"No, it's not. Let's keep looking. Sandpit, how's Mobile Two doing?"

Chua responded immediately. "There's a guard in their location, they're waiting for him to leave."

"Roger, we haven't found anything. We're going to keep looking."

"OK, move fast. You've got a patrol due in thirty minutes."

―――

MITCH FREEMAN HUMMED a simple tune as he watched a drab brown, three-story office block through the windshield of his hire car, a Volkswagen Golf. He and Ice wore similar clothes to Mobile One, dark pants and shirts. The bearded technician also carried a satchel, containing the tools he required. "What the hell are they doing in there?"

Ice shrugged. "Their job."

The pair was parked on the opposite side of the road to the headquarters of Global Aid Initiative. They'd arrived twenty minutes earlier but had been waiting for the night guards to finish their rounds and move on.

"Well, I wish they'd do it a little faster. I'm in dire need of some rack time. How you holding up?"

"I'm great. Happy to be in the field again." The former CIA operative turned to Mitch. "I've meant to thank you. The only reason I'm here is because of your work."

"Don't mention it. Any of the gear giving you problems?"

Ice held up his bionic hand and clenched his fist. "Nope, everything's G to the G."

"Ace." He nodded toward the building. "Looks like they're done."

They watched as two uniformed guards climbed into their white SUV and departed.

"Sandpit, this is Mobile Two, we're all clear and about to make entry," transmitted Ice.

Flash replied, "Roger, I've killed their security and cameras. I can't take down the power because there's a hospital on the grid."

"Fair enough. I mean we're the good guys, right," said Mitch as they navigated an alleyway that ran behind the building.

"Sometimes, you need bad men to do bad things to evil people," said Ice as they passed a row of bins and arrived at the rear entrance.

Mitch glanced sideways at the big man. "Ice, I'm not sure I'm comfortable being in a dark alley with you."

"What are you talking about? You gave me life." Ice twitched his head, rotating his artificial hand.

"You sir, are a dick."

They located the back door and Ice inspected it. "This looks pretty high tech."

Mitch reached into his satchel. The device he withdrew

looked like a flashlight. He pressed it against the lock and activated a switch.

Ice stared at Mitch's satchel as it emitted a faint hum.

The technology guru grinned, stowed the device and pulled out a canister the size of a takeaway coffee cup. Unclipping the lid he removed a resin printed key.

"You're shitting me."

Mitch slid the key into the lock and turned it gently. "Portable 3D printer." There was a click and the door opened.

"That's insane." Ice slipped in through the door, and Mitch closed it behind them.

They moved quietly along a corridor, through a kitchenette, and into a large open plan office. "Sandpit, we're in," reported Mitch.

"Good stuff, GAI's office is on the second floor."

They reached a set of stairs and climbed up a level into a long corridor with doors either side.

Mitch used a flashlight to check the names. "This is the one."

Ice inspected the lock.

"Need my help?"

Ice shook his head as he reached into his pocket. "No, I've got a special tool of my own." Sliding a credit card into the door jam he popped the bolt and pushed the door open.

"Nicely done."

Four desks equipped with computers, a couch and a coffee table occupied the cramped office.

"Flash, remind me, exactly what are we looking for?" asked Mitch, his voice transmitted through his earpiece.

"A stand-alone computer or network," came through Flash's voice. "I managed to hack into their online stuff, nothing suspect. If they're up to no good, they're keeping it local."

Ice positioned himself so he could see through the door and down the corridor as Mitch inspected the computers.

"I've got one here that's not hard-lined in."

"Does it have a Wi-Fi card?" asked Flash.

"Negative."

"That's the one. Hook me up."

As Mitch pulled a thumb drive from his pocket, he noticed a flash of light through the blinds behind the desk. He split them with his fingers and glanced through. "Shit." The security guards had returned. "Ice, we've got company." He jammed the drive into the back of the computer. "Quick, hide."

At six foot five and two hundred and forty pounds, there wasn't anywhere in the office that Ice could hide. He shot Mitch a bemused look and pulled the door closed.

"Flash, are you in yet?" Mitch asked.

"That's what she said," the PRIMAL hacker said chuckling. "Wait, no that's not right."

"How long?" snapped Mitch. "We could have company."

"A couple of minutes. Maybe more."

"Mate, that's not going to cut it."

Ice turned from the door and held a finger to his lips.

Mitch frowned and lowered his voice. "Get a move on."

The sound of footsteps echoed down the corridor along with voices. He crouched behind the desk. Ice made a token effort to hide alongside the door.

A light shone through the opaque glass, and Mitch held his breath. The voices were louder now and the footsteps directly outside. His mouth went dry as a key was inserted into the lock.

Ice reached across and grabbed the door handle with his artificial hand.

The men on the other side tried to turn it and failed. They spoke to each other in what Mitch assumed was Arabic then tried the door again.

He peered over the desk at Ice who calmly held the handle.

A moment later the guards gave up and continued along the corridor.

Minutes had passed before Ice spoke. "I think they're gone."

"Flash, are you done?" asked Mitch.

"Yeah man, get out of there."

He yanked the drive from the back of the computer and pocketed it. "We're good. Let's roll."

AS MITCH and Ice made it clear of the GAI office, Bishop and Mirza were still searching the warehouse.

They moved quietly down the last of the aisles.

"There're no TOW crates here," said Bishop as they reached the far end.

"None on my side," added Mirza.

"Sandpit, we've found nothing," he transmitted.

"Alright, the security patrol is due in your location in the next fifteen minutes. You need to exfil," replied Chua.

"Moving now." Bishop turned to Mirza. "I hope the boys had better luck at the office."

They made their way back through the dark warehouse to the exit. As they left the building and passed through the security gate, the lights flickered, and the power came back on.

"You could have waited till we got out," transmitted Bishop.

"That wasn't us," replied Chua. "The locals worked out the glitch Flash put in the system."

"Yeah, we barely made it out." As they walked back toward their sedan Bishop spotted another vehicle coming up the street. It stopped opposite their hire car.

Mirza grabbed Bishop's arm and pulled him into the shadows. A spotlight illuminated their car. They watched as a security guard stepped out and peered in through the windows. The figure lifted a radio to his mouth.

"This doesn't look good," said Bishop as a second vehicle pulled up behind the first. "I think we've been rumbled. Might be a good idea to ditch the wheels and head back to the hotel on foot."

"Do you think they're aware of the break in?"

"There could have been a silent alarm."

"It is possible."

"Sandpit, this is Mobile One," Bishop transmitted. "We've got a potential compromise. We're abandoning the car and extracting on foot."

It took a moment for Chua to respond. "Acknowledged, do you want me to coordinate an RV with Mobile Two?"

Bishop pulled his **iPRIMAL** from his pocket and checked the screen. Mobile Two's icon flashed in the vicinity of the office building. If he and Mirza moved one block west, it would be simple for Ice and Mitch to pick them up. "Yeah, sounds good. We'll move to the main road."

As they slunk away into the shadows neither he nor Mirza realized they were being watched. High on the wall of another building, a tripod mounted remote surveillance device zoomed in on them. The stubby antenna on the back of the camera broadcast the image to an old-model Mercedes sedan parked a block away. In the passenger seat, a broad-shouldered woman with short dark hair turned to her bearded partner. "We need to find out who these guys are."

"There's only one way we can do that."

"Let's pick them up."

ICE LED the way to the back door of the office block and into the alley. He waited for Mitch to lock the door, then headed back toward the car. As they rounded the building, a powerful floodlight illuminated them.

Ice caught a glimpse of the white SUV that the security guards were driving as he broke into a run. Mitch didn't need prompting, hot on Ice's heels. They reached their car together, Ice diving into the driver's seat. As he started the Golf, the rear window shattered and bullets thudded into the trunk.

Mitch ducked low. "Holy shit."

Ice gripped the steering wheel tight as he gunned the engine and dropped into gear. They rocketed out of the alleyway, wheels squealing on the asphalt. He glanced in the wing mirror and spotted the SUV following with blue lights flashing. "Sandpit this is Two. We've been compromised and have a tail. We're not going to make the RV with One anytime soon."

Chua's voice replaced Flash's in his earpiece. "OK, let us know when you're clear."

Ice checked the mirror; the guards were gaining on them. "That SUV's got us beat for power." The headlights illuminated a side street. He wrenched the wheel sideways and hit the throttle.

The nimble Golf slid around the corner with a screech, wobbled and took off like a rocket.

Mitch turned so he could see through the shattered back window. "They're still on us."

They raced around another corner and into an industrial zone of warehouses, shipping containers and trucks.

He glanced at the mirror again as the SUV careened around the corner. "We need to lose them before the cops join the chase."

Mitch grinned. "I know someone that can help with that. Sandpit, this is Two, I need you to activate contingency plan Romeo Romeo Four."

"Roger, already active."

"What is Romeo Romeo Four?" Ice asked as he spun the wheel, sending them screeching around another corner.

"One of Flash's babies. Complete overwhelming of Police resources through automated systems. I doubt if anyone will be responding to the security company's call now."

"Good, because if these guys can actually drive I'm going to have to ramp things up."

He spotted two sixteen-wheeler car carriers parked alongside the road. Checking the mirror he braked and wrenched the handbrake hard, flicking the Golf sideways into the gap between the trucks. They hit the curb with a loud thud as he killed the headlights.

A split second later the SUV screamed past, lights flashing.

Ice spun the wheel, stomped the accelerator to the floor and gave chase.

The driver of the SUV must have been fixated on the

road because he failed to see the blacked out Golf as it slipped in behind him.

Ice closed the gap as they raced around another corner. He waited for SUV to off-weight then rammed the inside.

The driver responded exactly how Ice wanted him to, slamming on the brakes and skidding sideways, out of control. Ice slowed as the security car slid into the curb. Its wheels stopped dead but the momentum flipped it, and it smashed roof first through a sheet metal fence.

"Woo hoo! They're not coming back from that," Mitch yelled excitedly. "Job well done, mate."

Ice flicked the headlights on and drove the Golf back toward the main road. "Sandpit this is Mobile Two, we've neutralized our tail and are on the way to RV with Mobile One."

BISHOP STARED AT HIS IPRIMAL. "I don't have a signal." He shook the device then turned to Mirza. "How about you?"

"Same, could be some kind of interference. There's a lot of heavy industry around here."

Bishop stuffed the phone back into the pocket of his cargo pants. "Yeah, maybe. The RV's about half a mile, that way." He pointed west through a fenced vehicle yard. "We'll have to box around."

They walked along the fence, careful to avoid any street lighting. Reaching the corner, they found a storm water drain that offered a concealed route to their rendezvous point. Bishop slid down the concrete wall with Mirza behind. When he hit the bottom, he checked his iPRIMAL again. "Whatever's blocking the cell phone signal is powerful."

"It could be jamming," said Mirza.

"Maybe, either way we need to get to the RV." Bishop stepped off, avoiding a pile of debris. The ambient light cast long shadows across the concrete, and their footsteps echoed.

At the next road the drain ended at two waist-high pipes. Bishop crouched next to them. "The RV is one block over. Give me a leg up."

Mirza stood with his back to the concrete wall and boosted Bishop so he could grab the railing above. Bishop clambered up the concrete slope and slid under the rail.

A car skidded to a halt alongside him. Before he could jump back into the drain a door opened and an Uzi Pro submachine gun was aimed at his face.

"Show me your hands," an accented voice growled.

Bishop rose to his feet and locked eyes with the gunman. He had a dark complexion, a week's growth and wore a baseball cap pulled down low. The Uzi was unwavering, held with the casual confidence of a trained operative.

"Where is your friend?" The man's eyes never left Bishop, a professional.

Bishop glanced into the drain, Mirza was gone. He shrugged as the driver's door of the car opened and a second figure appeared.

"Hands behind your back."

He felt something on his wrists and then the distinctive ratchet of plastic cuffs as they tightened. A hood and earmuffs were placed on his head. Strong hands guided him into the back of the car, and a moment later he sensed they were moving. The only consolatory thought in his head was that they hadn't captured Mirza.

AS MIRZA POPPED out of the pipe on the opposite side of the road, he heard a car door slam shut. Scrambling up the culvert, he managed to spot the car's plates as it drove away. He pulled his iPRIMAL from his pocket and made a note of the seven numbers. There was still no reception.

He sprinted in the opposite direction, rapidly covering the half-mile to the RV point. When he arrived, he spotted Mobile Two's hatch parked by the side of the road. He noticed the shattered rear window as he approached and climbed into the back seat.

"Someone snatched Bishop," he managed breathlessly.

"Security guards?" asked Ice.

Mirza shook his head. "Gray Mercedes sedan." He checked his iPRIMAL. "Number plate 3569870."

Mitch glanced over his shoulder. "What, when, how?"

"Five minutes ago. They went west, toward the city."

"We need to go after him," said Mitch as Ice pulled away from the curb.

Ice shook his head. "No, they could be halfway across town by now. We need to get off the street and get back into contact with the Sandpit."

Mirza frowned as he stared at his phone. It now had a full signal. "My phone's working."

"Yep, we were being jammed," said Mitch. "The buggers that grabbed Bish, they're pros."

THE ODOR of freshly laid carpet hung heavy in the air as Bishop was directed into a room and shoved into a leather chair. He relaxed ever so slightly. This wasn't the first time he'd been captured, and he was mentally prepared for the interrogation that would follow.

The hood was ripped off; he squinted, anticipating bright lighting. There was none. He turned his head and surveyed the room. It looked new, or at least freshly renovated. The walls were white, and there was a cream leather sofa behind a glass coffee table.

The person who had removed his hood appeared in the corner of his vision. It was a woman. She took a seat on the sofa opposite him and smiled pleasantly.

Bishop guessed her age at early thirties. She had a broad forehead, gray eyes, and a full mouth. Her hair, a shade of brown, was tied in a short ponytail. The fitted shirt she wore revealed strong shoulders and an athletic build. She reminded Bishop of an MMA fighter.

"Hello." She had a faint accent that Bishop couldn't quite identify.

He met her smile with a frown. "So, what's this all about then? You kidnap a lot of randoms?"

"Only those who break into warehouses."

"I don't know what you're talking about."

"So, it wasn't you at the GAI facility?"

"GAI? What? I was literally out walking my dog."

Her eyebrow arched. "Walking your dog? And where exactly is that dog?"

"He ran down the storm drain. That's what I was doing when your buddy stuck his pea shooter in my face."

She held out his wallet. Opening it up she removed his Abu Dhabi International Airport security card and inspected it. "It says here you work for Lascar Logistics. Tell me, Mr. Bishop, what is someone based in the Emirates doing walking their dog in an industrial zone of Amman?"

Bishop knew he was going to have to give her something. Clearly she was a professional, and for some reason she was playing nice, for now. "I work for a specialized wing within Lascar. We are contracted to fly GAI medical aid into Syria. Turns out we were actually smuggling weapons. I was trying to find out who's responsible."

She nodded thoughtfully. "Go on."

"We hired a car. Came out to the warehouse and we were snooping around when the power went out. Must have freaked out their security so, we took a peek inside."

"Did you find anything?"

He shook his head. "No. A complete waste of time." He noticed she kept glancing over his shoulder, and turned his head. Someone stood in the doorway of what he assumed was the kitchen. "OK, so how about you tell me who the hell you are and why I'm here."

Her eyes flicked to her partner and then back to Bishop. "We're investigating the same thing you are."

He raised his eyebrows. "And...?"

"We work for a government agency trying to stop high-tech weaponry getting into the hands of extremists."

"CIA?"

"Who we are is irrelevant."

"Not to me, it's not. You're not Jordanian, that's for sure, which means you don't have legal jurisdiction to hold me, much less interrogate me. So, how about we ditch the cuffs and talk like adults."

She nodded and a second later Bishop felt a hand on his. There was a snap, and he was free. Rubbing his wrists, he glanced over his shoulder at a swarthy dark-bearded man who could have passed for a native in any number of Middle Eastern countries. "Thanks, you can call me Aden." He turned back to the woman. "I don't suppose you two have names?"

She relaxed into the couch. "I'm Keila, and this is Thomas."

"Keila, that Hebrew?"

She ignored the comment. "We've been investigating weapons smuggling into Syria for some time."

"How did you find out about GAI?"

"That doesn't matter. What is important is we know that weapons are being smuggled in through Jarjanaz. There's a facilitator there who's supplying a number of extremist groups."

"The guy we've been delivering our aid to?"

"Salim Wayeed."

"That's him. So, he's not the hero he lets on."

"You've met him?"

"Yeah, he receives our shipments personally."

She glanced across at Thomas. "That's interesting."

"Look, you guys know a shit load more about these clowns than I do. How about you let me go and we forget this ever happened."

Bishop watched as Keila and Thomas exchanged another glance. They interacted silently, a sure sign they'd been working together for some time.

She slid Bishop's wallet across the coffee table. Then she reached into her pocket, removed a cell phone and placed it beside the wallet.

"That's not my phone."

"Thomas, give him his phone."

Her partner handed Bishop his iPRIMAL. He checked the screen. No reception.

"This cell phone will work across most of the Middle East. We'll use it to contact you."

"Contact me? You want me to provide you with information?"

"Yes, Aden. This is a war. A war between good and evil and we need your help."

He tried not to smirk. "Really, I could make a difference?"

"Yes, by providing us with information you could help us shut Salim down."

As amusing as Keila's pitch was, it did have merit. PRIMAL could potentially use her agency to neutralize Salim and recover the TOW missiles. "OK, how's this going to work?"

Chapter Nine

ABU DHABI, UAE

CHEN CHUA OPENED the refrigerator in the kitchen of the PRIMAL headquarters and grabbed a can of energy drink. Cracking it open he glanced at his watch. It was a little after four in the morning; no wonder he felt like rubbish.

Taking a second can, he made his way back upstairs to the operations room where Frank and Vance were manning their iPRIMAL terminals. He passed the extra can to Frank. "Any news from the team?" Vance didn't drink what he referred to as toxic waste.

The former British paratrooper shook his head as he opened the drink. "No. The guys are setup at the hotel and ready to go, but we've got no target."

Vance glanced up from his own terminal. "Has Flash got anything?"

"Not on Bishop. However, Jordanian police have issued an alert for the car Ice and Mitch were driving."

"Which they've subsequently abandoned?" asked Vance.

Frank nodded. "Correct. They ditched it outside of town. Both vehicles were rented under a pseudonym and had fake plates."

"So, who the hell has Bishop?" asked Vance.

Chua took a seat. "Mirza mentioned that their communications were being jammed during their exfil. That's an indicator it was someone with significant technical capacity. I'm thinking state level at a minimum."

"Do the Jordanians have that sort of capability?" asked Vance.

"Yes, but it could be the Israelis, Saudis, or even someone from the Emirates. They all have the ability to locally jam specific frequencies and even individual devices."

A shout sounded from the corridor. "I've got a hit!" Flash appeared in the doorway wearing his trademark flat brim cap tipped back. With a childlike grin he thrust a tablet computer out in front of him. "Bishop's iPRIMAL just pinged the network."

"Where is he?" asked Vance.

Flash turned his attention to the screen. "He's still in Amman, it's trying to get a tighter location."

Frank, Chua and Vance leaned forward expectantly.

"A few more seconds." Flash screwed up his face. "That can't be right."

"What can't be right?"

Flash smiled. "He's at the hotel."

AMMAN, JORDAN

Ice leaped from the armchair and was halfway to the hotel room door when it swung open, revealing Bishop. He skidded to a halt, lowering his fists.

"Where the hell have you been?" demanded Mitch. He and Mirza were sitting on either side of a table.

"Nice to know I was missed," responded Bishop as he closed the door.

Ice grabbed him in a bear hug. "We were worried."

"Easy, Terminator, you're going to break a rib." Bishop extracted himself from the big man's grasp.

"Mirza got the plate number of the car that took you but Flash couldn't track it down," said Mitch. "They were running fake plates."

"Who were they?" Mirza asked.

Bishop made a beeline for the mini bar in the corner of the room, removed a tiny bottle of whiskey and poured it into a glass. "They were Mossad."

"Mossad!" exclaimed Mitch.

Bishop downed half the whiskey. "Yeah."

Mitch shook his head. "Hang on. Mossad is smuggling weapons into Syria?"

"No. Like us, they're investigating who's responsible."

"Why did they let you go?" asked Mirza.

"Because," he took another swig of the amber liquid, "I agreed to work for them."

Ice frowned. "Exactly how will you do that?"

"I'm going to feed them information from our deliveries into Syria."

"Because you're a loadmaster with Priority Movements Airlift," said Mirza.

Bishop raised the empty glass. "Exactly. Now, when are we due to takeoff for Jarjanaz?"

Mitch checked his iPRIMAL. "Our parts have arrived. It will take me an hour to fit and test them. We can be wheels up at 0800 hours."

"Sounds good. First, I'm going brief the Sandpit and grab a bite to eat. Mirza, can you sort some room service?"

AS THE PRIMAL team prepared for their departure, Captain Momani of the Jordanian General Intelligence Directorate was at the offices of Spider Security interviewing two employees. Despite the early hour, he wore a crisp white shirt and an expensive business suit. As he reached for a cup of hot tea, his cuff slid back, revealing a golden Rolex, a gift from a wealthy family friend.

"The two men who escaped from the office block, describe them."

One of the guards made to reply, but the other cut him off. "One tall with a baseball cap, the other medium height with a satchel."

Momani took another sip from his cup and waited for the man to continue.

He didn't. Instead, he turned to his partner who proceeded to nod. "Yes, one tall and one medium."

The counter-intelligence officer sighed. He'd left a very attractive woman in his bed, and was keen to return to her warm embrace. At this rate, that wasn't likely to happen anytime soon.

"Did you also respond to the incident at the warehouse?"

The two men shook their heads in unison.

"Is there any CCTV footage that I can view?"

Again, the two men shook their heads.

"There is no camera footage?"

The first guard to speak answered. "The CCTV cameras and the security systems were off. It could have been because of the big power failure."

"What power failure?"

"The one at the warehouse."

Momani shook his head and sipped from his mug of tea. He felt his phone vibrate in his pocket. "One minute." He fished it out and answered the call as he left the office. It was his assistant.

"Sir, I have the information you requested."

"Go ahead."

"The Israeli embassy registered three additional consular staff last week; two men and a woman. They were listed as working for MASHAV. Our embassy surveillance team followed them when they visited a not-for-profit organization based near the airport."

"Do you have the name of the agency?"

"Yes, wait." He could hear the man ruffling through the mountain of paperwork that usually occupied his desk. "Global Aid Initiative."

He checked the name against the one scrawled in his notebook, the location of the break-in. It was the same.

"Does that help?"

"Perhaps. I need you to source copies of any photos from the surveillance team. I will see you back at the office." Momani terminated the call. He wasn't going to bother to continue his interview with the security guards. He had all the information he needed. There was no doubt in his mind; Mossad was sniffing around the Sheik's Jordanian interests.

ABU DHABI, UAE

Tariq sat at a conference table within the recently completed headquarters for the Ministry of International Cooperation and Development. He slid back the sleeve of his bespoke suit and checked the time on his Breitling watch. He'd been waiting for Mr. Kashif Totah for twenty minutes.

Returning his attention to one of the windows he watched as a delivery truck left Pepsi Cola's Emirati factory. The irony of the MICAD being located next door to a soft drink company was not lost on him. Companies like Pepsi had more reach and influence than the government agency could ever hope to attain. What's more, they made billions of dollars at the same time.

The sound of the door to the room opening caught his attention. An overweight balding gentleman entered and flashed him a smile.

"Mr. Ahmed, I am so sorry to keep you waiting. My previous meeting ran over."

Tariq rose and shook the man's hand. "Not a problem."

"Can I get you some tea or coffee?"

He shook his head. "No, this will have to be short. I have another meeting in half an hour."

The rotund government bureaucrat took a seat opposite Tariq.

"Thank you again, Mr. Totah, for agreeing to meet with me."

"Please, call me Kashif, and it is a pleasure to meet the man responsible for flying much of our aid to where it is needed."

"And that is exactly why I am here today."

"Yes, your assistant mentioned you were thinking of donating some of your services?"

"Not only services but also finances. My aircrew have told me how well received the medical supplies are in Syria. If it is possible, I would like to become more involved in that project. I thought Lascar Logistics could provide the airlift for free and also help with the purchase of medical supplies."

Kashif's ample features broke into a smile. "Excellent, I can add your donation to those provided by the Emirates Aid Fund. Together you will make a considerable difference to our brothers and sisters in Syria."

"The Emirates Aid Fund, I don't believe I've heard of it. Who are the major contributors?"

"It's an anonymous fund. It allows generous Emiratis to donate without the usual media circus. They feel that the emphasis should be placed on those with need."

Tariq nodded in agreement. "Understandable."

"Indeed. Now, how will you be making your donation?"

Tariq rose from the table. "I will have my assistant organize a check." He offered Kashif his hand.

"Excellent, your generosity knows no bounds, Mr. Ahmed."

Neither does my vengeance, thought Tariq, as he left the building and joined his driver in a long-wheelbase Range Rover.

As they returned to Lascar Towers Tariq placed a call. "Emily, can you find out who the major contributors to the Emirates Aid Fund are?"

"Yes sir, I will look into it. When do you need the information?"

"As soon as you can. And Emily?"

"Yes, sir."

"This needs to be discreet. Very discreet."

"Understood."

Tariq ended the call and relaxed into the Range Rover's plush seat. A list of names ran through his head; men he either knew or suspected harbored extremist ideals. At least one of them had to be funding the operation. The problem was they were all very powerful and influential Emiratis. He would need to be very careful how he approached this; he had enough enemies without making another.

Chapter Ten

GAZIANTEP, TURKEY

SALIM RAISED a cup to his nose and inhaled the rich aromas of the Turkish coffee. Commodities like coffee beans and sugar were becoming harder to acquire in Syria. It was almost worth sneaking across the border into Turkey for breakfast, although the bribes at the frontier would make it an expensive meal.

The ancient city of Gaziantep was located a mere thirty miles from the Syrian border. Occupied by everyone from the Romans to the Ottomans the city was a veritable melting pot of culture and subsequently fantastic food and drink. Salim always took the opportunity to visit his favorite cafés and restaurants when in town. Given that Gaziantep was the closest international airport to his home base of Jarjanaz, it was fairly regularly.

The café he had chosen to enjoy his morning beverage was the Tahmis Khavesi, an ancient coffee house first opened in 1635. He sat beneath an ornate chandelier in one corner of the sandstone building. Today's paper lay across the table under a plate of white cheese and olives. As he sipped his coffee, the phone in his pocket buzzed. He fished it out with his free hand and checked the screen. It was the Sheik.

"Did the missiles arrive?"

"Yes, my men took delivery a few hours ago." Salim sipped his coffee.

"Your men? Where are you?"

"Gaziantep."

"Why?"

"I'm on the way to Benghazi," he replied.

"I thought we lost our contact there?" Their supply line from the Libyan town had recently been disrupted, allegedly due to inter-tribal conflict. Salim suspected CIA intervention.

"I have a different trader. I thought it prudent to secure another line of procurement."

There was a moment of silence on the other end of the call. "A wise decision considering I have decided to suspend the missile shipments from Amman."

"Suspend the missile shipments?"

"We have been compromised."

He placed the coffee down. "How? Where?"

"Mossad broke into GAI's office."

Salim looked down into his cup. He knew better than to question the Sheik. The wealthy prince had an extensive informant network, with reach into foreign agencies that only extreme wealth could buy.

The Sheik continued, "The question on my mind, is why the interest from Mossad?"

"What do you mean?"

"A handful of missiles are hardly of interest to the Jews.

Why do you think they are sending operatives to investigate GAI?"

"I don't know," Salim replied with an even voice.

"You wouldn't be doing any deals on the side, would you?"

"I would not dare. My loyalty is to you and Mohammed."

"I hope so." There was a pause. "You will investigate supply from Benghazi. The medical aid will continue to flow from Amman. However, you must remain vigilant. I will send you the intelligence my people have gathered."

"I eagerly await it."

"Salim, without my support the Caliphate will wither and die. Continue to perform and you will be rewarded. Fail me, and you will find that my reach has no boundaries."

The call ended and Salim downed the rest of his coffee. The threat didn't bother him; the Sheik was a spoilt prince playing games. Mossad, however, was a serious concern and he knew exactly why they were after him. Gaziantep was not a safe place from their assassins. He needed to get on his flight to Libya.

ABU DHABI, UAE

When the team returned to the PRIMAL hangar, they'd immediately convened a debriefing in the planning room. In an hour they had covered the infiltration into GAI, their close call with the security guards, Bishop's kidnapping by Mossad, and the completion of their delivery mission into Syria.

"That's pretty much everything. You guys got anything

else you want to add?" Bishop asked turning to the other members of his team. Mitch, Ice and Mirza were sitting around a long table, drinking beers. Vance and Chua sat at the head of the table.

"Nah, that's about it," replied Mitch. He had already briefed his and Ice's component of the mission.

Chua glanced up from the laptop he was using to record the information. "Very comprehensive. I've got a few questions regarding the drop off in Jarjanaz. You said you found another six TOWs in the shipment?"

"That's correct," replied Bishop.

"We sabotaged the missiles and fitted a tracking device to one," added Mitch.

Chua nodded. "Good work. Who received the shipment, Salim?"

Bishop shook his head. "No, a new guy. Mirza, what was his name?"

"He introduced himself as Joran."

"Yeah, that's it, Joran." Bishop dragged out the vowels making it sound Spanish. "Joran of Jarjanaz."

"Sounds like a gay hair stylist," said Ice.

Mitch snorted into his beer. "Use a lot of them, do you?"

"No, but my mechanic's a little dubious." Ice wiggled the fingers on his bionic hand.

Vance slapped the table with his palm. "OK, that's enough." Despite his gruff voice, he wore a smirk.

Bishop took a sip from his beer and grinned. It felt good to be back with the team, in the field with men he trusted with his life. "What are we doing next, boss?"

Vance frowned. "Not a goddamn thing. There's no way we're going to risk getting involved with Mossad. Our job is done. We're going to sit back, track the missiles and leak the intel into the coalition targeting cycle."

"I take it we didn't get anything from the hack at the GAI office?"

Chua shook his head. "No. Flash has gone right through their records and there's nothing suspicious. We've got no idea how those weapons are getting into their aid shipments."

"We could stake it out?" suggested Mitch.

Vance shook his head. "Not with Mossad sniffing around."

Bishop put his beer down. "We've got a unique opportunity here. We can use them to target the smugglers."

"Bud, I've worked with Mossad before. They're ruthless. We expose ourselves to them, and PRIMAL is cactus. The risk is too damn high."

Bishop considered the comment. "Yeah, OK."

"That doesn't mean we ignore Mossad. They're looking at us now, whether we like it or not. Do you have their phone on you?"

He presented the device Keila had given him. "Mitch has already ripped it for Flash."

"Good. We'll be monitoring from HQ. You're not authorized to agree to anything."

"Roger."

"And that phone doesn't come anywhere near the Sandpit," Chua added.

"Got it."

The room went silent for a moment before Ice spoke. "So now we wait?" It was the former CIA operative's first hit out with the team since being captured and injured. "Are we back on stand down?"

Vance nodded. "Yeah, get some downtime. We're done here for the day."

Mitch, with a beer in hand, disappeared back into his engineering workspace. Ice and Bishop stepped outside to discuss something, leaving Vance with Chua and Mirza.

"What's up, bud? You've got the weight of the world on your shoulders," asked Vance.

Mirza reached into the pocket of his cargo pants, withdrew a folded piece of paper, and slid it across the table. "I received this email yesterday. I know you said we were stood down, but I need to help my friend."

Vance took a pair of glasses from his jacket and examined the printed email. A moment later he passed it to Chua. "Sonia Jayaram is the woman you saved in India before you were sent to Sierra Leone?"

"Yes, she was a public prosecutor in New Delhi. She took a stand against a corrupt senior police officer."

Chua looked up from the email. "The one who facilitated the terrorist attack you thwarted."

Mirza nodded. "Colonel Prasad proved to have friends in low places. Sonia escaped to England. She has been working there ever since."

Chua handed back the piece of paper. "What does she know of PRIMAL?"

"She thinks I'm a security contractor. I've helped her out from time to time, but we're just friends."

"The girl who is missing, do you know her?" asked Vance.

Mirza shook his head. "No, but if Sonia has asked for my help, then I cannot say no. I've already booked my ticket."

"Sentiment I can understand. Mirza, this mission is

exactly why PRIMAL exists." He turned to Chua. "Can we throw any intel muscle at this?"

Chua nodded. "Flash and I have some capacity. However, I think Mirza is going to need significant technical support. I recommend sending Mitch forward to assist."

"Good call. Mirza, when's your flight?"

"In four hours."

"Damn, you don't mess about do you, son. Once you meet up with your lady friend, make an assessment on what support you need. Give Mitch a few days to sort his gear and then he can RV with you in the UK."

Mirza nodded. "I did not expect help."

"Well, ordinarily I'd send Bishop with you. But, with the Mossad piece on the boil, I need him here."

"I understand." Mirza left the room, leaving Vance and Chua alone.

Vance stretched his neck and sighed. "So much for winding back ops. I swear we've been busier since we left the island."

Chua nodded. "Yeah, and now I've got less staff. Maybe we should consider getting the whole team back together."

"Yeah, perhaps. In the meantime, we make do with what we've got."

"Don't we always?"

TEL AVIV, ISRAEL

Keila Bachman strode purposefully down one of the sterile corridors inside Mossad's Tel Aviv headquarters. She had stepped off a flight from Amman and rushed directly to the offices of the world's most secretive intelligence organization.

Officially named the Institute for Intelligence and Special Operations, Mossad's headquarters consisted of five floors of analysts, agent handlers, liaison officers, and technicians. Keila walked through the bustling hive of workers, and down a quiet corridor to another part of the 'Institute'.

Stopping at a security door, she used a retina scanner to gain access into the *Metsada*, or Special Operations Department. Inside worked the support staff for Mossad's elite, field operatives known in popular folklore as *Kidon* and within the Israeli intelligence community as 'The Team'.

Keila placed her bag next to an empty desk and approached the Counter-Proliferation Cell where a gaggle of analysts had their eyes glued to computer screens.

"Hey, guys."

Three sets of red eyes focused on her.

"Hello, Keila. Welcome," said Abel, the lanky leader of the group. The other two analysts, Jacinta, a middle-aged motherly type, and Fahim, the bespectacled new kid, added their own greetings.

Keila gave them a smile. "Team, your lead on GAI was spot on. Good work."

"I just finished working on your recruitment proposal for this Aden guy," said Abel.

"It's rushed, I know, but this could be our chance to get Objective Charlie-Three-Three." Keila referred to Salim Wayeed, the Syrian arms trafficker. He'd made the *Metsada* High Value Target list a year earlier, the result of selling high-end weaponry to both Hamas and Hezbollah.

She rolled her chair to Abel's terminal. "OK, so what have we got on Aden of Lascar Logistics?"

Abel waited for her to sit while Jacinta headed to the

kitchenette in the corner of the room to make coffee. Fahim joined them at the computer.

Abel had a presentation ready to go. He advanced the slide to a picture of the man Keila's team had snatched in Amman. "His full name is Aden Bishop. A former Australian Army officer who was discharged in 2003 and started working with Lascar Logistics in 2004."

She studied the file photo. The shot didn't do the Australian justice. In real life, his dark eyes were far more intense.

"We hacked into Lascar's personnel server and downloaded his file. He's had a somewhat interesting career but hasn't progressed far through the company. There have been numerous disciplinary issues." Abel advanced the slide to a breakdown of Aden's career.

"He's worked in almost every major conflict zone since he joined," she observed.

"Yes, he moved to their Priority Movements wing in 2005. They deliver humanitarian aid to war-torn areas."

"Interesting. Do we have any information regarding his career in the Australian Army?"

Abel turned to Jacinta as she handed him a coffee. "Jacinta, what did you dig up?"

"Not a lot. He left military service as a lieutenant following an incident in Sierra Leone. Details are sketchy, but it looks like he refused an order and was sacked."

"So, our boy's got a problem with authority," said Keila.

"Most definitely. It's a theme throughout his entire profile and something you can target," reinforced Jacinta.

A newspaper headline filled the screen.

Australian Journalist and Wife Killed in Terrorist Attack!

She scanned the text. "You're kidding. His parents were killed on flight LY395?"

"Yes, they were on their way to Spain to meet with him."

Keila remembered back to her interview with Aden. There had been an intensity in his eyes as he held her gaze. She understood now. "He's going to be butter in our hands."

The next slide showed a network analysis diagram connecting Aden's close associates. She noted that most of them were his work colleagues.

"Nothing out of the ordinary here, except…" Abel zoomed the screen in on a photo of Aden with a woman.

She looked Middle Eastern, with exotic features, high cheekbones and long raven hair. She was gorgeous.

"This is the only evidence we have that Aden has a partner. Fahim used facial recognition to trawl the web for images. This is the only one we found."

Keila inspected the photo carefully. The couple had been snapped in front of a canvas tent in what had to be Africa. Aden had his arms wrapped around her protectively. The pair looked very much in love. "Do we know who she is?"

"Someone does," said Fahim.

She turned to the analyst. "What do you mean?"

"I ran the image through our databases. It came back with a hit."

"And?"

"She's on a blackout list. We can't get any intel on her."

"And we can't target her," added Keila.

"That's correct. Someone inside Mossad has put her completely off limits," said Abel.

"Right, well that's an issue." She considered the facts for a moment. "OK, what else do we have?"

"That's all we've got right now. Do you want us to keep digging?" asked Abel.

"Yes, but I want you to focus on the woman. Find out who she is and where she is."

"Keila, that's going to be tough. We won't be able to use any of the Mossad databases or technologies."

"You'll work out a way. Aden Bishop gives us access to Salim, and this woman may be the key to manipulating him."

"We'll do our best."

"I know you will, that's why you're the sharpest nerds around."

Fahim, the new guy spoke up, "So if you get Bishop on board, what's the plan to take down Salim? Infiltrate into Jarjanaz? Kill or capture?"

Abel shot the junior analyst a dark stare.

Keila stood, ignoring the question. "I'll be in the Emirates tomorrow to meet with Bishop. If you find anything on the girl send it through immediately.

A BLACK SUV would have been far too obvious. The meet went down in a battered sedan on the outskirts of Tel Aviv, far from the corridors of Mossad's headquarters. The driver, tall with thinning silver hair, had picked up his passenger on street corner. As he drove along a dark road, he glanced in the rear view mirror. "It's been a long time, Caleb."

Caleb was a few years younger. "It has Benjamin, and you haven't aged a day."

"I wish that were true, my friend. Every morning my bones let me know I'm an old man. Now, what's so important that you could not come to my home?"

They cruised the empty streets.

"Someone is searching for the Mantis," said Caleb.

Benjamin spun to face the current Mossad director. "Who?"

"One of my *Kidon*. She's targeting an arms trafficker in Syria."

He turned his attention back to the road. "That doesn't explain why she's looking for someone who's been dead for six years."

"We made an assessment based on the evidence presented at the time. No one ever saw a body."

"Regardless, why is your officer searching in the first place? I take it the Tiberias program is still compartmented?"

"Of course. She ordered a facial recognition assessment of this image." Caleb reached into his jacket, took out a piece of paper, and passed it forward. "It returned a ninety percent probability."

"What imagery of the Mantis is on file?" Benjamin asked as he drove.

"Only a passport photo. Aside from Manfred, you're the only one I know who ever met her."

The former Mossad director stared at the printed photo for a moment. "If it's not her then the resemblance is uncanny." He exhaled. "I think we need to assume the Mantis lives."

"I was afraid you would say that."

Benjamin handed back the photo. "We can't have any loose ends here, Caleb."

"I know, I'm going to finish what you started."

POOLE, ENGLAND

Sonia sat at a desk in the upstairs study of her family's holiday home. She had her laptop open and was reading everything she could on Imam Rahman. An open tin of tuna sat on a plate surrounded by dry biscuits; her dinner.

She hadn't left the house since Padak had dropped her off. Her office had no idea of her location. There was no way that Rahman or any of his cronies could find her.

She opened a news article on the beheading incident in Coventry. The image of the murderer was an old one, showing a typical white English teenager and his brother. No doubt Rahman had twisted the boy's mind with hateful lies. She reached for a bottle of water then froze as a thump sounded from downstairs. Her mouth went dry as a second thump sent her heart racing.

Leaving her chair, she opened a dresser by the door and withdrew the pistol that Padak had given her. She racked the slide and checked a round was chambered. Then she eased through to the corridor and made her way silently to the staircase.

Another loud crash from downstairs halted her in her tracks. Gathering herself she descended the stairs, the pistol held ready in both hands. The polished hardwood creaked under her feet.

A clatter sent her heart into overdrive as she reached the ground floor and approached the dark kitchen. She found the light switch outside the entry and rested one hand on it.

Exhaling slowly she flicked it on and stepped into the doorway. She screamed as a flash of orange rocketed across the floor of the modern kitchen. A tabby cat dashed for an open window and squeezed through the narrow gap, disappearing outside into the darkness.

Sonia lowered the pistol and took a deep breath. It was only then she realized her finger was on the trigger and had taken up the slack. She had nearly shot the cat.

A feeling of remorse overcame her, and she placed the gun on the table. She took another tin of tuna from a box on the table. Emptying it onto a plate, she slid it out to the sill and shut the window.

Padding back upstairs with the pistol, she tried not to cry. Imam Rahman and his thugs had reduced her to a quivering mess. They had made her a prisoner inside her family's holiday home. What's more, there was nothing she could do to help Padak find his daughter.

She placed the pistol on the dresser and slumped into the chair behind her desk. Drinking from the bottle of water she noticed a new email in her inbox. She opened it.

As she read the short message, elation replaced her distress. Mirza was arriving in London, tomorrow. If anyone could find Eshita, it was the former Indian Special Forces operative.

Her thoughts immediately turned to arranging the trip back to London. Mirza wanted to meet at the office. As she typed a response, she felt her excitement building. It had been two years since they'd last been together. Perhaps, this time, she could tell him exactly how she felt.

Chapter Eleven

BENGHAZI, LIBYA

SALIM CLUTCHED the grab handle in the back of a Toyota troop carrier as it bounced along a cracked and potholed road. His head slammed into the window as the driver swerved to avoid another crater-sized hole. The front seat would have been the safer option but it was occupied by an AK-wielding guard who had no intention of relinquishing it.

Salim had boarded the four-wheel drive at Benina International Airport, Benghazi, twenty minutes earlier. They'd driven east out of the city, along the coast road. According to his GPS the last town they passed through was named Ad Dirsiyah.

He glanced out the window at the rugged escarpments that ran parallel to the coast. Salim had heard of the Jabal al Akhdar hills, they had long been the domain of smugglers. Even when Gaddafi ruled Benghazi his forces had never pacified this harsh terrain.

Minutes later they turned off the main road and drove into a wide valley. Scrubby bushes replaced abandoned fields as the hills closed in on each side. "Hey, how long till we get to the compound?"

The toothless driver grinned in the mirror. "Not long, not long."

It was the same response the man had given him the last time he'd asked. Salim slumped against the bench seat, his feet braced against the opposite side.

The four-wheel drive slowed before being waved through a checkpoint. Salim glimpsed robed men wearing chest rigs and carrying AKs. They turned onto a winding rutted track that climbed into the hills.

"We are here," the driver grunted as they rounded a corner and approached the high mud walls and wooden gates of a compound.

Guards eyeballed them as they drove in and parked next to a row of vehicles: technicals mounted with heavy machine guns, utility trucks, four-wheel drives, and an old yellow school bus.

Salim climbed stiffly from the back of the troop carrier and adjusted his aviators as he gave the compound the once over. It was larger than he anticipated, about a football field in length and another wide. The wall on one side was lined with a linear cinder block structure with evenly spaced wooden doors. He assumed it was a storage facility. In the center of the compound stood a two-story building with a flat roof, bristling with satellite dishes and communications antennae.

He spotted half a dozen armed men sitting in front of the main building in the shade of a faded Carlsberg umbrella. None of them paid him any attention as he strode toward them; they were focused on a card game. "Hey, I'm here for Huron."

One of the men, a black African, glanced up from his hand and gestured to the entrance. Salim shrugged and pushed open the weathered wooden door.

The sound of cheering echoed off the walls as he made his way along a dusty corridor into a large open room crammed with people. Nearly thirty men of varying ethnicities and ages sat on crates, old couches and plastic chairs in front of a massive flat-screen television. Everyone was fixated on the soccer game being played somewhere in Europe. Salim scanned the rabble until he spotted who he was looking for.

Abdul Huron sat on a stack of ammunition tins in the corner. A short Arab, with gray hair, and a bulbous nose, Huron wore chocolate chip camouflage pants and a bright red Manchester United jersey.

As Salim worked his way through the crowd, the former warlord turned arms trafficker glanced across and saw him.

Huron ejected one of his men from a plastic chair and offered it to Salim. "How was your trip, brother?" he said before turning his attention back to the game.

"The flight was as bumpy as the drive."

The room exploded into a cacophony of cheering as one of the teams scored. Judging by Huron's excitement, it was Manchester United. Huron turned to Salim, his face flushed with excitement. "Two-nil and only three minutes to go. This game is ours."

Salim watched with mild interest as the match finished and the room exploded into an uproar. Hardened warriors jumped up and down like excited school children, hugging each other and whooping.

"I didn't realize you were such a fan of the crusader's game," quipped Salim.

"Please, I know for a fact that there are many *kafir* vices that you enjoy." Huron gestured for him to follow and they headed upstairs into an office. He sat at a dusty table as Huron closed the door and joined him. "So, you want anti-tank rockets and brides?"

Salim nodded.

"Both are in short demand, my friend. They will be expensive."

"The people I work with have deep pockets."

"Ah yes, the Sheik. I hear he is very generous when it comes to arming our brothers."

"So long as the weapons you supply are quality. How many TOW missiles can you get me?"

Huron frowned. "We have no TOW. Only the FSA have TOW. I can sell you 9K11 Basson and 9M133 Kornet."

He contemplated the offer. He was not familiar with the Russian systems but no doubt they would be simple and reliable, the Soviet gear always was. "What about women?"

"Like I said, they're harder to come by. I have some Jihad brides that have arrived in the last few days. You are welcome to purchase them if you chose. I only ask one thing in return."

"What do you want?"

"If you're going to be smuggling weapons and women it would make sense to send fighters as well."

"You want me to ship your foreign fighters into Syria?"

Huron nodded. "The Caliphate would be indebted to you."

"I'm not interested in their goodwill. I'm interested in the bottom line. Give me the brides for half price and I will consider it."

"Twenty percent off?"

Salim sucked his gums as he considered the offer. "Show them to me."

TEARS RAN down Eshita's cheeks as she sat cross-legged in the corner of a tiny room. Four other girls, including Vashti, shared the dark space with her. Their only item of furniture was a plastic bucket that served as their toilet.

The others didn't speak English or Hindi, further adding to Eshita's loneliness and despair. What's more, Mubarez had been taken from them not long after they arrived at this isolated compound. Hard-looking men had led him away to train for his Jihad. The girls had been herded into the room, like cattle.

The empty space was not designed for human habitation; it was originally a storeroom. Stacks of crates lined one wall. There were two doors, an inside one that she assumed led to other rooms, and the chained exterior door. The only light came from cracks in the weathered wood. There was no hiding what it was, a prison.

She sniffed as Vashti put an arm over her shoulder.

"Don't cry. Everything is going to be OK. Soon we will be in the Caliphate, and we will meet our husbands."

"I don't want a husband. I want to go home," sobbed Eshita.

"Not even Mubarez? He likes you. He will probably ask for you to be his wife."

She wiped her eyes. "Really?"

"Yes, I have heard that the bravest warriors have the first choice. He has already committed great acts of heroism. Surely they will reward him."

Eshita sniffed again. "You're probably right."

The clatter of the padlock and chain at the door caught their attention, and they clambered to their feet. It swung open, and Eshita squinted as sunlight streamed in.

"All of you outside," a harsh voice barked.

Eshita and Vashti led the way and they shuffled outside into the glaring Libyan sun.

Two men were waiting in the courtyard with half a dozen armed guards. She'd seen one of them before, the short one with the Manchester United jersey. From the way the others respected him, she figured that he had to be the boss. The other man was dressed like a Westerner; he wore jeans and a khaki shirt with the sleeves rolled up. Aviator sunglasses perched over a narrow face with a scraggly beard.

The guards pointed for the women to form a line. Eshita stood next to Vashti and clutched her hand as the man with aviators inspected them.

"They're young," he spoke in English.

"Of course. No lion of the Caliphate wants a wife as old as his mother," responded the man with the Manchester top.

"You keep them all in there?" the visitor asked as he peered inside.

"Yes, we don't want them changing their minds and running away."

Out of the corner of her eye, she spotted another group of men walking from the main building. Two of them carried weapons, the others followed. She turned her head and caught a glimpse of Mubarez. His smile instantly reassured her that everything would be alright.

"This one already has an eye for the fighters," the man

with the aviators said with a laugh. "They'll do nicely. Now, how many of the men do I have to take?"

The conversation faded as they walked away, leaving the girls under the watchful eye of the guards. Eshita caught one last glimpse of Mubarez as she was pushed back inside the room. Then the door slammed shut and once again they were alone.

LONDON, ENGLAND

It was with a sense of trepidation that Sonia walked from a private parking lot to her office. Only forty-eight hours had passed since the threats from Rahman's men. She hoped that was enough time for them to believe they'd scared her off.

She entered the foyer of her building, checking over her shoulder to make sure she wasn't being followed. Entering a waiting elevator she pressed the button to close the doors.

As they slid shut, an arm shot inside, stopping them. Sonia froze as a hooded, bearded young man stepped inside. The doors closed, and he turned and faced her, his forehead creased with a frown.

"Miss, you going to choose a floor or you here for the social life?" he asked in a cockney accent.

"Oh, yes. Level eight please."

He gave her a wink and hit the button along with his own. The elevator stopped on the third floor.

"Have a good one, yeah." He stepped out and the doors shut with a clunk.

Sonia clutched the handrail and almost broke down crying. She gathered herself as the elevator reached her floor. Swiping through a security door, she avoided eye contact with the young woman sitting behind the reception counter and made directly for her office.

Slumping into her chair, she fought the tightness forming in her chest. Panic almost overwhelmed her as she relived the attempted attack in the parking lot and finding the severed goat's head in her car.

A soft knock on the door brought her focus back to the present.

"Miss Jayaram, you have a visitor," said the receptionist from outside.

"A moment, please." She exhaled deeply and dabbed at the corners of her eyes with a tissue.

A sense of relief washed over her as she opened the door and looked directly into the bearded face and kind eyes of Mirza Mansoor. He stepped inside and wrapped his arms around her. "Sonia, I am so happy to see you."

In his strong arms, she finally felt safe. Burying her face in his shoulder, she wept.

"It's OK, no one will hurt you now."

He held her until she let go. Then they sat on a sofa in the corner of her office and she told him everything that had happened.

It took Sonia well over an hour to tell the story of Eshita, Padak, and most importantly, Imam Rahman. She finished with the notoriety the preacher had gained by converting the two English boys who had attacked the police. Throughout, Mirza took notes on his phone. When she concluded, his usually calm demeanor had changed to one of anger.

"This Imam betrays every aspect of my faith. He is using it as a tool to manipulate and control," growled

Mirza. "However, my priority is the recovery of the two girls."

"Do you want me to arrange a meeting with Padak?"

He shook his head. "No, first we need to get you somewhere safe. I've organized an apartment for you nearby."

"Will you be staying with me?"

"No. I have a room in Birmingham."

"Birmingham?"

"Yes, if I'm going to infiltrate the Imam's inner circle I'm going to need to be amongst them."

Sonia reached into her bag and handed him the pistol that Padak had given her. "Mirza, please be careful."

His brow rose as he inspected the weapon, a Glock 19. "I don't want to know where you got this."

He checked the pistol was unloaded and stowed it in his backpack. Then as he stood, she stepped in close. Wrapping her arms around him, she kissed his bearded cheek. "Thank you so much for coming, Mirza. I didn't know who else to turn to."

He locked eyes with her and smiled softly. "There's no way I could say no to you."

They held the gaze for a full five seconds before Mirza spoke. "OK, let's get you to the safe house."

ABU DHABI, UAE

Bishop swiped into the Priority Movements Airlift hangar and made his way past a G650 business jet and an AW609 tilt-rotor. Reaching the workshop container, he knocked before entering.

Inside Mitch was sitting at the counter, hunched over a laptop. "Bored again, Bish?" he said without looking up.

"Hey mate, I was going to ask to borrow the e-bike."

"Sure thing." Mitch closed the laptop. "First, I need your thoughts on something."

"Shoot."

Mitch hefted a MK48 machine gun from the bench and led him out of the workshop. "Check this out," he said placing the machine gun next to what looked like a pile of camouflaged parts. He flicked a switch, grabbed a handle and hauled an A-TACS backpack from the floor. Hydraulic limbs unfolded and Bishop realized it was the exoskeleton.

"You painted your Iron Man suit," he said.

"Yep, I removed the claws and added load carriage." Mitch flicked another switch and the backpack power unit began a low hum. "I'm converting it into a heavy weapons platform. What do you think?"

"I think it looks like a liability."

"Don't knock RALF till you've tried her, she's the duck's nuts. Give her a roll."

Reluctantly, Bishop allowed himself to be strapped in. He raised an eyebrow as the arm covers snapped closed, locking him in. The exoskeleton gave a hiss as he tentatively lifted an arm.

"How about you move around a bit?"

He pushed his right leg forward and was rewarded with an electronic whine and movement from the suit.

"Come on, first the right, then the left will follow. They call it walking."

He shook his head and took a few steps. Clad in the suit, he felt like the terminator. The heavy steel feet clumped on the concrete floor, servos whined, and hydraulics hissed. "This is awesome."

"I told you. Grab the MK48."

The exoskeleton crouched effortlessly as Bishop picked up the machine gun. The belt-fed weapon weighed roughly twenty pounds but with robotic assistance it felt like a water pistol. A grin spread across his face as he tore around the hangar jumping and aiming the weapon. He leaped onto one of the shipping containers. The steel structure groaned under the weight.

"Easy!"

He dropped off the roof onto the floor. Hydraulic pistons in the robotic legs absorbed the impact.

"Awesome. You've outdone yourself, Mitch." Bishop lowered the gun. "Now, how the hell do I get out of it?"

"There's a toggle on the shoulder harness."

He found the switch and the arm mechanisms opened, releasing him. The exoskeleton powered down as he undid the straps then stepped out. "I reckon if you could integrate this into our CAT assault armor it would be a game-changer."

"I thought you'd say that. Once I get back from London I'll look into it."

"Sounds good. Any chance I could take RALF to the range while you're away?"

Mitch began folding up the exoskeleton. "Fill your boots. You'll find spare hydrogen gas tanks in the magazine. Try not to break her."

"Sweet."

"Want a beer?" Mitch asked once he'd finished packing his new toy away.

"Yeah."

They headed across to the planning room, where there was a bar fridge.

"You got an update from Mirza?" asked Bishop as he passed a can of ale to Mitch and cracked his own.

"An hour ago. He's got Sonia to safety, and he's establishing a safe house in Birmingham."

"What's the plan? Is Mirza going after the hate preacher?"

"No, he's aiming to infiltrate the human trafficking pipeline into Syria, locate this girl that Sonia's trying to track down, then exfil."

Bishop sipped his beer. "Through Turkey or Libya?"

"Flash has broken out some of the network from the Imam. He says they're taking the route through Marseille, across the Med into Libya."

"So Mirza could end up in Raqqa?"

"Hopefully it doesn't come down to that. Anyway, I was wondering, are those two an item?"

"That's a question you'd have to ask Mirza."

Mitch nodded and sipped his beer. "I'm going to take Sleek this afternoon and meet them in London," he said, referring to PRIMAL's customized business jet.

"Looking forward to catching up with a few mates?"

"If I get a chance. Been a few years since I've been back in old London town. What about you?"

"I'm stuck here. Vance wants me on hand in case the missiles move or Mossad makes contact."

"Raw deal. Would be great to have you on team."

"You and Mirza will do fine. Ice and I will keep ourselves amused here."

Mitch swigged a mouthful of beer. "So, you heard anything from Saneh?"

Bishop shook his head. "Nope." He finished his beer and tossed the empty in a crate by the door. "Right, so you need any help prepping your gear?"

"Nah, I'm sorted. How about you take some time off? I hear that the Underwater Zoo in Dubai is shit hot."

He frowned.

"Not your thing? Fine, take the e-bike out to the desert and try not to kill yourself."

Bishop grinned. "Good luck and take care of Mirza."

He left the office and grabbed the black electric bike from where it leaned against a shipping container. Leaving the hangar, he pushed the bike to a gray Mercedes G500 Squared. As he lowered the rear seats of the four-wheel drive, a phone in his pocket vibrated. He fished out the phone Keila had given him and checked the screen.

He smiled as he read the message.

You made a good impression. I would like to see you again. Tomorrow, 0830 at the following coordinates 23.269375° 54.923289°

Bishop loaded the bike, climbed into the four-wheel drive and started the engine. Hopefully Vance would give him approval to go to the meet. It wasn't fair that Mitch and Mirza were the only ones who were going to be having fun.

Chapter Twelve

ABU DHABI, UAE

TARIQ RAN his hand over the smooth white paintwork on the Lascar Logistics LM-100J Hercules' nose and turned to the crew that had delivered the new aircraft. "How did she fly?"

"Like a dream, sir," the American pilot said with a southern drawl. "I've been driving these birds since 2000, and they just keep getting better. This girl's a dreamboat."

Tariq shook the man's hand and walked around the latest addition to the Lascar Logistics fleet. The airframe took the number of 100's in his inventory to three, including the modified version being flown by Priority Movements Airlift. An impressive cargo aircraft, the first Hercules had entered service in the USAF nearly sixty years earlier. This particular model was very different from the original variants. It boasted a high-tech digital cockpit and the latest turboprop engines from Rolls Royce.

Having completed his inspection Tariq joined his

employees and guests in a marquee erected on the tarmac. The arrival of the new transporter was a significant event within Abu Dhabi International Airport, and many officials had turned out to welcome it.

"What does an airplane like this cost?" asked a bureaucrat from the UAE General Civil Aviation Authority.

"About sixty-five million, delivered," answered Tariq.

"A lot of money to fly into a war zone," responded the official.

"Indeed."

He did a round of the guests thanking them for their attendance before excusing himself. A minute later he sat in the back of his Range Rover on his way home. A few miles down the highway his phone rang, it was his personal assistant.

"Sir, I have the information you requested regarding the Emirates Aid Fund. I'm sorry about the delay; the requirement for discretion extended the time frame."

"Not a problem. Now, what names do you have for me?"

"There are some minor donors. However, the primary contributor is Sheik Sayeed bin Khalifa Al-Hasher."

Tariq shook his head. It made sense. Sheik Al-Hasher was a bored young prince with a bent for fast cars, beautiful women and risky business ventures. No doubt supporting ISIS was another game for him, and a chance to prove his manhood to his father, a traditionalist.

"Sir, that's all the information that is available."

"It's sufficient, Emily." He paused in thought. "I need to have a talk with the Sheik. Am I correct in assuming we have a box at the Formula One this weekend?"

"Yes sir. Team Ferrari will be in attendance."

"Excellent, extend an invitation to Sheik Al-Hasher."

"Is that all, sir?"

"Also, I would also like to invite you and your parents to attend." Tariq knew that his English assistant's father was an avid motorsports fan. "Please put their flights on my Emirates account, First Class of course."

"Tariq, they are going to be thrilled. Thank you so much."

He smiled. Emily was a stickler for formality and rarely called him by his first name. "It is my pleasure. Thank you for obtaining the information I need. Now, take the evening off and call your parents." Returning his phone to his pocket, he stared out the window at the passing city skyline. The young Sheik posed a significant problem. He was a member of the royal family, well connected and very, very wealthy. If he was to make an enemy of him, it could prove lethal. But sometimes it was better to keep the snake where you could see it rather than let it lurk in the garden.

TEL AVIV, ISRAEL

The room was swept daily for bugs, accessible only by highly vetted individuals, and located five stories below Mossad's Tel Aviv Headquarters. Know as the 'Tomb' it protected the most sensitive of the intelligence organization's secrets.

As the Mossad Director, Caleb Atzmoni regularly convened meetings in the secure space. Today, the man in charge of the Special Operations Department joined him.

Manfred Lisker was lightly built, wore spectacles and had lost most of his hair. Forgettable, he could move through the streets of Tel Aviv unnoticed. However, inside

Mossad's headquarters, he was respected for his lethality. The unremarkable looking man held responsibility for the elimination of Israel's most high-value targets. He and his staff ran the *Kidon*, teams of Mossad's most elite operatives, capable of conducting assassination, capture or sabotage operations in almost every corner of the globe. A master of planning and execution, Lisker's reputation was reflected in his kill count. Since taking over the program eight years earlier, he had been responsible for the demise of exactly one hundred and seven of Israel's most dangerous enemies; a number he wore with pride.

Lisker took a seat at the conference table, depositing a brown satchel on the chair beside him. "Good morning, Caleb."

The director sat opposite, placing a manila folder on the table. "Manfred, I hear your team was successful in Croatia."

"Correct. The target was pronounced dead on arrival at a hospital in Zagreb." He clasped his hands in his lap. "The Doctor's assessment; heart attack."

"And your team has extracted?"

Lisker nodded.

"Excellent." Caleb pushed the folder across the table.

Lisker removed spectacles from his jacket and donned them. He took a few minutes to examine the file then looked up. "Are you sure?"

"Not entirely, which is why I am here."

"Interesting. Mantis was reported to have been killed in Ukraine in 2003."

"And yet the image in the file was taken less than nine months ago."

"Do we know if it's actually her?"

"It has been corroborated."

"And the man, what is his connection?"

Caleb leaned back in his chair. "His name is Aden Bishop. Works for an air freight company. One of your teams has recruited him to gain access to a target in Syria."

"Which team?"

"Keila Bachman's"

Lisker nodded and looked back at the file. "Hmmm, Bishop likes to keep dangerous company. Certainly not the type of woman I would want in my bed."

Caleb laughed. "Manfred, you and I could never get a woman like that in our bed. Unless she was trying to kill us."

He grinned. "It might be worth it." Then, in the blink of an eye, his poker face returned. "So, what do you want done?"

The Mossad director rose from his seat. "We can't have the Tiberias program coming back to bite us. If you can capture her alive I need a full interrogation." He made to exit.

"And then?"

Caleb paused at the door. "Do I need to answer that?"

"She was one of the best. Perhaps her DNA would be useful for the Proteus project."

The director frowned. "One Mantis is more than enough."

Lisker shrugged. "As you wish."

ABU DHABI, UAE

Bishop left his penthouse apartment wearing a ratty T-shirt and floral board shorts. He'd left behind the cell phone from

Keila; the only items he carried were a security key card, iPRIMAL and the key to his jet ski.

Waving to the concierge, he strolled onto the building's private jetty. The Bangladeshi security guard flashed him a broad smile as he swiped through a gate and strolled along the wharf. He passed expensive motor cruisers and yachts until he reached a berth with a solitary jet ski.

He'd always wanted a boat but the racy black lines of the HSR Benelli had caught his eye. Unshackling it from its mooring, he stowed his T-shirt and iPRIMAL under the seat, swung a leg over and started the turbocharged 3-cylinder engine. The craft rumbled to life before shooting out from the wharf, water rooster-tailing behind it.

The sea was glassy as he sped at eighty miles an hour toward the private gated community of Nurai Island. Easing off the throttle, he turned down a narrow channel and slid under a bridge. He gave the throttle one more burst before carving a tight U-turn and heading back the way he came. Confident he wasn't being followed he headed toward a private villa and ran the ski onto the sand.

He grabbed his T-shirt and iPRIMAL from under the seat, crossed the beach and strolled across the front lawn of PRIMAL's headquarters. Finding a towel in the pool area, he dried himself.

Ice waited for him in front of the glass doors. "You know you can drive here, like everyone else."

He tossed the towel on a sun bed and slipped on his T-shirt. "Where's the fun in that?"

Ice chuckled as he led him upstairs to the intelligence room where Flash, Chua, and Vance were waiting. Bishop greeted the men and dropped into a spare chair. "So, what's the plan?"

Vance spoke first. "We're going to turn Mossad down."

He frowned. "Why wouldn't we hear them out? They could have a lead on the weapons."

"Chua and I have discussed it. We think the risk is too high. If you decline, what are they going to do? We all know how source handling works. Without leverage, they ain't got shit."

Bishop considered Vance's viewpoint and shrugged. "I guess. So, who's going to tell Keila?"

Flash looked up from behind his laptop. "Do you want me to send the reply now?"

Vance turned to Chua. "You happy with it?"

The intel officer gave thumbs-up. "Good to go."

Flash's fingers raced across the keyboard as he used an application to replicate the phone Keila had given Bishop. "And it's gone."

Bishop couldn't help but feel disappointed. He glanced up at Ice, who stood in the doorway. The big man looked on impassively.

Flash's computer chimed. "They've responded."

"That was quick," said Chua.

Flash wore a shocked expression as he looked up from his computer. "They just raised the stakes."

Everyone gathered around the laptop. On the screen was an image of Bishop and Saneh, in Africa.

"Those motherfuckers," hissed Bishop.

He felt Ice's hand on his shoulder. "This changes things."

"Now they've got leverage," said Vance. "Chua, I want a detailed assessment of the proposed meet site. Flash, I want a trace on the Mossad number." He turned to Ice. "You're on overwatch." Finally, he turned to Bishop. "I need you level headed. You're going in to gather intel, and that's it."

He exhaled. "Yeah, I got it."

"Good. Because, as far as Mossad is concerned, you're a loadmaster who happened to fall in love with a beautiful woman. You know nothing about her background."

"Vance, we need to find her," said Bishop.

Vance nodded. "We can try. But, if we can't locate her, then Mossad won't stand a chance. OK, team, let's get to it." He checked his watch. "We'll run a back briefing at 1800 hours."

Bishop and Ice left the intel room and headed downstairs to the villa's kitchen. "You want a coffee?" asked Ice as he stepped in behind the dual head espresso machine.

"Yeah, that'd be sweet mate." Bishop sat on a stool at the kitchen counter. "You think they know where Saneh is?"

Ice shook his head as he ground beans. "Nah bro, they pulled that photo from some dark corner of the net. They're clutching at straws."

"So you don't think we should go to the meet?"

"Damn straight we should. These guys are going to give us the opportunity to hit that missile smuggler." Ice tamped the freshly ground coffee and twisted the group head into the machine.

"I concur."

Ice pulled a container of milk from the fridge. "I know you miss her, but Saneh's more than capable of taking care of herself."

The milk steamer filled the kitchen with a shriek as Bishop gazed out through the windows at the blue ocean. His mind wandered back to Africa, back to the incident that cost him the woman he loved and their unborn child.

Ice's voice snapped him back to the present. "Here's your latte, buddy."

He took the coffee and sipped from it. "Not bad, Terminator, not bad at all."

Ice leaned against the counter with an Americano in hand. "Alright, so how are we going to play this?"

Bishop sipped. "These guys are probably the best in the world at this sort of thing. So, we play it by the book. Nothing that could lead them to PRIMAL: no covert comms, no hidden weapons. We're going to have to rely on good old-fashioned hand signals and timings."

"Old school."

"Yeah, you OK with that, Robocop?"

"Have you seen the terrain out there? My biggest issue is going to be inserting without compromise."

He downed the last of his coffee. "I've got something for that."

BIRMINGHAM, ENGLAND

Mirza's rented room was little bigger than a walk-in wardrobe. The paint on the walls and ceiling was peeling. Dandruff-like flakes covered the mattress and floor. He dumped his rucksack on a stained chair and lowered himself onto the bed. The old springs groaned under his weight, and he sank a few inches.

Dressed in filthy torn jeans and an oil-stained jacket Mirza looked every part the illegal immigrant he was pretending to be. The only technology he carried was a cheap phone Mitch had given him, and a miniaturized satellite tracker built into his hiking boot. The cover story Chua and Flash had developed was roughly based on his actual background. Zufar, a former Indian Army soldier, had fled India in pursuit of a better life. Four years later, jaded and homeless he had turned to faith. A man of action, he had been drawn to Birmingham by the attack in Coventry.

English media had been reporting the presence of an Islamic enclave in Birmingham for some time. With the murder of the two policemen attributed to fundamentalists from the area, it made sense that other extremists would seek to join them.

He pulled the phone from his pocket and checked the messages. His network provider had sent him an offer for a cheap upgrade. That meant that Mitch had left the UAE and would soon land at a private airstrip outside of London. Then he would move to the safe house where Sonia was staying. Mirza would feel a lot more comfortable when Mitch was on the ground, and Sonia protected.

Rising from the bed he took a worn multitool from his pocket and used it to pull up the moth-eaten carpet in the corner of the room. Exposing the floorboards he found a loose one and pried it free.

Taking Sonia's pistol from his backpack, he wrapped it in an old T-shirt and slipped it in through the gap. Then, replacing the board and the carpet, he stepped back and inspected his work. Confident that if his room were tossed they would find nothing, he exited, locking the door behind him.

The Mosque was only a short distance from where he was staying. As he walked along the red-brick house-lined streets the brisk British winter cut through his thick jacket and he shivered. Ahead he spotted a group of youths clustered in front of a residence. There were five, all young men, dressed in casual clothes. Three of them were dark skinned with full beards and piercing eyes. The other two were Caucasian. They all stopped talking and eyed him suspiciously as he approached.

"Peace be upon you, brothers. Do any of you have a cigarette?" Mirza asked.

One of the dark-skinned men reached into his duffel coat and produced a packet. "What is your name?" He tapped out a cigarette and gave it to Mirza.

"Thank you. My name is Zufar." Mirza lit the cigarette and inhaled.

"Where are you from, Zufar?"

He exhaled. "London."

"No, before that?"

"Deoband, in India."

"What brings you to Birmingham?" one of the Caucasian men asked with a distinctly English accent.

"I've come to hear the Imam preach."

"You heard what happened here?"

Mirza nodded as he smoked.

"We knew them," the first youth admitted proudly.

"Brave young lions," said Mirza.

"Are you going to the mosque now?" asked the one with the English accent.

"Yes, I heard the Imam is giving a sermon?"

"Yes, he is. Tomorrow there is going to be a big rally to honor Saifan and Mubarez. You should come to that."

Mirza nodded. "I will. Thank you for the smoke, brothers."

He left the youths and discarded the cigarette as he continued along the street. Around a corner he spotted a crowd gathering in front of what had to be the mosque; a stream of men and burka-covered women filed into a converted community hall.

Mirza joined the line and shuffled inside. As he climbed

the stairs, a pair of tough looking heavies eyeballed him. He dipped his head, entered the foyer and kicked off his shoes.

The inside was not unlike places where Mirza had previously worshiped. Long carpets patterned as prayer rugs covered the floor. A throne-like chair was occupied by a middle-aged man sporting a long beard, crisp white robes and cap, and a conceited expression; Imam Rahman.

Mirza sat and listened for an hour as the Imam preached hate to his attentive audience. He glanced sideways at the men and women around him and noted the rapt attention they gave the preacher. He'd seen anger on faces like these before, in film from the Nuremberg rally where Hitler spewed forth his evil. This was not the Islam that Mirza practiced. His faith focused on helping those less fortunate, charity, and being judged by one's actions.

When the lecture concluded, he made to leave. However, as he waited for the crowd to file out a heavy hand grasped his shoulder.

"Who are you?" one of the two heavies from the door asked in Arabic. He wore a thick unkempt beard, the upper lip trimmed short.

"My name is Zufar."

"Come with me." The man directed him through a side door into a small room. He offered him a seat then questioned him along the same lines as the youths on the street. Mirza answered confidently, careful not to provide more detail than was required.

"What did you do in India, Zufar?"

"I was a soldier."

The man's bare lip lifted in a scowl. "You were a puppet for the *kafir*?"

"This is true. I had lost my way. But, now I have found it again."

At that moment a separate door to the room opened, and the other thug poked his head inside. "The Imam wants you."

Mirza's interrogator nodded then turned back to him. "Welcome to Imam Rahman's congregation, Zufar. We will be watching you closely."

As he left the Mosque, a burka-veiled woman thrust a pamphlet into his hand, a flyer announcing the gathering to celebrate the sacrifice of Saifan. If he was going to break into Rahman's inner circle then he needed to attend.

Walking back to the guest house, he checked his phone. He didn't have a confirmation message from Mitch yet. He needed his fellow PRIMAL operative on the ground if his plan was going to work.

Chapter Thirteen

ABU DHABI, UAE

BISHOP SLOWED and turned his four-wheel drive off the highway onto a sandy track. A quick check of his GPS confirmed he was still on route to reach the coordinates Keila had sent. He knew from Chua's analysis that this was the only way to the isolated compound.

He took his iPRIMAL from the center console and activated a comms link with Ice. "Hey mate, how you looking?"

"Nice of you to join the party." Ice had inserted on Mitch's e-bike the night before. He'd dug into a dune, establishing a hide that had line-of-sight on the meet location. From there he had used the bike to run a thin fiber-optic cable six hundred yards out into the desert and connected it to a small satellite dish. The offset communications array ensured he could talk to the Sandpit undetected. Hidden in the dunes, with comms and a sniper rifle, he was Bishop's only backup.

"I'm in position," continued Ice. "One of the vehicles

left the compound about fifteen minutes ago with two targets inside. They're parked about a mile along the road, looks like a security checkpoint. The other two targets are waiting in their vehicle at the compound. I'm able to engage them all."

Bishop smiled. "Ice, maybe we should call them something other than targets."

There was a pause. "OK, we have four potential targets."

"Oh, that's heaps better." Bishop felt confident knowing that the former CIA paramilitary operative had his back. "Sandpit, do I have a go ahead on the mission?"

Vance answered, "Roger, we've got a drone in a loiter pattern to the west. It can be on station in minutes."

"Armed?"

"Two Spike missiles. My preference is that this doesn't go kinetic. Try not to provoke the female Mossad agent."

"Easier said than done," said Ice.

Bishop frowned. "What the hell is that supposed to mean?"

"I believe Ice is implying that you frustrate women," added Chua.

"Not just women," said Vance.

"Hey, I'm about to meet up with lethal Israeli operatives. So, if you could lay off the Bish bashing that would be great."

Ice replied first. "Roger, Bish bashing. I like that."

Bishop let out a half-assed cry of anguish and dropped his four-wheel drive into off-road mode. "Right, I'm going comms silent. Ice, if you see my signal then the 'potentials' have switched to 'actuals'."

"Acknowledged."

Bishop accelerated along what remained of the track. The wind had blown sand across the crushed gravel. It clung to the wheels, slowing his progress. In the early morning light he could barely make out the tire tracks of the Mossad vehicles. He followed them between the dunes, staying in their tracks.

A few minutes later his GPS announced that his destination was a mile ahead. As the track snaked around a large dune he spotted the security checkpoint that Ice had mentioned. A gray SUV blocked the road. Two figures stood either side of it.

Bishop slowed to walking pace then came to a complete halt. He could now see that both men wore similar clothes to him, light colored pants and long sleeve shirts. There was no evidence of weapons but, no doubt, they were close at hand.

He opened his car door, and the hot desert air felt like a hairdryer to the face. "Hi, you guys with Keila?"

One of the men nodded. "I need you to step away from the vehicle and raise your arms."

Bishop grinned as he complied. "You the fluffer? Getting me all worked up for the main event?"

The man gave him a thorough pat down as his partner conducted a vehicle check. He found the iPRIMAL in the console beside the phone Keila had provided. "These your only phones?"

"That and the iPad in my ass."

The body checker stood in front of Bishop and shook his head.

He swallowed. "Guys, that was a joke."

The man frowned and jerked his chin in the direction of his SUV, a Ford Explorer. "Get in."

The other man directed him to the back seat of the

Ford then climbed in alongside him. The body searcher drove them along the road.

"So, you guys spend much time in the Emirates?"

Neither man replied.

"Yeah, good chat." Bishop stared through the windshield at the compound that approached. It was a typical setup with a chain link fence and transportable buildings. They drove into the compound and parked alongside a second, identical vehicle. The driver opened Bishop's door and pointed to one of the structures.

"Thanks, lads." He walked toward it, turned the door handle and entered. Inside the air-conditioned room was a TV, couches and kitchenette. His gaze was immediately drawn to the familiar female figure sitting on a ratty couch.

"Hello, Aden." Keila flashed him a bright smile. "Please, have a seat."

"Nice digs," he murmured, lowering into the couch opposite her.

"Tea or coffee? Water?" Keila asked as he scanned the room.

He spotted her partner, the bearded swarthy-looking guy, leaning against the wall next to the kitchenette. "Ah, Thomas. How are you champ? Coffee, white with two if you will." He turned back to Keila and stared directly into her gray eyes. "So, what can I do for Mossad?"

"Not one for small talk?"

"Not when it comes to being fucked over. Tell me what you want or I walk."

Her glance at Thomas suggested the request was going to be significant.

"We need you to help us transport a team into Syria."

Bishop laughed. "Why would I do that?"

"You wanted to know how you can help us defeat evil.

This is how you do it. You transport a medical team to Jarjanaz."

He scrunched up his face. "A medical team? You seriously think I'm going to believe that bullshit?"

"We have the same interests, Aden; stopping weapons getting into the hands of extremists."

Bishop clenched his jaw. "Priority Movements have not shipped any operational TOW missiles since we discovered them. The gig is over. My involvement is over."

She shook her head. "We're not concerned about the TOW missiles. We want Salim."

He shrugged.

"Do you have any idea what he's involved in?"

"He's a piece of shit smuggler. They're a dime-a-dozen around here."

"You work for a high-risk air-freight company, Aden, I'm sure you're familiar with the threat from MANPADS," she said referring to man-portable air defense systems.

He frowned.

"Salim initially became of interest to Israel when he sold FN-6 missiles left over from the Libyan civil war to Hamas," Keila continued. "The FN-6 is the latest generation of Chinese surface to air missile technology. It is roughly equivalent to the SA-18 that shot down Israel Airlines flight LY395 in 2004."

"You fucking bitch," Bishop growled.

"We've both felt the pain inflicted by men like Salim," she said in a soft voice. "I too have lost family to terrorism. My point is that he needs to be neutralized. Before supporting ISIS, he supplied advanced RPG-30 rockets to Hezbollah, rockets designed specifically to defeat the active protection systems on our tanks. That signed his death warrant. All we're asking from you is transportation. My people will do the rest."

"I don't want any part of this."

As he made to rise, Thomas strode across from the kitchen and tossed a photo in his lap.

"We know you've got strong feelings for this woman," said Keila.

Bishop clenched his jaw as he stared at the picture of Saneh. "Don't bring her into this."

"I don't want to. Help us and nothing happens to her."

He managed a snort. "You have no idea where she is."

"Aden, we find people. It's what we do. Right now no one's looking for her. That could change very quickly. Help us and I'll make sure she stays off our radar."

Bishop wanted nothing more than to reach out and snap Keila's neck. He ran through the scenario. It would start with a kick to her chest then a flying leap at Thomas. The Mossad operative would be trained, but Bishop would overwhelm him in seconds. Then he would dispatch the girl, leave the building, give the signal and Ice would kill the other two. Instead, he exhaled softly, lifted his gaze from the photo and locked eyes with Keila. "Right. Let's talk through how this is going to work."

She pulled out a tablet and moved around to sit beside Bishop. "You're making the right decision, Aden."

He shook his head. "I hope so." Because, he thought, it might be easier to let Ice slot you and bury you in the dunes.

"SO, bottom line, they're not asking much; an extra few hours layover when we do our next Jarjanaz run. All we're adding to the cargo is the four-person WHO medical team and a pallet containing their vaccine storage units," concluded Bishop's briefing to Vance and Chua in the Sandpit's operations room. The photo of Saneh lay on the counter between two workstations. Frank, the watchkeeper, sat monitoring a drone feed of Ice's extraction from the desert.

"It's a good cover," Chua said. "They're not the first medical team to set up a vaccination clinic in the area. Dealing with the polio and measles epidemic is a top priority for WHO."

"That's all good, but what happens when they snatch Salim or assassinate him?" Vance said.

Chua exhaled through his teeth. "It could burn Priority Movements in the region. We should run this past Tariq."

"I'll back brief him later."

"There's only one choice here, Vance," Bishop said intensely. "We have to play their game until we track down Saneh."

"I know, bud."

"The Israelis are after the same thing as us. Taking down an evil bastard and disrupting the supply of high-threat weapons to terrorists. I don't see an issue here."

"Hey guys," Frank interrupted. "Letting you know that Ice has withdrawn and is making his way back to his insertion vehicle."

Vance shot him thumbs-up. "Cheers, bud."

"Bish, risk is the issue here," said Chua. "And it's at its highest when the aircraft is on the deck in Jarjanaz. All it takes is a stray burst from a machine gun then our team, and theirs, are trapped."

"Could we fly the aircraft remotely?" asked Bishop.

"Not without recalling Mitch," replied Vance. "What

about holding a loiter pattern till they're ready for extraction?"

"I suggested that, but they insist we're on standby to exfil," Bishop said. "Understandable considering they don't want to be waiting around if they've offed Salim."

There was silence before Vance spoke, "Look, this is a shit sandwich, there's no way around it. You'll taxi Mossad to Jarjanaz but the first sign of trouble, you're out, understood?"

"Roger. And the threat to Saneh? What are we doing about that?"

Vance turned to Chua who spoke. "We're working on locating her. So far we haven't had any success. I assess that Mossad's threats are hollow. They're not going to put much effort into tracking down a former Iranian asset who's no longer active."

"Yeah, I figured as much."

Chua continued, "We'll keep looking though, Aden. I'll let you know if we get anything."

"Thanks, Chua. Right, I'm going to meet Ice at the hangar. We'll go through our contingency packs and reconfigure the Herc."

"Remember," said Vance. "Discretion is the key. If Mossad gets a sniff of PRIMAL we're screwed."

THE LASCAR LOGISTICS ATV sat low on its axles, its rear bed heavily laden with gear bags as Ice drove from the PRIMAL hangar. Bishop sat in the passenger seat with Daisy, the explosives detection dog, perched on his lap.

"Daisy seems to enjoy these missions," Ice said as they approached PRIMAL's Hercules transporter.

Bishop ruffled the border collie's fur. "She's a good pup. I'm thinking about bringing her on full-time."

"Where would she stay?"

"The Sandpit? Those guys never go anywhere."

"I actually think they'd enjoy that." Ice pulled in alongside the aircraft's ramp.

A figure dressed like them, in a flight suit, sunglasses and a baseball cap, appeared from inside the hold. "Hey guys, the bird is fuelled and ready to roll when you are."

"Cheers, Mike." Bishop let Daisy run into the cargo hold as he helped Ice unload their bags.

"What ya got there?"

"Gear for the contingency pod." Like PRIMAL's business jet, Sleek, the Hercules had a concealed compartment where they kept any sensitive cargo hidden from airport authorities.

"Not a problem." Mike grabbed one of the bags. "Goddamn, how much hardware are you packing?"

He smiled. "Enough."

They crammed their bags of weapons and tactical equipment into the pod concealed beneath the floor, before heading to the cockpit.

"So, I'm running solo on this one," said Mike as he strapped into the pilot's seat.

Bishop patted his shoulder. "It's OK; Ice has a little time on the stick. He can help you out."

The pilot nodded as Ice lowered himself into the copilot's seat. "Good to know. Got any time on the J model?"

"I've jumped from a few," Ice returned.

"OK, that's not particularly useful up front."

Bishop laughed. "Ice has run a couple of hundred hours in the sim, and he's been up with Mitch and Mirza." He leaned forward and passed a thumb drive to the pilot. "Here's your flight plan."

Mike frowned as he plugged it into the navigation system. "I thought this was the standard milk run from Amman to Jarjanaz?"

"It is, with a slight modification." Bishop rose to leave the cabin. "After Amman we're picking up some travelers in Tel Aviv."

Mike chuckled. "Tel Aviv, good one. We running death squads for Mossad now?"

Bishop slapped his shoulder again. "You worry about the bird. We'll handle the cargo. Now, let's get airborne."

Chapter Fourteen

BIRMINGHAM, ENGLAND

THE CROWD WAS LARGER than Mirza had anticipated. It seemed that both hardline Islamists and right-wing thugs were not perturbed by gray skies and a little drizzle.

He estimated that close to three hundred members of the Imam's parish had turned out to pay tribute to their martyr. Not only bearded men, the crowd also included hijab-wearing women and their children. Another fifty or so right-wing activists had parked themselves at the opposite end of the street armed with placards calling for Islam and Sharia law to get out of Britain. Much to Mirza's surprise, he couldn't see any police in attendance.

He hung on the fringes of the Islamic crowd, the hood of his jacket pulled up. Tensions were running high as the Imam walked out of the mosque, down the stairs and stood on a podium placed in the middle of the blocked-off street. Dressed in white, he raised his hands and was greeted by cries of adoration from the crowd. Mirza recognized the bodyguard that hung back to one side; the heavy-set thug was the one that had questioned him earlier at the mosque.

The radical cleric's message was the usual diatribe of hate, blame, and entitlement that Mirza had heard before. Regardless of the religion or political ideology the core themes remained the same. Tell the people that their problems were someone else's fault, give them a sense of entitlement, and aim their hatred at a fall guy. Today the villains were the police and their unjust execution of the martyr, Saifan. There was no mention of the two officers who had been slaughtered in cold blood by the brainwashed English youths.

"Good to see you here, Zufar."

Mirza turned and recognized one of the youths from the previous day. The bearded teen's eyes shone, and he wore an excited smile.

"Looks like things are about to get heated." Mirza gestured up the street toward the right-wing crowd. The angry demonstrators waving Union Jack flags were moving toward the Imam's ceremony. A Britain First banner led their charge, with chants of 'Islam Out!' carrying through the chilly morning air and echoing off the brick walls.

Sensing that things were about to turn hostile Mirza pushed through the crowd till he was close to the Imam and his bodyguard.

There was a roar as the front line of the placard-waving mob reached the Muslims. Women screamed as the demonstrators pushed forward, fuelled by rage and anger. Behind the crowd, Mirza caught a glimpse of a police car and a media van.

The Imam's people may have outnumbered the right-wing thugs, but they weren't going to win a confrontation.

Shaved-head hooligans formed their front line and they were spoiling for a fight.

Despite the imminent threat, the Imam remained on his perch inciting the crowd. It looked like the fanatical Islamists were going to hold the line. Mirza reached into his jacket, pulled out a cylinder and tossed it underhand into the crowd.

The gas grenade ignited with a pop. Screams echoed down the street as the harsh metallic stench of tear gas filled the air.

The Imam's bodyguard shepherded him away from the threat, down from the podium, and back toward the mosque. Pandemonium broke out with both sides throwing punches and objects through the thickening cloud of gas.

As Mirza made a beeline for the Imam he spotted a burly man with a thick hooded jacket approaching from the mosque. As the hulking figure waded through the crowd his hood fell back, revealing a Caucasian with a lumberjack beard and shaved head.

The bodyguard realized the threat too late. The man could have been an Islamic-convert until he launched a savage right cross that dropped the bodyguard to the pavement.

Mirza was still a few yards away when the intruder palmed off another guard and grabbed the Imam by the robes. "Fuck off back to the desert you sick, ISIS-loving, sharia-law preaching wanker!" he bellowed in a thick Geordie accent, a knife clutched in his fist.

Mirza shoved Rahman to one side and leaped into action. He grasped the knife hand and drove his knee into the attacker's chest, knocking the wind out of him. As the man toppled backward, the knife clattered onto the pavement. A right cross finished the combination, stunning the attacker.

Breathing hard Mirza turned to the Imam. The preacher was shaking, his face a mask of fear. "Come on, we need to go."

As he led the Imam up the stairs to the mosque, he glanced over his shoulder. The attacker had recovered and retreated across the road to a parked scooter. The wail of sirens filled the air as the hardcore thugs from both sides clashed.

Mirza bundled Rahman through the front door to the mosque and it was slammed shut behind them. They walked through to one of the rooms in the back and the Imam lowered himself into a chair.

"You, you saved my life," Rahman said, visibly shaken. "What is your name?"

"Zufar."

The middle-aged cleric bobbed his head. "Ah yes, the Lion. That is an apt name for you, my son. You are new to my congregation, aren't you?"

"Yes, Imam. I traveled from London."

A broad smile split the hate preacher's wrinkled face, exposing yellowed teeth. "Welcome, welcome to my family, Zufar."

BUSHEY, LONDON

Sonia sat at the dining room table of the rented house and studied the tablet that Mitch had left her. He'd given her a quick overview of the system they were using to track Mirza, explaining that they could locate his phone and clothing.

Pinching the screen she zoomed in on the icon that denoted Mirza's position. She sighed with relief; he was back at his guest house.

Zooming out, she noticed that Mitch's icon rapidly approached her location. The radio on the table crackled, and his voice came through, "Sonia, I'm on my way back."

The technology and the confidence of the two men had gone a long way to reassuring her that they could find Eshita. She picked up the radio and pressed the transmit button. "Um, OK, I can see you on the map."

"See you soon," Mitch said with a laugh.

She searched the icons at the bottom of the tablet and pressed one with a camera on it. The screen divided showing the feed from the cameras Mitch had set up outside of their residence. She watched as he rode a scooter into view and stopped in front of the garage. The rattle of the automatic opener filled the house, and a moment later she heard the door to the garage open.

"How did it go?" she asked as he entered.

Mitch had removed his helmet and jacket and was tentatively probing his rib cage with his fingers.

"Oh no, are you OK?"

"I'm fine, but Mirza didn't pull any punches. He needed to make it look real and damn, he did just that." He pulled out a chair and eased himself into it.

She opened the refrigerator and took a bag of frozen peas from the freezer compartment. Wrapping it in a clean towel, she passed it to him.

"Thanks." He winced as he held it against his T-shirt. "So, I think our boy's in with the Imam."

"That's good news. What happens next?"

"That's up to Mirza. The basic plan is he gets himself

into the pipeline to Syria, and I'll track him. When he finds Eshita he'll extract her."

She nodded.

"I'm a little worried we're rushing it," Mitch said.

"What do you mean?"

"When we do this sort of thing, infiltrating groups, it usually takes more time."

She considered the situation for a moment. "According to the media, radicalization is happening much faster now. It makes sense that the smuggling speeds would increase."

"Yeah, that's what Mirza said."

She rose and headed to the kitchen. "Do you want some tea?"

"Cup of char would be fantastic."

Sonia filled the kettle and placed two cups beside it. "So, have you been working with Mirza for long?"

"A few years now. He runs the security teams, and I handle the technical side of the house. He's a rock solid lad. I'd do anything for him."

She turned and flashed a smile. "Which is why you are here, Mitch. I want to thank you again for helping."

"Think nothing of it. That guy has saved my skin and the skin of my mates more times than I can count. There's no way I could let him down."

The kettle whistled then clicked off. Sonia poured two cups. "How do you have it?"

"Black with one."

She added sugar, handed him the cup and took a seat at the table.

"Now, I know a little about you, Miss Sonia Jayaram, but not much. How did you meet Mirza?"

"That's a long story."

He pulled out one of the other chairs, put his feet up,

and made himself comfortable with his tea and frozen bag of peas. "Well, we might have some time to kill."

"OK, well it all started in New Delhi. Back then Mirza worked for a special unit within RAW, our national intelligence agency. He and his partner had uncovered a terrorist plot to conduct a Mumbai-style attack on the city."

"No shit." Mitch listened with rapt attention as she spoke.

Two hours later, and as many cups of tea, Sonia had finished, and he'd run out of questions.

"That's a pretty amazing story," he said. "It would make a great action novel. I can see the cover, Mirza standing with his sniper rifle ready to take down the bad guys."

"He's the most amazing man I know," added Sonia. "Completely selfless and utterly giving."

"Yeah, he's one of a kind." An alarm sounded from the tablet. "And he's on the move."

BIRMINGHAM, ENGLAND

Mirza knelt on a prayer rug in a private room at the back of the mosque. One of Rahman's heavies had knocked on his door at the guesthouse and insisted that he accompany him to see the Imam.

"Do you have anything to eat?" Mirza aimed the question at the man guarding the door.

The guard shook his head. "The Imam will be here soon."

On cue, the door opened, and Imam Rahman appeared in his robes and cap. "Zufar, my son. Rise and embrace me."

Mirza stood and hugged the Imam, fighting the urge to snap his neck.

"You saved my life today," continued Rahman. "My so called protectors were felled like straw. You, the lion, had the fortitude to ensure I was safe. For that, I will always be grateful. Now, please join me for a meal." He led Mirza from the room, through a short corridor into the residence linked to the mosque.

In the Imam's dining room a woman dressed in a burka arranged plates of food on the table. As the men arrived she silently departed.

"Please, sit." The Imam took his place at the head of the table and gestured for Mirza to sit on his right. Another guard sat beside him along with the man he recognized as the Imam's security chief, who now sported a swollen black eye. Rahman gave thanks for the meal then proceeded to help himself to the traditional Pakistani dishes. "I am told that you came from India, where you were a soldier."

"Yes, this is true. I came to England four years ago to find a better life," replied Mirza.

They conversed over the meal, with the Imam asking questions about his military service, family, education and time in England. When the table had been cleared the four men moved into the living room and reclined upon cushions. The woman returned with a tray of tea and offered cups to the men.

"So, Zufar, what brought you to my congregation?" asked the Imam, his eyes piercing over the top of his cup. "There are many other mosques. Why did you seek out mine?"

Mirza sipped and then lowered his tea. "Because of what happened in Coventry. Because I want to fight for

Allah." He watched as the faintest hint of a smile appeared on the Imam's lips.

"You want to make the *kafir* pay for oppressing us?"

"I want to join my brothers and push them from our lands. I want to fight the jihad in Syria and Iraq. I want to help build the Caliphate." Mirza's eyes were wide, and he spoke with vigor. "There is only one god and his name is Allah." He raised a single finger and proclaimed, "Allahu Akbar."

The other men joined the chant. When they had finished, the Imam posed another question, "Would you not consider an attack on the *kafir*, here in their heartland?"

Mirza shook his head. "No, I am a trained soldier. I want to fight in the Caliphate. If you cannot help me with that then, Allah will provide another way."

They chatted for another few minutes before the Imam gave Mirza his leave. While Mirza returned to his guest house the other men remained to discuss Zufar and his request.

"Do you think he's a police informant?" Rahman asked the men.

The guard responded, "No, if he were police he would want to stay. This man seeks to be a warrior of the prophet."

The third man, the security chief with the black eye, poured himself another cup of tea. "It doesn't matter who he is. If we send him to the Caliphate, they will either make him fight or become a martyr. There are no spies among them."

The Imam nodded in agreement. "This is true. How many other fighters are waiting to go?"

"There are two, the Pakistani boys."

"Send Zufar with them. No need to use the boat this time, no one will be looking for them."

Chapter Fifteen

ABU DHABI, UAE

TARIQ STARED through the plexiglass footwell as his private helicopter commenced its descent toward the Yas Marina Circuit. The billion dollar motorsport complex, with its white-capped grandstands, glimmered in the afternoon sun. The helicopter flared alongside the metal shrouded Yas Viceroy hotel and touched down.

The pilot turned to him with a broad grin as the scream of high-performance Formula One engines overwhelmed the noise of the helicopter and penetrated their headsets. "Damn they're loud," he transmitted. "Have a great day, Mr. Ahmed."

"You too, Richard."

Tariq stepped clear of the Eurocopter, adjusted his shirt cuffs, straightened his suit and strode across the helipad. An assistant greeted him and led him to a golf cart. A short drive later and he entered the Lascar Logistics corporate box at the top of the Main Grandstand.

Tariq had attended the inaugural Abu Dhabi Grand Prix in 2009. He hadn't returned since. As a primary sponsor, Lascar Logistics had a corporate box, one of the largest at the race. Managed by his Events Director, tickets were highly sought after among the Emirati social elite.

A waiter handed him a glass of chilled orange juice as he weaved his way through the crowd to the windows that overlooked the main straight of the circuit. As he sipped, the F1 cars screamed past, the noise kept to a minimum by the triple-glazed glass.

"Mr. Ahmed, I'm so glad that you've finally decided to join us."

He turned to face Penny Rider, the petite New Zealander who ran Lascar Logistics events and marketing. "I always hear such good things. I had to come and see it for myself."

"Thank you, sir."

"Penny, can you tell me if Sheik Al-Hasher is here?"

"Yes, he is. I do believe you invited him. He's over in the lounge area."

"Thank you." Tariq exchanged greetings with friends and associates as he crossed the main viewing area to a lounge. Stepping inside he spotted Al-Hasher seated on a couch.

The Sheik wore traditional robes complete with a white keffiyeh. He sat engaged in an animated conversation with a gentleman dressed in a team Ferrari jacket.

Tariq stood a few yards away and watched the man he believed responsible for using Priority Movements Airlift to smuggle weapons to ISIS.

The Sheik was in his late twenties. Handsome, with a pronounced angular nose, immaculately groomed beard and eyes that were almost black, he looked every inch the young Bedouin ruler. He glanced up, flashed Tariq a charming smile and rose.

Tariq took another glass of juice from a passing waiter and approached.

"I must thank you for your gracious invitation," said Al-Hasher.

"My pleasure, Sheik Al-Hasher. I hear that you are a talented driver." He was already aware that the young prince owned a garage of supercars that he regularly raced at this circuit. The man had a bent for danger, embodied Wahhabi ideals and had near unlimited resources; a dangerous combination that had led him down the path of supporting extremists.

Al-Hasher shrugged as he rose. "It is merely a hobby that I enjoy from time to time."

They moved to the windows leaving the Ferrari employee in the company of Penny. Outside below, another group of cars screamed past.

Al-Hasher watched them with a hawk-like gaze. "Such incredible reaction times. At any moment they're a tenth of a second from utter destruction."

"There is no denying their skill," agreed Tariq. "But, I did not invite you just for the racing."

Al-Hasher turned to him. "I am not so naïve as to think that would be the case. I am aware that you have shown interest in my support to the crisis in Syria."

He made a mental note regarding his contact in the MICAD. Clearly, Kashif was on the Sheik's payroll. "You're very well informed. I made some inquiries regarding the shipments my people were delivering. It turned out that the majority benefactor was a fellow Emirati."

"Indeed, and now I hear that you have provided funding in addition to volunteering your aviation services." Al-

Hasher locked eyes with him. "It surprised me. I did not take you for a man of action."

"Perhaps if you had have asked for my support from the start you may have been even more surprised."

Al-Hasher held his gaze. "It is well known that you harbor, moderate ideals."

"My personal beliefs are irrelevant. Increased Iranian influence in both Iraq and Syria is bad for business. Your friends are the only counter to this. We may have different motives, but our end game is aligned."

Al-Hasher raised his chin as he considered the comment. "So, you are not opposed to providing assistance to the Caliphate?"

"As the MICAD, no doubt, have already informed you. My assets are at your disposal."

The corner of Al-Hasher's lip turned up in a sinister smirk. "Excellent. I'm actually in the process of coordinating a large shipment."

"Into Syria?"

"Correct, I require air transport from Benghazi. Your assistance would be greatly appreciated."

Tariq raised his glass as the next pack of Formula One cars raced past. "Send through the details and I'll make the necessary arrangements."

TEL AVIV, ISRAEL

Keila sat in the waiting room outside Manfred Lisker's office with her hands on her knees. She'd been summoned to answer the head of *Metsada's* questions regarding her plan to snatch Salim from Jarjanaz.

She was nervous, despite having briefed Lisker on a number of occasions. This was the first time she'd submitted an operational plan for his authorization.

A speaker attached to a wall buzzed. "Agent Bachman, come in."

Pushing open the door she saw Lisker at his desk. He glanced up from an open folder, adjusted his glasses, and gestured to a chair. "Keila, I don't have much time so I'm going to cut to the chase. I've been over your plan. I have a few questions regarding the risk profile."

She sat. "What in particular, sir?"

"Your infiltration plan. What makes you think you can trust this man…" He glanced at the file in front of him. "Aden Bishop?"

"Our investigation has revealed that he is intimately involved with a former Iranian operative named Afsaneh Ebadi. We're using that as leverage over him."

He folded his hands. "And you have access to this woman?"

"No, sir."

"So you're bluffing him?"

She nodded. "However, his parents were also killed on flight LY395. I believe he has a vested interest in our success."

"Success." His brow furrowed. "Your team is new, you're inexperienced and your plan has been classified as medium to high risk. Enlighten me as to why this shouldn't be handed to one of my 'proven' elements."

Keila swallowed. "Sir, my team may be new but they are hardly inexperienced. Thomas and Daniel are both from Sayeret Matkal and James has recent experience in Lebanon working under WHO cover. Jarjanaz is not Aleppo, there are a number of not-for-profit organizations operating within the town." She paused. "Sir, I assess that our plan has a very high likelihood of success. What's more I believe the capture of Salim is worth the risk."

He stared at her through his thick glasses. Then, right as she was feeling uncomfortable he spoke. "Your mission is approved."

"Thank you, sir."

Lisker lowered his eyes back to the file in front of him. "I want you to pay particular attention to this Aden Bishop. I expect a full debriefing post operation." He glanced up. "You may leave now."

As Keila made her way down to the department she pondered Lisker's interest in Aden Bishop. As far as an asset went he had limited use. Once her mission was complete it was unlikely that he could provide much, if any, additional support to Mossad.

She pushed the thought from her mind as she headed directly to Abel's desk. "We got approval, the mission is a go. Any intel updates?"

The lanky lead analyst looked up from his terminal. "No change to the security situation. There haven't been any major incidents in the vicinity of Jarjanaz."

"And our cover?"

"The profiles we worked up are solid. The last communications between Salim and his WHO manager confirms they're expecting the team."

The alibi for Keila's operatives traveling to Jarjanaz was a fabrication built on Abel's generation of online personas combined with the work of one of Keila's operatives, James, on a legitimate WHO program in Lebanon.

"Can you pull up the intercept?"

Abel brought up the report, generated by their signals intelligence partner Unit 8200. She scanned it, confirming it aligned with what she'd planned. In addition to establishing the vaccination clinic, her team leader, James, had an appointment with Salim to discuss his requests for further medical aid. The prospect of more of the critical, and valuable, medical shipments would ensure the arms trafficker's presence.

"Perfect, thanks Abel," she said. "Is there anything else?"

He shook his head.

She smiled. "We're going to get this bastard. I can feel it."

Fahim, a junior analyst, leaned over from his terminal. "Keila, what do you want me to do with the Afsaneh pack?"

She crossed to him. "Afsaneh?"

"Afsaneh Ebadi, she's the female in the photo associated with Bishop."

"You managed to get into her file?"

"Not directly. I trawled through the archives and Afsaneh was the one person of interest that fit her profile and description. She's been presumed dead since 2012."

Fahim showed her the biographical profile and a brief history of what appeared to be an operative of the Iranian Ministry of Intelligence and Security. "She's a nasty piece of work. Was once one of our top counter-intelligence threats; she assassinated a number of Mossad operatives."

"Were you able to dig up anything recent?"

"Not really. I found another photo. It's from Kiev in the Ukraine, a week before the alleged death."

Keila leaned in and studied the image on the screen. It was a grainy shot from a CCTV camera in what could be a nightclub. Afsaneh, dressed in an elegant evening dress, resembled a movie star. I'd kill for legs that good, Keila thought.

"Interestingly the day this image was captured the nightclub was raided by a tactical team. They tore through the place like a hurricane." He brought up a grainy video that showed armed men breaching a door and engaging targets.

"Any luck locating her?"

"No, if she's still alive, she's disappeared off the grid."

Keila took a moment to consider her options. Aden had agreed to help them and she'd promised not to touch Afsaneh. The earnest look in his eyes when she threatened the woman told her one thing, he was in love and that was something she respected. "Fahim, I want you to put everything you have into a single file and send it to me. Delete the original."

He nodded. "We're not going after the girl?"

"No, we're focused on Salim."

THOMAS HAD ARRANGED the staging area in a government hangar at Ben Gurion airport. It was a facility that a range of government agencies utilized including Mossad and elements of the Israel Defense Force.

Keila was the last of the team to arrive. Jacob, the ground commander, greeted her at the entrance to the hangar. The tall former IDF medic had disarmingly boyish features behind his black-framed spectacles. It was a feature that had helped him infiltrate the WHO and operate without suspicion in Lebanon, under the name James. Keila knew that, despite his pleasant bedside manner, he was actually a lethal operative with nearly ten years of operational experience.

"How are we looking on the civilian side?" asked Keila

as James led her across to where Thomas and Dan were checking their equipment. Both men were former operators in Israel's elite counter-terrorism unit, Sayeret Matkal. However, today, instead of combat fatigues they wore civilian clothes and navy blue ballistic vests marked with the letters WHO.

"I spoke to the operations director at WHO's Eastern Mediterranean office. We're good to go as far as they're concerned."

"Excellent." She joined the rest of the team at a long steel counter where their equipment was laid out. Thomas glanced up from a backpack and shot her a nod.

Dan, a hard-faced operator, shook her hand. "Hey boss." He directed her to a black bag.

She checked everything she needed was inside. "Is the medical gear ready?"

James pointed to a cargo carrier parked next to a van in front of the hangar doors. "The vaccines are in portable coolers. Everything else is stowed."

"OK, there's no change to the orders I briefed at HQ. However, I do want to go over the key points again."

The men stopped what they were doing and gathered around her. "As you all know, the mission is Salim. If we don't get him, we fail. So, it's critical we've go over all the courses of action."

All three men nodded in agreement.

"If Salim receives the shipment personally and we can detain him within the aircraft, we'll exfil immediately. I'll be calling the shots. According to Aden he usually enters the cargo hold, and his men aren't openly armed. This is the most likely scenario.

If we enact the contingency plan and actually establish the vaccination clinic, then James has command on the ground. I'll be monitoring your cell phones for location and audio." She looked at James. "At the interview, your task is to inject him with the sedative and get him back to the aircraft. However, you need to play the situation as you see it. If it's too risky we fall back to the third course of action."

"You do know this could burn the WHO in the area," James said hesitantly. "The UN will lose access."

She fixed him with a cold stare. "Jacob, the mission is Salim. He's a direct threat to the lives of your fellow Israelis," Keila said using his Hebrew name. "WHO will recover."

"If we can't take him from the ramp, I'd prefer to maintain our cover. We can achieve a close recon and follow up with an airstrike. Leak intel blaming it on the Russians."

"As I said, if you get out on the ground, then it's your call," Keila said firmly. "But command is reluctant to strike a UN facility and has directed that our priority is the snatch. The endgame here is Salim's interrogation to break out his suppliers."

James shrugged. "Whatever's best for Israel."

She nodded. "Good, let's get this done."

THE PRIORITY MOVEMENTS AIRLIFT HERCULES touched down at Tel Aviv with a screech of tires and puff of smoke. Roaring, reverse thrust slowed it to a walking pace and it turned onto a taxiway. An airfield attendant in a fluorescent yellow vest waved the transporter toward the freight terminal where it swung in a tight circle until its tail faced a row of warehouses.

As the ramp lowered Bishop spotted a minivan and a freight handling truck emerging from a hangar. They drove across the tarmac and halted a dozen yards away. He identified Keila as she emerged from the van along with Thomas and two other men. All wore navy blue body armor over khaki clothing.

"Hey, you do know Syria's a patriarchal society. They're not going to welcome a female medic."

Keila shot him a withering glare. "I will be staying with you in the aircraft. Now, can you help us get the vaccine storage units loaded?"

The truck approached carrying half a dozen white waist-high cylinders. Ice and Bishop took charge, lashing the containers to a pallet in front of the GAI medical supplies.

Bishop checked the load was secure before turning his attention to the four Mossad operatives sitting in the web side seating. "OK guys, listen up. While you're on my bird, you follow my instructions." He looked at Keila. "That clear?"

She made to say something, and he cut her off. "You stay in the cockpit till we've offloaded your people. I don't want Salim or any of his people smelling a rat."

Keila pressed her lips together.

"Now strap in. In the unlikely event of an emergency, there are pony bottles above your head and life jackets under your seat."

"What's on the in-flight menu?" quipped one of the men. "A beer would be great." The man was lightly built with thick-rimmed glasses. He looked the part of a WHO medical professional.

Bishop grinned as Keila elbowed the man.

"Ignore James, he's joining us from a stint with WHO in Lebanon," she said.

She gestured to the others. "Thomas you've already

met." The quiet olive-skinned operative met his gaze. "And this is Dan."

Bishop thought he recognized Dan as the driver from his kidnapping in Amman. At first glance the Mossad operative could pass as a humanitarian aid worker but, to Bishop's trained eye, the man's hard features and wiry build had Special Forces written all over them.

He gave the team a nod then continued his briefing. "If we hard land, the aircraft has multiple exits. There are the side doors." He pointed. "The ramp and an exit in the roof." He shot Ice thumbs-up and the big man disappeared into the cockpit.

"Did you check the supplies for missiles?" Keila asked.

"Yep. No missiles." Having completed her job, Daisy was napping on a bunk in the cockpit.

Keila's brow furrowed and she whispered a few words to James.

"What's the flight time?" she asked.

"A little over two hours. We'll head out over the Med and then come in from the northwest. Once we're airborne, you can make yourself comfortable. We've got a few yoga mats you can put on the floor."

As the aircraft rolled forward, he unstrapped a cooler from the kitchenette behind the cockpit. He pulled out four cold cans of Coors Light and handed them to James. "Here ya go."

The Israeli operative nodded his thanks and passed one to each of the team. Keila shook her head as he offered her one.

"You don't drink?" asked Bishop as he strapped in next to her. "It's light beer."

"It's American. You know what American beer and sex in a canoe have in common?"

Bishop's brow rose. "No, what?"

"They're both fucking close to water."

Thomas snorted beer from his nose, and Bishop chuckled.

"And here's me thinking you were a real kill joy."

She smiled. "Looks can be deceiving."

BENGHAZI, LIBYA

Mubarez sat in the shade cast by the compound's central residence watching the building that housed Eshita and the other girls. The long cinder-block structure had no windows, only a series of doors that led into storage rooms. In front of the door that led to the girls, one of Huron's guards sat on a stool.

Dipping a piece of flatbread into a spicy stew, Mubarez watched as the guard left his post in search of a meal.

Carrying his bowl, he ducked behind a row of battered four-wheel drives and made his way to the makeshift detention cell. A quick scan confirmed no one was around. He cautiously approached the chained door. "Eshita, are you there?" he whispered. He could hear movement inside.

"Mubarez, is that you?" a feminine voice replied.

"Yes, it's me. Are you alright?

"It's so good to hear your voice. I'm fine but Vashti is not well. She has a fever."

He pulled the door to the limits of the chain and took her hand. It felt so good to feel the warmth of human contact. He slid his bowl of stew under the door. "Here, share this with Vashti. It might make her feel better."

"Thank you, Michael."

The sound of his real name almost reduced him to tears. Michael was what his brother had called him right before he was shot.

"Have you heard anything about what will happen to us?" Eshita asked.

"The man who came to see you, he is making arrangements for us all to be sent to Syria."

A soft sob came from behind the door. "I want to go home, Michael. I want to take Vashti home where we will be safe."

The despair in her voice cut deep, and he held her hand tight. "It's going to be OK. This is what we wanted, remember? Soon we will be amongst friends in the Caliphate."

He heard voices coming from the main building; the guards were returning. "I'll bring you more food when I can. Look after Vashti, and everything will be better when we get to Syria." He gave her hand one last squeeze then dashed away from the cell. When he reached the row of vehicles, he slowed to a walk.

As he rounded the last of the four-wheel drives, a hand grabbed him by the collar.

"What are you doing?" demanded one of his trainers.

"Nothing."

The veteran fighter scowled. "They told me you killed an unarmed policeman in London. I want to see how well you fare when they shoot back."

"They shot my brother," he snapped.

The warrior spat in the dust. "He died a martyr, and if you're lucky you might get the same. Now, join the others. There is training to be done."

JARJANAZ, SYRIA

Salim watched through the window of his Red Crescent marked Land Cruiser as his driver took them through the outskirts of Jarjanaz, toward his base. He spotted two young children, dressed in rags, playing among the rubble of a bombed-out cottage. The scene sparked a glimmer of nostalgia. He'd been raised in a white painted house not unlike the ones that dotted the weed-infested fields on either side of the road. The son of a farmer he'd roamed the low-lying hills in search of treasure and adventure. He'd found both, but not as a child, not until war had come to his homeland.

As they reached the town center Salim was reminded how resilient the Syrian people were. Five years of conflict had left its mark on the city. Buildings had been destroyed, cars burned, and lives lost. And yet the streets were alive with residents going about their daily activities.

His satellite phone buzzed drawing his attention from the window; the Sheik was finally returning his call.

"Tell me about Benghazi," the Sheik demanded.

"Huron has what we need; weapons and suitable women. He has an airstrip if you can arrange transportation."

"The aircraft is easy."

"The supplier, he also made a request of us."

There was a pause before the Sheik responded, "Go on."

"He wants us to transport men. Fighters from Europe who wish to wage jihad."

"What did you say?"

"I said it would not be a problem."

"Good, the Caliphate needs these men. I understand you are receiving the WHO team this afternoon?"

"Yes, they are due to arrive in an hour."

"My contacts have confirmed their legitimacy. I will send you their names."

Salim's lips turned up in a slight smile. "Your intelligence assets never cease to impress, Sheik."

"The vaccination program is vital. Disease is killing more of our brothers than jihad."

"I will accommodate them. Do you have any further updates on the Jews?"

"The Mossad team is no longer in Amman. I expect the Jordanians have expelled them."

"They should have hung them."

"True. I will arrange the transport for Benghazi. Let me know how the vaccination program progresses."

The call ended and a few seconds later a text message appeared with the full names, dates of birth, and passport numbers of the WHO team.

"Every day there are more of them," Salim's driver said as they approached his compound on the outskirts of town.

Bedraggled civilians clustered around the front gate of the WHO logistics node that served as his headquarters and arms warehouse. Salim wound down the window and waved at his men who guarded the entrance. "Get them out of the way!"

He lit a cigarette as the crowd was forced from the gate. They drove in past a World Health Organization sign and parked alongside a white roofed office building.

The yard was stuffed full of crates, boxes, pallets and white UN vehicles. Food, medical supplies, ammunition, and weapons were stacked under white plastic sheeting adorned with the Red Crescent. The international symbol had become an important component of Salim's brand; a life-saving ruse that protected him and his assets from the drones and their bombs.

Salim got out with his bag and walked stiffly to his office building. It had been a long journey by plane from Benghazi to Turkey then across the border by four-wheel drive. It was good to be home. Pushing open the door to his office he spotted Joran lounging on a couch with his boots on the polished wooden surface of the coffee table.

"Comfortable, Joran?"

"Boss!" The former Syrian policeman sat upright. "How was your trip?"

Salim sat at his desk. "Arduous, but useful. Huron has the girls we need and the weapons."

"Excellent. Mohammed has been bitching about his missiles."

"We'll send them to Al-Bab soon. Did you have any problems with the last shipment?"

Joran shook his head. "No, it went smoothly."

"Good, now I need you to get off your ass and ensure all the weapons are concealed. The vaccination team is landing in an hour and I don't want to explain to them why half the compound is an arsenal."

Joran jumped to his feet. "Do you need me at the airstrip?"

"Yes, you'll bring them to my office. Apparently they want to discuss the requests we've been making for more medical supplies."

His assistant made for the door.

"And Joran? Ensure all our men in the compound are armed."

"Everyone, boss? Even those in WHO uniforms?"

He nodded. "Everyone."

Chapter Sixteen

ABU DHABI, UAE

TARIQ ACTIVATED the remote attached to the sun visor of his Range Rover and waited as the heavy steel security gate opened. The isolated compound was a short distance out of town, a location he kept 'off the books' for circumstances such as this.

He drove the up-armored SUV through the gate, which closed behind him. Another vehicle already occupied the tiled courtyard, and he stopped beside it.

The villa was understated but secure with thick walls topped with razor wire, and a comprehensive security system that included multispectral jamming. It was designed specifically for discreet meetings with trusted associates.

A biometric scanner confirmed his identity and the front door opened with a click. Stepping into the foyer he joined his guests in a living area.

"Gentlemen, sorry I'm late."

Chua and Vance rose and shook hands with the third director of PRIMAL before taking a seat.

"I apologize for the location, but I thought it might be a better idea to meet here rather than in my office or at the Sandpit."

Vance nodded. "Given the circumstances, that's wise."

Chua dipped his head in agreement.

"I read your reports. To say that I am disappointed regarding the involvement of Mossad in our operations is an understatement. Why was I not consulted before Bishop met with them here in the Emirates?"

"We had no choice, Tariq," responded Vance. "Once they played the Saneh card we had to maintain contact."

"I understand this, but you still should have consulted me. Any association with Israeli intelligence services not only has the potential to compromise PRIMAL but also undermine the reputation of the Lascar group."

"We've taken actions to mitigate the risks," Vance said. "Might I remind you that we're cleaning up after Lascar. Chua and I were in no way involved in the decision to conduct aid shipments into Syria. In fact, you borrowed PRIMAL personnel for those activities to ensure your aircrew's safety."

Silence settled on the room as Tariq and Vance glared at each other.

Chua broke the tension. "Gentlemen, what's done is done. We're here to find solutions not lay blame."

Vance's features softened. "He's right. Tariq, I'm sorry brother. Chua, why don't you give us the latest intel and we can go from there."

Tariq nodded.

Chua cleared his throat. "OK, so the intel collection op

into Jordan wasn't as successful as we would have hoped. We found no evidence of weapons or related transactions. However, Flash has been crunching the data we stripped from GAI's files. He's identified their primary aid contributor as the Ministry of International Cooperation and Development, here in the UAE."

"Yes, I am aware of that," said Tariq.

"And?" prompted Vance.

"I am investigating the source of the funding and possible ties to extremist elements."

"Do you need assistance from Flash?"

Tariq shook his head. "No. Discretion is required. I will continue to handle the investigation."

Vance frowned. "You're not going to share your findings?"

"When they become relevant. What is the latest regarding the missiles in Jarjanaz?"

"They haven't moved," said Chua. "They're still in the UN warehouse."

Vance checked his watch. "Bishop and Ice will be on the ground with the Mossad team in the next half hour."

Tariq shook his head. "I am still not comfortable being involved with Mossad."

"If the job goes bad our people are out. We're not responsible for the Mossad team's actions. We have complete deniability. This is just another one of your aid runs," assured Vance.

"As you keep reminding me. However, we all know that plans have a way of going awry, especially when Bishop is involved."

"Tariq, if you've got problems with how we're running operations feel free to speak up, it's why you're a director," said Vance.

Tariq shook his head. "No, Vance. I apologize if it sounds that way. I have responsibilities outside of PRIMAL. Lascar is my priority. I have over five thousand employees that rely on me."

"We get that. Chua and I are trying to keep our involvement to the bare minimum, and we still have most of PRIMAL on stand down," Vance said. Ever since the CIA nearly exposed their island headquarters in the South Pacific, they had scaled back operations and focused on counter-intelligence. Monitoring the threat from the CIA and other foreign intelligence services, such as Mossad, was their main priority.

Vance shook his head and continued, "It seems that every time we close something down another job pops up. We're busier than a one-legged man in an ass-kicking competition."

Tariq managed a chuckle. "What of Mirza's operation in London?"

"Progressing well. He's created an in with the local Jihad community. We anticipate him entering the smuggling pipeline in the next twenty-four. As soon as he finds the girl, we'll pull him out, and it's job done."

"Interesting. I may have a connection to the network that we can explore. Lascar has been requested to provide transportation of volunteers from Libya into Jarjanaz."

Chua cocked his head. "Who is the request from?"

"MICAD, they've asked for movement of humanitarian aid and personnel for a non-government organization based near Benghazi."

"Benghazi!" exclaimed the intelligence officer. "Well, we can safely assume they're not shipping bandages and medics."

"How do you want to play this, Tariq? This is more risk but, potentially, another lead."

"The shipment request is scheduled for three days from now. I will delay committing to it until the mission in Jarjanaz is complete, and we have a better idea of where Mirza is heading."

"Good idea."

"Do you have any more information regarding Saneh?" asked Tariq.

Chua shook his head. "I've got Flash monitoring all her email and banking accounts, the ones we know of. She doesn't want to be found."

"Understandable." Tariq shot each man a questioning look. "So, are we done here?"

Vance nodded. "We'll keep you posted on the operation in Jarjanaz."

They left the building, shook hands and climbed into their vehicles. Vance and Chua left first, heading east in their SUV.

"I don't like this at all," said Vance as he stomped the accelerator to the floor. "He's withholding information."

"This is close to home. You heard him, he's worried about Lascar."

"Yeah, and since when are we the enemy? We're transparent with him, damn it. The UAE end of this has to be big. I've never seen him afraid. Not even his father made him this jumpy."

"It's safe to assume that he knows who is supplying Daesh, and they're influential, very influential," said Chua.

"Yeah, that's what I'm afraid of."

JARJANAZ, SYRIA

Bishop waited for the ramp to touch the ground before jumping out and checking their surroundings. The five Land Cruisers were parked at the usual spot beside the cracked and dusty dirt airstrip. Apart from the Red Crescent-marked four-wheel drives, the rudimentary airfield was deserted, a mile out of town along the main highway.

He raised a hand and waved the group over. As they approached, he recognized Joran, Salim's assistant. The arms trafficker was nowhere to be seen, eliminating any hope of a quick snatch.

"Hello, Mr. Aden." Joran offered him his hand, and he shook it. "What's wrong? You look worried."

Bishop gestured to the right-hand wing of the aircraft. "One of the engines is running a little rough."

Joran grinned. "No problem, you have three more, and we will take out all the cargo."

He laughed. "Good point. Let's get this gear unloaded." He introduced Joran to the three WHO medical workers then helped load their equipment into the four-wheel drives. Keila remained up front, with Ice and Mike.

As the medical supplies and vaccination storage units were being unloaded, James, the bespectacled WHO worker, exchanged a few words with Joran. Bishop noticed he disappeared toward the cockpit for a minute before returning and giving the two other WHO personnel a nod; the Mossad operatives were going in.

Once the cargo hold was empty Bishop shook Joran's hand. "Good doing business with you."

The Syrian nodded. "Hey, next time, can you bring me some Coca Cola?"

"I can do better than that." He strode to the rear of the cargo hold and opened the cooler. Grabbing a carton of the caffeine-laced soda, he gave it to Joran. "See you soon."

Watching from the ramp he waited until the convoy had departed, with the three Mossad operatives, before raising the ramp and making his way into the cockpit where Mike, Ice and Keila were waiting. "They're away."

Keila climbed from her seat and brushed past Bishop. He caught a hint of her perfume as she pressed against him.

"Do you need anything?" he asked.

She shook her head and disappeared into the cargo hold.

He waited till she was out of earshot then turned to Ice. "Can you get a bird up?"

"Will do." Ice activated a hidden menu on the digital cockpit screen in front of him.

Mike leaned across. "I've been itching to play with this." The newly recruited PRIMAL pilot had only recently been familiarized with the full suite of upgrades built into the aircraft.

On the roof of the Hercules a panel slid back and an object rocketed into the sky with a puff of gas. Thirty feet above, a set of wings snapped into place and an electric motor powered propeller hummed. The drone climbed rapidly before setting into a loiter pattern.

Back in the cockpit Ice projected the image from its camera onto a screen.

Mike shook his head. "You guys and your toys."

"Did Mitch show you all the mods?" Ice asked.

"Yeah, we've got a Skyhook, RATO launch, ECM, air-droppable contingency pod..."

Bishop grinned. "Our old bird, the Ilyushin, had claws but we've got to play it a bit more low-key now."

"Yeah I've heard the Pain Train stories."

He slapped Mike's shoulder. "OK, let's keep the bird scanning a one-mile perimeter around the Herc. If anything gets closer than that you give us a warning, punch the RATO, and we get the hell out of here."

"No problems."

Bishop made his way down the short ladder and into the cargo hold. Keila sat in the web-seating hunched over a tablet, an earpiece in one ear, her eyes glued to the screen.

SALIM WAS STARING INTENTLY at his laptop when the door to his office opened and Joran's face appeared. "Boss, the medical team is here. You want me to bring them in?"

He shook his head. "No, I'll come out and talk to them." He grabbed his phone and followed Joran out into the yard.

The WHO workers were standing with their equipment, scanning various parts of the compound. There were three of them: one tall with glasses, another short and wiry looking, and the third swarthy, potentially Lebanese or even Syrian.

"Gentlemen, welcome to Jarjanaz. I hope my men haven't inconvenienced you too much with our security measures. These are testing times and many people object to the work we do here. They would prefer our meager resources be used on those who least deserve it."

The man with the glasses offered his hand. "My name is James. I take it you are Salim?"

He grasped the man's hand. The shake was firm, confident. "Yes, that's correct. I run the distribution operations."

"It's good to finally meet you. We've needed to set up a

clinic in the region for some time." James glanced around. "Is there somewhere we can discuss how this is going to work?"

"Of course. My office is small; Joran will make your men comfortable here." He turned to his assistant. "Arrange refreshments for them."

He gestured for the WHO team leader to join him in his office, followed closely by one of his guards. Offering James a seat he took his own behind the desk. "So how does the vaccination program work?"

"We'll set up a clinic where there's some space. It would be good if it were under cover. My men have brought leaflets that can be distributed throughout the town."

"And your intention was to run it here?"

"Yes, unless there is a better place. I recently ran a mission in Lebanon. We used a school close to the aid warehouse."

"Lebanon; your entire team was working there?"

"No, just me. Dan and Thomas have been on other projects."

"Interesting. Did you find the immunization program in Lebanon to be successful?" Salim watched as James glanced over his shoulder at the AK-wielding guard in the doorway.

"Yeah, very. In fact, we should probably start with you and your men. There have been outbreaks of measles, chicken pox and polio throughout the region. If you're traveling to deliver aid you will all be at risk."

Salim nodded. "Yes, I have heard that the diseases have spread as far as Amman."

James frowned. "Amman, as in Jordan?"

"Correct. That would explain why two of your men were there. Would it not?"

"I never mentioned Amman."

"No, you said 'other projects'. I assumed you meant their work in Jordan."

James shook his head. "I'm sorry, I'm confused. My colleagues were both working in the WHO regional office in Cairo."

Salim fixed him with a cold stare. "Is that right?" He spun the laptop on his desk so that the aid worker could see the screen. On it was a grainy photo showing two men and a woman. "This photo was taken in Amman last week. I would say that the resemblance to your men is uncanny."

James leaned in and examined the image. "Salim, that could literally be anyone. I can personally vouch for both Dan and Thomas. I have their passports in my bag and their WHO credentials. I assure you we are exactly who we say we are."

Salim opened a drawer, pulled out a pistol and racked the slide. "I don't believe you."

KEILA HEARD Salim's words through the active microphone in James's phone as clearly as if she was sitting in the room with them. Her heart leaped into her mouth, adrenalin kicked in and her thoughts raced at a million miles an hour. How the hell did Salim get the photo of her team in Amman? Who had compromised her mission?

"What's going on?" She glanced up and saw Bishop staring at her.

She held up a hand to silence him as she listened. Through her earpiece she could hear Salim's men yelling. There was no doubt, they were compromised. Suddenly the audio feed died and the location icon on her screen flashed red. James's phone had been destroyed. In a matter of seconds the two other phones followed suit.

"They've been compromised," she stated. "Somehow they knew Thomas and Dan were in Amman."

"Amman? We could all be compromised. You need to enact your recovery plan and we need to get airborne."

Keila dropped the tablet, rose and grabbed her equipment bag. Unzipping it she pulled out a Micro Tavor assault rifle, body armor and a bundle of black cloth. "A recovery element is never going to get here in time. If I don't do something they'll be dead within the hour."

Bishop grasped her by the shoulder. "You go out there alone and you're dead. It's a suicide mission."

She shrugged him away. "I know the risk. We're a team."

The door to the cockpit swung open and Ice approached. He eyeballed Bishop and Keila. "What's going on?"

"My team's been compromised," she snapped, strapping on her body armor and unrolling the bundle of black material.

"She's doing a fucking Rambo," replied Bishop as he locked eyes with his partner. The two men had been working together long enough to know what the other was thinking.

Bishop flipped up one row of netting seats. Twisting a hidden latch he removed a panel revealing a hidden compartment. Ice helped him haul out a number of gear bags.

Keila, now dressed in a black burka with her face unveiled, watched them. "What are you doing?"

He unzipped a bag revealing a customized AK assault rifle and low profile armor. "We're going to help get your team out."

TO ONE SIDE of the yard Joran used a hammer to smash apart the last vaccine refrigerator. So far he had found three pistols and spare ammunition. He tossed the weapons into a bucket and carried it across to where the so-called WHO workers knelt, their hands bound behind their backs. "So. Are you still medics?"

An assassin glared up at him with defiant eyes. He took a pistol from his belt and jammed it into his temple.

"How did you know Salim would be here? How did you know about the smuggled weapons?" Enraged by the man's silence he clubbed him in the temple with a sickening thud. The would-be assassin slumped forward into the sand.

"Joran, leave them be."

He glanced at Salim who sat watching from a pile of crates.

"Have you sent anyone back to the airfield?"

Joran shook his head.

"Might be smart, considering the aircraft hasn't taken off yet."

As if on cue there was a roar as the transporter buzzed the compound and climbed away.

"Never mind then." Salim lit a cigarette and took a long drag. "Looks like they're on their own now." He paused in thought. "Joran, put them in the trucks." The corner of his mouth lifted. "I'm sure Mohammed will pay handsomely for three Jew assassins." Exhaling a cloud of smoke he pulled his satellite phone from his pocket. The ISIS leader wasn't the only one who would be impressed with their captured prey. The Sheik would want to know that his air delivery service was compromised.

THE BATTERED Toyota sedan bounced along the potholed highway that ran alongside the airstrip, Middle Eastern music blaring from its open windows. A middle-aged man dressed in a traditional robe sat behind the wheel, a cigarette hanging from his lip. Another man, younger and also smoking, sat in the passenger seat, an AK resting on his knees.

Through the bug-splattered windshield the driver spotted a figure standing in the road. He eased his foot off the accelerator as he saw it was a woman in a burka. She waved her arms up and down as the car came to a halt.

He glanced sideways at the man next to him and shrugged. They were miles from the town. The younger man smirked and opened the door, leaving his AK in the footwell. As he got out he glanced around then flicked his cigarette into the dust.

The driver, not one to miss the fun, joined his partner at the front of the car. "What are you doing out here?" he asked the woman in his native tongue.

She took a few tentative steps toward them. "I got lost. Can you give me a ride back into town?" she replied with the faintest of accents.

"I'll give you more than that," growled the younger man as he grabbed her arm.

Her reaction took them by surprise. She punched him in

the throat, breaking his grip. Then, as the driver lunged, she snapped a front kick to his groin.

Pain shot through the driver's body. He dropped to a knee, moaning as he watched her dispatch his friend with another vicious kick, this time to the head.

"No, no, please don't," he managed as she whipped a compact assault rifle from beneath her burka.

"Put your hands behind your back," she snarled.

Out of the corner of his tear-filled eye he spotted two figures appearing from the ruins of a building. The armed men moved swiftly toward him as her boot sent him sprawling face down into the dust.

Bishop let out a chuckle as he took over from Keila and cable-tied the driver's hands behind his back. "Remind me not to piss you off."

He and Ice wore local garb: black and white-checked keffiyehs, dirty jeans, boots and worn canvas chest rigs over a long shirt. The shirts covered their covert armor and pistol belts. From a distance they resembled local fighters, but wouldn't pass a closer inspection. Their customized AK-104s sported infrared lasers and state of the art optics.

Ice bound the hands of the other man and they dragged them into the shade of the ruins.

"She's lethal," said Ice as they propped them against a wall.

"Mossad aren't known for kid gloves."

They gathered the heavy packs they'd stashed, dumped them inside the sedan and climbed in. Ice sat in the back, Bishop behind the wheel and Keila rode shotgun.

The rusted Toyota smelled heavily of tobacco and when Bishop turned the ignition it sounded like it was running on three cylinders.

Ice produced a tablet from his vest and checked the screen. "Three more hours of drone time and then we're blind."

"Excuse me," asked Keila as they drove into the outskirts of Jarjanaz. "But who the hell are you people? Weapons, armor and drones; you're not loadmasters from a logistics company."

Bishop eyeballed her in the rear view mirror. "We dabble in personnel recovery. What we need now is eyes on the compound." Bishop checked his watch as they drove through the war-ravaged town. By his calculations, they only had about a half an hour until nightfall.

Ten minutes later they parked a block away from the compound where the Mossad team had been captured.

"OK, what now?" asked Keila.

"Now, we wait till it gets dark. Then Ice and I are going to infiltrate the compound, recover your guys then get the hell out of here."

"What about me?"

"You are going to be driving the getaway car."

"We're going back to the airfield?"

"That's the plan. Once we have the guys, we'll contact our pilot in the Herc and he'll RV with us there." Bishop turned to her. "Does the plan meet with your approval? Because once we do this I don't want to ever hear from you again. You leave me alone, you leave Saneh alone. You got that?"

"Deal."

"Guys," interrupted Ice. "There's a problem."

"What's that?"

He thrust the tablet forward. On screen, the Mossad operatives were being bundled into a truck. "They're moving them."

"Damn, that complicates things."

ABU DHABI, UAE

"You're kidding me, right? Tell me you're fucking kidding me?" Vance sat on the bench in a singlet that barely contained his bulging chest. He'd slipped away to the gym in the garage and had been on his third set of three hundred pound bench press when Frank had interrupted him.

"No joke, boss. The Mossad guys got rumbled. Bishop, Ice and the female Israeli operative are tailing them now."

"Jesus, Tariq is gonna freak. What about the Herc? Where the hell is that?"

"Safe in Turkey. Mike is standing by to recover the team once they have the Israelis."

"I should have known this would happen. I should have known. You put Bishop and a woman into a high-risk environment and of course he's going to go charging in." He grabbed a towel and wiped his face. "Exactly where are they?"

"About fifteen miles east of Jarjanaz. They're tailing a pair of trucks."

"Are we in contact with them?"

"Sort of. Bishop has been broadcasting but hasn't responded directly to any of our questions. He's most likely trying to maintain a low-profile presence because of the Mossad operative."

"Bit late for that."

"Well, I guess I better let Tariq know. What about Mirza, any movement on that front?"

"Negative. He's still in Birmingham. Mitch and Sonia are in the safe house in Bushey. There's nothing going down in the UK."

"Yeah, well we'll see about that. In my experience, shit never goes south in one place. Nope, it likes to whip itself up into a storm. Brace yourself, it's coming."

Chapter Seventeen

BIRMINGHAM, ENGLAND

MIRZA LAY on the lumpy mattress in his room reading a battered copy of the Koran. His mother had given him the book when he was a child but it had been years since he'd opened it. She had been a devout Muslim, a strong woman well regarded in her community. Her interpretation of the word of Mohammed was based on love, tolerance and justice. They were ideals that had served him well throughout his life, and that he would continue to embody since she'd passed.

He lowered the Koran onto his chest as he contemplated the difference between his faith and that of men like Imam Rahman. No, faith was not the right word to describe the hate preacher's beliefs and teachings. Faith was an intensely personal thing. Rahman's interpretation of Islam was purely control and manipulation; manipulation of religion, beliefs and ultimately, innocent people. He was not a preacher, he was a criminal, and criminals deserved one thing, justice.

His phone vibrated on the windowsill, and he reached for it. The message was from a number he didn't recognize.

Come to the corner of Smith and Warton at 0230. Tell no one.

Mirza checked the time on his phone; it was a little after ten pm. Four hours before, what he assumed, was the start of his journey to Syria.

He dialed a number and lifted the phone to his ear. A series of soft beeps confirmed the call was secure. "We're on. Corner of Smith and Warton at 0230."

"Got it. I'll be there," replied Mitch.

"How's Sonia holding up?"

"She's good, real trooper. Got friends in France. I'll drop her there once you're in the pipeline."

"Roger. Mitch, I'm not going to be able to contact you until this is done. If anything happens, promise me you'll get the team to follow up and recover the girls."

"Nothing's going to happen, mate."

"Promise me."

"Yeah, I promise. Stay out of trouble."

"You too." Mirza terminated the call and placed the phone back on the sill. He lay with his hands folded, staring at the ceiling. Despite what lay ahead he felt no fear. Instead, he was calm, centered on the task at hand; ready to find Eshita and bring her home.

ALEPPO GOVERNATE, SYRIA

Mohammed pressed his hands to his ears as the T-55 tank's main gun fired, belching flame into the darkness. The shockwave from the cannon resonated through his chest, and he grinned. Using armored vehicles captured from the Iraqi army, his men had quickly overrun the Free Syrian Army position on the outskirts of Aleppo.

Emboldened by American airstrikes and armed with their weaponry the FSA had begun encroaching on his territory. Forty-eight hours earlier they had overrun one of his bases, killing twenty men and seizing weapons and stores. In retaliation he had mobilized one of his companies and, under the cover of darkness, quickly repelled the incursion. Now, the FSA fled as Mohammed's forces hammered them with the T-55 and the last of his TOW missiles. Burning vehicles lined the main road, flames illuminating shattered buildings.

He lit a cigarette and watched from inside his armored Humvee as the tank rattled forward into a new firing position and continued to engage targets.

A radio crackled and the voice of his lieutenant, Malik, emanated from the speaker. "Our base is secure. We have captured Masif."

Mohammed flashed his teeth in a broad smile. Mullah Masif was once one of the rebellion's most notorious commanders. A legend among the rag-tag forces of the FSA, his Wolf Brigade had overrun more than a dozen of Assad's outposts. Recently however, under pressure from his US backers, he had taken a stand against the more fanatical rebel forces. Turning his men against Salafists such as Al-Nusra and ISIS, he had surprised his one-time allies and had rapid success. Masif's capture was a significant victory for the Caliphate, and for Mohammed's reputation within the Islamic State.

Leaving the Humvee, he waited for his protection detail to gather before walking toward the captured outpost. Despite the absence of the moon he had no difficulty finding his way. A row of vehicles burned fiercely, lighting the path to his recaptured base, a former Syrian police compound. Bodies littered the demolished street. He recognized some of his men among the dead fighters.

The front gates to the compound had been blown wide open by a suicide car bomb but the cinder block fortress within was still intact.

The deep staccato thump of heavy machine gun fire reverberated through the air as his men continued to engage the fleeing FSA fighters. Over the noise, Mohammed recognized the roar of a coalition fighter-bomber. "Hurry with the human shields!" he bellowed at his men, shepherding women and children into the compound. "Get the tank under cover!" He flicked his cigarette into the dust as he searched for Malik.

His lieutenant appeared from the corner of the main building. In the flickering light of the fires he resembled the devil incarnate, face filthy with the grime of combat, yellow teeth displayed in a manic grin. "This way, Mohammed." He waved him around the corner.

Five men sat, heads bowed, in the sand as he approached. He recognized the grizzled features and short-cropped salt-and-pepper beard of Masif and almost cried out in excitement. "Mullah Masif. It is a pleasure to meet the legend."

The FSA commander glared at him defiantly, his eyes burning with hatred. "Burn in hell Daesh scum," he growled.

Mohammed wrenched his pistol from its holster and aimed it at the older man's face. "If you had joined us we would have defeated Assad by now. But you chose to forsake Allah. You chose the Americans over your own."

Masif's expression didn't change.

Mohammed jerked the weapon to one side and fired, hitting one of the FSA prisoners in the neck. The man managed a weak gurgle as he clutched the wound and toppled over. He twitched and convulsed in the dust as his blood stained the sand.

Still, Masif's eyes remained defiant.

The ring of Mohammed's phone broke the silence, and he turned away to answer it. "Salim, you better have my missiles."

"I have that and more," the arms trafficker replied.

"Women?"

"The women are coming. No, I have captured three *kafir* spies."

Mohammed scowled. "Cut their throats and bring me the missiles."

"They are Jew spies."

His brow rose. "How? Explain how you have them."

Salim gave him a run down on how the would-be assassins had attempted to infiltrate his organization posing as WHO workers.

"Bring them to me."

"My convoy is already on its way. You will have the missiles and the Jews in your hands soon."

"Excellent." He terminated the call and turned to his lieutenant. "Brother, take the FSA scum to Al-Bab. Salim's trucks will meet you there with weapons and three captured spies. Secure the prisoners. When I return, I will deal with them."

"What about Masif?"

"Take him with his men. Execute them at dawn, film it so the FSA dogs can see their hero die. I will return in the morning with the brigade."

Malik nodded and turned to issue orders to his men. Mohammed left him and continued his tour of the police compound. His T-55 tank was now hidden inside a partially destroyed building. His Humvee and the technicals were parked in the open with Red Crescent-marked sheets draped over their heavy weapons, women and children shackled to their sides. He anticipated an FSA counter attack. It would come in the early hours of the morning and he would personally crush what remained of Masif's Wolf Brigade. Then he would return to Al-Bab and spend the day wringing information from the Jewish *kafir* spies.

BUSHEY, LONDON

Mitch packed the last of his gear and dropped the bags in the hire car parked in the garage. Closing the trunk he handed the keys to Sonia. "Right, I need you to drive this to Gatwick. Park at the private terminal and I'll meet you there in a few hours."

She nodded. "Do I need to return the car?"

"No, I'll do that when I arrive." He grasped her shoulder. "And don't worry about Mirza. He does this kind of thing all the time."

She hugged him. "Please keep him safe."

Mitch squeezed her tight. "Listen, we're all over it. This is going to be a real simple job. OK, I'll see you at the airport."

He waited for her to get in the car then raised the roller door. A quick check up and down the dark street confirmed it was clear. He waved her out and watched as her tail lights drove away. Donning his helmet, he swung his satchel around to the back and mounted his scooter.

A chilling thirty-five minutes later he arrived in Birmingham. Checking his watch he saw he had ten minutes to get into position. Parking the scooter he unslung the satchel and pulled out a black case. Unzipping it, he retrieved a tiny disc-shaped drone. He activated it with his iPRIMAL then slipped it into his pocket. He rode around the corner, pulled over behind a parked car and watched the street.

A minute later a van stopped at the curb. A man stepped from the passenger side and lit a cigarette. Then a figure approached; Mirza.

Mitch watched a brief exchange between the two men. The smoker held out his hand, and Mirza dropped something in it. The item was thrown to the ground and crushed underfoot. Then Mirza ducked into the back of the van.

Mitch launched the drone, tilting his iPRIMAL to guide it toward the van. The vehicle pulled away from the curb and accelerated up the street.

"Shit." He sent the drone racing after it. The van turned a corner, and he lost sight of the tiny aircraft. Dropping his eyes to the screen gripped in his gloved hands he used the drone's camera to guide it. The grainy image flickered as the device reached the extent of its range.

"Come on." He started the scooter and twisted the throttle riding out onto the street with one hand. The other hand gripped the iPRIMAL as he tried valiantly to stay in range.

The van filled the grainy screen as he managed to get the scooter around the corner without crashing. Tilting the screen he sent the drone soaring over the van then brought it down on the roof, where it stuck.

"Thank God." Mitch let the scooter slow to a halt and checked his iPRIMAL. A flashing icon appeared on a map. The tracker in the drone was working. He slipped the iPRIMAL into his jacket and gunned the scooter. Now he could locate the van from anywhere in the world.

ALEPPO GOVERNATE, SYRIA

Bishop took one hand from the steering wheel of the Toyota and adjusted the head-harness of his night vision goggles. They were driving without headlights, tailing the convoy for over an hour, and his left eye was twitching with fatigue.

Behind him, he could hear Ice rummaging in a bag. Suddenly the rich aroma of coffee overwhelmed the stale stench of cigarettes and Ice leaned forward, handing him a thermos cup. "Get some of this into you."

Bishop took the sweet black liquid and sipped it as they continued along a rutted highway. "Thanks, mate." The coffee immediately perked him up. He handed back the empty cup and Ice offered one to Keila, who sat in the passenger seat beside Bishop.

A few hundred yards ahead Bishop spotted the convoy coming to a halt at a cluster of buildings. He pulled the car over while Keila observed with a thermal scope.

"It's a checkpoint," she said.

Through his NVGs he could see a barricade manned by armed guards. "We've got to be close to the Daesh front line."

She lowered her scope and turned to him. "If we lose the trucks now we're not going to find them again."

Bishop raised his NVGs, closed his eyes and drummed his fingers on the steering wheel. Trying to bluff their way through the checkpoint was not an option. They would have to box around it. However, that would mean losing sight of the convoy.

"The weapons," said Ice from the back.

Bishop glanced back at him, confused for a moment. "I'm an idiot. They're not just moving the prisoners."

"They're also shipping the TOW missiles," finished Ice.

He pulled his iPRIMAL from his vest and opened the mapping app. A side menu showed him PRIMAL's current live tracking devices. He turned on the overlay for the TOW missile trackers. Sure enough, the last location lay on the road they had been following.

"Missiles? How does that help us find my men?" asked Keila.

"Trust me, it does." Bishop looked up and saw that the trucks were through, their headlights continuing along the highway. Then he waited for the next location update. A split second later the missile icons appeared on a road curving away from the checkpoint.

He used the map to find an alternate route a few miles away. "We're in business."

Chapter Eighteen

ABU DHABI, UAE

CHUA OPENED the door to the operations room, spotted Vance standing in front of a wall-mounted screen and moved across to join him. "How are things looking?"

Vance's eyes were glued to the battle-tracking map. It showed the location of Ice and Bishop along with the TOW missiles and, he assumed, the kidnapped Mossad operatives.

"When it rains it pours. We now have Mirza in the smuggling pipeline and Bishop and Ice heading into Daesh controlled territory. Shit is rapidly spiraling out of control, and we've got zero redundancy."

"Mitch is in France with Sleek. Worst case scenario he could be over Turkey in a matter of hours."

"To do what? Fight with USAF for airspace? We need more shooters in case shit hits the fan." He reached out and touched an icon on the edge of the map. It zoomed out to a global view. Colored dots appeared showing the locations of PRIMAL's active and inactive operatives.

"Don't you mean, 'when' shit hits the fan," Chua added dryly.

Vance turned to his fellow director. "You're even starting to sound like me."

Chua chuckled. "You say it like it's a bad thing."

"It is. Someone has to be the ray of sunshine around here and it sure as hell ain't gonna be me." Turning back to the map he pointed at a pair of flashing icons. "What's the status on Miklos and Pavel?" He referred to two PRIMAL operatives on stand down following the organization's compromise by the CIA. The pair had formed the core of the Critical Assault Team, a heavy hitting in-extremis force.

"They've opened a guest house outside of Barcelona."

"You're shitting me? Together? You sure it's not a cover for an assassination service or a halfway house for special ops veterans?"

"Nope. According to Trip Advisor, it's legit and highly rated. Flash tells me their marketing is slick. He's thinking about booking in for a weekend away."

Vance shook his head. "Well, at least they're adaptable. OK, let's bring them back online and hook them up with Mitch. Then if things get hairy we can re-task them as required." He turned to the man sitting in the corner of the room. "Frank, does Mitch have a contingency pod loaded on Sleek?"

The watchkeeper looked up from his screen. "Yep, he's got guns, ammo, armor, and all the usual kit. Sleek is currently airborne but will be on the ground in Avignon in forty-five minutes."

"Excellent, Pavel and Miklos can meet him there. Do we still have a firm fix on Mirza?"

"Yeah, he's clear of the tunnel and heading south toward Paris."

Chua used his finger to draw a line from the north coast of France down through the capital and across to the Mediterranean. "They'll head for Marseille, where Imam Rahman has associates. There's a large militant Islamic population there. Then they'll board a boat and head across to Libya."

"Might be a good idea to scope a vessel," added Frank.

"Do it," said Vance. "We need to be ready for all contingencies. And get in contact with Bishop. I want to know what he's planning. I mean, apart from chasing a Mossad team around Daesh controlled territory."

ALEPPO GOVERNATE, SYRIA

Bishop pulled the cab to a halt at a long trench and mound of earth; an anti-tank ditch. Checking his iPRIMAL, he saw he had three missed calls from the Sandpit and a message demanding that he get in touch, ASAP. Ignoring them, he checked the satellite imagery and confirmed what he already knew. "This is as far as we can go with the car."

Keila looked across. "How do you know?"

"Google Earth. Your people are five miles past this ditch. We need to get a hustle on."

He left the vehicle, slung his AK and grabbed one of the backpacks from the trunk. Ice joined him, shrugging the heavier of the packs over his broad shoulders.

"What can I carry?" Keila had removed her burka, revealing cargo pants and boots.

"Just keep up," said Bishop as he adjusted his NVGs and slid down into the ditch. He paused at the bottom, waited for the others then clambered up over the berm on the other side. As he crested, he spotted a series of flashes to the west. Twenty seconds later a rumble filled the air.

"That's not a place I'd want to be," said Ice.

"No, someone's copping a pasting."

They waited for Keila to join them then set off into the darkness. For the next three hours Bishop led them through fields, skirting farms and war-scarred dwellings. They moved fast in the cold night air, despite the heavy pack each man carried. By the time Bishop called a rest stop their shirts were damp with sweat and they were breathing heavily.

He sat in a copse of trees and scanned ahead, his weapon laid across his thighs. He sensed someone moving behind him and gave Keila a quick glance as she slid in beside him.

He showed her his iPRIMAL. The missile icons had not moved. "Not far now."

They sat in silence before Keila spoke. "Why are you helping me?" she asked softly.

"Because it's the right thing to do. We should get moving, we've got two miles to cover." He climbed to his feet and waited for the others to join him. As he did his iPRIMAL vibrated, reminding him he needed to reply to the Sandpit before Vance had an aneurysm.

LLOFRIU, SPAIN

The doors to the barn burst open, and an angular faced man in his mid-thirties charged inside. He was followed by a shorter, darker individual of the same age. The first man, Miklos, kicked straw from the floor revealing a brass latch recessed in the floorboards. He grabbed it as the other man, a Russian named Pavel, watched. Lifting it, he uncovered a steel door with a combination pad. His fingers danced over the keys and the door opened with a click.

"Alright, we've got passports, cash, and pistols," he said in a thick Czech accent.

Pavel knelt alongside him. "Leave the guns. Mitch will supply what we need."

Miklos pulled the bagged documents and cash from the safe and handed them to Pavel, who shrugged off a backpack and stuffed them inside.

After closing the safe they left the barn and returned to the renovated Spanish villa that they ran as a homestay. A rotund, elderly woman waited at the front door, Miklos's mother.

"When will you be back?" she asked.

"In a week, maybe less," replied her son.

She grasped the sides of his face as he reached for a backpack. "Be safe." She turned to Pavel. "You too."

He threw the backpack over his shoulder. "Yes, mother. Try to be pleasant to the guests while we're gone."

She placed her hands on her hips. "The guests love me. Why do you think we have five stars? It is my cooking that makes them stay. Which reminds me..." She reached for a pair of brown paper bags on a table and handed them to the men. "Sandwiches for your trip."

A short time later they were in a hire car and heading for the French border. Miklos drove as Pavel read the mission briefing from his iPRIMAL.

"So, Mirza has gone undercover to infiltrate the jihadi smuggling pipeline into Syria. He's trying to find a girl who ran away from her family. We're going to meet Mitch in France and act as backup."

"Sounds like Taken," replied Miklos as he overtook a truck.

"Taken what?"

"Taken, the movie. You know, with Liam Neeson. Someone kidnaps his daughter and he goes after them."

Pavel frowned. "The girl is not Mirza's daughter."

"I know that. I said it's like Taken, not the same."

"No, I don't see how it is." Pavel shook his head and turned his attention back to his iPRIMAL. "According to this, Ice and Bishop are in Syria helping to recover a Mossad snatch team."

"Mossad," spat Pavel. "Why would you help Mossad? You can't trust them as far as you can throw them."

"If Bishop is helping them they must be a team of beautiful Israeli women." Miklos laughed.

"No. He still loves Saneh. Poor fool."

"Either way, I think we're going to see some action."

Miklos broke into a broad grin. "Very good. It's been too long."

Pavel laughed. "It hasn't been three months."

"Like I said, too long."

AVIGNON PROVENCE AIRPORT, FRANCE

Mitch touched the Gulfstream G650 down at Avignon airport in France at three in the morning. Taxiing across to his designated parking bay he powered down the jet's turbines, left the cockpit and joined Sonia in the luxurious cabin.

She was sitting in a plush leather armchair, her eyes glued to a tablet.

"We still got our boy?"

She managed a half smile. "Yes, he's passing through Paris."

"On schedule then." He lowered himself into a chair opposite. "Did you want me to order you a cab?"

She checked her watch. "It's probably a little early for my friends. Is it OK if I stay here until morning?"

"Of course. It would be good to have some company." Pavel and Miklos were still at least five hours away. "These chairs are tip top." He yawned as he hit the controls, reclined and closed his eyes.

"Mitch, I don't want to seem nosy but what sort of security firm can afford an aircraft like this, much less having it operating without payment?"

He opened one of his eyes. "It belongs to the boss. He and Mirza are pretty tight. Your lad has saved the old man's bacon more than once."

"Mirza does have a way with people."

Mitch opened both eyes. "So, what's the go with you and him? I mean clearly, there's something between you. How come the two of you aren't an item?"

Sonia blushed and dropped her eyes back to the tablet. "It's not like that."

"Like what? You're the only woman I've heard Mirza talk about, other than his mom. Clearly the guy has feelings for you and, if I'm not mistaken, you feel quite strongly about him."

She shook her head. "In India, we come from very different backgrounds. Different religions, families, it's complicated…"

"Yeah, maybe. But, both of you have dedicated your lives to helping those less fortunate."

"That's true." She looked out the window at the lights

of the airport terminal. "I guess we've both been so wrapped up in our careers, we've never had the chance to…"

Mitch closed his eyes and leaned back. "Well once this is all done and dusted; maybe you two should make the time."

AL-BAB, SYRIA

Bishop checked his iPRIMAL and confirmed that the building he had eyes on was the last reported location of the TOW missiles. He lifted a thermal scope to his eye and surveyed the compound. The cool early morning temperature allowed the sensor to detect hot air rising from the cooling engines of the trucks that had transported the Mossad operatives.

They were on the outskirts of a town the mapping program called Al-Bab. Judging by the town's lights it was still occupied, despite the conflict. Fortunately, their target backed onto the countryside with the buildings surrounding it shattered by airstrikes. Bishop frowned, why was the walled compound the only structure still standing?

"That it?" Ice whispered next to him. They'd established their observation post in the ruins of what had once been a home a little over five hundred yards from the target.

"That's it. For some reason, it's still standing."

"Worth a closer look?"

"Yeah, what's Keila doing?"

"She's making some coffee."

"Handled the walk in well," Bishop said matter of fact.

"Got a lot to lose." Ice disappeared into the darkness as Bishop continued to observe through his scope. He estimated that the razor wire topped perimeter wall stood at a little over nine foot tall. Above it loomed the roof of a warehouse. He guessed it had originally been a storage facility for the farms they'd walked through to get into position.

A whirring noise behind him signaled the launch of an electric tactical drone. The quadcopter climbed above them and disappeared into the sky. A moment later Ice appeared next to him.

Equipped with an infrared camera, the quadcopter soon beamed an overhead image of the compound to the iPRIMAL that was strapped to Ice's wrist. Ice showed it to Bishop. A quick glance verified why the building was still standing; it was a makeshift hospital. Tarpaulins emblazoned with the Red Crescent were draped across the roofs of all the structures. Trucks parked alongside the warehouse were also marked with the medical symbol. Among the vehicles they could see people wrapped in blankets. In one corner a huddle of figures warmed themselves around a glowing fire pit.

Ice zoomed the camera, confirming that many of them were women and a few, children.

"Either this is an actual hospital, or they're using them as human shields," said Ice. He used the stealthy drone to inspect every inch of the compound from a distance. "Couple of guards on duty at the front gates."

"Yeah, now's the time to strike." Bishop activated his iPRIMAL and sent a short message from the interface.

"Check it out. More visitors." Ice had focused the camera on the front gate where a six-wheeled armored truck and a pickup had stopped to wait for the gates to open. "Looks like an MRAP," he said referring to the armored vehicle.

"Might be useful," said Bishop.

The vehicles drove inside and stopped in front of a two-story building that butted up against the rear wall. Half a dozen men alighted and a moment later three others were manhandled from the MRAP.

"Eyes on the prisoners," said Ice as the three Mossad operatives were shoved toward the building. "Now we know where they're keeping them." The iPRIMAL emitted a beep. "Nearly out of juice." He jabbed the return button on the screen.

A whisper from behind startled the men. "Coffee's up."

Keila handed over a cup of hot black coffee. Bishop took a sip then handed it to Ice. "Damn that's good, thanks."

"What's the plan?" she asked.

"The Herc is going to drop us some extra gear. Then we're going to hit the compound, grab your guys and head for the airstrip."

"You make it sound simple. How long till the drop?"

He checked his iPRIMAL. "Should be overhead in under an hour. We're aiming to hit these guys at dawn."

"What do you need me to do?"

Bishop handed her the thermal scope. "Surgical fire support. How are you with a long gun?"

"I was a marksman in the IDF before I joined Mossad."

"You ever fired a G28?" asked Ice.

"No. But, I'm a fast learner."

Bishop turned his attention back to the compound. "Ice will get you up to speed. We're going to need all the help we can get."

"VANCE, I'VE GOT BISHOP!" Frank bellowed into the corridor.

The hulking African American was half way down the stairs to the kitchen. He spun and charged back into the operations room. Frank tossed him a headset.

"Bishop, what the hell's going on?"

"Vance, good to hear your voice," Bishop whispered.

"I wish I could say the same," he growled. "What's this about you planning to take down an ISIS hospital?"

"The Mossad operatives are located inside."

"Right; good job finding them. We'll pass the information to the Israelis, and they can take it from here."

"Listen, we're pulling the location from the missile tracking chips. Once they separate them from the Mossad guys… they're done. The IDF is never going to be able to respond in time."

Vance knew he was right. Assets as valuable as Mossad operatives would be moved quickly and most likely executed for the propaganda victory. He slammed his fist down on the desk, making the laptop jump. "What's your plan?"

"I'm expecting delivery of our contingency pack from Mike. Once it arrives we're going to bang in. He should be here any minute."

"And your exit strategy?"

"Steal vehicles and head back to the airfield where Mitch will pick us up."

"And if you run into trouble?"

"I've got a tac radio in our contingency pack. Flash can get us into the JTAC network, and we'll whistle up some CAS."

"It might not be that simple to call in an airstrike."

"Flash will sort it out. Look, our package is on its way. I'll let you know when we're kicking this rock show off."

"Bish, Bish…" Vance said, but the line was dead. He turned to Frank who stood in the doorway. "Get Flash to see if he can arrange the frequencies, fill and call signs for Bishop." He paused in thought. "Then let's get everyone in here for contingency planning. I want Tariq dialed in as well. This has the potential to go to hell in a hand basket."

Chapter Nineteen

AL-BAB, SYRIA

THEY COULDN'T SEE or hear the Hercules. It flew forty thousand feet above them, blacked out in a moonless sky. However, Bishop could track its position on his iPRIMAL. His eyes were glued to the screen as the aircraft's icon moved swiftly across the map. As it passed over his position a message appeared.

Green light. Package inbound.

High above, a concealed hatch beneath the transporter opened and a carbon fiber pod fell toward the earth. As it hit ten thousand feet a small drogue chute deployed, steadying it. A few seconds later as it approached five thousand a canopy blossomed, slowing its descent.

On the ground, Bishop heard the snap of the canopy and monitored his iPRIMAL. Then he heard a thud as it touched down a hundred yards away. Leaving Ice and Keila to cover him from the ruined house, he moved to investigate.

As he jogged over the weed-infested field, he raised his night vision goggles. Shades of gray began replacing the black of night; dawn was fast approaching. He reached the cargo pod and released the straps holding the parachute in place. Then he punched a code into a keypad before opening the lid, exposing the gear bags he and Ice had packed back in the UAE.

Unzipping one of the bags he hauled out Mitch's prototype exoskeleton.

Checking his kit he found the Link 16 radio and slid it into his rig, extending the antenna. He synced the radio with the iPRIMAL strapped to his forearm, donned a helmet containing the integrated comms, and strapped into the exoskeleton. A check of the radio's frequencies and fill confirmed he could communicate with coalition airpower. "Good work, Flash."

He lifted the heavy weapons bags effortlessly and strode at high speed across to where the others were waiting.

Ice didn't flinch as Bishop dumped the gear bags. He peered through their thermal scope, his focus on the target compound. "Bish, we've got movement at the eastern wall. Four shooters and three prisoners."

"What's the go?"

"At a guess, a morning execution. The lighting's softer at dawn."

"Very professional."

Keila grasped his shoulder. "Is it them?"

"I can't tell. Bishop, what do you want to do?"

"Can you neutralize the shooters without alerting the compound?"

"Yeah, with Keila's help."

Bishop unzipped one of the bags and withdrew a suppressed G28 marksman's rifle. He handed the rifle to Keila along with a bandolier of magazines.

She threw on the chest rig and lay down with the weapon.

Bishop withdrew a MK48 machine gun from the other bag and containers of ammunition.

"All three prisoners are on their knees. Tango one is ranting at them and waving a sword. Tango two has a video camera and tangos three and four have pulled guard duty," Ice reported calmly.

"They're going to execute them," said Keila peering through the scope of her own rifle.

"She's right, as soon as it's light enough they're going to off these guys."

Bishop loaded a belt of ammunition and racked the cocking handle of his machine gun. "Roger, let's get as close as possible before engaging."

Ice turned to Keila. "You ready?"

"Yes," she whispered. "Let's take these fuckers out."

MASIF FELT no fear as he gazed defiantly into the cold eyes of his executioner, Abu Malik. He knew death was moments away but he wouldn't give the stocky Daesh fighter the satisfaction of fear.

As Abu Malik waved his sword, his lips peeled back revealing a sickly grin. "The great Mullah Masif of the Wolf Brigade. How does it feel to know you will die here, in a ditch where the dogs will gorge themselves on your guts?"

Masif hacked a ball of phlegm from his throat and

launched it. It hit the ISIS killer's pant leg, smearing across the camouflage pattern.

His fellow prisoners snickered, and Abu Malik's face turned a bright shade of red. "Your head will be the last to fall." He gestured to his guard, and one of Masif's lieutenants was dragged forward and propped on his knees in front of them. "Is the camera ready?"

His man held the device focused on the condemned. "Yes."

Abu Malik pointed the blade at the cameraman. "Start filming." He waited for a nod then began his speech. "This man is a member of the Free Syrian Army, a traitor, a dog, a *kafir* and an enemy of the Caliphate. In the name of our glorious leader Al-Baghdadi I sentence him to death." He hefted the sword over his head.

Time slowed for Masif and sadness washed over him as he braced for the death of his friend and loyal lieutenant. A ray of sunlight glinted off the blade as he whispered a prayer.

As the sword dropped a high-velocity round cracked through the air and struck the wall behind him. He flinched and felt warm fluid spray across his cheek. Diving forward he lay flat in the sand as more shots hit the cinder blocks. When the shooting stopped, he rolled onto his side, raised his head, and found himself inches away from what remained of Abu Malik's face.

A round had torn the would-be executioner's head apart, mangling his features into a grotesque bloody death mask. Glancing around he saw that all four of the Daesh men were dead. Swiveling his head, he searched for the source of their salvation.

He caught a glimpse of movement across the fields. A

bulky figure ran toward them at breakneck speed. The man skidded to a halt, effortlessly wielding a machine gun. The warrior eyeballed Masif before sprinting toward the compound. His mouth dropped open as his savior leaped skyward, cleared the nine-foot razor wire topped wall and disappeared. "What in god's name was that?"

"That was your guardian angel," said a female in softly accented Arabic.

Masif managed to rise to his knees and turn to the voice. Two more heavily-armed figures had appeared from the field; a woman carrying a long rifle and a tall man with a modern-looking AK and a keffiyeh wrapped around his head.

"Then praise be to Allah," he exclaimed as the man freed his hands and the woman did the same for his lieutenant. "We owe you our lives."

"We're calling in that debt," said the woman as she collected one of the dead fighter's weapons and thrust it into his hands. "Your angel needs backup."

BISHOP STEPPED off the crushed hood of the pickup truck, where he'd landed, and scanned the inside of the compound. A group of unarmed civilians huddled around a fire in the far corner staring at him, slack-jawed.

"It wasn't the Mossad team," he transmitted. "I'm inside the compound, heading to the front gate now."

An AK-47 barked and bullets stitched the ground as he headed for the front gate.

He aimed the MK48 at the gunfire and let loose a burst. The gun barked and full metal jacket rounds punched through a wooden crate in the storage shed, killing a Daesh fighter.

The gun shots were like a whistle to hungry dogs. More shooters appeared from among the boxes and vehicles. Bullets cracked through the air.

"Crap!" Firing the machine gun with one hand he wrenched a smoke grenade from his vest with the other. Crouching behind a crate he tossed it toward the shooters. With a hiss it flooded the area with thick gray smoke, reducing visibility to inches. He lowered his goggles.

The gunfire ceased, replaced by panicked yelling.

Using his thermal enhanced night vision, Bishop strode through the smoke, his machine gun belching flame and death. He reached the sliding steel front gate, wrenched the locking mechanism from its mountings and threw it wide open. Instinctively he ducked as a rocket screamed past. He spun, identified the shooter and cut him down in a hail of lead.

"Ice," he transmitted. "Front gate is open. You sort transport, I'm going after the Mossad team."

Ice responded immediately. "Roger, be aware we now have three friendlies with us; the prisoners are now armed."

The smoke started to dissipate as Bishop moved toward the two-story building at the rear of the compound. As he ran a machine gun fired from one of the upper windows. A round struck his helmet, smashing his night vision tubes. Hefting the MK48 he blasted the upstairs window while sprinting toward the entrance to the fake hospital.

Kicking the door, he smashed it off its hinges and tried to enter. With the extra bulk of the exoskeleton, he wedged firmly in the narrow frame. A gunman appeared inside and aimed an AK at his face. Bishop let off a burst from the machine gun, cutting him in half.

"Bish, we've got this." He stepped back and saw Ice and Keila moving through the compound accompanied by the three prisoners. The big man swept past him, through the doorway with Keila close on his shoulder.

Bishop knelt and covered the front of the compound as he tore the useless NVG's from his helmet.

The sound of gunfire echoed through the building along with the booms of flash-bangs. He considered abandoning the suit to back up Ice and Keila. More shots sounded from behind him. He glanced back to see the former prisoners engaging a Daesh truck that had appeared at the gates.

The heavy machine gun mounted above its cabin swiveled toward him, and he leaped sideways as the ground exploded. His MK48 spat lead as he sprinted into the warehouse. Running between rows of crates he spotted the markings for weapons and ammunition. Boxes of rocket launchers, machine guns, and surface to air missiles were stacked to the ceiling.

Reaching the end of the shed he burst from cover, spraying the technical with more gunfire.

"Bishop, we've got the Mossad team," Ice's voice came in over his earpiece.

"Get the civilians away from the facility. I'll clear the front gate." He clanked across to where the shattered technical blocked their exit. The men inside were riddled with bullets, their blood splattered across the windshield and cabin. Bracing himself against the rear of the pickup, he used the suit's powerful servomotors and hydraulics to shove it forward. With the gate clear, he strode back toward the building. Women, men, and children screamed in terror as they fled past him.

He spotted Ice hustling the three rescued Mossad operatives into the six-wheeled armored MRAP.

"Grab the gear from the OP!" he yelled. "I'm going to call in the fast air."

Bishop checked the iPRIMAL on his wrist and accessed the communications interface. Flash had come through; he now had access to the JTAC radio network. He could talk to any coalition aircraft within twenty miles of his location.

EIGHT MILES southwest of Al-Bab a USAF F-16, call sign Baron, cruised at twenty-eight thousand feet. The pilot, waiting to strike ISIS targets of opportunity, hummed as he banked his aircraft and began another circuit of his allocated airspace. His mind wandered to the cute Australian intelligence officer he'd met on the base in Jordan. He'd been pestering her for weeks, and she'd finally relented and agreed to go on a date with him.

The crackle of his radio brought him back to the job at hand.

"Any call sign; this is Slammer One. I require immediate Close Air Support." The accent sounded Australian; he wasn't aware of any Australian special forces operating in the area.

The pilot flicked through the notebook attached to his knee and found 'Slammer' in a list; an in-extremis call sign allocated to 'Intelligence Assets.' He thumbed his mike switch. "Slammer this is Baron, I am on station and able to assist."

"Roger, Baron; stand by for coordinates."

A moment later Slammer read out the coordinates and he entered them into his targeting system. Adjusting his orbit he slewed the LITENING pod under the belly of the jet onto the target. Glancing at the screen, he saw a flashing red icon over the compound. "Slammer, I've got bad news, bud. Your target's on a no-strike list, I do not have authority to engage."

There was a moment of silence before Slammer came back with a hard edge to his voice. "Baron, I can confirm that the location is not a hospital, it's an ISIS C2 node and weapons cache."

"Bud, I can't hit it based on your word. It's gotta be struck from the no-strike list. Call made by higher paid dudes than me."

Another pause. "Baron, are you running a full suite of countermeasures?"

Behind his visor, the pilot frowned. "Yeah, what sort of question is that?"

There was no response.

"Slammer, this is Baron, do you read me?" The pilot shook his head and turned his attention back to the display screen for his LITENING pod. He could clearly see the Red Crescent markings and white paint of the hospital compound.

An alarm snapped his attention to the aircraft's Electronic Counter Measures. A calm female voice declared, "Missile launch detected."

"Fuck me!" He rolled the jet and sent it into a dive. A quick glance at his screens confirmed the missile's point of origin, Slammer's target. He keyed his mike as the jet shuddered, spitting flares to divert the missile. "Firebird, this is Baron, I have been engaged by a Surface to Air Missile. I have positive identification of the launch site. Request permission to engage."

He registered a faint shudder in the stick as the SAM detonated behind the F-16. Having defeated the missile, he focused his attention on the launch site.

"Baron, you are cleared for engagement of TAI-0619," replied the terminal controller.

"Here comes the rain, Slammer. I hope you've got your head down," he transmitted as he hit the bomb release."

BISHOP HEARD the pilot's warning and tossed the empty missile tube. He picked up his machine gun and made to sprint for the open gates of the compound. As he moved he noticed the suit felt heavy and sluggish. Jogging through the front entrance, he was suddenly confronted by two pickups equipped with heavy weapons. Bullets snapped through the air and a projectile exploded against the wall next to him.

He fired a burst instinctively, riddling one of the technicals with bullets. An armored Humvee joined the pickups and he caught a glimpse of a commander yelling orders from the cupola, black keffiyeh trailing in the wind. Behind it a tank rattled into view. Bishop turned and made for the corner of the compound, putting the thick wall between him and the Daesh reinforcements.

A warning alarm sounded, and the exoskeleton ground to a complete halt. Panicked, he dropped the MK48 and grabbed the release toggle on the shoulder harness. Nothing happened. He was trapped in the dead suit and the airstrike was imminent. Surely Mitch would have put in an emergency eject, he thought. Frantically, he clawed at the arm mechanisms. One unlatched, then the other, freeing his hands to release the remaining straps.

The exoskeleton fell to the ground as he sprinted in the direction of the abandoned house they'd used the night before.

He registered a loud series of clacks from above as the

bomb made its final adjustments. His only hope, that the thick walls would contain the blast.

Covering a little over sixty yards, he was well within the lethal radius of the bomb when it detonated. The earth shook, and he was thrown forward by the blast. The last thing that passed through his mind as he fell into an inky black void was regret; regret that he hadn't gone looking for Saneh.

FROM THE RELATIVE safety of the armored MRAP, Ice saw the blast wave overtake Bishop and launch him through the air. Rubble and shrapnel pelted the laminated windshield. The maelstrom had barely abated when he pushed open the door and leaped out.

The air was thick with acrid black smoke, and the stench of explosives filled his nostrils as he sprinted to where his friend had disappeared. His eyes stung, lungs burned, and he almost lost his footing as he blundered through the dust and rubble. Ignoring the debris falling around him he searched frantically.

"Bishop!" he screamed once he reached the spot where he'd seen him fall. "Bishop!"

As the dust settled and the smoke blew clear, he spotted a broken body. It was severely mangled with the head almost severed. His heart lurched and tears ran down his cheeks as he knelt by the corpse.

"That guy's proper fucked," croaked a voice from behind.

He turned and spotted a Bishop stumbling forward. Ice grasped him in a bear hug. "You OK?"

"Yeah, but go easy, I think I broke a rib." He prodded

the pouches on his side and pulled out the shattered tac radio. The device had been hit by shrapnel.

Ice helped him limp across the field to where Keila and the three Mossad operatives were waiting at the MRAP. "What happened to the FSA guys?" asked Bishop as they walked.

"Soon as we got Keila's people out they hit the road. Told us the base belonged to some guy called Mohammed Al-Bab. Allegedly he's a bit of a bad ass. The guy we rescued, his name is Mullah Masif, a local brigade commander."

"Well, Mohammed is going to be pissed we blew the crap out of his cache," said Bishop as they reached the armored vehicle.

Keila shot him a concerned look from where she stood in the turret, behind a machine gun.

Bishop waved at her. "I'm OK."

At that moment an explosion blossomed in the field immediately behind them. He glanced over his shoulder, past the smoking ruins of the compound and spotted a T-55 tank at the head of a column of vehicles.

"And that would be Mohammed."

The blast of the Keila's machine gun filled the air as he climbed into the back of the MRAP. Ice dove behind the wheel as Bishop dropped into a seat alongside the Mossad team. "I'm pretty keen to get the hell out of here. How about you guys?"

Thomas shot him thumbs-up. "You saved our asses in there. We won't ever forget that."

He and the rest of his team still wore their blue WHO vests but now they also had chest rigs and carried AKs looted from the ISIS arms cache.

The armored truck shuddered as another tank shell

exploded close by. Ice revved the engine and they bounced across the rutted field with the turret gun hammering. "Mike's standing by to grab us from the airfield. We need to find our way back."

"Easier said than done," managed Bishop as he clutched at his ribs. "Something tells me the fun has only just begun."

MOHAMMED SCREAMED with rage once the dust had settled and the full extent of the damage to the hospital facility was revealed. The air strike had completely destroyed it, leaving only remnants of the compound wall. He had witnessed the explosion from the safety of his Humvee. The lead elements of his convoy had not been so lucky; the T-55 was unscathed but two technicals had been incinerated by the blast.

The tank fired at the cloud of dust that trailed the MRAP fleeing into the distance, a pointless gesture with the rudimentary aiming system.

"Use a TOW," Mohammad ordered one of his lieutenants. The technical with the TOW-launcher pulled out of formation and a fighter in the back readied the missile launcher.

He squinted as the missile fired, racing off across the desert, trailing its guidance wire. Seconds passed; the explosion never came. He frowned. "Fire again!"

"That was the last one, Al-Bab," his lieutenant replied.

"Alert all of the checkpoints. Have your men close every road. Chase them down and kill them."

The man nodded, turned and snapped a series of orders. A moment later technicals raced off in pursuit.

Mohammed took his satellite phone from the Humvee and dialed Salim.

The arms trafficker answered in a matter of seconds. "I hope you are enjoying your gifts, brother."

"The Israelis came for their people. They have destroyed my headquarters. You set me up." His voice was flat and lethal.

"No, no that's not possible."

"All of my weapons are gone. You are going to replace them." He paused. "Or I'm going to kill you." He terminated the call and tossed the phone into the Humvee.

"Al-Bab," said his lieutenant. "We've found Malik."

He followed the man across to the blast site. They skirted the edge of the crater and pushed past what remained of the perimeter wall to where a body lay in the dust.

Mohammed inspected the corpse. Malik had been shot neatly through the head. A few feet away were the bodies of three of his most trusted men. That confirmed the worst; Mullah Masif had escaped along with the Mossad operatives. "Get the convoy moving. I'm going to kill them myself."

JARJANAZ, SYRIA

Salim stormed from his office, found Joran among the rows of trucks and workers, and screamed at him, "Hurry up and get everything loaded. These Jewish dogs have probably already passed our location to the Americans." He glanced up at the sky. "Make sure every load has WHO or Red Crescent Markings."

"We're moving as fast as we can," snapped his assistant. "Perhaps you could help us with the work."

He scowled but before he could retort his phone rang. He glanced at the screen before answering the call. "I've been trying to contact you all day."

The Sheik's voice was icy. "I have been busy."

"While you have been busy the Mossad agents have escaped."

"How? Did you deliver them to Mohammed?"

"Yes, but they destroyed his headquarters and fled into the desert. He's hunting them as we speak."

"They cannot be allowed to get away."

"Al-Bab will find them. Then he will want more weapons. He is not a man I want to disappoint." Salim took a breath. "Do we have transport for my Benghazi shipment?"

"We? There is no we. You work for me, Salim, or have you forgotten who is the master and who is the servant?"

He clenched his jaw. "I have not forgotten."

"I have made arrangements for an alternative aviation provider, one that is not a puppet of Mossad."

"Should we be concerned with how they uncovered our operation? I can't stay here in Jarjanaz."

"You should not be concerned with anything other than what I tell you. I will deal with the security at this end. Mohammed will butcher the assassins, and you will focus on ensuring you can deliver arms to him and his fellow commanders, is that clear?"

"Yes, Sheik."

"Make your way to Ankara, I have a contact there who'll provide an aircraft and cargo. You'll then fly to Benghazi and load the rest of the shipment. Is that clear?"

"Yes, Sheik."

The call ended. Salim stared at the men loading the trucks for a moment. Then he headed to his office to grab his bags. As he walked across the compound he glanced up at the sky. He hoped like hell that the American drones were not already watching.

Chapter Twenty

SOUTHERN SYRIA

BULLETS RANG on the side of the armored MRAP as Ice turned away from a checkpoint and accelerated along a narrow rutted track. In the turret, Keila fired a long blast from the machine gun. An RPG screamed overhead and exploded against a building.

In the co-driver's seat, Bish looked up from his iPRIMAL. "Damn, that was our last route."

The team had been trying to find a way around the urban sprawl of a Syrian town back to the airfield. Every time they pushed down one of the access roads they took heavy fire from a Daesh checkpoint.

"How are we for fuel?" Bishop asked Ice as he searched for an off-road route.

"Not great. We've got less than a hundred miles in the tank."

"We need to find somewhere to hold up and establish comms with the Sandpit."

"You're getting nothing on the iPRIMAL?"

Bishop shook his head. "There's no phone network out here, and I can't get a satellite fix. We need to set up an antenna. I've got local mapping cached but that's it."

There was a cough and Bishop turned to see Keila crouched behind them. A glance past her confirmed that one of the Mossad operatives had replaced her in the turret.

"Guys, I wanted to say thanks. No matter what happens you got my guys out."

Ice gestured through the windshield at the bleak landscape outside. "I'm not sure I'd call this, out." The track was leading them away from the small town, through abandoned fields into the desert.

Bishop managed a smile as he studied her face. Her eyes were bloodshot, cheeks blackened with grime, and wisps of hair stuck out in every direction. "You did well."

She nodded. "So what's the plan now, hotshot? I take it we're not going to make your pickup."

He turned his attention to the road ahead. "Nope. We're going to find somewhere to hole up, establish comms and work out an alternate extraction plan."

"When we stop I'll contact my headquarters. They'll be working on a recovery operation."

"That's fine, except every minute along this road takes us further from Israel and closer to Iraq. I'm not sure your people are going to be able to help in time."

"Do not underestimate the determination of my people. Have you not heard of Entebbe?"

Bishop was familiar with the daring Israeli raid into Uganda. A hundred Commandos, spearheaded by Sayeret Matkal, had flown four thousand miles to rescue hostages from Arab terrorists.

"We're not hostages, yet. Let's work on an alternate extraction plan first."

In the distance, Bishop spotted a lone cluster of buildings. They loomed larger as they raced toward them. When they were less than half a mile away, Ice slowed the MRAP to walking speed. Bishop took a pair of binoculars from the dashboard and focused on the settlement.

It was a farm; squat mud brick buildings clustered around a well. The lack of livestock or inhabitants suggested it was abandoned. A number of walls had been smashed in by heavy weapons or blasted full of holes. A charred pickup jutted from what might have once been a barn.

"Looks all clear," Bishop said.

Ice drove slowly into what remained of the desert community. They came to a halt alongside the largest of the buildings, as the Mossad operative in the turret swiveled back to cover the road.

Bishop climbed into the rear compartment where Keila and the others were sorting through the weapons that they'd stolen with the MRAP. "What have we got?"

Thomas looked up from a crate he'd opened. "RPGs, PKMs and lots of ammo."

"Set yourself up covering the road. If Mohammed's people follow us up, we're going to need to hit them hard and bug out."

The steely-eyed Mossad operative nodded as Bishop opened the PRIMAL gear bags that had come from the contingency pod. Inside among the ammunition, batteries, short-range radios, medical kit and ration bars he found the bag containing a miniature satellite dish.

As he stepped outside to set up the device, Keila walked past with a satellite phone pressed to her ear. "You call yours, I'll call mine," he murmured as he plugged the dish into his iPRIMAL.

ABU DHABI, UAE

Vance paced the operations room like a panther in a cage. He stopped and leaned over Frank's shoulder. "So what do we know? Run over the facts again."

The watchkeeper accessed the log used to track all activity. "At 0615 local Mike reported that he'd completed his drop. At that stage, we still had a track on Bishop, Ice and the TOW missiles. Then, at 0625, Bishop assaulted the target facility, followed by Ice. They stayed on target till 0638 when Ice moved back to their original OP. Bishop remained in the location till 0643 then returned to the OP a few minutes later. Now they're all offline."

Chua looked up from where he sat across from Frank. "Vance, the TOW trackers aren't active. The last ping was at 0643. I'm downloading the latest imagery of the compound now. Flash, what have you got?"

The electronic intelligence analyst sipped from a can of energy drink. Wiping his chin, he checked the screen. "Nothing since they dropped off at the edge of cell phone coverage. If they're in a vehicle or building the satellite chips in the iPRIMALs won't come through."

Chua pointed up at the main screen. "Overhead shots are ready."

The screen blinked twice, and an image appeared.

"Ah shit," said Frank.

Flash wore a half-smile. "Looks like our boy smoked it."

The compound was a cratered ruin. The team was silent as they studied it.

Vance leaned closer. "What is that?" He pointed to an object on the western side of the picture.

Chua zoomed in, and a man-shaped object appeared. He sharpened the image until it revealed the shattered remains of the exoskeleton.

"That must have been in his special delivery," Vance murmured. "Mitch is not going to be happy."

The room's silence was interrupted by an alert on Frank's computer. "It's Bishop calling through," announced the watchkeeper.

"Put him on speaker," said Vance.

A moment later a voice filled the room. "Team, I'm going to keep this short. You've got my location; we need an extraction plan for six pers."

"What direction are you heading?"

"East, into Iraq."

"Good plan, worse case you can RV with the Iraqi army."

Bishop chuckled. "That's not a course of action I'm looking to explore."

"What about the Israelis, can they get their people out?" asked Frank.

"They've enacted some sort of plan but I don't have a timeframe," replied Bishop.

Gunfire emitted from the speakers along with shouting.

"Bishop, what's going on?" asked Vance.

"We've got company. Look, whatever you do, you need to be coming in hot. We've got half the Daesh brigades looking for us and they're going to be pissed we blew up their arms cache."

"Do you have coalition air support on call?"

"Negative, radio is trashed." More gunfire sounded in the background. "I've got to go, I'll check in as soon as I can." The call terminated.

The room fell silent.

"Vance, the UAE is running bombing missions against ISIS," Chua said.

"We need transport not an F-16."

"No, that's not what I'm getting at."

Vance turned to him. "CSAR!" All nations involved in the air campaign in Syria had Combat Search And Rescue contingencies in place for downed pilots.

"I happen to know that Tariq is close friends with the head of Special Operations Command."

Vance nodded. "I'll make the call."

SOUTHERN SYRIA

The T-55 sat by the side of the road, its turret orientated south along the highway. A woman, two children and an elderly man sat chained to it as a fuel tanker pumped gas into its tanks.

A short distance away Mohammed crouched beside his Humvee, a cigarette dangling from the corner of his mouth. The tank was probably overkill for the pursuit, he admitted, but with the number of armed groups in the area it was wise to have the firepower on hand. So far his hunt for the Jewish spies and their friends had been in vain. Two of his checkpoints had reported contacting the stolen MRAP but had not been able to stop it. His men had given chase, and yet somehow they had remained elusive. He frowned as one of his commanders approached, holding a map.

"They've found them," the man declared.

Mohammed sat upright. "Where?"

"East of As Sukhnah."

He grabbed the map and studied it. "They fled?"

"Yes, toward the South East. They damaged one of our vehicles and injured two men."

Tracing his finger in the direction indicated he stopped at the Iraqi border. "They're trying to reach Iraq. They think the armies of the Shia dogs will save them. Contact the Ahl Al Athar Brigade and have them block their escape. Our men are to continue driving them toward the border."

"Yes, Al-Bab." The man turned and ran back to where his soldiers were waiting with a half a dozen technicals and trucks.

Mohammed turned his attention to the men refueling the tank. They'd completed their task and were uncoupling the hoses. He strode across to where the crew sat beside the armored vehicle. "Start up. We leave at once for As Sukhnah. I want you ready to destroy the *kafir*."

The men sprang into action, clambering up and into the tank. It started with a rumble, coughing out a thick cloud of black smoke. The human shields scrambled on board without a word.

Mohammed glanced up at the sky as he strode back to his Humvee. The airstrike on his hospital base had unnerved him but he wasn't about to let his quarry escape.

"Where are we going?" asked his driver has he got in.

"South, toward As Sukhnah, and then to the border. We will crush them in the desert between us and the Ahl Al Athar Brigade. Then, when their corpses adorn my tank, I will deal with what's left of Masif and his dogs."

RECLOSES, FRANCE

Mirza's eyes snapped open as he felt the van slow. A sharp turn jolted him against the two would-be jihadists traveling with him. Then the van continued along what felt like a rutted country road.

One of the men grunted as they bumped over a pothole. There was a vibrating shudder as the van crossed what Mirza guessed was a cattle grid and then they came to a halt. A moment later the doors at the rear of the van opened, and the driver appeared.

"Ten-minute break," he announced.

Mirza waited for the other two to scramble out. Younger than him, they had the dark skin and hair of the subcontinent. Through their limited conversation he'd determined they were English-born of Pakistani descent. He squinted in the bright sunlight as he stepped from the van, stretched his legs and took in his surroundings.

They were parked between a dilapidated farmhouse and a row of sheds. A road led away from the farm through a thick grove of trees and bushes. A good safe house, it was isolated, hidden and unobtrusive. As he swept the area, his eyes came back to the van, and he noticed that the plates had been changed. He committed the new sequence to memory.

The co-driver dumped a bag filled with takeaway burgers on the ground. "There is a toilet in the house."

The two men traveling with Mirza dove on the bag and attacked the burgers with gusto. He chose to use the farmhouse's facilities to relieve himself and wash his face before returning to the van.

Taking a burger from the bag he watched as the driver and his associate smoked a dozen yards away. He already knew the men were more criminals than jihadists. They'd been paid by Imam Rahman to deliver him and the others to a location that he assumed was on the Mediterranean coast. As he watched, the driver cracked a can of cola and downed it in one hit. Wiping his mouth on his sleeve, he then gestured to them.

"OK, get back in the van. We're leaving."

Mirza finished his burger, gave his calves one final stretch and climbed inside with the others. The doors clanged shut and the van started. A high-pitched whine filled the cabin as the driver reversed. They turned and a second later something hit the top of the van with a thud and screeched across the roof.

A shout sounded from the cabin and the van shuddered to a halt. Then they jolted forward and the roof screeched again for a few seconds.

Mirza shook his head, leaned against the side of the van and made himself comfortable.

The other men did the same. "Idiots," one of them mumbled as they jolted back over the cattle grid and along the pot-holed road.

AVIGNON PROVENCE AIRPORT, FRANCE

In the south of France, Mitch sat in one of the leather recliners in the back of PRIMAL's business jet, Sleek. Lifting his tablet from the coffee table, he shook it.

A few feet away Pavel opened an eye from where he napped in another of the chairs. Miklos was doing the same further back in the cabin. "What's wrong?" asked the Russian. "Are you playing Fruit Ninja?"

"No, the signal for the van transporting Mirza has dropped out."

Pavel sat upright, and Miklos' eyes shot open. "Is he in trouble?"

"Not necessarily. The tracking beacon could be damaged, or it may be faulty." He checked a second program. "His secondary tracker is still active but hasn't updated since their last stop. He's probably still in the van." The low-power satellite receiver in Mirza's shoe would not register from inside the vehicle.

"You have a description of the van?"

Mitch nodded. "Yeah, I've got the make, model, plate numbers, their last location and likely route to Marseille."

"We could use our car and watch a choke point. Then when the van passes we could tag it or tail it to their destination," said Pavel.

Miklos stood. "It beats sitting around here waiting for something to happen."

Mitch frowned. "You'd be sitting around out there waiting for something to happen."

"*Da*, but at least we get to go for a drive."

Mitch rose from his chair and moved to the back of the cabin. Rolling back the plush carpet he uncovered a hidden compartment beneath the floor. Lifting a panel revealed a foam inlay laden with weapons and equipment. He removed two pistols, paddle holsters, suppressors, magazines, night vision goggles and what looked like a spear gun. "You've used the tagger before?" he asked Miklos.

"Yeah. No problem. We drive up alongside, and I shoot a dart into the truck."

"Bang on. I'll send the route through to your iPRIMAL along with a likely time frame given their average speed." Mitch popped an overhead locker and removed a bright red life vest. He stripped off the outer cover revealing covert body armor. Passing it to Pavel, he found another for Miklos.

"Is there someone you want us to kill?" Pavel asked.

"No. I just want you to be prepared. Now, don't get pulled over by the cops. The last thing I need is to bail you out."

"That reminds me, comrade. Any chance we can have some cash for expenses?"

Mitch sighed as he pulled out his wallet and removed a thick wad of Euros. "You guys are cheep, cheep like a budgie." Then he dropped the aircraft's stairs and watched as they walked across the tarmac to where their car was parked.

As he closed the door, his phone beeped. It was a message from Sonia. Staying with family friends, she wanted to know how the mission was progressing. He thumbed a reply:

No Change. Everything is fine.

As he hit send the device lit up with a secure call from the Sandpit. Mitch answered and was greeted by Frank.

"Mate, what's the go with the tracker on the van? Our feed has dropped off."

"Mine too. I've sent Miklos and Pavel out to locate the van, tag it and track it."

"OK. And if they can't find it?"

"Then we wait till his secondary tracker pings and follow that."

"Right, I'll brief Vance and Chua."

"Any news on Bishop and Ice?"

There was a pause before Frank responded. "They got in a bit of trouble. We're sorting an extraction now."

"Anything you need from me?"

"It's well in hand. You and the boys focus on Mirza and your mission. We'll keep you in the loop regarding Bish and Ice. Sandpit out."

ABU DHABI, UAE

Major General Henry Gawler, the Commander of the UAE Presidential Guard, reined in his favorite polo pony and trotted across manicured turf toward the Ghantoot Racing and Polo Club's stables.

As he entered the stables and dismounted he spotted a figure leaning casually against the pony's stall. His eyes adjusted to the gloom revealing his friend Tariq Ahmed dressed in a sharp suit.

"Tariq, not riding today?"

"No, I'm afraid I'm here on business."

The former commander of the United Kingdom Special Forces frowned as he led his horse into the stall and released its girth strap. An accomplished military commander, Gawler had been recruited by the Crown Prince to raise the country's inaugural Special Operations capability. Although he and Tariq were friends, there had never been any formal business between them.

He slipped the saddle from his horse and dumped it over a railing. "Are you meeting someone in the club rooms?"

Tariq shook his head. "No, I am here to see you. I need a favor."

The short, gray-haired general handed the pony's bridle to a waiting orderly. "Give her a full rubdown, thanks Raul." He left the stall. "Let's head to the club."

Tariq strode alongside him. "I'm afraid this is time critical." There was an edge to the businessman's voice that Gawler had never heard before.

"Are you in trouble?"

"No, but some of my people are. One of my aircraft was attacked while delivering aid in Syria. Six of my crew are now inside Daesh territory and may soon be captured."

Gawler stopped and turned to face Tariq. "Aid? What type of aid?"

"Medical supplies, we've been making deliveries on behalf of a UAE-based charity for the last few months."

He studied the transport tycoon's face for a moment. "There are many in the UAE who support Daesh," he stated.

"We are good friends, Henry. Believe me when I say I am no friend of the Caliphate, far from it. Now, can you help my people?"

Gawler nodded. "I have a CSAR program in place. It's a contracted solution, and a job like this is not going to be cheap."

"I'll pay all the costs… twice over."

He extended his hand, and they shook. "Tariq, if this goes bad we never had this conversation."

"It goes without saying."

"Send me the coordinates and any intel you have. I'll forward it to the contractor. I'll get back to you with the associated costs."

Tariq looked relieved. "Henry, I won't forget this. You truly are a good friend."

The general frowned. "Don't let me find out there's more to this than you've let on."

"I'll have that information to you within the next thirty minutes."

"CSAR is on twenty minutes standby. As soon as we have the details I'll get the ball rolling."

He watched as Tariq turned and walked away. Something told him there was far more to this than his friend had revealed. Once the CSAR mission was complete, he would make some subtle inquiries. Resuming his journey to the bar he called his operations officer and warned him of the pending mission. Then, having reached the luxurious settings of the Polo Club bar, he reclined in a lounge chair and ordered a gin and tonic.

Chapter Twenty-One

SOUTHERN SYRIA

BISHOP WIPED sweat from his eyes as he studied the map displayed on the iPRIMAL. The MRAP's air conditioning unit had failed an hour earlier and under the unrelenting Middle Eastern sun, the steel box was an oven. They'd opened every vent and the rear door but it made no difference.

Glancing through the windshield, he spotted a smudge on the horizon. As they approached, it grew into buildings and a fence line. "That's the border."

Ice slowed the MRAP. "Daesh have been here."

The mud-brick buildings were pockmarked with bullets, walls blasted with high explosives and blackened by flame. Bishop spotted a charred skeleton lying in front of an obliterated guard post. The dead soldier's arms were outstretched, clutching at the desert sands that were slowly engulfing him. "Welcome to Iraq," he said grimly.

"How far are we from the Iraqis?" asked Keila from the rear.

Bishop wiped his brow and checked the map again. "The latest reporting had their forces in control of Rutba. That's about forty miles from here. How are we for fuel?"

Ice checked the gauge. "We should be OK."

They weaved around a burnt out tank, technicals, and a truck before exiting the border settlement. Gathering speed Ice aimed the MRAP south, toward Rutba.

"Have you guys got any identification?" asked Bishop as they drove through the desert.

"I've got New Zealand passports for all of us."

He glanced over his shoulder at her. "Oh, that's handy. Didn't you guys get busted stealing passports in NZ?"

She shot him an icy glare.

"Yeah, that's right I remember the news articles. What year was it, 2004? A couple of your agents got busted applying for a passport in the name of a disabled guy."

"That was never proven."

"Well, we've got the proof now." As he spoke, the cabin rocked with the dull thud of an explosion.

"What the hell was that?" asked Keila.

Shrapnel sang against the MRAP's armor. Bishop squinted through the windshield. Suddenly the laminate surface cracked as heavy caliber bullets slammed into it. He flinched as Ice spun the wheel.

The Israeli manning the turret hammered away as they drove off the track into the desert sand. The MRAP slewed sideways as rounds slammed into its flank.

"It's an ambush!" yelled Bishop. "Get us back to the outpost."

In the rear of the cab, Keila and her men braced themselves against the seats as they turned. Crates and weapons rattled around on the floor as the truck bounced over rocks.

Something struck the side of the MRAP with a clang and it rang like a bell. There was another explosion as Ice wrestled it back onto the road and accelerated toward the abandoned border outpost.

Another blast, a jolt, and the MRAP slowed. "We lost a wheel," Ice announced calmly.

"Get us to the outpost," said Bishop as he climbed from the cabin into the back. "When we get there we're going to need to find a stronghold and fast."

Another blast shook the MRAP, and a moment later it shuddered.

Ice turned and bellowed over the sound of the turret gun firing. "We're down to one rear axle."

Despite being mortally wounded the six-wheel drive armored truck lumbered on. Bullets ricocheted and mortar rounds exploded around it. RPG's streaked across the desert, barely missing them.

Ice's artificial foot stomped the gas pedal to the floor as he tried to squeeze power from the engine. Finally, as their speed dropped below twenty miles an hour, they reached the abandoned border outpost.

"Focus our firepower south," yelled Bishop as he leaped out the door. He pointed to the largest of the remaining structures. The single-story building bore the scars of battle, but its thick mud-brick walls had withstood the onslaught. "That's our stronghold."

He grabbed a PKM machine gun, his backpack, a tin of ammunition and sprinted across to the building's shattered doorway. Inside, through the gloom, he made out earthen stairs leading up to the roof. Throwing the PKM down, he dropped to his stomach on the sunbaked rooftop and readied the gun.

The gunfire from the south had ceased, along with the mortar bombs. The silence made Bishop uneasy as he scanned the desert for their attackers. He spotted them a mile distant. A long line of vehicles was arrayed facing him.

"What have we got?" Ice asked as he dumped a bag containing RPGs and a launcher alongside him.

"Looks like more of Mohammed's friends." Bishop fished in his backpack for a pair of binoculars. "Can you set the dish up?" he asked as he focused on the distant vehicles.

"Roger." Ice rushed back down the stairs.

The Israelis joined them on the roof as Bishop identified heavy machine guns, recoilless rifles and antiaircraft guns mounted on over a dozen vehicles.

Keila lay beside him, resting the G28 on its bipod. "What are they waiting for?"

Bishop lowered the binoculars. "They've got enough firepower to have wiped us out already." He left the machine gun and hurried to where Ice was setting up the satellite dish on the opposite side of the roof. Lifting the binoculars, he scanned the horizon. "They're a blocking force. They were never meant to kill us. Just stop us from getting to Rutba." He spotted a cloud of dust on the horizon.

"And hold us here?" asked Keila.

"Yep. And here comes Mohammed to seek his retribution. Ice, ETA on comms?"

"Searching for a bird."

"As soon as you get online pass our location to HQ." Bishop turned to the four Israelis who had set themselves up to defend both directions. "The rest of us are going to prepare our defenses. We're going to be attacked from the north." He checked his watch. "We've got less than three hours of sunlight left. If we can hold them off, our night vision will give us a slight advantage."

THE HUMAN SHIELDS shackled to the sides of the T-55 held their hands against their ears and sat with their mouths open as its cannon belched flame. It amazed Mohammed how resilient humans could be. Two of the older men had been attached to the tank for well over a week. Usually, they lasted a few days at most.

Turning his attention to the tank's target, he raised his binoculars and watched as the round exploded against a mud-brick wall. "Come out, come out, wherever you are." He lowered the binoculars and frowned. The Jews and their friends weren't taking the bait.

"Mohammed," said a voice behind him. "We have the mortar ready."

He faced the warrior who had replaced Abu Malik as his second-in-command. "How are we for ammunition?"

"Not good, we have thirty bombs for the little one and eight for the big." The man shrugged. "We also have the TOWs."

He scowled; this batch of missiles had proven useless. They'd already fired two at the building and both times they had veered off target and disappeared into the desert.

"And the tank?"

"A dozen, maybe less."

"We will use five mortar rounds and then assault with the tank."

The warrior nodded and strode away to coordinate the attack.

Mohammed raised his binoculars back to the border outpost. With Al-Nasr and his men blocking the escape to the south the Jews and their friends had nowhere to go. He had hoped they would make an attempt at escape. They would have been far easier to kill exposed in the desert. Still, they were few, and had no heavy weapons. The assault would be short and their deaths bloody. He glanced out to the west where the sun sat low on the horizon. There was only an hour of light left. He lifted the radio from his belt. "Everyone listen. We start the attack in ten minutes."

BISHOP LAY in the rubble of the destroyed security outpost a few yards from the building that he had designated as their stronghold. Hidden in his makeshift foxhole, he checked the sniper scope on the G28 he'd taken from Keila.

"Any updates from HQ?" he asked into the short-range radio Ice had given him.

"Negative, I got our location out but there's been no reply. I think the satellite dish is screwed."

What else could go wrong? thought Bishop. "How about our friends to the south?"

"They're holding firm."

In the distance, he could see the outline of the T-55 in the fading light. Raising his thermal scope he spotted the bloom of the tank's exhausts. "Ice, they're beginning their assault." He registered the whistle of a mortar round. "Take cover! Get off the roof."

The first bomb exploded in the desert in front of them.

On the roof, Ice grabbed Keila by her chest rig and dragged her across to the stairs. The next mortar bomb hit the rooftop and the blast knocked Ice sideways. His helmet clipped the lip of the roof and he managed to crawl downstairs before the next round hit.

Outside Bishop hugged the earth as shrapnel sliced through the air around him. His ribs ached as the shockwave washed over him. Dust and smoke assaulted his lungs and he fought for breath. He counted five explosions before the barrage ceased.

"Is everyone OK?" he asked into the radio.

Coughing emitted from the speaker. "Yeah, everyone's OK," said Ice.

"Good, because Mohammed's about to hit us with everything he's got."

The mortars were soon replaced by machine gun fire as the tank approached, supported by half a dozen pickups armed with heavy weapons. Heavy caliber bullets cracked through the air as Bishop aimed through the scope of his rifle. "What I wouldn't give for air support," he murmured as he focused on the tank. He could make out people on the armored vehicle's side skirts and turret. "You sick bastards." He squeezed the transmit button. "Ice, the tank is covered by human shields. Don't hit it with the RPGs. I repeat, do not hit it with the RPGs."

The radio crackled. "Roger, we'll target the technicals. You take the tank."

"Easier said than done," said Bishop as he focused his scope on the T-55. The main gun spat flame, and a round screamed into the outpost and slammed into the MRAP. The armored truck exploded, flipping onto its roof.

Bullets smashed into the remains of the buildings behind Bishop, and debris lashed his legs as he searched for a target. The Russian tank had been modified; a steel plate with thin slits was welded in front of the commander's cupola and the driver's hatch. The original periscopes must have been long since destroyed.

The tank and supporting trucks were less than three hundred yards from them when Ice and the Mossad team opened fire. RPGs and small arms fire lashed the ISIS advance. One of the technicals took a direct hit and exploded into a massive fireball.

The tank's turret rotated, searching for one of the Mossad operatives who'd fired an RPG from a flank. Bishop winced as rocket screamed over him and slammed into the stronghold.

With the turret rotated a sliver of the commander's head was exposed. Bishop exhaled, took up the slack in the trigger, balanced the crosshairs on his target and fired.

The turret slewed away from the compound and the tank ground to a halt. Bishop caught a glimpse of the driver and fired again. He missed, but the tank suddenly braked and began reversing. Switching his aim to the remaining technicals, he shot a gunner through the face.

It took a moment for the fighters in the technicals to realize that their heavy armor had withdrawn from battle. When they did, they swung their pickups around and fled across the desert.

Bishop climbed to his feet as the ISIS force disappeared into the fading light. Returning to the smoking stronghold, his radio crackled.

"Bishop, we need your help," transmitted Ice.

He dashed for the doorway. Inside he spotted Ice and Keila crouching in the darkness. In the beam from Ice's headlamp, he spotted a body, one of the Mossad operatives. "What happened?"

Keila was holding the man's head. It was James, her infiltration team leader. She looked up, her face pale. "A shell from the tank. Shrapnel caught him in the lower abdomen."

"Ice, how does it look?"

The big man had a trauma kit open and was doing his best to stem the flow of blood from the Israeli's stomach. Bishop knelt alongside him and inspected the wound.

Ice shook his head.

A jagged piece of steel had lodged slightly below the belly. The entry wound was at least three inches wide with only a glimpse of metal showing.

"Cover it as best you can. I'll get a bag of fluid into him and dose him with painkillers and antibiotics." He reached for the trauma kit and found what he needed. As Ice bandaged the wound, he inserted a cannula and injected a cocktail of drugs.

James slumped against a backpack and passed out.

"If we can't get him to a medical facility he'll be dead inside twelve hours. I don't have enough plasma to keep him alive longer than that." He left Keila to tend to the casualty and climbed the stairs to the roof. The sun had disappeared behind the horizon leaving the desert in darkness. He spotted one of other Mossad operatives, Thomas, lying at the lip of the roof, watching out to the north.

"How's James?" asked Thomas as he knelt beside him.

"He'll be alright if we can get him to a medical facility. You guys did a great job. We gave those Daesh pricks a bloody nose."

"But they're going to be back, and ammo's low."

"We need to get the hell out of here."

"How do we do that without a vehicle? The MRAP is trashed."

"Don't worry about that. Let's sort out a roster for keeping watch. I'll send Ice up with some warm gear; it's going to get real cold out here." He rose, walked back across the roof and down the stairs.

Keila had wrapped James in a space blanket and was monitoring his vital signs. Ice had laid out what he had managed to salvage from the destroyed MRAP next to the gear from their packs. Bishop retrieved a set of night vision goggles, grabbed his AK-104 and retrieved a suppressor from a pouch on his vest.

"You mind holding the fort?" he asked Ice.

"You going to find us some wheels?"

Bishop snapped the suppressor in place. "That's the idea."

THE TANK CREW dragged their dead commander from the turret and laid his body in the headlights of one of the technicals. The man had been popular among the brigade and his death had shocked them. Mohammed stood next to the body, his face a twisted mask of rage. "Nizar is dead because you failed to kill the Jews!" he screamed.

The thirty fighters who had taken part in the attack stood in a semicircle around him, the shame on their faces hidden in the darkness. The ISIS 'brigade' had withdrawn to a wadi to deal with their casualties and plan their next move.

"They're in that village laughing about how they defeated the caliphate's finest warriors. You assault them with mortars, a tank, and they beat you back with rifles." He paused. "At dawn, we attack again. Anyone who retreats will die."

He strode across to his newly promoted second-in-command. "Post sentries and contact the Ahl Al Athar

Brigade. I don't want these dogs trying to slip away in the night." He lit a cigarette. "When will our reinforcements arrive?"

"They have left Al-Bab. They will be here before dawn."

"As soon as they arrive we will prepare for our attack." He sucked on the cigarette. "We will use all the mortars; Salim will replenish us from his holdings.

The man nodded and reached for his radio.

Mohammed left him and walked through the darkness to where his armored Humvee was parked. His driver crouched behind the vehicle brewing coffee on a gas burner. He took a cup of the sweet Turkish brew and stared into the desert in the direction of the outpost. "Tomorrow you all die," he murmured as he sipped. "Tomorrow I will slaughter you like goats."

Chapter Twenty-Two

AVIGNON, FRANCE

MIRZA FELT his chin drop and involuntarily jerked it back up, waking himself in the process. Shaking away the fatigue he exhaled and stretched his legs. His stomach rumbled reminding him that it was past dinnertime.

Pressing his ear against the side of the van he listened to the hum of traffic; they were still on the highway. In his head, he worked out the time and space. They'd been on the road for a little over ten hours, including the half hour rest stop. That put them a few hours from Marseille if Chua's assessment on the likely destination was correct.

"Do you know if we're getting on a boat?" one of the other men spoke from the darkness.

"How else do you think we're getting there?" snapped the other.

"I mean, we could fly?"

"We'll take a boat to Libya," replied the other man.

"My cousin traveled a few months ago. He said there is a safe house near Benghazi. Maybe we'll fly after that."

The conversation reassured Mirza that he was on the right track. Chua had briefed him that Imam Rahman's network extended through France to Libya. The only question was whether Eshita had been smuggled into Syria yet, and if so, where she'd been taken.

"Your cousin, where is he now?" asked Mirza.

"Raqqa, he is with the Jaysh Mohammed brigade."

He could tell by the tone of the young man's voice that he was immensely proud of his cousin's exploits.

"Does he have a wife in Raqqa?"

"He has a wife, but he has also been rewarded with the women of men he has slain."

"It sounds too good to be true," said Mirza.

"Believe me brother, it is the truth. He has sent me many photos. If we fight well, we will be rewarded with—" The wail of a siren cut him short.

Mirza held his breath as the siren gained in intensity. The sound came from directly behind them. He couldn't tell if it was an ambulance, fire truck or a police car.

The van slowed and pulled off to one side. He heard a door open followed by loud voices. Seconds turned into minutes.

"What are we going to do?" asked the man with the cousin in Raqqa.

"We sit tight," said Mirza in a low voice. "If they've taken the drivers in for questioning they might not check the back. We give them enough time then we can escape."

A few more minutes passed and he began to think they were in the clear. Suddenly the van's doors were wrenched open and he found himself blinded by a bright flashlight. An angry voice issued a series of commands in French.

Mirza held up his hands as he squinted. "English, no French. Only English."

"Get out of the van. Keep your hands where I can see them," the officer snapped.

A moment later Mirza found himself cuffed in the back of a police patrol car along with one of the other men. The driver and the third jihadist had been placed in another vehicle. As they sped along the highway, Mirza felt overcome with failure. There was no way he could talk his way out of custody and back into the smuggling pipeline. He had failed Sonia and worse, he had failed Eshita.

PAVEL HAD PULLED over their sedan into a service bay alongside the A7 highway. A mile outside of Avignon, the van would have to pass the chokepoint on its way to Marseille.

In the passenger seat, Miklos slurped noisily from a frozen cola as he watched the stream of evening traffic under the lights of the *autoroute*. Twisting the straw, he struggled to get the last traces of the caffeinated liquid from the bottom of the cup.

Pavel glared at him, but the Czech operative slurped on. Finally, the Russian leaned across, grabbed the cup and tossed it into the backseat.

"Hey, I wasn't done with that."

"*Nyet*, you were done five minutes ago," snapped Pavel.

Miklos folded his arms and focused back on the road. "I thought this would be fun. I didn't know you had turned into a grumpy old man."

A siren wailed and he spotted flashing red and blue

lights approaching. A split second later a police car sped past.

"Someone's in a hurry," said Miklos.

Pavel glanced at his watch. "Our van's not. They should have passed us an hour ago."

"They might have been delayed. Could have gotten a flat or needed to stop for fuel."

"Those things don't take an hour."

"That's not true. Once my mother got a flat tire and had to walk for an entire day to get help."

"Didn't she have a spare?"

Miklos shook his head. "No, my father swapped it for a bottle of vodka."

Pavel sighed as he took his iPRIMAL from the car's console and contacted Mitch.

"How are you lads doing?" asked the Brit.

"No sign of the van."

"You've had eyes on the highway the whole time?"

"Ever since we arrived. Could it have passed before then?"

"Not unless it was traveling at over ninety miles an hour. On the way down from the UK, it averaged thirty-five."

"We can stay here as long as you need."

"Give it another hour then check in again," said Mitch.

"Acknowledged." He terminated the call and turned to Miklos. "Do you want to take a nap? I can watch for the next half an hour and then we can swap."

Miklos shook his head. "I just drank a gallon of cola. I need to pee."

"Make it quick. If the van goes past I'm going to leave you here."

"In that case hand me the container."

"You're not pissing in the car. Get out and do it fast."

As Miklos stepped from the car, he noticed a flashing orange light approaching along the highway. He watched it as he relieved himself on a shrub.

The light was attached to the roof of a flatbed truck, the type used to transport crashed cars. This one wasn't carrying a car. Secured on the back of the transporter was a white van that matched the description Mitch had given them. He zipped up his fly and jumped back into the passenger seat. "Did you see that?"

Pavel started the engine and spun the wheel. "That's why they're late. The van is broken down."

They accelerated onto the highway and gave chase.

"What if Mirza isn't in it anymore? They could have moved him to a new truck," said Miklos.

"Either way this is the only lead we have," replied Pavel as they gained on the transporter. He indicated and moved into the outside lane so they could pass it.

"The plates are different," Miklos commented.

"They would have changed them."

"We better be right."

"I don't see any other vans that meet the description."

"Good point. Do you want me to contact Mitch?"

"Not yet. He will know we're on the move. Tag the van and then we'll give him an update."

"OK." Miklos leaned over to the back seat and pulled a soft weapon case from under a blanket. Unzipping it, he pulled out a gas powered spear gun. Elastic loops in the cover held projectiles that resembled shotgun cartridges.

"Remember to arm it," said Pavel.

"Thank you, comrade obvious." He used his iPRIMAL to activate a projectile. A tiny red LED flashed twice as he loaded it into the weapon. Lowering the window, he aimed up at the van and fired. Compressed air drove the canister through the air, and it shot into the wheel arch of the van and stuck to the metal. "Bullseye." Miklos checked his iPRIMAL. "The tracker is live. You can break clear."

Pavel accelerated, and they passed the truck, leaving it in the darkness behind them. "I really hope Mirza is still in that van."

MARSEILLE, FRANCE

An hour later the truck carrying the van reached its destination, a fenced yard on the outskirts of the coastal town of Marseille. Pavel drove slowly past as a sliding metal gate closed behind the truck. Bright security lighting illuminated the compound but black sheeting attached to the fence blocked their view.

"It must be a safe house," observed Miklos as he snapped a photo with his iPRIMAL and forwarded it to Mitch.

"It would make it easy to change vehicles," replied Pavel as they drove around the block and parked.

"Do you want to have a peek?" Miklos asked.

"Break in?"

"No, we can use Mitch's little toy." He left the sedan and walked around to the trunk. A moment later he returned with a soft case the size of a laptop computer. He opened it, removing a control unit and something that looked like an oversized dragonfly. Activating the drone, he lowered the window and tossed it into the darkness. It hovered, emitting a low buzz. Then, using the joysticks on the controller and watching the built-in screen, he piloted the drone into the air, over warehouses and beyond a fence.

On screen, he could see the van being lowered from the truck's bed.

"What do you see?" asked Pavel leaning over.

"They've unloaded the van."

"That's it?"

"That's it." Miklos watched as the driver walked into a transportable office. He lowered the insect-like drone until it could see in through the window. The man was making himself a coffee. Adjusting the heading he flew around the building and saw a desk and computer through a window. "This doesn't look like a safe house."

Pavel reached for the controller. "Isn't that the point of a safe house? Let me see."

Miklos put the drone into a hover and handed the controller to Pavel. The Russian studied the screen for a moment then fiddled with the joysticks. "How do I make it turn?"

The drone zoomed around the building and flew directly at one of the windows. The image of the driver loomed until the aircraft bounced off the glass.

Miklos grabbed the control. "Don't do that." He flew it backward as the man's face appeared at the window. "Way to go, comrade, you've compromised us." He launched the drone skyward, switching to the downward looking camera. On screen, the driver left the office and inspected the window. He hunted around on the ground then went back inside.

Pavel grinned. "No harm done. He thinks it was a bird."

Miklos sighed and flew the drone to the van, lowering it over the roof. "No sign of Mitch's tracker, but you can see marks where something scraped the paint."

At that moment his iPRIMAL chimed. He answered the

call, putting it on speakerphone. It was Mitch. "Lads, you sure that's the right van?"

"It has marks on the roof where something scraped your tracking drone off."

"Shit, that's not good news."

"Why?" asked Pavel.

"Because it's in a police impound yard."

AVIGNON PROVENCE AIRPORT, FRANCE

Fifty miles away in the Gulfstream, Mitch ended the call with the surveillance pair and immediately opened a line with the Sandpit. Vance's face appeared on screen. "Mitch, this better be good, we're kind of busy."

"Not good. Mirza's been picked up by the frog fuzz."

Vance frowned. "The what?"

"The French police, they've arrested Mirza. I think he's in Marseille, but I can't be sure."

"Shit, that's just what we need." He paused. "Right, we'll get Flash onto it."

"I want to recall Kurtz. His knowledge of European policing will be invaluable. I can fly over and grab him."

Vance considered the idea. "Approved, I'll leave it to you to work out the details."

"Thanks, look, is everything OK with Bishop and Ice?"

"Yeah, we're right in the middle of coordinating their extraction. Mitch, I hate to do this but can I get back to you?"

"Sure boss, I'll get in contact with Kurtz and put something together at this end. If I get any more information I'll drop you a line."

"Appreciated."

Vance's face disappeared, and Mitch slumped in the leather recliner. A plan formed in his mind as to how he would boost Mirza from detention. First things first, he needed to get in touch with Kurtz. The former German police officer was spending time with his family in Denkendorf, only a short flight away. He unlocked his tablet, typed out a message and hit send. The response from Kurtz came through almost immediately, 'Ack'. Mitch smiled, like every other PRIMAL operative, Kurtz itched to get back in on the action.

Rising from the chair he strode to the aircraft's galley and put the kettle on. A hot cup of char always helped clear through the fog of fatigue. As he waited, his civilian phone buzzed. It was a message from Sonia asking for an update. He considered telling her everything was OK, but instead opted for the truth:

Transport was intercepted. Mirza may be in police custody. Will update you when we know more.

He hit send, made his cup of tea then entered the cockpit. Settling into the pilot's chair he activated the navigation system and plotted a route to the closest airfield to Denkendorf. He uploaded it to Kurtz and then submitted his flight plan to Euro Control Network Manager Operations Center. As soon as he received approval, he would takeoff, and a little over two hours later he'd pick up Kurtz. In the meantime, he needed to come up with a cunning way to free Mirza.

Chapter Twenty-Three

SOUTHERN SYRIA

BISHOP CROUCHED behind an outcrop of limestone five hundred yards to the north of where the ISIS forces had camped. He clenched his teeth to stop them from chattering and rubbed his gloved hands against the sides of his cargo pants.

It had taken him the better part of the night to work his way east and then north to make sure he avoided any patrols. He had scanned the terrain ahead with his thermal scope between moving in short bounds. In the freezing nighttime conditions the scope's sensitive imager could detect the heat from a man almost a mile away.

Looping around he'd put the Daesh camp between him and the outpost before making his approach. His assessment that the sentries wouldn't be focused to the north proved correct. Through the scope he could see that a two-man guard detail was facing away from him, manning a technical and its heavy machine gun. Checking his watch he confirmed it was less than two hours from daybreak. He stowed the scope in a pouch; time to make his move.

He cradled his customized AK as he wrapped a black and white keffiyeh around his face. Taking a deep breath he walked slowly across the desert toward the camp.

Once among the vehicles he realized that they must have received reinforcements. Now there were at least a dozen technicals, the T-55 tank, a tracked BMP infantry fighting vehicle, an armored Humvee and two trucks, all parked in a rough circle. In the center, wrapped in blankets, were over fifty fighters and what appeared to be human shields shackled to the vehicles.

As he passed a pickup mounted with a recoilless rifle, a blanket moved and a man spoke in Arabic. Bishop froze and slowly turned toward the noise.

The Daesh fighter sat bolt upright and stared at him. Bishop's heart pounded as he locked eyes with the man and took up the slack on the trigger.

The man mumbled again, ignored Bishop, lay back down and pulled his covers over his head.

He sighed, released the trigger and continued moving between the vehicles. The armored Humvee was the only vehicle in the fleet suitable for their escape. Fast with protection from bullets it was their only hope in punching through Daesh forces to the south and reaching Iraqi lines.

As he passed the T-55 tank he nearly trod on a body huddled against the tracks. An old man, on the end of a chain, lay shivering in a pile of rags. In the moonlight, Bishop could see sad eyes peering out from under a scrap of blanket. Reaching into his vest he took out an energy bar and pressed it into his hand. Then he walked around the tank and strode the final few yards to the Humvee.

Moving to the side of the armored vehicle he glanced

through the inch thick rear windows; he couldn't see anyone inside. Checking the driver's side door he eased it open and inspected the interior. The air inside smelled heavily of body odor and tobacco. A closer inspection of the controls revealed that the ignition system was intact.

Leaving the door slightly ajar he left the Humvee and made his way back to the sentry point. The two men on duty were easy to find; they were standing alongside the pickup, smoking.

"Amateur move, boys," Bishop murmured as he raised his suppressed AK.

The weapon coughed twice and the bodies hit the sand a split second apart. He paused, waiting to see if the noise had woken anyone. A minute passed with no response. He took an explosive charge the size of a D-cell battery from a pouch, twisted the pickup's fuel cap off and slipped it inside.

He strolled back to the Humvee, climbed into the driver's seat and pulled the door shut. The four-wheel drive was in neutral so he placed a gloved hand on the starter. Taking a deep breath he pushed the lever and the engine coughed to life. Dropping it into gear he eased his foot onto the accelerator and drove off.

A harsh voice barked from the rear of the cabin, startling him. Although the question was in Arabic Bishop guessed its nature. He reached for his pistol as a flash of light lit the interior, the sentry truck exploding in a ball of flame.

A hand grabbed Bishop's keffiyeh and tore it from his face as he drew his Glock from his hip holster.

"You're one of the Jew dogs!" screamed the man.

Bishop thrust the pistol over his shoulder. The fanatic grabbed the weapon as it fired. A nine-millimeter slug punched through his hand and impacted against the back of the cabin. The man screamed in rage and used his other hand to try and wrestle the weapon away.

Firing again, Bishop heard the bullet ricochet and felt it tug the edge of his armor. It felt as if someone had stubbed a cigarette out a few inches below his right armpit. As he fought for the gun he felt a trickle of blood running down his torso. Releasing the steering wheel he turned and locked eyes with the fanatic. He would never forget the pure hatred that burned through his gaze.

"You're going to die here," the man hissed.

Bishop punched him in the face and snatched the pistol free. "Shut the fuck up." The Glock slipped from his grasp, falling into the footwell. He grabbed the fanatic by the collar and dragged him over the seats. Punching him again he then grabbed the wheel and searched for the Glock with one hand. As his fingers closed around the grip the fanatic grabbed the door handle, pushed it open and tumbled out into the darkness.

"Not on my watch." He dropped the handgun in his lap, spun the wheel and sent the heavy truck into a skidding turn. In the faint glow of dawn he spotted the man sprinting back toward the ISIS camp. "One less Daeshbag." Bishop lined him up and stomped the accelerator to the floor. The diesel engine roared and the truck bounced across the rocky desert.

Suddenly the Humvee shuddered as bullets struck the hood and windshield. The thick glass cracked and Bishop spun the wheel again away from his quarry. "Shit balls."

He spotted the border outpost through the spider-webbed glass and turned toward it. Fishing his radio from his vest he lifted it to his mouth. "Ice, is everyone ready to go?"

The reply was instantaneous. "Yeah, you woke the whole neighborhood. I take it you're coming in hot?"

Bullets ricocheted off the back of the Humvee. "Yeah, you could say that."

MOHAMMED SLAMMED into the ground as one of his heavy machine guns fired, bullets snapping through the air barely inches from his head. He lay in the sand with his injured hand jammed into his armpit. The pain inflamed his rage to the point where he could barely think. A pickup skidded to a halt next to him and he glanced at the man who climbed from the cab.

"Mohammed, are you alive?" asked his second-in-command.

He climbed to his feet. "Are the reinforcements here?" he hissed through his teeth.

"Yes."

"Good, attack!"

"I need to coordinate the mortars."

"Fuck the mortars. Attack now, before the Jewish scum escape."

The man raised his radio and gave the order. A few seconds later the rumble of the T-55 filled the air.

Mohammed felt the ground shudder under its tracks. "I will command the tank!" he yelled as it appeared from the gloom followed by the tracked BMP infantry fighting vehicle.

"Mohammed, let me see your hand."

He winced as he pulled it from his armpit and held the palm out. The rising sun shone through the bloody hole the bullet had punched through his palm.

His second-in-command reached into his vehicle for a medical kit as the tank rumbled to a halt next to them. "Let me bandage the wound. It will take a moment."

Mohammed gritted his teeth as his hand was wrapped. As he endured the pain more technicals lined up on either side of the tank. Using his good hand he climbed onto the T-55. "Ten thousand for anyone who brings me a Jew's head!" he screamed. "Begin the assault."

BISHOP SKIDDED the Humvee to a halt alongside the wrecked MRAP. Jumping from the cabin he sprinted into the stronghold. "We've got to roll people."

Ice and one of the Israelis, Dan, had the wounded man on a makeshift stretcher. His face was waxen in the light cast from Ice's headlamp but he was conscious.

Keila wore one of the backpacks and had the other under her arm.

"Where's Thomas?" Bishop asked as he grabbed one of the bags from her.

Above them, an RPG boomed followed a moment later by the rattle of a PKM.

"He's keeping them occupied." Keila hefted another machine gun from the floor, wedged it against the doorway and fired a long burst. Bishop grabbed an RPG and a bag of rockets as Ice and Dan shuffled the casualty outside.

"Thomas, it's time to go!" screamed Bishop.

The building shuddered as an explosive round struck it. Choking on dust he dashed out the doorway. As he left the building, a machine gun sounded from directly above him. He glanced up, spotted Thomas, and waved him down.

Ice already had the casualty loaded and was firing the

fifty-caliber machine gun in the turret of the Humvee. Keila stood in the open door shooting her PKM.

Bishop fired his RPG at a line of vehicles approaching from the desert. "Everybody in!" he screamed as he glanced up at the roof.

Thomas was grasping the edge, lowering himself down. A shell struck the building and Bishop flinched as the explosion threw Thomas through the air, slamming him against the side of the Humvee.

"Thomas!" Keila screamed.

Bishop was the first to reach the crumpled body of the Mossad operative. The man's head was rotated almost entirely to the rear. "Get her inside!" he bellowed at the others.

He grabbed the body and hefted it onto the hood of the Humvee. Bullets and explosives hammered the stronghold as he wedged Thomas behind the bull bar. Fighting back his grief he swung into the driver's seat, slammed the door and stomped on the accelerator.

In the wing mirror he spotted the first of the Daesh vehicles, a technical, only fifty yards behind them. Silhouetted by the rising sun he watched as Ice hammered it from the turret. The unarmored pickup lurched sideways and collided with the remains of a guard post.

Bishop's foot was jammed to the floor as he turned them onto the sandy road, kicking up a cloud of dust.

He turned to Keila who was sitting in the passenger seat. "I'm so sorry."

Her eyes were glassy, but she wore a determined look.

A flash ahead of them caught his eye. He backed off the accelerator. "Shit!" Blocking the road were more vehicles.

"Can we punch through?" asked Keila.

Bishop shook his head as he turned the wheel. "No, we need to outrun them."

The Humvee bounced off the road, over a shallow drain, and into the rocky desert. It slowed as its wheels sank into soft sand.

Behind the wheel he searched for the central tire inflation system. Bullets clanged off the armor as he hunted. Finding the toggle he adjusted the pressure and gunned the engine.

"They're getting closer," said Keila as she glanced through her window at a cloud of dust billowing from behind their original pursuers.

"Those pickups won't get far in this," Bishop said as he wrestled with the steering wheel and aimed for a dune.

She reached across and grasped his arm. "Aden; the tank."

FROM THE COMMANDER'S cupola of the T-55 Mohammed saw the Humvee swerve off the road onto the soft sand. The corners of his cruel mouth turned up in a wicked grin and he raised his radio. "Halt the trucks, they will bog down. I will finish them myself."

The speaker crackled and his second-in-command replied, "The BMP can follow."

He glanced over his shoulder at the infantry fighting vehicle. Filthy black smoke was billowing from the tracked vehicle's exhaust as it rolled over the sand. He donned sunglasses and wrapped his black keffiyeh around his face, warding off the wind and sand as they gained momentum. Ahead, his stolen Humvee had slowed as it tackled a dune. Reaching for the DShK machine gun he thumbed the trigger. Bullets splashed the sand around his target as it scrambled up the side of the dune. He lowered himself inside the turret. "Are we loaded?"

The man who sat in the loader's chair gave thumbs-up.

Mohammed placed his eye against the main gun's sight. Rotating the turret and elevating the cannon he aligned the crosshairs where the Humvee would crest the dune. His injured hand throbbed as he clutched it to his chest, his other grasping the trigger. "Now you die."

Something shook the tank as he fired and the shot went wide. He flinched as blow after blow rained down on the armor. The noise was deafening. Then, as suddenly as it started, the clanging stopped.

Cautiously, Mohammed poked his head out the cupola. Over the rumble of the tank's engine he heard a dreaded sound, the beat of helicopter blades. A gray gunship raced into the distance having completed its attack. He spun, scanning the sky, knowing they usually flew in pairs. The second aircraft was a speck on the horizon, heading directly for him. Grabbing the DShK heavy machine gun attached to the turret he made to aim it at the approaching threat.

As he swiveled on target he spotted puffs of smoke either side of the helicopter. He abandoned the weapon, grabbed the edge of the turret with his good hand and climbed out. As he made to jump from the tank a hand grabbed his leg. He looked down at the person holding his ankle, one of the pathetic human shields. Kicking the old man in the face he leaped clear.

Rockets slammed into the T-55 and it exploded in a ball of flame that hurled Mohammed through the air. He landed sideways, the force knocking the air from his lungs. Heat washed over him as the T-55's ammunition exploded and the turret shot skyward. A second later it landed a scant twenty yards away. He barely registered the object that hit the ground next to him. When he managed to open his eyes he stared at the molten face of the driver's severed head.

BISHOP WATCHED in disbelief as the BMP infantry fighting vehicle slewed away from them. A drab gray Battlehawk roared overhead and gave chase, unleashing a fusillade of rockets. Seconds later the BMP exploded into a fireball, its crew incinerated.

A second helicopter, a Blackhawk, flew toward them a few hundred yards distant, its door gunner firing a minigun toward the Daesh forces. The six-barreled weapon sounded like tearing canvas as it spewed lead into the unarmored technicals and trucks.

Bishop skidded the Humvee down the dune as the Blackhawk flared and touched down, kicking up a wall of dust. A moment later soldiers clad in MultiCam uniforms, helmets and body armor appeared through the haze and ran toward him. They aimed their M4 carbines directly at the battered vehicle.

Bishop exited with his hands held high. "We need a medic!"

Keila and Dan had the Humvee's doors open when the men reached them. A soldier carrying a large backpack moved in and crouched next to the casualty as they lowered him to the ground. His teammates formed a perimeter around the Humvee as the Battlehawk thundered overhead, hunting for prey.

Ice joined Bishop at the front of the Humvee and helped him lift Thomas's body from the bull bar.

"You guys work for Lascar Logistics?" one of the soldiers asked in an American accent.

Bishop recognized the voice but couldn't place it. He turned to face the man, then struggled to contain his surprise as he found himself staring into the hard features of Charles King.

"Well, I'll be damned, Aden." King extended his hand. "I didn't expect to run into you out here."

The former CEO of Ground Effects Services had previously gone head to head with the PRIMAL team. Bested by PRIMAL, he'd come to realize the organization he worked for was rotten to the core. Bishop had been responsible for saving his life on more than one occasion.

He managed a grim smile. "Same; I didn't expect Charles King to come to my rescue."

"God knows I owe you." His eyes dropped to Thomas's limp body. "Looks like you guys did it pretty rough. I'm sorry for your loss." He waved two of his men across. "Let's get you folks to the chopper."

Bishop watched as they slid Thomas into a body bag. Then he helped them carry the corpse to the waiting Blackhawk where Keila, Dan and James were already loaded. Ice was the last to board having prepped the Humvee with a demolition charge.

As they climbed into the air, and the side doors slid shut, Bishop locked eyes with Keila.

"Thank you," she mouthed.

He nodded and turned his attention out the window. The Battlehawk swooped in beside them. Far below the Humvee exploded in a ball of fire, destroying the weapons and the last of their PRIMAL gear. In the distance Mohammed's 'brigade' beat a hasty retreat, leaving more than half their vehicles burning on the road. As the two helicopters gained speed, King handed Bishop a headset.

"So, what in god's name were you guys doing out here?" he asked through the communications system.

Bishop shrugged. "You know me, Charles. Wherever there are bad guys, I'm not far away. The big question is why you're running a CSAR package?"

"My new firm won the contract with UAE Special Operations."

"Your new firm?"

King grinned. "Don't worry, this is a more discerning organization." He touched the side of his nose. "If you know what I mean."

His eyes narrowed. "It better be."

"So I know who you and your ex-CIA buddy are," King continued. "Your Lascar Logistics profiles were on our mission orders but who are these guys?" He jerked a thumb at the Mossad team.

Keila and Dan eyed them wearily.

"They're New Zealand aid workers." He glanced at the pilots in the cockpit. "We need to talk about our destination."

"Sorry bud, that's not negotiable, I'm under strict orders to drop you at an airstrip outside of Rutba."

"What about the guy who's wounded?"

"He's stable. Your people anticipated potential casualties. There's an air ambulance and medical team at the airfield. We're about ten minutes out."

Good, thought Bishop. Vance and the team in the Sandpit were all over it. He sighed and slumped back into the web seating. For the first time in forty-eight hours he allowed himself to relax.

RUTBA, IRAQ

The UH-60 Blackhawk and its AH-60 Battlehawk escort cut a lap of the isolated desert airstrip before coming in to land. Bishop glanced out the window and spotted a gray C-130J military Hercules parked a short distance from the almost identical civilian variant, the PRIMAL Hercules.

The helicopter touched down and the crew opened the side doors.

"We're done here," King said. He'd taken photographs of the passports of Bishop, Ice and the 'New Zealanders'. "You're good to go."

Bishop removed the radio headset. As he stepped onto the sand a medical crew approached from the C-130J. He and the others were waved across to the aircraft by a guard dressed in khaki fatigues and armed with an M4. Bishop followed Keila to the ramp.

He and Ice watched as Thomas's body was loaded and the stretcher carrying James was secured. Then he turned to Keila. "We're done. I don't want to hear from you again, remember the deal we made."

She nodded. "I owe you my life, Aden."

"Saneh; no one goes after her. Not now, not ever."

"We never had anything on her. I told you that. We, I, just needed the leverage over you."

"Yeah, I get how it works." He turned to walk away.

"Aden!" She reached out and grabbed his body armor.

When he faced her she wrapped her arms around him and buried her face in his neck. He felt her body shudder and raised his arms in an embrace. She clung to him for a moment then broke, cleared her throat and turned to Ice. "You're the bravest men I know. I won't ever forget what you did for us."

Bishop swallowed. "No problem."

Ice reached across and grasped her shoulder. "You held your own, Keila. Your audacity got your team out."

"But not Thomas."

"In war, there are always casualties," said Bishop. "Now, we've got a flight to catch."

As he and Ice left the cargo hold they found themselves facing four armed men wearing khaki fatigues.

"I'm sorry. I didn't want to interrupt your farewell," called out a voice from behind. "But you won't be needing your own transport."

"What the hell?" snapped Ice.

The man who spoke walked down the ramp with his M4 slung. He wore the same clothing as the guards but was older with lean, angular features. "I apologize for the weapons but it's a necessary evil in this business." Despite the civilian attire Bishop had him picked as Israeli Special Forces.

Keila turned to the man. "They saved my team."

"And in turn, they will be rewarded and released. However, they will need to be debriefed in detail." He gestured to his guards. "Load them in the aircraft; wheels up in two minutes."

"Yeah, I thought it was a little strange that the New Zealand government was flying an unmarked J model," King's voice sounded from behind Bishop and Ice.

The PRIMAL operatives turned to see the military contractor and his men arranged in a rough semi-circle, their weapons aimed at the guards.

The Israeli commander stepped forward, smiling. "Look, this is—"

"Shut it," snapped King. "Aden, you and your man are free to go."

Bishop shot the Israeli commander a wink and he and Ice walked past the guards and joined the contractors.

"Feel free to take your people and leave," King yelled at the man.

The khaki-clothed operators stood defiantly for a moment before turning away and returning to their aircraft. Bishop and Ice waited as the Israeli C-130 taxied onto the airstrip and roared off into the distance. Bishop called out to King as he and his men headed toward their helicopter. "I owe you, Charles."

The former mercenary shook his head. "Negative, bud. Now I feel like the slate is clean."

He nodded and waved as the contractors boarded their helicopters. They lifted off as he and Ice headed toward the waiting PRIMAL transporter.

"That was an exciting forty-eight hours," said Ice.

Bishop managed a laugh. "You think that was exciting? Wait till we get on the ground in Abu Dhabi. Vance is gonna go high level on me."

They climbed the side stairs and were greeted by Mike. The pilot looked exhausted but wore a relieved grin. "My first official mission with PRIMAL. Are they all like this?"

"Mostly," said Bishop as he grasped his shoulder.

"Sometimes worse," added Ice as he passed.

A few minutes later the Hercules cruised southeast toward the Emirates. Bishop sat in the cargo hold with his mind racing at a million miles an hour. He glanced sideways at Ice; the big man was asleep on the floor. As he tried to relax he felt a sharp pain under his ribs. Then he remembered he'd been shot. Tentatively he felt under his armpit for the wound. Dried blood covered the spot where the bullet had nicked the flesh. An inch closer and it could have been fatal. Shaking his head he turned his attention to the window and gazed out in the direction of Israel. He trusted Keila but Mossad had revealed their ruthlessness. He immediately forgot his injury. He needed to find Saneh and warn her.

ANKARA, TURKEY

Salim stood in the light cast by a street lamp and checked the address he'd scribbled on a piece of paper. The Sheik had made it perfectly clear that he was not to bring telephones or any other electronic device to the meeting. He'd had to check the address on his phone and then commit the route to memory.

He glanced over his shoulder for the third time in less than a minute. The Mossad assassination attempt had put him on edge. The Sheik's contact better be worth the effort. Consulting the paper again he double-checked the address against the number on the gate post. He was in the right place.

The house was two stories high with curved balconies and a flat roof that bristled with satellite dishes. In the soft glow of the lone street lamp the building looked to be bright orange with red trimmings. Some people have no taste, he thought.

The lack of security baffled him as he pushed open the

gate and walked to the front door. The home was poorly lit and there wasn't a CCTV camera in sight. He was starting to doubt if he was in the right place.

Taking a deep breath he knocked on the heavy wooden door and waited. A moment later a security panel in its center slid open revealing a hijab-covered woman. "Hello, how may I help you?" she asked in Turkish.

"I'm here to see Omer. Tell him, Salim is here."

"Very well." The woman closed the shutter.

He waited what felt like five minutes before the door opened and the woman gestured for him to enter.

The inside of the home was as tasteless as the exterior. It smelled of cheap perfume and shisha smoke, with tacky furniture and garish pieces of art.

She led him to the back into a large room adorned with rugs and pillows. Through a smoky haze, he spotted three men lounging around an ornate shisha pipe.

One of the men, the largest of the three, gestured for him to join them. As Salim got closer the man's features gained clarity through the smoke. He had a pudgy round head with a shiny bald patch. Two beady eyes were perched above a bulbous nose and a full, beard-framed, mouth. If Salim had been asked to sketch a Turkish Islamic crime boss this is pretty much what he would have drawn. The other two men looked as if they had stepped out of the same B-grade action thriller as their boss. Like Omer, they sported shaved heads and were dressed in T-shirts, cheap jeans and sneakers. In the corner of the room their leather jackets hung from a coat stand.

The crime boss finished exhaling a mouthful of smoke. "Welcome to my palace, Salim. Please sit."

Salim crossed his legs on a cushion and took the shisha hose that was handed to him. Inhaling he savored the sweet watermelon-flavored tobacco. As he exhaled, he locked eyes with his host and gave him a nod. "I am honored that you would invite me into your home."

Omer chuckled. "Our friend the Sheik is paying me a lot of money to extend the honor."

Salim smiled. "It is good to know that I am amongst businessmen."

The joviality slid from Omer's features. "What? You are mistaken, my friend. We are all here to serve Allah and ensure that his warriors have the weapons they need for the jihad."

He swallowed. "I never meant to imply that this was not the case."

Omer fixed him with a withering gaze. Then a smile crept onto his flabby face and he chuckled, jowls wobbling. "I am messing with you, friend. Of course we are businessmen. It is all about supply and demand. The Caliphate needs weapons, food, medical supplies and women. We can provide them with these things. For the right price, of course."

Salim nodded. "Of course."

The Turk licked his lips. "Now, the Sheik tells me you need TOW missiles. How much are you willing to pay for them?"

"That depends on how many you can get."

"My cousin is a General in the 7th Corps. I can get you as many as you need. I assume that the Sheik will be footing the bill?"

"Yes, he has deep pockets."

"May Allah bless his generous soul."

Salim took another toke on the pipe and exhaled a cloud of smoke into the air. "And girls? Can you get me girls?"

Omer gestured to one of his associates. "Dundar handles that part of our business. He can provide whatever you desire."

The bald-headed thug spoke, "Blondes are in high demand at the moment. If you want them you will have to pay a premium."

"The Caliphate needs jihad brides, not western sluts."

"That I can do. We can get you truck loads of bitches from the Balkans. Good Muslim virgins with tight little assholes." The man chuckled. "Your Daesh friends can dress them up as little boys."

All three Turks broke into laughter.

Salim managed a smirk as he thought what Mohammed would do to the three gangsters if he heard them disrespecting his faith. That reminded him; he needed to replace the ISIS commander's depleted ammunition stocks, and fast.

"Omer, the Sheik mentioned that you would also provide air transportation."

The crime boss nodded. "It can be arranged, for the right price. To Jarjanaz?"

"Yes, I also have a shipment that needs to be moved from Benghazi."

Omer licked his lips. "That will be expensive, but, achievable."

"When?"

"I will make some inquiries and get back to you. In the meantime, perhaps you would like to sample some of our products?"

Salim frowned. "Your products?"

A smile spread across Omer's face. He clapped his hands and barked an order. A moment later the door to the room opened and three figures dressed in burkas entered.

He clapped again and the women lifted the full-length outfits, revealing young curvaceous bodies clad only in underwear.

He sucked back another lungful of the sweet smoke and grinned. The things he had to do to serve the Caliphate.

Chapter Twenty-Four

MARSEILLE, FRANCE

MIRZA SAT on the edge of a stainless steel bed, topped with a thin mattress, and stared at the concrete wall four feet away. There wasn't a clock in the room. He estimated that he'd been in the cell for at least eight hours, possibly more.

So far the police had been stern but courteous. He'd refused to give them his name or answer any questions. Subsequently all of his possessions and clothing had been confiscated, replaced with blue prison coveralls, and he'd been locked in the isolation cell.

The sound of a sliding latch caught his attention and he turned to the door as it rattled and swung open. A police guard gestured for him to place his hands together and a set of cuffs were snapped shut on his wrists. Mirza gave them a cursory glance and confirmed that they were standard police issue. His record for removing them was less than ten seconds.

The guard led him along a corridor to the interview

room he'd been questioned in earlier. Once again he was told to sit at a table and wait. Minutes passed before a uniformed police officer entered and placed a cordless phone on the tabletop.

"I've got some bad news for you," the officer said with a French accent. "One of your friends from the van has been identified as an extremist with links to jihadists. That means we can hold you, without charges, for three weeks."

The news was a punch to the gut. He'd been hoping to be released soon and find a way back into the smuggling pipeline. In three weeks the missing girl would be as good as dead. "I want to contact my lawyer."

The officer smiled. "Oh, so he speaks."

"My lawyer," he repeated.

The man pushed the phone across the table. "One call."

Mirza thumbed in a number. Holding the phone close to his ear with cuffed hands he waited for it to connect.

"Hello?"

His heart skipped a beat when he heard the soft voice. "Sonia, it's me."

"Where are you? No one knows what happened to you."

"I'm in custody in Marseille."

She paused. "OK, don't say anything else; I'll take care of everything." The confidence in her voice went a long way to quell his anxiety. "Stay safe."

"You too." He ended the call and slid the phone back. "Thank you."

"So, you want to tell us why you were in the back of that van?"

Mirza sighed, stared him in the eye and said nothing.

The officer smirked. "I guess this is going to be a fun three weeks then."

DENKENDORF, GERMANY

Mitch lowered Sleek's stairs and stepped out into the crisp night air. He spotted a tall figure, rugged up in a Russian style cap and a down jacket, at the edge of the private airfield. Raising an arm, he waved him over.

Wilhelm, or Kurtz as he was known, was a former German police officer who, like Miklos and Pavel, had been placed on hiatus when PRIMAL had scaled back operations. He'd been staying with his parents in Denkendorf for the previous two months. Mitch guessed that the high energy operative had long grown tired of that.

"Good to see you, my friend," said Kurtz in his thick German accent. He offered his hand but Mitch enveloped him in a bear hug.

"Great to see you too, you filthy Kraut."

They parted and Mitch gave him a once over. The German operative sported a thick blonde beard and his hair stuck out from under his cap. "You look like a bum."

Kurtz laughed as they climbed inside the warmth of the business jet's cabin.

"So what's the situation?" Kurtz asked as Mitch made them coffee in the galley.

"Mirza infiltrated an Islamic smuggling network to track down a young girl who ran away. Something went wrong on the move from London to Marseille." He was interrupted by the beep of his civilian phone. "Excuse me." Taking it from his pocket, he checked the screen. It was a message from Sonia.

Mirza is detained by National Police in Marseille. He has requested my representation.

He quickly typed in a reply.

Stick to Mirza's story. Pass through any details of your point of contact and Mirza's exact location.

"OK, we have a lawyer that's going to meet with Mirza. She's going to try and get us more intel."

"If Flash updates my credentials I could get inside and see him."

Mitch nodded. "Yeah, and find out when they're going to transfer him. Then we hit the transport and snatch Mirza."

"That's going to take more than two of us."

"Miklos and Pavel are already in France."

The corner of Kurtz's mouth twitched then he smiled broadly. "I like this plan."

"Good, then we're off to Marseille. You contact the Sandpit and get Flash working on your Interpol profile. Any luck we can get Mirza out of prison and back on the job in the next twenty-four hours."

ABU DHABI, UAE

As Bishop and Ice walked toward the Priority Movements Airlift hangar at Abu Dhabi International Airport, they spotted a black SUV parked beside Bishop's four-wheel drive. The driver's door opened and Vance appeared.

"I'm surprised you two came out of that clusterfuck in

one piece," he said shaking his head. "Every fucking time, Bish. What did I say?"

"You want to discuss this in the hangar?" Bishop asked.

"I ain't got time. We're literally jumping through our asses."

"Vance, this wasn't Bishop running ops off his own back," Ice said. "It was a team decision to go in."

"Really? A fucking team decision that didn't include Chua or me." He sighed. "Sometimes there are bigger issues at stake than what you see on the ground."

Bishop and Ice glanced at each other.

"Look, I'm proud of you for rescuing Keila's team, slapping those ISIS pricks and trashing the TOWs. Yeah, Chua reckons we got them all. You showed audacity and initiative and got the job done." He paused. "The problem is in doing so you've exposed both PRIMAL and Tariq to an increased level of risk."

"Should we have let Daesh lop off their heads?" asked Bishop.

Vance shook his head. "No. We should have never agreed to give them access."

"Well we did," replied Bishop. "We did and then we got them out. They owe us now."

Vance snorted. "Mossad doesn't owe us a fifteenth of fuck all. Your friend Keila might but I guarantee she'll forget that pretty damn quick. They're exactly like the CIA, Bish. As soon as you stop being useful they won't want to know you."

"Is Tariq upset?" Ice asked.

"You could say that. He's concerned word will get out that he assisted Mossad."

"So long as UAE special operations remain discreet the

only person who could link us to Mossad is Salim," said Bishop.

"We'll consider addressing that once we bust Mirza out of prison."

Bishop's brow rose. "Mirza's in prison?"

"The van he was being smuggled in got pulled over by the police. He's detained in Marseille. Mitch and Kurtz will be leading the mission to recover him."

"How did that happen?"

"We're not sure. The cops in France are extremely vigilant. Chua believes it may have been a random inspection. Mirza's release is our priority."

Bishop shot a look at Ice, who nodded. "If we go now we can be in France tonight."

"No, Mitch and his team have it well in hand."

"What do you need from us?"

"Stay away from the Sandpit; Mossad could have you under surveillance. You and Ice need to lay low."

"And what about Tariq's investigation into the funding coming from the UAE?"

"It's ongoing. Look, I've got to run." Vance opened the door to his SUV. "You did a good job, Bish. Now rest up and sort your gear. You too, Ice."

Vance slammed the door and drove away.

"He's stressed," Bishop said as they entered the hangar.

"About Mirza?"

"No, I think it's more Tariq and Mossad."

They dumped their bags and headed to the planning room. Opening the fridge Bishop pulled out a beer. "You want one, mate?" he asked as Ice clumped inside on his artificial leg.

"Got a Coors in there?"

Bishop tossed him a can, popped his own and took a

swig as he sat at a computer in the corner of the room. Ice pulled a chair in next to him. "What now?"

"Vance is right. We can't trust Mossad. I need to send a message to Saneh. I need to warn her."

"You know where she is?"

He shook his head. "No, I've got an email address. I just hope she still checks it."

TEL AVIV, ISRAEL

Keila sat in silence as Lisker made a note. She'd been summoned to the Head of Special Operations' office for a comprehensive debrief as soon as her aircraft had touched down in Tel Aviv. She'd wanted to go with Dan to the hospital but Lisker's staff had bundled her into a waiting car.

She fought the urge to fidget as she watched him write. It had taken her over an hour to outline the mission from start to finish. In that time he'd asked questions without revealing what would happen to her team.

Finally he looked up from his notes, adjusted his glasses and fixed her with an unnerving stare. "How do you think the operation was compromised?" he asked deadpan.

"We must have been under surveillance in Amman," she replied.

"By whom?"

"I assess that Salim is receiving external support. Possibly from someone within Jordanian Intelligence."

His gaze never left her face. "Tell me more about the Lascar Logistics staff, Aden and…" He checked his notes.

"Ice, Aden called him Ice."

"Right, Ice. You said they had specialist equipment."

She nodded. "Covert armor, weapons, drones, communications and some kind of powered exoskeleton."

"The suit Aden wore when he leaped over the wall?"

"Yes sir. I saw a similar setup at an IDF innovation conference last year."

His brow furrowed as he considered the information. "Is it possible that the two men were working for the CIA?"

"It's possible, but I got the feeling that they were independent. They made decisions without consulting a higher authority. I also don't think the CIA would risk compromising an asset of this nature to rescue us."

"Most likely true." He nodded then returned to scribbling notes.

"Sir, those men put their lives on the line to save my team."

"Yes, and I assure you no harm will come to them."

"And Afsaneh Ebadi?"

His forehead wrinkled. "His girlfriend?"

"Yes." Keila swallowed. "I used her as leverage to get Aden to help us. The deal was if he worked with us then we wouldn't go after her."

Lisker looked her in the eye. "That's the problem with subterfuge, isn't it? You have to tell a lot of lies." He jotted down more notes and then lowered the pen. Exhaling he folded his hands in front of him. "Your mission was a failure. Yes?"

Keila's mouth was suddenly dry. "Yes sir."

"You managed to kill one of my *Kidon*, wound another and missed your objective." His expression had not changed but there was an edge to his voice. "Until further notice you are being reassigned to an analytical desk."

"Yes sir."

"That is all."

Leaving the office she made her way to a bathroom and locked herself in a stall. Grief for Thomas, the stress of the mission and concern for Dan finally broke through her tough exterior and she wept.

UBUD, INDONESIA

Saneh lay on her back, long lycra-clad legs extended, arms out to her side and exhaled every last breath of air from her lungs. She waited for a count of three and then inhaled again. Yoga session complete, she opened her green eyes and stared at the straw roof of the Balinese hut.

She rolled her mat, thanked the yogi and stepped off along the narrow path that wound through terraced rice paddies before joining a single lane road that continued through the hills.

The picturesque Indonesian mountain town of Ubud had always been a second home for the former PRIMAL operative. A spiritual getaway that rejuvenated her body and soul, it was her refuge from a world of subterfuge and violence. She'd never shared it with anyone else, not even Aden.

After waking from a coma to find she'd lost her unborn child Saneh had fled Abu Dhabi. Aden had been off chasing vengeance, and she'd cut all ties, returning to the serenity of Ubud.

A few minutes down the road she turned onto another track that snaked its way through lush green paddies, over a stream, and up a hill to another grass-roofed gazebo. A sign hanging from the side of the hut identified it as the Yoga Monkey Juice Bar.

A broad smile split the tanned features of the native Balinese who stood behind the counter. "The usual, Miss Sarah?" he asked as she took a seat on a rough-hewn bench that looked out over fields and mountains.

She returned the smile. "Yes please, Wayan."

He set to work making her an avocado and coconut milk smoothie as she gazed into the distance.

Anyone who saw her sitting there would not have guessed that she was a highly trained intelligence operative. With her tanned skin, long raven hair and athletic figure, she could have been a yoga instructor or, with her ample bust, a swimsuit model. In fact, since she'd been in Bali she'd already been offered work doing both.

As she waited for her drink, her gaze lingered on the computer in the corner of the room. She hadn't checked her email since she'd left Abu Dhabi almost two months earlier.

While the pain of losing her child had begun to ease she still wasn't ready for contact with Aden Bishop or anyone else from that world. She managed a faint smile as her thoughts turned to her handsome Australian and his easy-going smile. She did miss him. Perhaps tomorrow she would take the plunge and check her messages.

BENGHAZI, LIBYA

Eshita sat with her back against the cold mud-brick wall with Vashti's head in her lap. Her friend mumbled and thrashed, her body burning as it tried to ward off a viral infection. It was a battle that she had been fighting for the last few days, a battle the teenage girl was losing.

She took a bottle of water, unscrewed the lid and pressed it to Vashti's lips. The girl mumbled, turned her head and refused the liquid.

"Vashti, you need to drink." She tried again with the bottle and once more her friend rejected the fluid. "If you don't drink you're not going to get better."

In the gloom of their cell she could see the other girls sitting in the opposite corner, staring. Since Vashti had gotten sick they'd refused to go near her for fear of being infected.

Re-capping the bottle she placed it with another that Mubarez had managed to smuggle her. The young English fighter had been visiting two or three times a day to give her food, water and even a blanket. If it weren't for him, Vashti would have been much sicker, or worse.

Their guards had shown no interest in helping her friend, refusing to step into the cell to deliver the slop that passed as their meals.

A soft knock on the heavy wooden door went a long way to improving her morale. She wiggled out from under Vashti, rested the girl's head on a bundled blanket and moved to the door. "Mubarez?"

"Eshita, how are you?" He pushed the door ajar, till the padlocked chain tightened, and reached through to grasp her hand.

"I'm fine, but Vashti is not doing well." She squeezed his hand gently.

"I found something that might help." A battered packet of aspirin appeared through the gap.

She took it, along with another bottle of water. "Where did you get this?"

"One of the men."

"Are you hurt?"

"I wrenched my knee in training. It's nothing."

Eshita squirreled the Aspirin away in her pocket. "Have you heard anything?"

"No, the men talk about a delay. I think they're trying to find a way to get into Syria. When I learn more, I will tell you." There was a distant shout from behind the door. "I have to go. I will come back later with food."

He left and, despite the other girls, Eshita suddenly felt terribly alone. She moved back to Vashti and shook two tablets from the packet. "These will make you feel much better."

She managed to get them into Vashti's mouth and coax her into drinking. Then she laid her head back down on her lap.

"I love you, mother," the sick girl mumbled.

Tears filled Eshita's eyes as her thoughts turned to her family. She took the photo of her family from her pocket and held it close to her face. "I'm sorry, papa," she whispered.

Chapter Twenty-Five

THE ARABIAN GULF

SHEIK SAYEED BIN KHALIFA AL-HASHER stood on the fly bridge of his Benetti motor yacht, the *Yarmouk*. He watched as the ship's teak-decked tender bounced over the waves toward them.

By Abu Dhabi standards the one hundred and forty-five-foot yacht was not considered large. In fact, it was almost conservative compared to the behemoths owned by other members of the royal family. Immaculately maintained the blue-hulled vessel could sleep ten and included two luxurious VIP cabins.

The yacht had been a gift from his father on his twenty-fifth birthday. As far as gifts went it had proved to be very useful. He tended to hold his most sensitive meetings aboard the ship and had it regularly swept for listening devices.

He waited till the tender came alongside and turned to the Captain. "Once the Colonel is on board have him escorted to my office."

"Yes Sheik."

Leaving the bridge, he descended two levels and entered his office. The cabin was lavishly appointed in polished woodwork with a desk and a sofa on the wall opposite. A minute after he sat behind the mahogany desk there was a knock on the door.

"Come in."

A uniformed crewmember opened the door. "Colonel Zaman, Sheik."

He nodded and the sailor directed a square-framed, short-bearded man dressed in a suit into the cabin.

"Colonel, please take a seat. Would you like any refreshments?"

The UAE Special Operations officer shook his head. "No, I would prefer to get down to business."

He smiled. "A man after my own heart. So, tell me what your investigations revealed."

The Colonel stroked his beard. "Yesterday, the Presidential Guard authorized the deployment of our contracted search and rescue capability. They extracted five people and one body from the Syrian-Iraq border. Two UAE citizens and four New Zealanders."

"New Zealanders?"

The Colonel nodded. "The contractor reported that one was killed and another severely wounded. They were transferred to an unmarked transport outside of Rutba. The CSAR package engaged a significant ISIS element in close vicinity to the extraction zone."

"That's fascinating, Colonel. Do you happen to know what the UAE citizens were doing in Syria?"

"It is alleged they were delivering aid when their aircraft experienced difficulties."

"By chance, are they employees of Lascar Logistics?"

"Yes, Sheik. They work for Tariq Ahmed."

Al-Hasher's face turned red, becoming a mask of pure hatred. "That man has interfered in my business for the last time. Colonel, the solution we discussed earlier, can you make the necessary arrangements?"

"I have a team that I trust. We can resolve the matter for you." The officer took a packet of cigarettes from his pocket and made to light one.

He raised a hand. "Not on my boat. I don't want it to smelling like a whorehouse. I will pass the target information when the time is right."

"I have a condition."

He frowned. "And it is?"

"We won't do it in the Emirates. The risk is too high."

He leaned back in his chair and clapped his hands in front of his chest. "Tariq Ahmed travels frequently. I will find an opportunity in one of our neighboring countries."

"I have contacts in Saudi and Bahrain; they would be the simplest."

The Sheik smiled, revealing a row of perfect white teeth. "I do believe that can be arranged."

MARSEILLE, FRANCE

The officer behind the counter of the central police station in Marseille hit a button and waved Kurtz through a door into the station. Dressed in a well-fitting suit, freshly shaved and sporting a smart haircut, the PRIMAL operative looked every bit the Interpol officer he was pretending to be.

A uniformed French policeman met him on the other side of the door. "Officer Müller, a pleasure to meet you."

"The pleasure is mine," responded Kurtz in French.

"This way."

Kurtz was led down a short corridor, into an interview room and offered a seat.

"So, you know who our suspect is?"

Kurtz nodded. "Yes, I believe his name is Kapil Sharma. Immigrated to the United Kingdom, illegally, in 2008. Since then he's moved around Europe attending a lot of hardline mosques."

"Has he ever been prosecuted?"

"No, not that I am aware of. He's a low-level guy. For him, the whole militant Islam thing seems to be more about fitting in than waging jihad."

"So, why make the decision to go to Syria?"

"That's where the others were going?"

"We assume so. The major smuggling route from France is out of the port here in Marseille. The driver of the van has been linked to an Islamic smuggling ring based in the city."

"How long can you hold Kapil?"

"Three weeks. If he chooses to cooperate it may be longer. It will be up to DGSI," he said referring to the French intelligence agency.

Kurtz frowned. "He is going to be transferred to DGSI?"

"Yes, tomorrow. With the others."

He feigned frustration. "If he disappears into DGSI, Interpol is never going to get a chance to question him."

The officer shrugged. "Interpol has no jurisdiction here. I can't even let you interview him. If you have questions, I can add them to my own. However, so far he is not very cooperative."

He sighed. "The joys of working for a toothless organization. I will contact my headquarters and see what they want to do. What time will the prisoner be transferred, in case they have questions for you to ask him?"

"The transfer is scheduled for nine-thirty tomorrow." The French man smiled. "I'm sure the pay makes up for lack of teeth."

Kurtz laughed. "The only perk to the job."

They chatted for another five minutes before the officer escorted him back to the station's foyer. "We appreciate you sharing what information you have. At least now we have a name."

"Sometimes that's all Interpol is good for. Thank you for your time, officer."

As Kurtz reached for the door, he spotted an attractive figure through the glass. The dark, exotic woman reminded him of Saneh; she wore that same look of determination. He held the door open. She smiled courteously and he caught a whiff of floral fragrance. Then he stepped outside and hailed a cab. They had timings, now they needed to come up with a plan to target the police transport.

TEL AVIV, ISRAEL

At an unmarked facility in the Negev desert, a row of satellite antennas glimmered in the midday sun. Aimed skyward the dishes relayed information captured from spy satellites in orbit high above the earth's surface. Intercepted traffic was beamed through them into an underground bunker where banks of supercomputers sifted through it, searching for particular snippets of digital information.

It was one of these computers that detected a phrase it

had been tasked to monitor. Packaging the conversation and all its metadata, it shot the information into a secure server that beamed it halfway across the country to a terminal in the headquarters of Unit 8200, the Israeli signals intelligence agency.

The analyst who received the package opened it and ran her eye over the information. Noting that the collection tasking had come from Mossad, she dropped it into a secure file-sharing platform and sent an email to the requesting officer.

The email landed in the inbox of an analyst working directly for the head of the Special Operations Department, Manfred Lisker. He reviewed it, printed the report and spoke into his phone. "Sir, we've got a report regarding Tariq Ahmed that you'll want to see."

A minute later the door to the intelligence cell opened and Lisker appeared with another man in tow. While his boss resembled an academic, this man looked and moved like an operator.

They made a beeline for the analyst's desk where Lisker was handed the report. Thirty seconds later he gave the file to his companion. The younger man was broad shouldered with a square, stubble-covered jaw, and slate gray eyes.

It took him slightly longer to digest it.

"Avi, we have a unique opportunity here," Lisker said.

"I concur, sir. If we move fast, we can use this information to leverage the whereabouts of our primary target."

"The *Rahav* is currently in the Persian Gulf. Can your team use her as a base of operations?"

"Yes, we're equipped for maritime operations." Avi turned to the analyst. "Do you have any additional information on this Colonel and the Sheik?"

The analyst nodded. "Yes, if you give me half an hour I'll have a detailed briefing ready."

Avi nodded. "Good." He checked his watch. "I'll return at 1345 for the update."

Lisker led the *Kidon* team leader from the intelligence room into the corridor. "Keila's team has already embarrassed us in front of Tariq Ahmed's people. I can't afford any more mistakes."

"I'll ensure that Tariq provides the information we need."

Lisker placed his hand on Avi's shoulder. "It is imperative that we find the Mantis. Director Atzmoni has made her our highest priority."

ABU DHABI, UAE

Inside the PRIMAL hangar, Bishop double-checked the equipment inside a canister the size of two forty-four gallon drums welded end to end. He slammed shut the watertight hatch. "This bad boy is ready," he said as he snapped down latches and activated an electronic locking mechanism. Then he turned his attention to Ice, who wheeled a pallet carrier across with a parachute in a large green bag. "You need a hand with that?"

"Nope." Ice hefted the hundred and fifty pound parachute effortlessly onto the canister and tightened the straps that held it in place.

Bishop linked the shackles that attached it to the canister. When he finished, he slapped it with a gloved hand. "Right, Mitch and the boys are going to have enough kit to wage a small war."

"Gym time?" asked Ice as they headed back to the planning room.

"Aren't your batteries flat? Three sessions a day is pushing it."

Ice shrugged. "Want to be a machine? Got to train like one."

"You've taken that way too literally. I'm going to check in with the Sandpit and find out what's going on."

"OK, I'll only be an hour."

Bishop shook his head as he opened the door to the planning room. Inside he grabbed a beer from the fridge and slumped into a chair in front of a computer terminal. Twisting off the cap he took a sip and then accessed his Gmail account. He had half a dozen messages from various contacts and online subscriptions but nothing from Saneh. "Come on woman, check your emails." He closed the account and logged into the iPRIMAL network.

Checking the battle-tracking map he saw that the icons denoting Mitch, Miklos, Pavel and Kurtz were all clustered on the south coast of France. Frank's designator in the UAE was green and he clicked on it. Seconds later he had a secure video call established with the Sandpit.

The watchkeeper grimaced when he spotted the beer in Bishop's hand. "I could crush one of those."

Bishop took a sip. "Vance running a dry HQ?"

"Yeah, only caffeine and guarana over here. Hey, you and Ice rigged that resupply already?"

"Packed and stacked. You give us the word, and we'll jump it in."

"Roger, I'll let Vance know."

"Any news on Mirza?"

"Yeah, Kurtz infiltrated the police HQ today and picked up some intel. The fuzz is going to ship him out tomorrow.

The boys are fine-tuning their plan on how to grab him and get him back in with the Islamists."

"Sounds like they're having all the fun."

Frank laughed. "You and Ice just shot your way through a couple of hundred Daeshbags, I don't think you can start whining about not having fun. Try being cooped up in here all day."

"Well, I'm grounded now, so I'm allowed to mope. Hey, is Chua around? I wanted to go over the intel we've got on Salim."

"Negative. He and Vance are on a call with Tariq."

"You know what it's about?"

Frank's eyebrows rose. "Damage control. They're talking through the implications of our exposure to Mossad."

He grimaced. "How's that going?"

Frank shrugged. "As well as can be expected. Vance and Chua seem pretty comfortable with it. Tariq's not particularly happy."

"You think they're going to approve an operation against Salim?"

"Bish, I wouldn't be surprised if Tariq tries to shut us down completely."

"He can try, but since we're all cashed-up now we can always set up shop somewhere else." Ever since PRIMAL had requisitioned the cash assets of a corrupt and unscrupulous Private Equity firm, it had gained a measure of financial independence.

Frank looked dubious. "Look, I gotta help Flash analyze the likely routes for the police convoy. I'll keep you posted."

"Roger." The call ended and Bishop took a sip from his beer. He had no idea what he would do if the directors made the decision to shut down PRIMAL. Without Saneh in his life, this family was all he had. Necking the beer, he drove the thought from his mind. There was no way that Vance or Chua would let that happen.

VANCE LOCKED eyes with Chua and frowned. They were sitting either side of a coffee table in the living area of their headquarters. A phone was on the table between them, with its speaker activated.

Tariq Ahmed's clipped voice emitted from the phone. "Gentlemen, this exposure is potentially more damaging than the previous incident with the CIA. Mossad has a vested interest in the Middle East beyond that of the US. Additionally, they have a direct interest in retaliation against Afsaneh for her previous activities as an Iranian intelligence operative."

Vance shook his head. "I disagree. Our exposure is limited to Ice, Bishop and Saneh."

"Vance, it connects them directly to Lascar Logistics. Our entire capability could be exposed. Chen, what is your assessment?"

Chua leaned in. "The likelihood of complete compromise is minimal. The Israelis are now aware that Lascar has a small in-house paramilitary capability. However, this fits with the Priority Movements Airlift cover."

"And Vance, what are our recommended courses of action?" asked Tariq.

"I recommend that once we conclude Mirza's operation we move back to a passive collection model," advised Vance.

Seconds passed before Tariq replied. "I would like to look at taking preemptive measures. There are two plans I believe we should develop in addition to watching and waiting. The first being the movement of your team to an alternate base of operations and disassociating from Lascar Logistics. The second," he paused, "is shutting down PRIMAL completely."

Vance's brow rose and he glanced at Chua.

"Gentlemen, I want to leave those options on the table for discussion when I return from Bahrain. I will be attending the airshow for the next few days; we should meet in person when I return."

"Yeah, OK," Vance replied.

"Tariq," added Chua. "I was wondering if you had any updates on your investigation into the source of the funding for Salim's weapons?"

Another pause. "Nothing concrete at this stage. We can discuss it further at our meeting. Gentlemen, I apologize, but I do have to run."

"No problems," added Chua.

A tone buzzed from the speaker indicating that the call had terminated.

"Shut down PRIMAL?" Vance mouthed. "Surely he's not serious?"

Chua shook his head. "He's spooked that's all. The worst-case scenario is a move to South America or Africa, and let's face it, that's not a bad idea. Having us here with Mossad sniffing around is a significant risk for Tariq and his empire."

"Since when has he ever put that first?"

"It's never faced a threat like this. He's holding back information on the UAE Daesh sponsor so it must be someone big. Throw Mossad into the mix and suddenly he's facing real threats to everything he's built."

Vance leaned back in his chair. "Do you think he's in danger?"

"Without an idea of who he's up against, it's hard to say. However, if he needed our help I'm sure he would ask."

He sighed and checked his watch. "It's 0830 in France. The boys will be making their move soon. I should get back to the ops room."

Chapter Twenty-Six

MARSEILLE, FRANCE

THE DRUNK SAT on a park bench a dozen yards from the police station. Dressed in a dirty trench coat and tattered watch cap he looked like a veteran of the streets. Placing his head in his hands he exhaled deeply before staggering to his feet.

As he stumbled along the footpath, a sliding steel gate retracted in front of him. It stopped as he reached the opening and stepped onto the driveway.

A police van stopped with a screech, almost hitting the drunk. He waved his fist at the officers inside, tripped and fell against the vehicle's hood. A horn sounded as he steadied himself, swore and continued along the sidewalk.

A hundred feet past the station, the drunk straightened and walked directly to a waiting sedan. Climbing into the passenger seat he shrugged off the jacket. "The tracker is in place," Miklos said to Mitch, who sat in the driver's seat.

Mitch opened an app on his tablet. On a digital map, he

could see the progress of the van. "Mobile Two, the trace is live," he reported over his iPRIMAL.

A beep sounded through his earpiece as Kurtz checked in. "Affirmative, we are moving."

Mitch passed the tablet to Miklos and started the engine. He pulled out onto the street and drove in the same direction as the van.

"They're heading onto the A7," Miklos announced. "It looks like Alpha is a go." He referred to the analysis the team had done on all the possible routes the van might take. They were identified as Alpha through to Echo.

"Mobile two, Alpha is go," transmitted Mitch.

A few minutes later they were on the A7 highway, heading northwest at fifty miles an hour.

Mitch slowed slightly as he saw their target. "There's the van."

Up ahead the police van drove in the inside lane.

Mitch glanced in the rearview mirror and confirmed that the car carrying Kurtz and Pavel cruised a few lengths behind them. "You ready?"

Miklos pulled out an electric nail gun and checked it was armed. "I'm going to nail it," he said in a perfect Schwarzenegger accent.

He laughed as they pulled into the outside lane. "Let's do it."

As they passed the van, Miklos raised the tool and shot two nails into one of its rear tires.

Mitch eased off the gas and dropped back. Miklos dumped the nail gun on the back seat and retrieved a cordless rescue saw.

"You sure you hit it?" asked Mitch.

Miklos stared at him with narrowed eyes. "I never miss."

Sure enough, a minute later the van began to slow and

the tire looked deflated. Then it indicated and pulled off the highway into a service bay.

"Irene, mother fucking Irene," transmitted Mitch as he slowed and parked behind the van.

Pavel passed and stopped in front of the van, blocking it. A balaclava-wearing Kurtz jumped from the car armed with a suppressed Tavor carbine. "Show me your hands!" he screamed in French at the driver and his escort.

Mitch left the car running, pulled his balaclava down and drew a Maxim 9 suppressed pistol. He covered the driver's side as Miklos started the rescue saw and used it to slice between the van's rear doors. The carbide blade screeched and sparks flew as it cut through the steel lock. Dumping the saw he drew his own Maxim 9 and grabbed the door with his other hand. Mitch did the same on the other side. "Ready."

Together they pulled open the doors, aiming their pistols inside.

Four prisoners dressed in blue uniforms stared at them.

Mitch scanned their faces twice before realizing that Mirza wasn't among them. "Fuck! Abort, abort! He's not here."

Seconds later they were back in their cars and screaming down the highway.

"I don't understand," transmitted Kurtz. "He was supposed to be in the van."

Mitch turned off the highway onto a side road and slowed to a reasonable speed. "We'll find him. But first, we need to ditch these cars and head back to Sleek." In the rearview mirror, the other vehicle turned down another street.

He parked behind a small hatchback and jumped out. Miklos transferred their gear from the sedan as Mitch removed the fake plates. Seconds later, transfer complete, they were on their way to Marseille airport in the hatchback.

As he drove, Mitch's civilian phone rang. He pulled it from his pocket and tossed it to Miklos. "Who's that?"

Miklos checked the screen. "Someone called Sonia."

"Bollocks. Pass it here." He answered the call. "Sonia, look I'm so sorry, I meant to get back to you."

"No, it's fine. I just wanted to tell you Mirza is with me."

Mitch's eyebrows almost reached his receding hairline. "What, how?"

"Let's say I lawyered the hell out of it. Now, Mirza has a way to get in touch with a local contact. He's going to try and get back into the pipeline."

"Right, but I need to see him first. Where are you?"

Sonia read out an address and Mitch repeated it so Miklos could load it into the iPRIMAL tablet.

"It's close," Miklos said.

"OK, sit tight, Sonia. We'll be with you in a few minutes." Mitch ended the call, tossed the phone to Miklos and transmitted to Kurtz. "Mobile Two, we've located Mirza, he's safe. We'll meet you at Sleek in an hour."

SONIA HANDED Mirza a cup of tea. "You sure you don't want more to eat?" She'd placed a spread of food on the hotel room table.

"No thank you, I'm good."

"I feel terrible about you getting arrested." She sat opposite. "Look, if this is too risky we don't have to go on."

He locked eyes with her. "I made a promise to you that I would find Eshita, that's what I'm going to do."

Her eyes misted. "I don't want to lose—"

A thump at the door interrupted her. Sonia rose, put her eye to the peephole then unlocked it.

Mitch greeted her with a smile. "If your call had been thirty minutes earlier it would have saved us a lot of heartache."

"Why is that?" she asked.

Mitch spotted Mirza. "Hey, champ, we just cracked open a police van to find you weren't inside."

Sonia's hands shot to her mouth. "Oh my god. Was anybody hurt?"

"No, but the police are probably wondering why someone went to the trouble of heisting their van only to leave all four prisoners inside."

Mirza reached out and shook his hand. "Those men would be the drivers and the other jihadis?"

"Most likely. Whoever they were, they're not about to blow your cover. They're on their way to DGSI." Mitch shrugged off a backpack and sat on the bed.

"That's good. So, I've got an emergency number they gave me in London. When we're ready, I'll make the call."

"Let me check your tracker first."

Mirza slipped off his boot, and tossed it to Mitch.

He pulled out the inner-sole and waved a wand over it. "Battery's low. He pulled another from his bag. "I've amped up the power on this one."

"Duress signal?"

"Same as before, bend the sole back on itself. We'll get it right away."

Sonia watched curiously as he slipped the sole into the boot and handed it Mirza. "If you can track it, can ISIS detect it?"

"Not likely," Mitch replied. "It's set to transmit every

five minutes and uses a very slim bandwidth. They'd have to have very specific equipment and perfect timing."

Mirza exhaled. "OK, if we're ready. I'm going to make the call."

Sonia leaned over and kissed him on the cheek. "You're the bravest man I know, Mirza Mansoor."

He managed a grim smile. "Let's hope I'm not too late."

IT TOOK Mirza less than fifteen minutes to catch a cab to the address he'd been given over the phone. The meeting point was a cobblestone-paved intersection in the northern part of the city.

He took a seat in a graffitied bus shelter and waited. Traffic along the narrow street was light and there was no sign of public transport. The buildings looked shabby: windows filthy, white painted walls flaked and crumbling. The only people he saw were bearded men and women with faces hidden behind veils. As the time ticked by he found himself worrying that Eshita would already be in Syria. Not that it mattered; he was committed to finding her even if it took him deep into Daesh territory.

The arrival of a battered sedan caught his attention. It stopped in front of him, and a dark tinted window lowered. "Are you Zufar?" asked a Middle Eastern male.

Mirza nodded. "Yes, that's me."

"Get in."

He opened the rear door and climbed in alongside a second man who handed him a hood. Mirza donned the covering as they drove away. It remained on his head throughout the ten-minute journey. As they slowed, he could hear the cry of seagulls. When the door opened, the salty smell of the sea filled the cabin.

As someone led him from the car the noises around him painted a picture. He could hear the sounds of heavy industry: cranes, trucks, men shouting and metallic clanging.

The noise subsided as he was shoved forward. Standing on what felt like a wooden floor he registered the thud and clunk of a door being closed and locked. Pulling off the hood, he saw he was inside a shipping container, dimly lit by an electric lantern. As his eyes adjusted he noticed a cluster of young girls huddled in the corner. He counted six scared faces fixed on him.

"My name is Zufar." As he spoke, the container rocked and lifted off the ground. He stumbled, bracing himself against the wall.

"It is better if you sit," said one of the girls.

He sat across from them with his back against the wall. Yelling penetrated the steel as the workers outside coordinated the loading of the container. Moments later they touched down with a thump, a clang, and more voices. The battery-powered lantern flickered and then died, plunging the space into darkness. Only a few slivers of light peeked through rusted holes in the steel roof. One of the girls whimpered and another cried.

"It's going to be OK," whispered Mirza. As long as the tracker in his shoe can penetrate the container, he thought.

IN A MORE AFFLUENT part of town Miklos and Pavel strolled along a private dock, hand in hand. They both wore matching blue blazers, chinos and boat shoes.

"I like that one," Miklos said pointing at a sleek cabin

cruiser. He glanced back at the salesman who accompanied them.

The slick-haired Frenchman wore a charming smile. "Ah, yes, she's a Sunseeker Predator; 72 feet of high-powered luxury."

Pavel pursed his lips. "What's her range like?"

"A very respectable three hundred nautical miles."

Miklos sighed. "Respectable, no one likes respectable. What if we want to sail to the Greek Islands? Or visit Venice?"

"Then you'll be needing a long range cruiser, I've got something that might interest you at the end of the wharf." The salesman led them past a vast selection of luxurious crafts before stopping at a motor yacht with a dark blue hull and white superstructure. Not as sleek as the Sunseeker, it looked more seaworthy than high speed. "This is the *Charlotte*. She's a Serenity by Cheoy Lee. She's got a longer range than anything else we have."

Miklos clapped his hands. "She's gorgeous."

Pavel looked equally enthusiastic. "What's the range?"

"We're talking true transoceanic capability, at least three thousand miles."

Pavel nodded. "That's what we want. Can we go aboard?"

"Certainly."

Miklos didn't need to feign amazement as the salesman gave them a tour. The build quality of the near-new vessel was evident in the polished teak, brass and leather. There wasn't a plastic surface in sight. They were shown the four staterooms, salon, galley, pilothouse and finally, the open air fly bridge with its second helm and controls.

Miklos studied the array of digital screens for a moment. "Can you start her?"

"Certainly." The salesman took a key from his pocket, inserted it, primed the fuel system and hit the ignition. The powerful diesel engines rumbled to life, the deck vibrating under their feet.

"It sounds fabulous," exclaimed Miklos.

Pavel's eyes never left the digital gauges on the console. The indicators for the fuel tanks showed full. "Very impressive."

The salesman killed the twin diesels.

"So what is the lovely *Charlotte* worth?" asked Miklos.

"A little over two million euros."

Miklos clapped his hands. "That's well within our budget."

Pavel elbowed him. "Is that the best price you can do?"

The salesman smiled. "Make an offer. I can take it to the owner."

"We're going to have to talk to our bank manager."

"Of course." He handed Pavel his card. "I look forward to hearing from you." The salesman said it in such a way that they both knew he didn't believe them.

"That guy was a douche," said Miklos as they left the marina and hailed a cab.

"I don't feel so bad about borrowing his boat now," replied Pavel.

BAHRAIN

Hundreds of heads turned skyward as the Lascar Logistics AW609 tilt-rotor circled the Bahrain International Airshow. Against the cloudless blue sky its silhouette resembled that of a conventional twin-propeller aircraft. However, as it banked, the oversized propellers rotated skyward, and it slowed. Then, when the blades reached horizontal, it came in low over the runway and hovered directly in front of the crowd. After rotating slowly, it flew sideways along the tarmac, with its nose facing toward the grandstand before touching down on the taxiway.

The pilots taxied the tilt-rotor to an area of the airport reserved for private business jets and then came to a halt. When the stairs lowered Tariq Ahmed stepped out into the stifling heat, looking immaculate in his usual suit, eyes shielded by designer sunglasses. Carrying a leather bag over his shoulder he strode across to a Black Bentley SUV and got in the back.

A short drive took him through the ultra modern city to the Ritz Carlton hotel. The accommodation wasn't Tariq's choice; the organizers of the air show had allocated it. Reservations were essential during the bi-annual airshow, the biggest event on the tiny nation's calendar.

Alighting from the Bentley with his overnight bag he waved off an eager porter. A concierge greeted him before he reached the counter. "Mr. Ahmed, we have you in a Royal Suite on the eighth floor." He handed over a gold embossed envelope. "This arrived for you this afternoon."

"Thank you, I know the way." He opened the envelope in the elevator. It contained an invitation to an event on the final night of the show. He sighed; it would be the first of many. His pulse quickened as he read the name of the host, Sheikh Sayeed bin Khalifa Al-Hasher.

By the time Tariq entered his suite he'd decided he would attend. He gazed out over the swimming pools and palm trees into the Arabian Gulf and made a call. "Emily, I'm going to need my security detail."

MARSEILLE, FRANCE

Wearing a black wetsuit, Pavel crouched at the sea's edge and contemplated the inky black water. It was a little over half a mile from the beach to the marina. In his mind, a half-mile of shark-infested waters teeming with pollution and disease.

Miklos thrust a pair of fins and a dry bag into his hands. "Come on, what are you waiting for?"

"You know I don't like water," growled the Russian. "I worked for the FSB, not the navy."

"Yes, that is why you can steal a boat. I would go, but you know what I'm like with security systems."

"*Da*, a bumbling fool." Reluctantly he pulled on the fins, checked his waterproof radio and slid into the water. He swam forward with a breaststroke so he could keep his head clear.

As he glided through the water his earpiece crackled, "We will see you at the RV," transmitted Miklos.

"Not if I drown," mumbled Pavel. Swimming through the water he tried to think of anything other than what could be lurking below. Angling toward the lights of the marina he took a little solace in the fact that he could see clearly. Additionally, the sea was calm with only the slightest ripple.

He reached the edge of the marina without incident. Bracing himself against a pylon he paused at the side of the floating wharf. This was the part he'd been dreading, diving under the structure to reach his target.

Pulling his mask down over his eyes he inhaled deeply and then ducked below the surface. Underneath the floating plastic walkway the water was murky; he had to swim blind. Panic assailed him, and he surfaced, gasping for air.

"Don't be such a child," he murmured to himself. "You can do this."

As he floated alongside the pylon, focusing on the job ahead, something bumped into him and he nearly leaped from the water. Spinning toward the threat, he drew a dive knife and thrust it at his attacker. The blade sunk into the side of a waterlogged plastic container with a dull thud. He sighed and sheathed the knife. He took a deep breath and dove under the walkway.

Reaching out with gloved hands he kicked with the fins. As he swam further, he could see the lights of the marina and the outline of a hull.

His head broke the surface, and he heard voices speaking French. Swimming in close to the hull of the boat he sank as low as he could in the water.

Two security guards strolled along the boardwalk, talking loudly as they inspected the boats with a flashlight. Pavel's heart pounded as they stopped directly in front of the *Charlotte* and ran the beam over her stern to the cabin. A moment later they continued their rounds.

He gave them a few minutes and then swam to the stern of the boat and clambered onboard. Relieved to be clear of the water he lay on the swim platform for a moment. Then he climbed onto the aft deck and checked the door that led inside.

The sophisticated tumbler lock and wireless alarm took him less than five minutes to crack. Inside, he headed to the pilothouse and studied the console. Using a cordless driver from his dry bag he removed a panel, gaining access to the vessel's electrics. Then he attached a pair of alligator clips and switches to a series of wires, bypassing the security system.

A quick scan of the dock revealed that the guards were back in the marina office. He cast off the lines securing the vessel and returned to the pilothouse. Swallowing hard, he flicked his makeshift ignition switches.

The twin diesel engines rumbled to life. He eased the throttles forward and crept away from the dock. He glanced out the side window as he turned the wheel away from the marina. There was no response from the guards. Once he'd passed the last row of boats he flicked on the running lights and turned into Marseille's busy shipping channel.

Pavel felt relieved once he'd made his way out of the packed marina without a collision. He didn't have a lot of experience with a craft this size; the motor yacht was practically a ship, designed for long ocean voyages. Back when PRIMAL was based on the island he'd skippered their workboats, but the *Charlotte* was next level.

Cruising between the channel markers he eased the throttles forward a notch and the engines vibrated with a low hum. A grin spread across his face as the hull cut smoothly through the swell. He adjusted the heading, following the coast to the Roucas Marina where Miklos would be waiting with Mitch and Kurtz. He keyed his radio, "Team, I'm inbound to the RV, pickup in ten minutes."

Chapter Twenty-Seven

THE MEDITERRANEAN

MIRZA HAD NEVER SUFFERED seasickness in his life. However, inside the confines of the dark shipping container, surrounded by the stench of bile, he'd begun to feel queasy. By his estimate they'd been underway for at least ten hours. He had dozed off for some of that time and didn't have a watch, but a sliver of light cutting through a hole in the roof told him the sun had risen.

The door to the container rattled and opened. Mirza squinted as light streamed in. He checked on the girls huddled in the corner. They were miserable, splattered in vomit, their faces green.

A sailor pointed at Mirza. "You, come out."

"They need water."

The man's face remained blank.

"The girls need water."

The sailor disappeared and reappeared a moment later

with a plastic bottle. Mirza took it and offered it to the girls. They looked at him with grateful eyes as they shared it between them.

"You need to come."

He followed the sailor out of the container and onto the deck of a freighter. The vessel was stationary. A quick glance at the horizon confirmed there was no land in sight. "Where are we?"

"At your stop," said the man as they reached the ship's rail.

He looked down at a fishing boat tethered alongside the steel hull. A crane lowered a cargo net filled with military crates onto the deck. The crew quickly unloaded, stacking them in front of the wheelhouse under a tarpaulin.

"Down the ladder."

Mirza followed the sailor's directions and climbed down a rope ladder that hung from the freighter to the fishing boat. When his feet hit the deck a member of the crew met him. "Welcome brother, make yourself at home in the cabin. Once we have the women onboard we will get underway."

"Do you mind if I stay topside and get some fresh air?"

The man shrugged and joined his companions helping the girls off the rope ladder.

Mirza stood at the railing gazing out to sea. From the position of the sun he knew he was facing northwest, back toward France. Scanning the horizon, he could see no other vessels.

FROM THE CAPTAIN'S seat of the *Charlotte*, Kurtz eased off the throttle and glanced at the tablet propped against the console. Following the freighter's AIS navigation beacon he'd been maintaining a separation of fifteen nautical miles, outside of visual range. The device pinged and he raised an eyebrow. Finally; it was Mirza's tracker. It had been silent for almost twenty-four hours.

"We've got a fix!" Mitch said as he rushed into the pilothouse.

"*Ja*, he's still on the freighter."

Mitch walked up and checked the screens. "That's strange, looks like he's stationary."

"Not if they're transferring him to another vessel. You said the freighter was bound for Greece."

"Good point. I wish we had a drone. We could throw it up for a bit of a look."

"I could use the radar?"

Mitch shook his head. "No, we don't want to risk spooking them. The radar is a backup. If we lose the tracker, we'll use it."

"Got it."

"OK, switch to following Mirza's beacon. According to Chua our most likely destination is Benghazi. I'm going to check in with the Sandpit."

Kurtz gestured to the travel mug of coffee sitting in one of the console's beverage holders. "I can handle this for a few more hours."

"Rock on." Mitch left the pilothouse, walked past the galley and sat at the salon immediately behind it. Here he'd established a mobile command center consisting of two tablets, central Wi-Fi hub and a cable that snaked outside to a portable satellite dish.

Accessing the iPRIMAL network he initiated a call to Abu Dhabi. A moment later Vance was on the line. "Boss, how's the weather in the Sandpit?"

"Hotter than hell itself," Vance replied. "I see we've got Mirza's tracker back on line?"

"Yep, finally. It's coming through loud and clear. He's currently stationary. We think they may be changing vessels."

"Makes sense. The resupply canister is good to go. Send through the coordinates and I'll have Bishop and Ice make the drop."

"They jumping in?"

"Not at this stage. We're holding them in reserve. How's the team going?"

"Good. Miklos and Pavel are getting some down time and Kurtz has the con."

"How are you for fuel?"

"We've got enough for now. May need a resupply on the way out."

"I'll have it on standby," Vance said.

"Anything else?"

"Negative, we're a hundred percent focused on your mission."

"Well, we better get you those airdrop coordinates then. I'll flick them through within the hour."

"Smooth sailing boys." Vance terminated the call.

Mitch headed back to the pilothouse.

"Mirza's on the move," Kurtz said as he stared intently at the tablet, "heading south."

"OK, maintain the distance. Let me know if he deviates off course from Benghazi, or if the tracker cuts out again."

"*Ja*, no problem," Kurtz said as he relaxed into the plush seat.

BENGHAZI, LIBYA

It was the following afternoon when the four-engine Antonov An-12 touched down on the dirt airstrip. Renowned for its ruggedness, it could haul twenty tons over two thousand miles and land on little more than a track. These attributes made it the perfect smuggling platform across Africa and the Middle East.

This particular aircraft left a thin haze of oily black smoke as it came to a halt. The makeshift runway had been built to the south of the Jabal al Akhdar hills, on the edge of an agricultural region that was unusually fertile for the desert nation. A rusted pickup drove out from under the shade of a cluster of palm trees and headed directly for the transporter.

The Antonov's side door opened and a figure jumped out. Dressed in tan slacks, boots, a khaki shirt and a keffiyeh wrapped around his neck, it was Salim.

He spotted the truck and walked across to it. He didn't recognize the man in the driver's seat. "Where's Huron?"

"He sent me to get you."

"Is my cargo ready?"

The man shrugged and wore a blank look. An armed guard rode shotgun so Salim climbed into the bed of the pickup. They took off at high speed along the runway and turned onto a road that led up into the hills.

Salim fumed as they bounced their way through a rocky valley then up a winding dirt road to the arms trafficker's compound. As they drove through the open gates, he saw men loading crates into the back of a battered two and a half ton truck. Huron stood a short distance away, watching the operation.

Climbing down from the pickup Salim confronted him. "Why isn't the truck at the airfield? That was the deal."

Huron's lip turned up in a snarl. "Because I haven't been paid; first the money and then the weapons."

Salim pulled a satellite phone from his backpack. He dialed the Sheik. "I'm in Benghazi with the aircraft. Huron says he hasn't been paid."

"That is unlikely."

"I sent the account numbers. Perhaps your people have overlooked it."

"Perhaps, I will have it checked." He sounded preoccupied.

"Is everything OK?"

"Nothing that concerns you. Tell your man the money will be transferred in the next hour." The Sheik ended the call.

He returned the phone to his bag. "I apologize. The money will be transferred soon."

"When it clears you can have the weapons."

"And the girls. I would like to see them before the shipment."

Huron stared at him. "Very well." He shouted an order to his men. Then he gestured for Salim to follow him, past the central building to the storage sheds.

There were six women lined up against the wall in burkas, their veils open.

Salim inspected them. "These are the same as before?"

"There are more arriving soon. If you wait a day, I can give you another six and another jihadi fighter."

He shook his head. "No, I want the shipment to leave today. These girls will do." As he spoke, one of them swayed and fell forward into the sand. "What's wrong with her?"

"She's sick."

"No one is going to want a sick wife. What if she spreads her illness?"

Huron drew his pistol and handed it to Salim. "Perhaps you would like to partake in quality control." His steely gaze told Salim that he would lose face if he did not do the job himself.

He took the weapon, flicked off the safety and aimed it at the girl. One of the others let out a scream. She dashed forward and threw her arms around the girl.

Huron snickered. "That's cute." He gestured for one of his men to remove her.

She fought the guard. "NOOOO, don't hurt her."

"Do it now," hissed Huron as she was dragged clear.

He raised the pistol and fired a single shot into the back of the sick girl's head. Applying the safety, he handed the weapon back. He gestured to the struggling girl who was now sobbing. "Load her and the others."

As he turned from the body, he locked eyes with one of the jihadists who would accompany him to Syria. Tears ran down his cheeks, his face twisted in pain. Salim shook his head and turned to Huron. "As soon as the money clears I want to be airborne."

TEL AVIV, ISRAEL

Seated within the *Metsada* counter-proliferation cell, Keila spun a pen on her palm. With Thomas dead, James in hospital and Dan on leave, she'd been relegated to analytical duties. She dropped the pen in frustration and turned her attention back to the file on her laptop; Aden Bishop's Australian Army service record. It was an interesting read.

His actions in Sierra Leone had been impulsive and heroic but ultimately cost him his career. She wondered if his boldness in Iraq had cost him his job at Lascar Logistics. Probably not, apparently Tariq Ahmed liked to have a few heavy hitters on the books to deal with contingencies.

"Excuse me, Keila." Abel's soft voice startled her.

She turned to face the leader of the analytical team. "Abel, how are you?"

"I'm OK. Look, Keila, I know your team isn't active anymore but..."

"But what?"

"8200 have got a new selector for Salim. Less than an hour ago he was active in Libya."

"Where?"

"Near Benghazi." He ushered her over to his screen that displayed the report containing the coordinates and date time stamp of Salim's call.

"He contacted his handler in the UAE with the new number," Abel explained as he scrolled through an extract of the conversation.

She scribbled down the key details on a piece of paper. "What do we need to authorize an airstrike?"

Abel shook his head. "Won't happen in Libya, not for someone like Salim. He'll need to return to Syria."

"I doubt he'll go back to Jarjanaz." She returned to her laptop and scrolled through the file on the screen. There, at the bottom, was a list of countries that Priority Movements Airlift had delivered aid to. Second from the top was Libya. "He might be able to do something," she murmured.

"What's that?"

"Nothing. Abel, if Salim's handset moves let me know."

"He'll probably drop the phone if he travels."

"Just keep me posted. I'll see what I can do." She

checked her watch. "I'm going to get some lunch. Do you want anything?"

He shook his head and sat back at his desk.

Minutes later she drove out of a secure parking lot onto the highway into Tel Aviv. A mile down the road she pulled over at a fast food outlet and took a phone from the glove box. The burn phone had no links to her or Mossad. She typed a short message that included Salim's location and sent it to a number in the UAE.

ABU DHABI, UAE

Bishop slid the bundled equipment canister along the rollers built into the cargo hold of PRIMAL's Hercules. When it reached the required location he raised a gloved hand. On the opposite side of the canister, Ice secured a tie-down strap and passed the other end across. Bishop locked it down and walked around to join him.

It was the second time they'd loaded the resupply canister, this time to pack two of the black e-bikes behind it. Idle hands were the devil's tools and the pair had nothing better to do.

Ice gestured to the e-bikes and bags of gear. "Anything else you want to load? Maybe a kitchen sink?"

Bishop shrugged. "Gotta be prepared. OK, has Mike got the coordinates for the resup?"

"Yeah, flight plan has been submitted. We're ready to roll."

"Roger, I'm going to grab something from the hangar. When I get back we'll go wheels up." He headed to the back, walked down the ramp and made his way across the tarmac toward their hangar. The sun was setting, drenching the hangar in a soft orange glow. He punched a code into the door, entered and made his way to the planning room. Logging into his email account he checked to see if Saneh had opened the message he'd sent; she hadn't. "Come on, babe."

As he walked out the iPRIMAL in his pocket vibrated. A text message had been auto-forwarded from the phone Keila had given him. As he read it, the ramifications became apparent. He established a secure call with the Sandpit.

"Bishop, you guys ready to go?" asked Frank.

"Yeah. Is Vance there?"

"Sure, I'll throw him on."

Bishop left the building and strode toward the waiting aircraft. The ramp was up but the side door was open.

"Bish, what's going on?" Vance asked.

"I just got sent a text message from Keila. They've got a new sat phone for Salim. He's in Benghazi."

"And you believe them?"

"Mossad wants him bad, and it makes sense that Salim has links into the Benghazi pipeline."

"Mirza's about twenty-four hours out from Benghazi."

"I know, and if Salim sees him, he's done." Bishop climbed through the side door into the aircraft's hold. "Boss, we need to extract Mirza, ASAP, even if he doesn't find the girl. Ice and I are good to go. We can drop in, neutralize Salim and assist the team."

There was silence as Vance considered the option. "I don't have to ask if your gear is loaded, do I?"

"We are G to the G."

"OK, I'm going to get Chua to work through the intel

and then I'll get back to you. Do not, I repeat, do not launch without my authority."

"You got it, boss." Bishop hung up the call as Ice appeared from the cockpit.

Ice spotted Bishop's grin. "What's going on?"

"Salim's in Benghazi and Vance is going to give us the green light."

Ice laughed. "Yeah, and I'm going to grow my hand back."

A high-pitched whine interrupted them as the aircraft's four turboprop engines turned over. "I've got fifty bucks that says we're going in," he yelled.

Ice gave him thumbs-up with his mechanical hand. "I'll take that bet."

BENGHAZI, LIBYA

The headlights of two pickups lit up the back of the An-12 and the two and a half ton truck. Salim and Huron stood in the darkness as men loaded crates from the truck into the aircraft.

Salim spat in the sand. "Could they move any slower?"

"You could help." Huron shot him a withering glare. "No? I didn't think so."

Salim shook his head and strode toward the An-12. He'd hoped to be airborne by sunset but it had taken all afternoon for the Sheik's funds to clear. Standing on the aircraft's ramp he watched as Huron's men finished stacking the crates, almost filling the entire cargo hold. The aircrew threw nets over the load and strapped them down. When they were finished, he waved Huron's men forward. "Bring the girls and the men."

The jihad brides were led from a battered yellow school bus to the fold-down seats on one side of the cargo hold. A moment later the fighters joined them on the opposite side. He spotted the young English man who'd cried when he'd shot the girl. The fighter now wore a grim look of determination.

Huron joined him at the ramp and shook his hand. "Good doing business with you, Salim. Let me know when you can arrange another shipment."

"I will discuss it with the Sheik." He turned and made his way to the aircraft's cockpit as the loadmaster raised the ramp.

The An-12 was originally crewed by five: two pilots, an engineer, navigator and a radio operator. The navigator and radio operator had been replaced by technology leaving their seats free. Salim had been allocated the navigator's seat in the nose. Through the clear plastic dome he had an unobstructed view of the airstrip ahead. As he strapped in he could hear the pilots going through their checks. The aircraft shuddered as the engines started. Landing lights turned on, illuminating the runway ahead of him. Engines roaring they rolled forward. Salim felt his pulse quicken as they gained momentum.

Suddenly a loud bang sounded from somewhere in the rear and the cockpit was inundated by a wailing alarm. He could hear the pilots yelling as they slowed dramatically and ground to a halt. Unclipping his harness, he poked his head into the cockpit. "What's going on?"

The mustached pilot glanced down at him. "We lost our number four engine."

"What do you mean lost?"

"Oil pressure dropped."

"Can we still fly?"

The pilot shook his head. "Not with all this weight. We need to leave half behind if you want to fly tonight."

Salim climbed out of the navigator's dome. "No. That will not do. We take all of the cargo with us." He searched for the engineer and found him inspecting a row of dials and switches. "How long will it take to fix?"

"Last time this happened it took a day. Out here in the desert, it will probably take two."

He pounded his fist against the cockpit wall. The last thing he wanted was to spend another minute in this shit hole. "I'll pay you an extra five grand if you can do it in a day."

"Five each," replied the pilot.

Salim glared at him. "Ten total. You split it how you think is fair." He stormed from the cockpit, past the terrified girls to where the loadmaster sat. "Drop the ramp."

The man scrambled to comply. The ramp dropped with a whine and Salim walked out into the night air. One of Huron's pickups pulled to a halt and the arms trafficker stepped out. "What's wrong?"

Salim shook his head. "We lost an engine. It is going to take a day to fix."

Huron smirked. "I guess you'll still be needing my services."

"Can you provide guards and men to help the crew?"

"I can provide anything, for a price. You can stay at the compound. We will discuss the cost of extra services there."

"What about them?" He gestured to the girls and the fighters.

"My men will bring them as well. This delay is a good

thing. You can take the next batch of girls and fighters arriving tomorrow."

DILMUNIA ISLAND, BAHRAIN

A black Bentley SUV turned onto the causeway to the recently opened Dilmunia Island Hotel. Crossing the bridge, it took its place in a queue of luxury vehicles waiting to unload at the foyer.

In the front passenger seat a square-jawed Arab in a black suit and tie turned to speak to the man in the rear. "Sir, do you want me to join you inside?"

Tariq shook his head. "No thanks, Farès. Stay with the vehicle. I have the alarm." He pulled a single-button duress alarm from a pocket in his tuxedo and checked it. Both Farès and the driver had a receiver along with their firearms.

The bodyguards were ex-Abu Dhabi police who had worked for Tariq when he headed Special Tasks Branch. Now they worked for Lascar Logistics, providing close protection for senior management.

When the Bentley reached the tree-lined entrance of the hotel a porter opened the rear door and Tariq stepped out. He adjusted the cuffs of his tuxedo as he entered the lobby and was directed to a restaurant entrance where smooth jazz played over the hum of conversation.

Sheik Al-Hasher was greeting his guests as they arrived. When he spotted Tariq he approached with a cocky grin. As usual he was adorned in his traditional attire, seemingly unaware of the hypocrisy between his lavish lifestyle and religious values.

"Tariq Ahmed, I'm so glad you could tear yourself away from your philanthropic pursuits to attend my little event."

He returned the smile and dipped his head. "I could never have ignored such a compelling invitation." He held open his hands and gestured back to the lobby where marble columns, chandeliers and manicured trees blended avant-garde design with traditional features. "The new hotel is most impressive; your family continues to gather extraordinary wealth."

They locked eyes for a moment until the arrival of the British Consul General redirected his attention. "Well done, Sheik Al-Hasher. You've done a fantastic job of converting wasted land into such a beautiful precinct."

"Oh," added Tariq. "And here is me believing that it was your father's project, my apologies."

Al-Hasher scowled. "A family undertaking."

Tariq shot him a wink before entering the restaurant, where the party was in full swing. He had to give the Sheik one thing; whomever he'd picked to design the hotel had a good eye. Despite the hundred-odd guests and a five-piece band, the restaurant still felt spacious with high ceilings and floor to ceiling glass. He took an orange juice from a waiter's tray and walked through the open doors into the garden.

The exterior of the hotel was a natural contrast to the sleek restaurant. Lush green grass and bougainvilleas lined either side of an infinity pool that stretched out to a beach of pure white sand. Beyond the pool a teak-decked motor launch bobbed next to a short jetty. Further out to sea he could make out the lights of a much larger vessel.

"You've made a terrible mistake, Mr. Ahmed."

He ignored the comment, took a sip from his orange juice and faced Al-Hasher. "The Consul General was right, this is a beautiful development. Your father should be very proud."

The young prince wore a fierce scowl on his dark features. "I'm going to make you pay for interfering in my business."

Tariq finished his drink and leaned close. "You should stick to fast cars. Extremist is not a label you want to wear." He turned and walked back into the restaurant.

After twenty minutes of greeting the who's who of the aviation industry, Tariq called for his car. As he left the hotel he caught Al-Hasher's eye one last time. The Sheik shot him a knowing smile that left Tariq a little unsettled.

"You all right, sir?" asked Farès as he got into the rear of the Bentley.

"Yes, I'm fine. Straight to the hotel please."

The car departed the foyer then slowed as they approached the causeway. Tariq glanced through the windshield and saw that a work crew had established a detour. It would seem that Al-Hasher's family had yet to complete their impressive estate.

The SUV bumped over a temporary road, slowing to a walking pace. A workman holding a sign waved them to a halt.

"Something's not right here," murmured Tariq. "Keep driving."

As the words left his mouth holes appeared in the windshield and bullets thudded into Farès and the driver. Tariq ducked, but there was no more gunfire. Slipping between the front seats he pulled back Farès' jacket and snatched a Glock from the dead man's holster.

The passenger window to his right shattered, a metal tool reaming out the glass. He thrust the pistol out and fired two shots. Someone grunted as a canister bounced onto the seat next to him, sputtering and hissing. He fired blindly as the CS gas burned his lungs and eyes. Opening his door, he rolled out onto the road and tried to scramble under the car. There was a sharp pain in his flank then a crackling sound. Pain shot through his body as he lost control of all muscular function.

"You're fucked now," growled a voice as hands grasped his legs. As he reached into his pocket for the duress alarm something hit him on the head and everything went black.

THE ARABIAN GULF

Tariq fought the urge to vomit as he came to terms with his condition. His eyes were blindfolded, hands cuffed behind his back, a firm seat underneath him. He wasn't sure if he was on a boat. The rocking sensation may have been a result of his concussion.

"So you're the Jew lover." The voice was the one from the attack.

Tariq sighed. "It would seem that you are very badly informed. Your employer is using you to remove his competition."

The man chuckled. "He told me you might say that. He also told me you'd offer to double what he's paying."

Tariq nodded. "Ah, so this is a business transaction." He paused. "You do realize that I have very powerful friends and limitless resources."

"I'll hedge my bets with the Sheik. Speaking of…"

He could hear the man typing a message on a phone. At a guess, he was on the yacht he'd seen from Al-Hasher's hotel. Tariq should have felt helpless. Instead rage coursed through his veins like lava, dulling the sting of CS gas still in his eyes and lungs. Al-Hasher had killed two of his most trusted men, men that were his friends. He made himself a promise that if he ever got off this boat he was going to do everything in his power to kill Sheikh Al-Hasher.

Colonel Zaman hit send on his phone, reclined in the Sheik's office chair and waited for a reply. He studied his captive as he pulled a packet of cigarettes from his tactical pants. Tariq had impressed him. The former policeman turned businessman had managed to kill one of his men before they subdued him.

Remembering that the spoilt Prince hated the smell of smoke, he left the office. One of his men was guarding the hallway to ensure the crew remained in their cabin. "Keep an eye on our friend."

Moving topside he checked the bridge where another of his men stood watch. Then he strolled to the stern and lit his cigarette. The fourth member of the team lay on the dive platform below, wrapped in a tarpaulin. Despite his death things had turned out rather well. Two million dollars split three ways was a hell of a lot better than four.

He lit a cigarette and gazed out at the hotel, a little over a mile away. The building sparkled like a Christmas tree and he could hear the music. As he took a drag his phone buzzed; Al-Hasher was going to be thirty minutes or more. With any luck, the Sheik would deal with Tariq and then go back to his party. Then he and his team could enjoy the cruise back to Abu Dhabi. All they had to do was deep-six the two bodies.

As he flicked his cigarette ash into the sea he noticed something in the inky-black water. A cylinder with a round object behind it bobbed in the swell. Recognizing a dive mask he grabbed the pistol on his hip.

He was too slow. The cylinder emitted a muted crack and a nine-millimeter bullet hit him between the eyes. He slumped next to his dead comrade.

A moment later a neoprene-hooded head breached the water at the rear of the yacht. The diver climbed onto the platform and checked the Colonel's body then waited for his partner to appear. Moving with the lethal grace of trained professionals the two operatives entered through the rear door, pistols ready. They killed the guard on the bridge with two suppressed rounds to the head. The final UAE operative fared no better, gunned down outside the office.

Inside they found their target cuffed and blindfolded. One man took him by the shoulder and guided him topside as the other checked the rest of the yacht.

"I'm going to release your hands," a voice instructed Tariq. "Follow my directions and you'll live."

The handcuffs fell away and Tariq's blindfold was removed. He found himself at the stern of Al-Hasher's motor yacht face to face with a neoprene-hooded operative. Tethered to the dive platform was a cylindrical craft slightly larger than a jet ski, a swimmer delivery vehicle.

The diver handed Tariq a compact rebreather. "Can you use this?"

He nodded and shrugged the backpack on over his tuxedo. As the man helped fit the rebreather his partner slid a number of dead bodies into weighted bags. One by one they were shoved over the side.

With the corpses disposed of Tariq waited on the dive platform wearing a full-face mask. His minder pointed to one of the seats on the mini-submersible. "Get on."

He hesitated and the diver pointed a suppressed pistol directly at his face. Reluctantly he mounted the craft.

Once all three were strapped in the submersible disappeared beneath the surface with a gurgle.

A few short minutes later the sound of a motor launch reached the yacht. The teak-decked tender from the hotel nudged up against the stern and Sheik Al-Hasher stepped aboard. He stood on the dive platform for a moment waiting for someone to meet him. When no one arrived he climbed the stairs into the main cabin. A glance at the bridge confirmed it was unmanned.

"Zaman, where are you?" he bellowed as he descended into the hull. Reaching the landing to the cabins he spotted a smear of blood on a wall. More of it covered the floor. "You better not have already killed him," he snarled as he shoved open the door to his office. The room was empty.

The scowl dropped from his face as he pulled his phone from his robes and dialed the Colonel. With the phone pressed to his ear he checked the master and guest staterooms; they were also empty. The call failed to connect as he unlocked the crew's quarters. He found the Captain and two stewards seated, playing cards. All three jumped to their feet at the appearance of their boss.

"The men who came aboard. Where are they?" he snapped.

They looked bewildered. The skipper managed a response, "They told us to wait in here. We haven't seen them since."

Al-Hasher felt his pulse quicken as he returned to the corridor with the crew in tow. They climbed to the bridge and he inspected the cockpit. Blood was splattered across the controls and windows. He followed a trail of it down the side of the boat to the stern. There was no doubt in his mind; Zaman and his men were dead. He panicked and glanced around searching for another vessel. There were none in sight. Turning to the Captain he snapped an order, "Take the boat offshore and scuttle it."

The Captain made to reply.

Al-Hasher cut him off, "I'll pay you a hundred grand. Dispose of the boat." He climbed back into the tender and gestured for the driver to return him to the hotel. As he raced across the water he made a call to organize his aircraft. He needed to get back to the relative safety of his father's estate and army of guards. Then he would figure out what to do about Tariq Ahmed.

Chapter Twenty-Eight

ABU DHABI TO BENGHAZI

IN THE CARGO hold of the Hercules Bishop checked his gear for a third time. He tightened the straps that held the black e-bikes to their parachute assembly. Then he inspected the canister they would soon be dropping to Mitch and his team. Satisfied that everything was in order he returned to his seat and tried to relax.

The problem was he had too much on his mind. Between trying to warn Saneh and wanting to go after Salim he was utterly preoccupied. He contemplated using the aircraft's satellite uplink to check his email but decided against it. The bandwidth was limited and he needed to keep it free for when Vance called.

He glanced across at Ice, who despite the drone of the aircraft's turboprops lay asleep on the cold metal floor. That guy was the ultimate soldier, he mused. He could catch zees anywhere and wake instantly ready for action.

"Quit staring, you're messing with my nap," Ice transmitted through their communications headsets. "Why don't you check your gear again; something might have changed in the five minutes since you last did it."

Bishop managed a half smile. "Hey, you're going to be handing over that fifty, mate."

Ice yawned and stretched his arms out over his head. He flexed the fingers of both his mechanical and organic hand and then folded them on his chest.

He was amazed at how quickly Ice had adapted to his bionic hand and leg. They had barely slowed the PRIMAL operative. In fact, they had probably enhanced his capability. There weren't many people that could punch their fist clean through a glass window with no injuries.

A beep in Bishop's headset told him that he had an incoming call on his iPRIMAL. It was Vance.

"You ready to make the drop?"

"Yeah, we're ten minutes out," replied Bishop.

"OK, so we've reviewed the intel. Salim's sat phone is still in the vicinity of Benghazi and we've assessed that there's undue risk of Mirza being compromised."

"So, we're going in?"

"You've got a green light on your mission into Libya."

Bishop punched the air.

"You're grinning like a dog with two dicks, aren't you?"

"Maybe."

"The plan is simple. You infil off target, get eyes on Salim and report to Mitch and his team. If it looks like Mirza could be compromised, you neutralize Salim."

"And extraction?"

"You'll RV with the team on the beach."

"Sounds good."

"I'm sending you the intel pack now."

"Our bandwidth is pretty tight. It might take a little while."

"That's fine. You've got to make the drop for Mitch first. Once you have the intel, I'll get Chua to talk you through it."

"Roger."

"Oh and Bish; try to stay out of trouble."

Bishop grinned as the call terminated.

"What's up?" asked Ice from where he lay.

"Change of plan."

The big man's eyes opened. "You're shitting me; Vance approved the job."

"Yep, better double check your gear. Oh, and I'm gonna need that fifty bucks."

THE ARABIAN GULF

Tariq studied the face of the operative who sat opposite him, perched on a black torpedo. He had a square stubble-covered jaw, with a cleft in the chin. His gray eyes had the same intensity as Bishop's. The man had Special Operations written all over him.

Judging by the uniforms of the sailors who'd helped him from the dive chamber the operative was Israeli. He had heard rumors that their Dolphin-2 submarines operated within the Arabian Gulf but they had never been confirmed.

"My name is Avi," the operative said. "As you have probably already guessed you are now a guest of the Government of Israel."

Tariq was wrapped in a blanket and sitting on a plastic

case in the submarine's forward weapons room. Behind him were the hatches that torpedoes and missiles were fired from. He'd never been on a submarine before and it was more confined than he expected. Looking Avi in the eye he nodded. "I want to thank you for coming to my aid."

The man winked. "No problem. We are grateful for enabling the rescue of our team in Syria."

Tariq shrugged. "That was not my decision. My men acted on their initiative."

Avi drummed his fingers on the torpedo. "Is that so? Look, Mr. Ahmed, I want to be very blunt with you. There is information that I require. If you give me that information, then I can facilitate your return to the Emirates. If you don't," he dipped his head in the direction of the torpedoes, "I can sedate you and dispose of you. The choice is entirely up to you."

He glanced back at the hatches. "Exactly what is it you want to know?"

A knock on the steel door interrupted Avi. He unlocked it and a sailor handed him two cups of coffee. He passed one to Tariq as the sailor disappeared, locking the door behind him. "Tell me about the two men who rescued our team in Syria."

Tariq took a sip of the black coffee. "I keep some former military staff on the books to deal with problems. The two men assisting your team were my best."

"And they usually fly around armed with state of the art weaponry and bombers on call?"

He frowned. "They have an element of flexibility and are very well resourced. I was not made aware that they were supporting your people until they got into trouble and required extraction. It would seem that your operatives benefited from their audacity."

Avi drank from his cup. "Indeed. But, one would ask what a transport tycoon would need with a hit squad."

He laughed. "Half the Middle East is at war, as you well know. What businessman doesn't employ hired guns?"

"Yes, but how many hire former Iranian assassins?"

Tariq lowered his cup. "I do not have any employees that fit that description."

"Really? How long has Afsaneh Ebadi been working for you?"

"Who?"

"Come now, Tariq. You don't remember a beautiful Iranian intelligence operative?"

"I have over fifteen thousand employees in my organization. I'm not aware of the background of all of them."

"You'd know this one. She's very cozy with your boy, Aden Bishop, the former Australian Army officer you referred to as one of your best."

"Saneh is no longer a part of my organization."

"So you don't know where to find her?"

He shook his head.

"Tariq, are you aware of WikiLeaks?"

"Yes."

"Good, because imagine a scenario where Mossad files, identifying your organization as a front for our operations, were released to Mr. Assange and his friends."

Tariq's brow furrowed. "That would destroy my company and jeopardize my employees."

"Yes, it would. And if you don't tell me everything you know about Afsaneh Ebadi that's exactly what is going to happen." He took a sip from his coffee. "After I shoot you through a torpedo tube into the Persian Gulf, that is."

"The Arabian Gulf," Tariq corrected him.

"Given the circumstances I prefer Persian. Now, let's start with a form of communication. How can I reach her?"

Tariq sighed. He was trapped and even with the assets of PRIMAL he saw no way out. "I have an email address."

"Excellent. I can see Mossad and Lascar Logistics are going to have a long and fruitful relationship."

THE MEDITERRANEAN

Bishop and Ice stood either side of the equipment canister in the back of the Hercules. Both wore oxygen masks and their cordless communications headsets. They slid the container along the cargo hold's rollers until it reached the rear ramp. Then they snapped a safety line from their belts to the floor.

"You boys all good?" asked Mike, the pilot, over the intercom.

Ice shot Bishop thumbs-up.

He hit the transmit button on the side of the headset. "We are good to go."

"Excellent, we're coming round on to our approach. Mitch has confirmed he is ready for pickup."

"Sweet, tell him that there's plenty of candy in the package." Bishop made a final check of the parachute system on top of the cylinder then cracked a glow stick and attached it.

"Two minutes out. Drop ramp," transmitted Mike.

A red light flashed on as Bishop pressed the button and lowered the ramp. Icy cold wind sucked the oxygen from the hold, chilling him to the bone.

Bishop pressed his shoulder against the heavy container,

eyes fixed on the red light. Ice mirrored his stance on the opposite side.

An alarm sounded as the light changed from red to green.

"Go!" yelled Bishop as he pushed the container. He reached the end of his tether as it dropped off the ramp and a static line ripped a pilot chute from the bundle atop it. He peered into the darkness and caught a glimpse of a silver chute blossoming behind them. Then he hit the button on the bulkhead raising the ramp.

"Bundle is under canopy and tracking toward the impact zone," reported Mike.

"How long have we got till we reach our drop point?" asked Bishop as he moved back to his equipment.

"We'll be in a holding pattern south of Benghazi in fifteen minutes. Got plenty of gas so take as much time as you need."

"Thanks brother, I'll let you know as soon as we're ready." Bishop gave his parachute harness, helmet and night vision goggles a quick check then centered his attention on the e-bikes.

"How you doing?" Ice said as he strapped on his helmet.

"I'm itching to get down there and sort Salim out." He stretched an arm and winced. "I still owe him one."

Ice nodded. "Let's do it then."

MITCH STOOD at the helm of the *Charlotte*, his eyes fixed to the iPRIMAL tablet propped against the console. According to the flashing icon they were almost on top of the resupply canister.

He glanced through the windshield at Kurtz. The German, wearing a wetsuit, stood at the bow attempting to spot the container in the increasingly rough seas. The dark clouds blocking the moon and stars were making the job near impossible.

He lifted a radio to his mouth. "Kurtz, if we don't find it soon the waterlogged chutes could drag it under."

The speaker crackled. "*Ja*, I know."

Mitch pulled the throttles back slightly, slowing their speed to less than a knot. "The transponder says it's right here." He flicked on the wipers to clear the spray from the window. As the blades swiped across he caught a glimpse of Kurtz diving over the railing.

"Man in the water! Man in the water!" he bellowed as he dropped the props into neutral. "Miklos, take the helm."

The Czech appeared at his side and took the wheel.

"Keep it in neutral till I radio." Mitch stepped out the door into the wind. He moved to the bow and grasped the line that attached to Kurtz's waist. Peering into the water all he saw was the choppy sea. A swell hit the hull with a crash jetting frothy spray into the air.

Suddenly Kurtz appeared, gasping for air. Mitch tried to pull the line but it was taut, attached to something other than the swimmer.

"I hooked the container. Saw the glow stick," Kurtz managed between breaths. "I've got to cut the chutes." He drew a dive knife, sucked a lungful of air and disappeared below the surface.

Mitch grabbed the line, hoping like hell that it would hold. If they lost the container, they'd have next to no chance of being able to extract Mirza. He checked back over the side. Kurtz was still underwater.

Another ten seconds passed without a sign. Mitch tried

pulling the line, it was taught. He raised the radio and was about to order Miklos to reverse the boat when he spotted something in the water. A glowing red light seemed to be rising toward him.

The container broke the surface directly alongside the vessel, smacking into the hull. Kurtz was nowhere to be seen. "Come on you Kraut bastard," he murmured.

Just as he thought his friend was lost a black shape surfaced, gasping for air. Kurtz held onto the webbing straps on the side of the container as Mitch untied the line and dragged it to the stern where Pavel waited. Handing the line to the Russian he hauled Kurtz from the water onto the dive platform.

It took Kurtz a moment to gain his composure. "That parachute tried to take me with it. Grabbed my legs and pulled me down. I had to cut the *schweine*."

Mitch grasped his shoulder. "Get inside and take it easy. Pavel and I can take care of this."

"*Nein*, I dove for it. Now I get to unwrap it."

"Right, well let's quit faffing about then, we're only half a day from Benghazi."

BENGHAZI, LIBYA

Bishop stood alongside Ice, in front of the gaping maw that was the aircraft's lowered ramp, waiting for the light to turn green. Standing with his legs wide to balance his gear bag he focused on breathing slowly from his oxygen mask. No matter how many times he leaped from an aircraft it still got his heart racing. Night jumps were even more terrifying given how many things could go wrong. A quick glance back at the bundled e-bikes confirmed that they were still in place.

"Thirty seconds," Mike's voice crackled over his headset.

Bishop checked the iPRIMAL strapped to his wrist and made a minor adjustment to the night vision goggles raised on his helmet.

Ice grasped him by the shoulder and gave him thumbs-up. Bishop could tell by the look in his eye that he was grinning behind his mask. "Nutcase," he murmured.

"Ten seconds," reported the pilot.

He grasped one side of the bundle while Ice grabbed the other.

"Green light is go."

They pushed the bikes and watched them disappear over the ramp. Heart pounding, Bishop counted five seconds and dove after them. Wind lashed his face as he stabilized himself in flight. An alarm sounded in his earpiece, letting him know his release point was approaching. His gloved fingers found the ripcord handle and he yanked it, bracing for the jerk.

The chute partially deployed then folded on itself forming a single streamer that slowed him but didn't arrest his fall. "Fuck." He released the handle and went for the cutaway, at the same time grabbing his reserve release.

"Ten thousand feet," a soft voice in his earpiece announced.

Yanking the cutaway he waited for the chute to detach. It failed. The main parachute still fluttered above him as he fell.

"Five thousand feet," the voice stated.

"Bish, you OK?" Ice asked over the radio.

He made a split decision to deploy the reserve regardless

and risk it wrapping in his main canopy. A shrill alarm announced his imminent impact with the earth as he yanked the handle.

The reserve chute deployed with a crack, tugging at his shoulders. He grabbed the risers used to steer the canopy. He flared hard then reached down to grab his equipment release.

Too late; he smashed into the earth, the full weight of his gear and body driving through his left ankle. His vision flashed red as the agony of the impact shot through his body and he cartwheeled over his gear and smashed down on his back, the wind driven from his lungs.

"Bish you OK?" radioed Ice. His partner would be high above him, still under canopy and gliding to their DZ.

"I'm alive." Bishop groaned as he detached his harness and untangled himself from his gear.

"Roger, I'm coming to you."

"Negative, head to the DZ and recover your bike. I'll head there on foot and you can pick me up." He glanced at his iPRIMAL and confirmed he was only a few miles off target.

"Affirmative."

Free of his gear Bishop tried to stand. Shooting pain in his right foot confirmed it was sprained, possibly broken. The dull ache under his ribs reminded him he was already wounded. "Damn it." Grabbing his gear sack he slid his G28 marksman's rifle from its sleeve, inserted a magazine and cocked it.

He then opened a medical pouch on his pack. Previous experience told him that taking off his boot was a bad idea. Instead, he popped two heavy-duty anti-inflammatories, injected a painkiller through his sock and taped the boot and upper part of his leg with black tape. Clambering to his feet, he tested the ankle; it was tender but held his weight.

Lowering his NVGs he scanned the terrain around him. He'd been lucky coming down in what appeared to be a wheat field. If he'd landed in the rocky terrain to the north, toward the hills, he'd probably be dead.

Abandoning his chute, he shouldered his pack, cradled his rifle and started off toward the DZ. He hadn't gone thirty yards before his ankle began to ache. Despite the cool night air sweat gathered on his brow. Gritting his teeth he limped on.

ABU DHABI, UAE

The zodiac came in under the cover of darkness. It cruised over a flat sea, the hull hissing as it slid up the beach. A man jumped over the bow and held it as Tariq and Avi climbed out and strode across the sand. Behind them, the little boat reversed off the beach and disappeared out to sea.

Tariq inspected his phone as he reached a track.

"Where's your man?" Avi asked abruptly.

"She would be here already if you had let me contact her earlier."

"She?"

"My assistant, Emily. I trust her explicitly."

"We should have used one of my people."

Lights appeared in the distance, gaining in intensity as the vehicle drove toward them. Avi crouched, grabbing Tariq's arm to pull him down.

Tariq shook his hand free. "It's Emily." He waved as a

Range Rover pulled up alongside them. Opening the door of the luxury SUV he gestured for Avi to enter.

When they were both inside Emily turned her head.

"Eyes to the front," snapped the Mossad operative.

She complied and focused on driving them along the track. "Sir, where have you been? Bahraini police found your hire car and your security detail but could not locate you. People are saying you're dead."

Tariq exhaled. "I made some new friends."

"No more questions," ordered Avi.

Tariq frowned at him. "You're my guest now. If you talk to her like that again that courtesy will end. This relationship goes both ways."

Avi's jaw clenched. "Fine. I'm sorry Emily, thank you for agreeing to pick us up at this hour."

"It's no problem," she replied with a glance at the rear-view mirror. She turned off the track onto a causeway. Within a minute they were cruising down a highway toward Abu Dhabi International Airport.

"Emily, is the jet ready?"

"Yes, sir."

Tariq gazed through the window at the city lights. He couldn't help but feel that he had betrayed everything he stood for. He'd given Mossad the breadcrumbs they needed to track down Saneh and, no doubt, terminate her. But it was necessary to protect the rest of the team, at least that's how he justified it to himself.

It wasn't far to the airport. Emily swiped them through to the freight precinct and drove into one of the Lascar Logistics hangars. She parked the SUV alongside a white business jet and got out, leaving Tariq and Avi alone.

"The jet will take you back to Tel Aviv, as you requested. Then we're done."

Avi smiled. "You and I both know this isn't where it's going to end."

Tariq gestured to the door. "You're going to miss your flight."

"Been fun, Tariq. You'll be hearing from us."

He watched as Avi left the car, strode across to the jet and paused on the stairs. The operative gave a wave then disappeared inside. Tariq hoped like hell it was the last he saw of him.

Emily climbed back into the car. "Sir, who was that man?"

"A new friend. Emily, can you please drive me home." She started the car and drove out of the hangar. "Did you bring my spare phone?"

"Yes, sir." She passed the device back to him.

He activated the hidden iPRIMAL menu and checked his messages. There were a series of updates from Vance and the team. He opened one and scanned it. They'd authorized the insertion of Bishop and Ice into Benghazi to support Mirza's extraction. His finger hovered over the communications button as he considered contacting Vance. No, he needed to keep Mossad as far from PRIMAL as possible; this was his problem.

BENGHAZI, LIBYA

Bishop had barely made it half a mile before he stopped. Even with the drugs and strapping his ankle ached. He checked his iPRIMAL and saw that Ice rapidly approached his position. Taking a seat next to a boulder, he waited. A short moment later he heard the soft hum of an electric motor then spotted the bike through his night vision goggles.

Ice stopped alongside him. "What the hell happened?"

He climbed to his feet. "My main candlesticked, cutaway failed."

"No shit. You're lucky to be alive. Any injuries?"

He slung his G28 and climbed onto the bike, behind Ice. "Strained my ankle a little. It'll be all right; let's get this show on the road."

Ice accelerated the bike through a barren field. They rode the mile to the drop zone in silence. When they arrived Bishop could see that the bundle had landed on target. Ice had already buried the chute and broken down the gear. Bishop's e-bike was configured and ready to go.

"I spotted lights northeast of our DZ," Ice said from his bike. "Should we check out the location Mossad gave us first or the lights?"

Bishop accessed his iPRIMAL. "We can make a dog-leg on the route to the target and check it out." He scanned the horizon through his NVGs and then referenced the satellite mapping on the device. "Could be an airstrip."

"Yeah, that would explain how Salim got from Syria to Benghazi."

"Let's check it out." He twisted the throttle and sent the bike racing along a dirt track, with Ice close behind.

They rode toward the lights, crossing a number of shallow streams. In the distance he could see the outline of rugged hills against the night sky. In less than ten minutes they had covered a mile and a half and stopped short of a rudimentary airfield. Stashing their bikes in a dry riverbed they crept forward on foot, climbed a small outcrop, lay among the boulders and observed the dirt strip.

"That's an Antonov 12," Bishop whispered as he peered through the scope of his rifle.

"Bird of choice for smugglers."

He focused on the plane's wing where a pickup parked below one of the engines. A man stood in the bed, his head and shoulders inside the aircraft's engine cowling. "Looks like they've got maintenance issues."

"How far are we from the location Keila gave you?" asked Ice.

Bishop checked his iPRIMAL, using his hand to shield the light. "A little over four miles."

"Too close for coincidence."

"Yeah, my thoughts exactly." Using the digital camera built into the scope he snapped a burst of shots and uploaded them to his iPRIMAL. Using the satellite relay in his e-bike he bounced the images to the Sandpit for the team to analyze. "The ramp's down. Let's see if we can make our way around and get a peek inside."

"You've got half an hour. Then we're moving on. Sun will be rising soon."

Bishop turned to his partner with a grin. "Look who packed their big boy pants."

"Someone has to keep you on track. Remember what Vance said about staying out of trouble."

He slid backward and climbed to his knees. "Vance always says that. You don't think he means it."

They made their way back to the bikes.

"Yeah, he knows trouble finds you because you go looking for it."

"Please, you're one to talk."

Ice climbed onto his bike. "I'm not the one that requires adult supervision."

Bishop shook his head as he rode slowly along the dry riverbed then accelerated up the bank. The mix of painkillers and anti-inflammatories had finally kicked in; he could no longer feel the throbbing in his ankle.

Chapter Twenty-Nine

TEL AVIV, ISRAEL

MANFRED LISKER and Avi both rose as Mossad Director Caleb Atzmoni entered the secure space known as the Tomb.

Caleb waved for them to sit. "Good morning gentlemen, I'm on a tight schedule today. You have five minutes."

Lisker adjusted his glasses, sat, and glanced at his notes. "Avi's mission in Bahrain was a success. They successfully foiled the attempt on Tariq Ahmed's life and gained information that may lead us to the Mantis."

Caleb nodded. "Excellent, tell me about Tariq Ahmed. Will he be a useful asset?"

"Extremely useful. His airfreight company has extensive reach. It can be utilized to move operatives covertly across most of the Middle East and Africa. In fact, Avi returned to Tel Aviv by that very means. Additionally, Ahmed maintains a small team of former military personnel to deal with 'volatile' situations."

"The men that extracted Keila and her team?"

"Yes, sir."

"It would seem that our new relationship has already been of benefit to us both. The way I see it, we would be remiss not to ensure that it remains so."

"I agree."

"And the Mantis, is she one of his hired guns?"

He checked his notes. "It would seem that way. Although, he claims that she is no longer in his employment. He provided us with a point of contact that should ultimately lead us to her."

"I want her picked up at the earliest possible opportunity. She's to be interrogated then neutralized. If she's compromised any aspect of the Tiberias program I'm to be notified immediately."

"It will take a few days. Her last known location was Indonesia."

Caleb frowned. "Do we have anyone in close vicinity?"

"We have a suitable operative in Hong Kong that can conduct the reconnaissance. Then I intend to deploy Avi and his men to make the snatch."

He gave a slight nod. "Approved."

"Excellent." Lisker gestured to the door. "Avi if you don't mind." He waited until the operative had left the room. "Caleb, I still think we should use her as a donor for the Proteus project." All formality had left his voice. "I reviewed her file again. Her lethality is undeniable."

Caleb pondered the request. "Fine, take what samples you need." He glanced at his watch. "That's your five minutes." Rising, he made to leave then paused. "If you manage to take her alive I'd very much like to speak with her before she's interrogated." He smiled. "I mean, the Mantis is a legend around here."

UBUD, INDONESIA

Every muscle in Saneh's body ached as she walked along a vibrant green rice paddy but she felt amazing. The two-hour yoga session she'd endured had worked every inch of her lean frame. Now she needed one of Wayan's avocado and coconut milk smoothies to re-energize.

She reached the Yoga Monkey Juice Bar, ordered and took a seat on a bench with a view over the green hills. Behind her the blender roared as her smoothie was prepared. Looking for something to read, her eyes fell on the ancient computer in the corner of the open-air cafe. She walked across to it. "Wayan, can I use this?" she asked when the blender fell silent.

"Sure Miss Sarah, anything you want."

Sitting, she opened explorer, activated private browsing and logged into her email account.

The computer and software were obsolete and the bandwidth terrible. It took nearly a full minute for her account to connect. In that time Wayan brought her the smoothie and she sipped it.

When it finally opened, she saw she had well over two hundred emails. The account was less than a year old yet somehow every scammer from Bombay to Nairobi seemed to have emailed her. She scrolled through offers of Viagra and opportunities to help smuggle gold out of Iraq until she reached a message from an address she knew by heart, susurro@gmail.com. Her heart lurched as she hovered the cursor over Bishop's email. She couldn't bring herself to read the subject line. Instead she closed the browser, wiped the history and took her smoothie back to the bench.

All the good work of the Yoga session was gone. Her stomach churned, her heart pounded and she felt tears welling in her eyes. Visions of the ambush in Africa flashed through her head and she could hear and smell the gunshots that had robbed her of her child.

"Are you OK, Miss Sarah?" asked the bartender. "Is the smoothie good? If it is bad I can make you another."

His voice and the concerned look on his face brought her back to the present. "No, it's wonderful, Wayan. I just over-did it in class."

She finished the smoothie and walked slowly through the fields. Part of her wanted to turn around, go back and read the email from Bishop. She missed him. No, she loved him, but the pain of losing their child still burned. Maybe she would read it tomorrow.

MEDITERRANEAN SEA

The first glow of the rising sun peeked through a window as Mitch finished his coffee. He rose, avoiding equipment cases as he made his way through the salon. Piled on the table and seats were all the equipment and weapons they'd need to extract Mirza including sniper rifles, combat vests, dive kit and a switchblade drone.

Walking through the galley he placed his cup in a sink then opened the door to the pilothouse.

"What's the progress on Mirza's boat?" he asked.

The German sat at the helm and glanced at the tracking app on the tablet. "Making a steady eight knots. Will reach shore in the next half-hour."

Mitch sat on the leather couch to the rear of the cabin, behind a table that held his mobile command center. He'd relocated his gear to make room for the equipment from the resupply canister. "Where are Bish and Ice?"

"They're in an observation post south of the target location."

As Mitch inspected the map the communications interface announced an incoming call. It was the Sandpit. He tapped the screen.

"Morning sailors," Vance's voice emitted.

"Hey boss," replied Mitch. "You've got Kurtz and me here. Pavel and Miklos are getting some shut eye."

"Roger; Chua's online too. He's going to give you a quick intel update based on the information Bishop and Ice have uncovered."

"Hi guys," said the intelligence officer. "As you're aware Bishop's Mossad contact passed on the location of Salim's satellite handset, which gave us his location near Benghazi. That prompted the insertion of Bishop and Ice and subsequent identification of an An-12 on an airstrip a short distance from what we've designated Objective Troy."

"You think they're linked?"

"Yes. We've run the tail number and the aircraft belongs to an air freight company based in Turkey with known ties to organized crime. With Lascar compromised it's probable that Salim has sourced a new provider. Objective Troy is likely to be a halfway house come weapons cache."

"And Mirza's on his way there?" asked Mitch.

"It's a possibility," answered Chua.

"Which is why we need to recover him tonight, before there's any chance he could cross paths with Salim," added Vance. "Your team will insert, link up with Bishop and Ice, recover Mirza and any girls then extract via your boat to Crete."

Mitch turned to Kurtz who nodded.

"We've got a Switchblade onboard. We can trash the An-12 as well." Mitch referred to a short-range kamikaze drone.

There was a pause as Vance considered the suggestion. "That might be a good diversion. Keep it in your back pocket."

"Roger. The lads will cross the beach some time after nightfall."

"Got it, keep us posted if anything changes, Sandpit out."

Mitch leaned back into the plush couch and sighed. "I'm going to need some more coffee."

"Get some sleep. I can run the boat," said Kurtz.

He stretched his arms above his head. "Yeah, you're right. I'll set my alarm for thirty minutes. Call me if anything happens."

Kurtz frowned. "We're in the middle of the sea. What could happen?"

Mitch chuckled as he rose. "You've been in this game long enough. Shit always happens."

BENGHAZI, LIBYA

A trickle of sweat ran between Bishop's eyebrows along the bridge of his nose to the tip. It hung for a split second before dropping onto the screen of the iPRIMAL that was strapped to his wrist. "Damn it's hot," he whispered as he smeared it away with a gloved finger. Before sunrise they had infiltrated up into the barren hills. Now they lay, exposed to the sun, on a rocky outcrop overlooking the target compound. "Any sign of Salim?" he asked Ice who lay beside him.

Ice had his eye pressed to the scope of his rifle. "Negative. Not a lot going on down there."

"Yeah, because it's hotter than Satan's crotch."

Ice chuckled. "You've got such a way with words."

"What can I say, I'm a poet."

"You're something, but it's not a poet."

He grinned. "Why are you so harsh?" A chime in his earpiece announced a message on his iPRIMAL. He quickly read it. "We've got timings and a location for an RV for tonight. We're getting Mirza out."

"So he's moving toward Objective Troy?"

Bishop checked the battle-tracking map. The Sandpit relayed the location emitted by the tracker in Mirza's shoe. According to the latest update he was a short distance from the coast. "It looks that way."

"But no sign of Salim. Hopefully the two don't cross paths before we extract him tonight," said Ice.

He tucked his own rifle to his cheek. Through the digital scope he could see the compound clearly. A row of vehicles, pickups, four-wheel drives and a yellow school bus were parked in the yard. Butted up against one wall a long rectangular building looked to be a storage facility. The heads up display told him the range to the main two-story building: four hundred and eighty yards. "Come on, Salim. Come out and play."

MIRZA STOOD at the railing of the fishing boat as the crew brought it alongside a concrete wharf that stretched the better part of a half-mile into the bright blue waters of the Mediterranean Sea. He guessed the structure was part of the oil infrastructure established during Gaddafi's regime. To the south, the white and ochre buildings of Benghazi could be seen in the distance.

It was high tide and the edge of the boat sat only a few feet from the top of the weathered concrete. He watched as the crew laid a gangplank to unload their cargo.

The honk of a horn drew his attention toward the shoreline. A battered green truck reversed slowly toward them. It stopped at the plank and two AK-wielding men emerged from the cabin. One of them pointed at Mirza.

"You help us put the crates in the truck," he said in broken English.

It was hard work in the hot sun but Mirza enjoyed the exercise, having been cooped up in vans, prison cells, shipping containers and boats for the last week. When the truck was loaded the girls were brought up from below and ordered into the rear. Mirza joined them in the shade of a bullet-riddled canopy.

"Where are we?" asked one of the girls.

"Libya." Mirza managed a fake smile. "We are now safe in the lands of the Caliphate."

As they drove off the wharf and turned onto a coastal road dust billowed from the wheels. Mirza covered his mouth with his T-shirt as the familiar smells of the Middle East filled his nostrils. Out the back he watched the outskirts of Benghazi disappear, replaced by arid coastal lowlands. Glancing skyward he scanned for any sign of a drone, any indication that the PRIMAL team was out there, tracking him. The sky was clear with only the hot sun beating down on them.

The truck rattled and bounced onto a pot-holed highway that followed the coast about half a mile from the sea. They passed through numerous villages before rugged hills loomed off to the side. A short while later robed men carrying AKs waved them through a checkpoint. The truck turned onto a winding rutted track that rose into the hills.

Mirza and the girls were jolted from side to side as the driver negotiated the dirt track. He held onto the side rails with one hand, and pushed against a crate with the other to stop it from sliding along the floor. One of the girls coughed as dust billowed up from the wheels.

A crunch of gears and squeal of brakes brought them to a halt. Voices came from the front as the driver conversed with someone. Then they jolted forward, through a gateway and parked in a high-walled compound. Armed men, dressed in a mixture of fatigues and robes, appeared at the back of the truck.

"Everybody out!" yelled an African wielding an AK.

Mirza climbed down and took in his surroundings. The compound was at least a hundred and fifty yards square. A two-story house constructed from cinder blocks dominated the center. Its flat roof was arrayed with satellite dishes and antennas. The compound wall to the left of the truck had a long storage facility butting up against it. He counted five doors; the two closest were open.

He watched as the girls were inspected by a gray-haired man wearing choc-chip camouflage pants and a red Manchester United jersey. From the way he swaggered around Mirza deduced he was the boss. The girls were shoved through one of the doors and it was chained behind them. If Eshita and her friend were at the compound, he thought, that's where they would be imprisoned.

The African gestured to the truck with his weapon. "Unload the boxes."

Mirza grabbed a crate and made to lift it from the back of the truck. A young Caucasian with a patchy beard placed a hand on his shoulder. "Let me help you," he said in a British accent.

"*Shukran.*"

They shuffled the heavy crate across the yard, through the remaining open door, and stacked it against a wall.

"Where are you from, brother?" asked the youth as they grabbed another crate from the truck.

"India, but I moved to England."

"What part?"

"London and Birmingham."

They placed the crate inside and returned for another.

"I'm from Birmingham." The young English man offered Mirza his hand. "My name is Mubarez."

"I know that name. You're the one who killed the *kafir* police officers in London." He feigned respect, suppressing the feeling of disgust that welled up inside him as he gripped the youth's hand. "I'm Zufar."

"And I'm Peter fucking Pan!" screamed the African. "Get the damn truck unloaded."

Mirza thought he caught a glimpse of regret on the English youth's face as he grabbed the other side of the crate and hefted it off the back of the truck.

"Did Imam Rahman send you?" Mubarez asked quietly.

He nodded. "Are there others here from his congregation?"

"Not fighters. But there are two girls…"

"The girls, are they still here?"

The boy swallowed. "One of them died."

His words hit Mirza like a bullet. "How?"

As they carried the box into the room Mubarez mumbled, "She was sick, and they killed her."

"What was her name?" Mirza asked quietly.

"Vashti."

Mirza shoved the crate into the corner of the room. Vashti was the other name that Sonia had given him, Eshita's friend. He followed Mubarez back to the truck. There were no more boxes inside. Task complete, they wandered across to the shade cast by the main building and sat.

"How long have you been here?" Mirza asked.

He sighed. "A week, maybe more. They tried to fly us out last night but the plane broke. Once they fix it we will leave. You will probably come with us."

For the first time since embarking on the mission to find Eshita, Mirza felt a glimmer of hope.

SALIM SAT in front of a rattling air conditioner in a room filled with Huron's men. In the far corner a massive television blared; another soccer match. He rose, grabbed a bottle of water from a refrigerator and sought refuge from the smell of stale sweat and cigarettes. Opening the bottle he walked into the corridor and entered the tiny room that Huron had allocated him. He contemplated calling the Sheik and requesting another aircraft, but dismissed the idea. The Emirati Prince was as ruthless as he was wealthy and Salim had failed him more than once already.

A voice in the corridor caught his attention and he stuck his head out of the room. Recognizing one of the guards from the airfield he approached. "Any update with the aircraft?"

The man shook his head. "Not yet. They said tomorrow morning."

"Lazy flea-bitten dogs. I need to get home."

"Is my hospitality so terrible?" The voice behind his shoulder startled him.

He turned and found himself face to face with Huron. "It's not like that. I have warriors waiting for these weapons."

Huron shrugged. "Another day won't hurt the Caliphate. In fact, they will benefit from the delay. A new shipment of girls and weapons has arrived."

"Really?"

"Yes, white phosphorus mortar bombs; a very useful addition to their arsenal."

"And the women; whores or brides?"

He shrugged. "That's your decision to make. Would you like to see them?"

"Why not." Salim followed him out through the front door into the scorching sunlight. As his eyes adjusted he spotted a group of men sitting in the shade of the building. He recognized the jihadists who had boarded the aircraft. Pausing, he studied the face of a newcomer. There was something strangely familiar about the bearded, dark-skinned warrior. Pushing it from his mind he followed Huron across to the storage facility.

A guard opened the door to the room where the girls were imprisoned. As he inspected the new girls the man's face continued to plague him.

"Do you want them all?"

"Huh, what? The girls, yes, of course, I will take them." Turning back to the doorway, he glanced through to where the men were sitting. The one he recognized had turned his head and shaded his eyes with one hand. Then it clicked. He was the Lascar Logistics loadmaster, part of the Mossad team sent to assassinate him.

"Huron," he hissed. "One of those men is an Israeli spy."

The arms trader's head snapped around. "What? How do you know?"

"Because he helped a team of Jews who tried to kill me."

"Which one?"

"The Indian. Do you know him?"

"No, he arrived today." Huron waved one of his men over. "The new guy. Take him into the house." He turned back to Salim. "If he's a spy, we'll make him talk."

BISHOP HIT transmit on his iPRIMAL and waited for it to open a call with Mitch. The device sent an encrypted signal to the e-bike that he'd stashed nearby. Its satellite booster, in turn, relayed it through the Sandpit to the extraction team based on the *Charlotte*.

"Mitch, we've got eyes on Mirza and Salim."

There was a slight delay. "Has he been compromised?"

Bishop had his eye pressed to his scope. Salim hadn't reappeared from where he'd entered the storage facility where the girls had been taken. Mirza was sitting against the wall opposite with a group of men. "No, I think we're still..." As he spoke an armed man appeared from the main building. He had his AK pointed at Mirza. "Shit."

He leveled the cross hairs on the gunman's body.

"Bish, if we take him out Mirza's done. They'll kill him on the spot," said Ice from behind his own weapon.

He watched helplessly as more armed men surrounded the group and Mirza rose to his feet. Even through the powerful scope he couldn't make out his friend's facial features but he knew the PRIMAL operative would remain calm. "Ice, we could drop these fuckers right now. Pin the rest down and Mirza could make a break for it."

"Negative, we've got no idea how many men are in there. We need to stick to the plan."

Bishop clenched his jaw as the armed men led Mirza around the corner of the building and out of sight. "We go in tonight. We get him and the girls out."

His earpiece crackled. "Lads, please confirm, has Mirza been compromised?"

Bishop thumbed the transmit button. "Yeah, he's now a captive in the main building."

There was a pause. "Don't worry, we'll get him out tonight."

BLOOD OOZED from the split in Mirza's brow and he felt it run down the side of his face where it coagulated in his beard. The room where the guards had left him bound to a chair was dark and stank of sweat, piss and stale cigarette smoke. He looked around, scoping his options for escape. There were no windows, only a single door leading out into the corridor.

The door handle creaked before Salim and another man, the one wearing the Manchester United top, entered. They switched on a single light bulb that hung from the ceiling, closed the door and stood in front of him.

"Look, I don't know what I've done but I assure you it wasn't on purpose," Mirza said.

The corners of Salim's mouth turned up in a sadistic smile. "Hello, Mirza."

He shook his head. "My name is Zufar, you have me confused with someone else."

Salim laughed. "So you're not Mirza, the man I met in Jarjanaz? The man that delivered a Mossad hit squad to my door."

"No, I'm Zufar. I came from Birmingham. Imam Rahman sent me to fight for the Caliphate. I have never met you before in my life."

Salim took a step closer to him. "You're a liar, you're a Mossad spy."

He anticipated the punch and rocked his head back with the blow. Salim hit him again, smashing his knuckles into Mirza's forehead. Screaming with rage, Salim clutched his fist to his chest.

"Stop wasting your time," snapped the other man. "If he is Mossad you won't break him like that."

"I'm not Mossad," wailed Mirza. "I'm here for my God, I'm here to serve Allah and the Caliphate."

"I have a man who is very experienced in making people talk," continued the Libyan. "He worked over many of Gadaffi's men to find out where they hid his gold."

"Did he find the gold?" asked Salim.

"No, but they told him all kinds of secrets to stop the pain." He laughed sadistically.

Blood bubbled from Mirza's nose and lips as he pleaded, "Brothers, I am not who you think."

Salim sucked his teeth in thought. "Have your man work on him. I need to get to the airfield and hurry the crew." He turned and disappeared out the door.

Huron stood staring at the captive for a moment longer. He doubted that the weeping fool was anything more than a brainwashed idiot. Salim was paranoid. Still, his interrogator would enjoy going to work. Stronger men had lasted days, but he doubted this one would make the break of dawn. Switching off the light he slammed the door behind him.

Chapter Thirty

UBUD, INDONESIA

MOSSAD'S HONG KONG based operative was an athletic Eurasian who went by the name Liberty. The daughter of an Israeli diplomat and his Chinese wife she had been recruited into Mossad following her compulsory service in the Israel Defense Forces. Following her training she'd returned to Hong Kong to work for a tech startup. Responsible for managing the fledgling company's website and social media platforms she worked from her laptop as she traveled on missions for her clandestine masters.

Ubud was a destination that she'd always wanted to visit. So, when the surveillance task had appeared in her secure email she'd booked a room in a boutique resort and jumped on a flight to Bali. From the airport it had been a three-hour bus ride into the mountains. Then she'd unpacked her bags, donned a sarong, let her long dark hair out and set about exploring the town.

The target pack on the Mantis was lean, only a few

photos and a general location. The SIGINT team in Tel Aviv had broken through her firewall and VPN but still hadn't been able to give much more than a football field-sized bubble. The file had also come with a warning that the target is lethal. The instructions were clear: observe, report and await the arrival of the snatch team. Liberty was more than happy to comply with those directions.

Her resort was a short walk from the search area. Perched alongside a river it consisted of quaint bungalows tucked under the jungle canopy. Narrow wooden walkways linked them to a reception area, restaurant and swimming pool.

She strolled out to the road with a satchel on one shoulder, SLR camera hanging from her neck. A minute down the road she emerged from the jungle onto a hillside planted with rice. It made for a great photo, the lush green rice paddy terraces contrasting against the vibrant blue of the sky. She snapped some shots with the camera and continued into town.

According to the intel pack she was looking for an internet cafe. Analysis indicated that it was a desktop computer that the target had used to access her email account, not a mobile device, which made Liberty's job a little easier.

She strolled along the potholed road to the outskirts of town, passing massage parlors and day spas, services she was definitely going to indulge in once the mission was complete.

When she reached an intersection, she noticed a small grass-roofed hut opposite, perched on the side of a hill. Lifting her camera she zoomed in on the sign that hung haphazardly above the door; Yoga Monkey Juice Bar. She snapped a shot and decided that it was as good a place as any to start her search.

Following a raised path through the rice paddies she reached the hut and stepped inside. A smiling local greeted her and directed her to the specials board. She ordered a smoothie called a Chunky Monkey and took a seat on a bench with a view of the fields and valley.

As she scanned the room she noticed an ancient computer in the far corner. She asked the Balinese vendor if she could use it. He grinned, pulling out the chair and offering her a seat.

Smiling she sat and unlocked the screen. A quick check of the control panel identified the computer's IP address. Taking her phone out she opened the intel pack and checked it against the address her target had used. Her pulse quickened; it was the same.

"This is very slow. Do you have Wi-Fi?" she asked.

Another grin. "Yes, we have the Wi-Fi." He pronounced it wifee.

"Great, do you mind if I work here?"

"Yes yes, you can work here. Wi-Fi is very fast and very cheap."

She took a seat at a table and pulled out her laptop. Opening her email she felt a little disappointed that it had taken so little time to find the computer. Still, once she located the target the snatch team would take over and she would have the opportunity to enjoy this tranquil little town. In the meantime, she would stake out the café and at the same time get ahead on work for the startup.

BENGHAZI, LIBYA

Mirza sat in the dark room evaluating his situation. His primary concern was freeing his hands and activating the duress alarm in the sole of his right boot. Twisting his hands he struggled against the thick zip-ties the guards had used to bind him to the chair. Unable to break them he came up with a different course of action. He'd use his other foot to push off the boot, topple the chair and use his bound hands to activate the alarm.

Digging the toe of his left boot into the heel of his right he focused on levering it off. As he did the door handle turned and it opened.

The figure that stood in the doorway was cause for concern. The man's hulking frame blocked most of the light from the corridor. His head alone looked to be the size of a bowling ball.

The behemoth stepped inside and flicked the light switch revealing his girth in all its glory. His arms were the size of Mirza's thighs, his head massive, completely bald and scarred like a pit-fighting dog. He had to be one of the biggest and ugliest men that Mirza had ever laid eyes on.

"Hello," he said as he shut the door behind him.

Mirza swallowed.

The interrogator wore a grubby white singlet that barely contained his gut, under which hung what looked like a carpenter's belt filled with tools.

"They told me to make you talk," he mumbled. "They told me you had lots of things to tell me."

Mirza shook his head. "No brother, I haven't got anything to say. This is all a mistake. I am a fighter, like you."

The man shrugged and grinned, a sickly flashing of his

teeth more akin to a grimace. "Who do you work for? CIA? Mossad?"

"I'm a servant of Allah."

The interrogator balled his fist and struck Mirza in the face. The blow felt like a sledgehammer and he toppled backward, smacking his head on the floor. He barely had time to gather himself as the behemoth grabbed his shirtfront and yanked him upright.

"Who do you work for?"

"I already told you, broth—"

A blow to the torso silenced him, driving the air from his lungs. A second punch followed, then a third.

As Mirza fought for breath he noticed that the grossly overweight assailant was doing the same. His face dripped with sweat as he lined up another punch, breaths coming in short gasps.

Mirza weathered another assault, turning his face to protect it from the man's fists. A blow split his eyebrow, another striking his cheek.

Exhausted the interrogator shuffled across to the wall and slid down till he was sitting slumped against it.

Mirza feigned unconsciousness, letting his head drop forward against his chest. His body throbbed with pain as he prayed that the PRIMAL team would rescue him. There was no doubt that, despite the interrogator's lack of fitness, he would most likely kill him in the next few hours.

BISHOP WATCHED through his night vision goggles as an inflatable boat bounced through the surf and slid up the beach. A figure jumped clear and wrestled the craft higher, securing it with a line attached to an anchor.

He raised his rifle and pulsed the infrared laser a few yards from the man. Dressed in drab colors and crouched in the dunes he was invisible to the naked eye. The flash of a laser responded in acknowledgment. A second figure joined the first and they moved swiftly across the beach toward him.

As they got closer Bishop could make out the details of their equipment. Both men wore black assault armor on their torso, shoulders and groin. Full-face helmets with integrated night vision, audio enhancement and respirators concealed their faces.

Bishop waited for the pair to crouch alongside him. They carried integrally-suppressed Tavor assault rifles chambered in .300 Blackout and were laden with ammunition, grenades and breaching charges.

"Lads, welcome to Libya."

Pavel grasped his hand. "It's good to be here, comrade." His voice was metallic through the helmet's vents.

Miklos shot him a nod. "How far is it to the target? This stuff gets heavier every time I put it on."

He suppressed a laugh. "Ice has eyes on the compound. It's about three miles away up in the hills."

"Three miles?" wailed Miklos.

"No change to the plan?" asked Pavel.

"Negative. We handle transport and the girls. You guys get inside and grab Mirza."

"No problems. Mitch and Kurtz are monitoring radio traffic and have a switchblade drone for fire support."

"Let's hope it doesn't come to that. OK, let's get moving." He rose and led them through the dunes. As they walked his ankle started to throb and he found himself limping. Taking a fistful of painkillers from his pocket he swallowed, chasing them with a mouthful of water from the bladder on the back of his armor.

The drugs kicked in as they crossed a road and began climbing the rocky terrain into the hills. Clouds covered the night sky, the limited ambient light making them invisible to the naked eye. However, they could see clearly through their goggles and the sensors in their helmets.

"Are you injured?" asked Pavel as Bishop paused.

"I rolled my ankle jumping in. Nothing I can't manage."

"How far to go?" asked Miklos. "I'm sweating like a Russian athlete at a drug test."

"Very amusing, douche bag," snapped his partner. "Maybe you wouldn't sweat so much if you laid off your mother's kolache."

"I'm not the one who steals it from the kitchen."

Bishop grunted. "You two bicker like a married couple. Let's get moving."

An hour later they reached the ruins of a mud house. Behind the eroded walls lay Bishop and Ice's e-bikes and their gear. Miklos nudged one of the bikes with his boot. "You made me walk when you had these?"

He sat to take the weight off his ankle. "I could only carry one of you. Were you going to make Pavel walk?"

Miklos chuckled. "I'm not that cruel."

He activated his radio as the PRIMAL operatives made final checks of their assault gear. "Ice, we're at the RV, anything going on?"

The radio crackled. "Negative, target is a graveyard."

"It will be when we're done," he growled. "We're moving to your location." Turning to the others he gestured them forward. "Let's go. Not far now."

He led them silently through the rugged hilly terrain, sticking to the folds in the ground where scrubby bushes and the occasional tree grew. Within five minutes they reached the mud-brick perimeter wall of Objective Troy. Bishop crouched at the base and looked up. A caving ladder slowly lowered from the roof of the storage facilities that butted against the inside of the wall. He pointed up with a gloved hand.

Pavel and Miklos hauled themselves up the flexible ladder then he followed. On the roof he saw Ice laying at the edge, his rifle aimed at a two-story building not fifty yards away.

"OK, lads," whispered Bishop. "Get Mirza out. We'll sort transport and take care of the girls."

Both the operatives with the full-face helmets nodded.

"Right then. You're up."

"You mean down," replied Pavel as he lowered himself over the side of the building and dropped to the ground.

MIKLOS TOOK point as he and Pavel made their approach to the two-story building. He held his suppressed Tavor firm against his shoulder, the point of aim displayed on the high-definition screens inside his helmet.

He paused at the corner, waited for Pavel to tap his shoulder, and then stepped around toward the entrance. Two men sat smoking to one side of the wooden door, their cigarettes glowing hot through thermal sensors. His Tavor spat twice and they toppled sideways, shot through the head. When it came to extracting one of their own, they were pulling no punches.

The front door was unlocked. He pushed it open with his boot and aimed through the gap. There was no one in the long corridor. He moved inside with Pavel at his shoulder.

He glanced at the tracking app on his iPRIMAL. It emitted a soft beep that would gain intensity as they closed with the transponder in Mirza's boot.

The pair crept along, pausing at doorways to see if the sensor changed in tone. They were almost halfway down when the pulsing increased in frequency. Miklos gestured to a door, keeping his weapon trained down the corridor as Pavel turned the handle and checked inside.

"He's not in there," Pavel whispered.

Miklos frowned. "You sure?"

"No, I don't know what he looks like."

"No need for the sarcasm."

"So where is he?"

Miklos extended a finger toward the ceiling. "He must be on the second level."

"I was afraid of that."

As they stepped off there was a noise from the far end of the hall. They froze as a figure appeared. The man stumbled blindly toward them.

Pavel's Tavor snapped, drilling a subsonic round through the man's skull.

Miklos lunged forward, caught the body and lowered it gently to the floor.

The corridor led into an open room with a large television in the corner. Miklos paused in the doorway, the thermal sensors in his helmet revealing men sleeping around the edges of the room. He counted eight in total. Each man lay next to his assault rifle.

He felt a hand on his shoulder and turned to his partner. Pavel pointed to the far side of the room where a staircase led to the next level.

As he crept between the men, a voice mumbled and a hand reached out, brushing his boot. Miklos froze. The voice declared something unintelligible. Glancing down he saw that the man was still fast asleep. Stepping through the last of the slumbering gunmen they climbed the staircase to the second floor of the building.

Upstairs they found another corridor with rooms running off each side. The sensor beeped rapidly in Miklos's ear as he continued forward, building up to a wailing alarm. Through his helmet the sliver of light under a door a few steps ahead shone like a beacon. He paused next to it as he pressed the iPRIMAL strapped to his wrist, killing the alarm. "This is it," he whispered as he checked the doorknob. It was unlocked. He shoved the door open and stepped inside with his Tavor held ready.

Mirza sat in the middle of the room; head slumped forward against his blood-drenched shirt. As Miklos moved toward him he caught a glimpse of someone sitting immediately behind the door. A behemoth grabbed his weapon, shoved him back toward the door, bellowing like a wounded bull.

Miklos struggled to wrestle his gun free. Shouts sounded from the room below. Pavel turned and covered the stairs as his partner fended off the hulking assailant.

The torturer snarled as he pinned Miklos against the wall, towering over him. Realizing he didn't stand a chance he released the Tavor and thrust his finger through the ring on the hilt of his Benchmade dagger. The knife slid from its sheath and he stabbed it into his attacker's eyes. The man screamed and backed away, clutching his face. Miklos released the knife, letting it hang from his finger as he snatched up his Tavor and fired twice.

The torturer collapsed in the corner. Miklos rushed to

Mirza, whose head was still slumped forward. The razor sharp dagger made short work of his bonds. "You OK?"

The bearded Indian lifted his head and struggled to speak through his swollen features. "The girls, we've got to get the girls."

Miklos helped him to his feet. "Bishop and Ice are taking care of it."

Gunfire erupted in the hallway along with the snap of Pavel's suppressed weapon.

He pressed the transmit button on the forward grip of his weapon. "Bish, we've got problems. We've recovered Mirza, and he's mobile. But we're on the second floor. Our exit is blocked by lots of angry men and they've got guns."

The response was immediate. "Yeah, you've really stirred up the hornet's nest. Head to the western side, there are multiple windows you can use as exit points. We'll pick you up in the bus."

THE SOUND of gunfire woke Salim and he clambered out of bed, searching in the darkness for his boots. Slipping them on he grabbed his backpack and checked the door. The gunshots seemed to be coming from above. Pushing open the door he glanced down the corridor in the direction of the television room. A grenade detonated and gunfire echoed off the walls, along with screams.

"What the fuck is going on?"

The voice startled him. He spun to see Huron standing shirtless with a pistol clutched in each hand.

"Have you brought Mossad down on our heads?" the arms trader snarled. The Libyan was intimidating despite his flabby torso and checked pajama pants.

"The spy arrived by boat. It has nothing to do with me."

More gunfire sounded from outside.

Huron turned to one of his men. "Radio Magafe in Ad Dirsiyah. Tell him to send everyone he has. Tell him we're under attack by the Jews. I'm going to fight from the bunker."

"We have to get to safety!" yelled Salim. "I need to get to the airfield."

Huron spat on the floor. "Run away, you scared little bitch. Take your cargo, you've paid for it. The girls, they stay here." He stormed along the corridor toward the exit.

Salim made to follow as two more men appeared from another room and moved toward the front door.

He was torn between staying with Huron and escaping in a vehicle. He decided on the latter and followed the men out into the yard. Beyond the pickups, four-wheel drives and a battered yellow school bus the heavy wooden gates were closed. As he considered his options the men moved around the side of the building, toward the storage facility on the far wall. One of them spotted something and raised his rifle. Before he could fire bullets tore into his body and he fell back, dead.

Salim dove behind a stack of crates. An explosion rocked the building. He huddled into a ball and dialed the aircrew.

OUTSIDE, Bishop and Ice moved through the compound, their weapons held ready. They'd shot one gunman and now the yard was clear. All the fighters were inside the main building, focused on the upper floor.

Bishop gestured at the yellow school bus. He covered as

Ice pried open the door and climbed inside. A moment later the diesel engine spluttered to life.

He stepped onto the stairs as Ice crunched through the gears, found reverse and backed toward the main building. The transmission whined as they approached the two-story residence, the brakes squealing before they scraped the cinder block wall.

Bishop swung up onto the vehicle's roof, his rifle slung.

"Miklos, we're at the west end with the bus," he transmitted as another grenade detonated in the building.

"We're about to move to your side," Miklos's voice came through over the chatter of gunfire.

He used the buttstock of his rifle to smash in a window on the second floor. Tossing in a flash-bang he waited for it to explode before entering. "I'm in the northwestern corner," he transmitted as he cleared the room. It was empty.

"Acknowledged, moving to you," replied Miklos.

He knelt in the corner of the room and waited. A moment later someone thumped on the door. "Party!" Miklos yelled from the other side.

"Pooper," replied Bishop, letting him know that a PRIMAL operative was inside.

The door sprung open and the black-helmeted operative entered followed by Mirza. Suppressed gunfire sounded from behind them followed by the thud of a grenade. Then another black-helmeted figure appeared, Pavel.

Bishop pointed at the window. "Lads, get out the window. There's a bus below."

"What about the girls?" croaked Mirza who was gripping an AK. The Indian operative's face was battered, his right eye swollen, beard matted with dried blood.

Bishop grasped his shoulder. "I'm going to get them now." He hit his transmit button. "Ice we're coming out."

"You're all clear."

As Bishop climbed through the window he spotted a group of men near the storage rooms where he'd seen the girls taken earlier. He aimed his laser and fired a shot. One of the men fell, sending the others scurrying into the long building that butted against the wall.

He jumped onto the roof of the school bus then dropped to the ground. As he scanned for additional targets, his earpiece clicked. "All call signs this is Mitch in the *Charlotte*. I've intercepted radio traffic. Hostile call signs in your area have requested support from a nearby militia. I'm vectoring the switchblade to cover the likely approach route. ETA of the hostiles at your location is less than fifteen minutes."

Ice joined him having given up the driver's seat to Miklos. Bishop offered Mirza a hand as he climbed down from the hood.

"Mirza is secure. Moving to the girls now," he transmitted.

ESHITA SAT HUDDLED with the other girls in the far corner of their cell. They cowered, away from the door.

"What's happening?" asked one of the new girls, her voice wavering.

She wrapped an arm around the girls either side of her. "We must be quiet. We'll be safe in here."

"How do you know that?" a hysterical voice asked from the darkness. "They will kill us if they find us."

"No one is going to kill you," she replied.

"They killed your friend."

The comment hit Eshita hard. A ball of grief formed in her stomach and tears welled in her eyes. As she fought back sobs she heard a rattle.

"What was that?" asked one of the girls as the interior door swung open and a flashlight shone into the room.

"Get out of the way," grunted a voice.

A girl scampered from the door. Eshita caught a glimpse of the face of one of their guards. Behind him, in the next room, she saw other heavily-armed men.

"This way. All of you, in here," the guard ordered.

She froze, unsure of what to do.

"Eshita, it's OK," said a voice she recognized; Mubarez. "We're being attacked. We need to get you all to safety."

"Quickly, through the door," she said, guiding one of the girls into the next room. As she made to follow she heard the chain outside jingle. One of the guards stepped past her and fired into the wooden door. The other girls dropped to the ground, screaming. Rough hands pulled her into the other room and slammed the door.

BISHOP DROPPED his electric bolt cutter and spun away from the door as bullets smashed through it. Girls screamed over the gunfire as the chain clattered to the ground. Ice charged past him, barreling through the door, his rifle spitting lead.

"Room clear!" Ice barked as he fired two more shots into a body. The battle rifle was deafening in the confined space. Both Ice and Bishop had removed their suppressors to make their long-barreled weapons more manageable.

Bishop moved into the dark room, scanning it with the

infrared flashlight mounted to his G28. A huddle of girls in burkas cowered in the corner, eyes wide with fear. Ice kicked an AK away from the dead man on the floor.

Bishop moved across to the girls. "It's OK, we're here to take you home. Do any of you speak English?" He raised his NVGs, took a glow stick from his vest and cracked it. The soft orange light seemed to reassure the girls.

One of them raised her hand. "Some of us understand."

Bishop guessed her age at around fifteen, possibly younger. Outside, the rattle of the school bus's diesel engine grew louder and he glanced back to see the silhouette of Mirza at the doorway.

"Is Eshita here?" asked the Indian in a gravelly voice.

"They took her," said the girl.

"Where?" asked Bishop.

She pointed to the wooden door at the rear of the cell.

"Mirza, you get the girls in the truck with Pavel and Miklos. Ice and I are going after Eshita." He lowered his NVGs, strode across to the interior door and checked the handle. It was unlocked. No sound could be heard from behind it.

With a fluid movement he swung the door inward and Ice charged through.

The next room was similar to the girls' cell but larger with crates stacked against the walls. In the center a set of earthen stairs disappeared into the ground.

As Ice checked the room Bishop aimed his weapon down the stairs.

"Bish, wait," whispered Ice from behind.

He paused long enough for Ice to catch him then moved silently down the stairs into a tunnel. He hadn't taken more than a dozen paces when he glimpsed the barrel of a rifle protruding from a corner. Activating the infrared laser he balanced the dot on it and fired. His bullet slapped the weapon away, its owner letting rip a burst of fire that ricocheted down the tunnel.

Bishop felt a round crack past his face as he dove forward, slid around the corner and shot the gunman in the chest. The body toppled backward, down another flight of earthen stairs. Below, another shooter fired a panicked burst.

He glanced back at Ice. "You OK?"

"Yep," Ice responded.

He lobbed a flash-bang down the stairs. Shouts echoed from below before the grenade detonated. AK fire sounded as he moved swiftly down to another turn in the tunnel. Crouching he leaned sideways, his weapon and head briefly exposed. His rifle snapped twice, drilling a waiting gunman. "We've got an underground storage facility," he reported to Ice.

"Come out or we kill the whores!" a voice screamed.

Bishop leaned out again. He couldn't identify the source of the voice. Suddenly lights flickered on washing out his night vision goggles.

"I said come out!" the man bellowed.

A shrill feminine scream penetrated Bishop's headset. "He's not fucking around," he whispered as he raised his NVGs. "OK, I'm coming out." He left his rifle, drew his pistol and slipped it into the back of his pants. "You got me?" he whispered.

Ice gave him a reassuring pat on the shoulder.

"Hold your fire. I'm coming out." Bishop stepped around the corner into the underground bunker. "OK, let's talk."

The room was the size of two shipping containers and

stacked with weapon and ammunition crates. In the center stood three men and two burka-clad girls. One of the men, an overweight shirtless slob, held a pistol to a young girl's head. Next to him a bearded fighter dressed in camouflage pants, T-shirt and a combat vest aimed an AK while holding the second girl. On the other side of the slob stood a younger Caucasian clutching a pistol nervously. Bishop prioritized them: AK-wielding fighter, slob with no shirt and then the terrified youth.

"What about your friends?" asked the slob.

"They're all upstairs," said Bishop. "But if you don't release the girls they're going to join the party."

"What do you want with these bitches?"

"I'm here to take them home."

He snickered. "You're not here for them. You want Salim."

Bishop clenched his jaw. "He's still here?"

The slob nodded. "Yes. If I give him to you, will you leave?"

"The girls come too."

"Fuck you. Leave, take Salim but the girls stay. If you come back, I'll butcher them like goats." He clicked back the hammer of his pistol, the barrel pointed at the girl's temple.

"No!" the Caucasian boy yelled, shoving his gun into the shirtless slob's face. "Let Eshita go."

The AK-wielding guard reacted by whipping up his weapon and firing. His bullets found their mark, ripping through the youth's chest.

Bishop dropped to a knee, snatching his pistol from his pants as the slob fired wildly. At the same time Ice stepped from the tunnel and shot directly over his head. Ice's bullets found the AK-wielder's chest while Bishop drilled the shirtless slob through the forehead.

The girl who'd had a pistol pressed to her head dropped to her knees next to the dying teenager and pressed her hands to his chest. "Michael, Michael," she sobbed as his lifeblood pumped out between her fingers.

Bishop rose to his feet as Ice moved forward to comfort the other girl. He considered pulling a bandage from his medical kit but could tell the kid was already gone.

"Bish, this is Pavel. Can you hear me?" The transmission came through broken with static.

"Yeah, send."

"We need to bug out. Mitch has eyes on a convoy of five technicals heading our way."

"Roger." Bishop grasped the distraught girl's shoulder. "Eshita, we need to go. We're going to take you home."

She held the boy's head in her arms, still sobbing. "He died for me. Michael died for me."

"Yes, and if we don't get you out he'll have died for nothing." He closed the dead boy's eyes and helped her stand.

Half a minute later they left the girl's prison and crossed to the bus. Bishop helped Eshita inside where the other girls were waiting with Mirza. Ice and the second girl were right behind them. He joined Miklos up front, wedging himself in the bus's doorway, aiming outward with his rifle.

"Pavel's got the gate," Miklos announced as he crunched the gears and the bus lurched forward.

As they gained speed, a pickup appeared from the flank. It accelerated across in front of them and Bishop caught a glimpse of the man at the wheel; Salim. He fired a snap shot, striking the truck.

The pickup fishtailed in the sand narrowly missing Pavel

as he shoved open the gates. Miklos jumped on the brakes and Bishop pulled back to make room in the doorway.

As Pavel jumped on board Miklos got back on the gas, accelerating away from the compound.

Bishop watched the lights of Salim's pickup turn off the main road then grabbed Miklos's shoulder. "Get everyone to the boat. I'm going after him." He gripped his rifle and leaped from the cab, rolling in the dust. Ignoring his throbbing ankle he hobbled toward the ruined building where they had stashed their bikes.

"Bishop, what the hell are you doing?" Ice's voice came through over the radio.

"Making that murdering bastard pay," he replied.

He could see the lights of the pickup bouncing along the track that linked with the road to the airfield. Breaking into a jog he reached the ruins, grabbed his e-bike and leaped onboard. As he flicked the starter switch he heard a noise behind him. Turning, he saw Ice jump over a crumbling wall and grab the other bike. "You didn't think I'd let you go after that asshole by yourself did you?"

Chapter Thirty-One

AS BISHOP and Ice blasted through the desert on their powerful e-bikes, Miklos struggled to keep the lumbering bus above thirty miles an hour. The tired engine clanked and wheezed as he coaxed all the horsepower he could from it.

"Come on you piece of shit," snapped Pavel from a passenger seat.

"That's not helping."

"No? Do you want me to get out and push?"

Miklos ignored him as he downshifted in search of more power.

"Guys, those trucks are almost on top of you," Mitch's voice came through in his helmet. "I'm going to intercept with the Switchblade." He referred to a single shot drone armed with an explosive warhead.

"Do it," replied Miklos as he followed the navigation icons in the heads up display in his helmet. He was driving without headlights, relying on the thermal sensors and navigation prompts to get him back to the beached zodiac.

"ETA to target is three minutes," updated Mitch.

Glancing out the left-hand side Miklos spotted the headlights of the approaching convoy. They were less than a mile away and closing fast.

They bounced over the coastal road and hit the softer sand of the dunes. Sinking, Miklos revved the engine to maintain momentum. "Come on old girl, we're almost there."

He and Pavel both saw the flash of light that announced the detonation of the Switchblade, followed by the rumble of an explosion. The deadly drone had done its work, knocking out one of the technicals.

"I hope that slows them down," said Miklos as the bus ground to a halt in the soft sand, "because this old girl is done." He turned to Mirza and the girls. "OK, everyone out. We're on foot."

They assembled the girls and led them through the dunes and onto the wide beach. With dawn less than an hour away the sky had already started to lighten revealing the white caps of breaking waves.

Pavel pointed out their inflatable, less than four hundred yards down the beach. "That's it."

Headlights shone behind them flaring in Miklos's helmet; the technicals were bouncing through the dunes. "Shit, they're on us. Run, run, run!"

They sprinted through the soft sand toward the zodiac as the roar of engines grew louder.

Miklos turned, knelt and fired his Tavor at the lead truck.

Pavel ran past him before dropping and doing the same. "Covering!"

Rounds zipped past his head as he ran past his partner and then turned, repeating the process.

Muzzle flashes lit up from the technicals as their heavy machine guns returned fire. Sand sprayed around them as bullets lashed the beach. One of the girls let out a scream as a round clipped her and she tumbled.

Miklos sprinted to her but Mirza was already there, heaving her over his shoulders.

"Mitch, we're going to die on this beach!" screamed Pavel into the radio.

"Not on my watch," came through Kurtz's voice.

Four technicals were less than two hundred yards away when Miklos raised his Tavor and fired again. Through his thermal sensors a pulse like a laser hit his target followed by a boom. A split second later another pulse tore through the truck's cabin. He switched to firing full-auto adding his bullets to the maelstrom. Alongside him, Pavel did the same.

The successive booms from a high-powered rifle rolled over them as high-velocity rounds struck the trucks. Miklos's Tavor ran dry and he turned to the sea, spotting the source of the fire.

As the *Charlotte* cruised toward the beach a sniper rifle flashed from high on the fly bridge as Kurtz continued his engagement. Then the vessel turned with a roar of engines and the boom of the sniper rifle was replaced with the distinctive retort of a grenade launcher.

High explosives rained down on the pickups tearing the first two to shreds. The trucks behind them skidded sideways in the sand as they tried to escape.

In literally seconds the battle for the beach had turned in their favor. Miklos dropped to his knees in the sand, panting for breath as he yanked off his sweat filled helmet.

Pavel punched him in the shoulder. "That was close."

"Not like your shooting." Miklos laughed as they climbed to their feet.

"What are you talking about? I hit the driver of the first truck."

The two men made their way to the zodiac where Mirza and the girls were waiting.

"You didn't hit shit," said Miklos as he recovered the anchor.

"Who's injured?" asked Pavel as he and Mirza shoved the inflatable back into the waves.

"One of the girls will need a few stitches," said Mirza. "But they're all safe."

Miklos held the bow of the boat as Pavel started the engine. Then he clambered in as they backed away from the coast.

"Any news from Bishop and Ice?" asked Mirza as they cruised toward the *Charlotte*.

Pavel shook his head. "Negative, but you know what those guys are like. They've probably blown up the plane and killed half of the militia in Benghazi by now."

BISHOP GUNNED his e-bike and sent it scrambling out of a rocky riverbed up a steep sandy bank. Behind him Ice followed his line, his rear wheel rooster-tailing sand into the air.

"He's going for the airstrip!" he yelled as he reached the top of a lip and gathered his bearings.

They'd taken a short cut to try and catch Salim but had been slowed by rugged terrain.

"Guys, we've got the team on board: Pavel, Miklos, Mirza and five girls," Mitch's voice came through in his earpiece. "We're standing by to extract you on completion of your task."

"If we complete it," mumbled Bishop as he twisted the throttle and took off down the ridge. His eyes stung as sand and grit whipped past the NVG tubes. The grainy green image made it hard to judge depth and it still wasn't light enough for the naked eye.

He skidded the bike around rocks trying to maintain speed and catch the technical as it made a beeline for the airstrip. Sweat ran down his face despite the cool air, his hands clammy as he gripped the handlebars tightly.

A jagged outcrop appeared and he swerved to avoid it, hitting a larger rock. The bike soared into the air, landing with a thud a good ten yards past the launch point. Bishop clung to the bike as it careened down a shallow embankment.

Heart racing he throttled back and glanced over his shoulder. Ice caught up, riding beside him, a broad grin on his face. "Now you're showing off."

Looking forward to the direction of travel Bishop caught a glimpse of lights a scant mile ahead. He also heard the faint whine of turbines starting. "They're taking off."

Twisting the throttle he sent the bike blasting across the field. As they closed with the An-12 he glanced down and checked his speed. The bike blasted along at nearly sixty miles an hour.

Ahead of him the An-12 loomed. The hulking transporter crept forward, the ramp rising. He reached the dirt strip and raced past Salim's abandoned pickup as the roar of the transporter's engines increased. Stones and sand blasted him as he gave chase. Bursting through the backwash from the turboprops he made for the closing ramp. The plane slowly pulled away from him.

Screaming in frustration, he twisted the throttle. As he did a shape went blasting past.

Ice hit the ramp at top speed and was thrown inside as Bishop remembered the boost button. He thumbed it and the front wheel lifted as the bike sped off like a rocket. The ramp started lowering as he gained on the aircraft.

Once again the Antonov inched away; any second it would have enough speed to takeoff.

The ramp was half down when a body sailed over it and disappeared in the dust. Then, Ice's face appeared over the lip. He shot Bishop a reassuring grin as he tossed a webbing tie down toward him. The heavy hook danced in the slipstream almost catching him in the head.

Bishop raised his left hand from the bars and grabbed it. The aircraft's speed yanked him off the bike, dragging him through the air by his arm. Managing to grab the line with his other hand he held on as the aircraft gained speed and lifted off.

It was then that he noticed that the webbing strap wasn't attached to the ramp but wrapped around Ice's forearm. His other arm stretched out behind him, clutching one of the steel tie-down rings.

Bishop's life hung in the balance as the An-12 gained altitude and its slipstream buffeted his body. There was no way he could pull himself along the strap, it would slip through his gloved fingers. His only hope was that Ice could somehow haul him inside.

And that's exactly what he did. Inch by inch the ramp got closer as the big man pulled him toward it. Even when he reached the aluminum surface Bishop didn't dare let go of the hook. He waited till he was well up the ramp, outside of the clutches of the slipstream before he scrambled on all fours into the cargo hold.

Finding the controls for the ramp, he activated them

and turned to watch it close. As it did he noticed that Ice wasn't letting go of the eyelet.

"What's going on?" he yelled.

Ice managed a smirk. "I think I broke it."

Bishop inspected the mechanical hand. Ice had crushed the steel ring closed in his effort to hold on.

"Hang on a second." Bishop squeezed his way past the stacked ammunition and weapon boxes and located a tool bag under a webbing seat. Inside he found a wrench.

"This won't hurt a bit," he said as he used the handle as a lever to open the ring, releasing Ice's mechanical fingers.

Free, Ice held his hand up. Two fingers were bent at almost forty-five degrees. "Mitch isn't going to be impressed."

Bishop grinned, still jacked on adrenaline. "He'll get over it. He loves fixing shit. Now, let's find that dickhead, Salim."

LIBYAN AIRSPACE

Inside the cockpit of the An-12 the engineer tried for the third time to contact the loadmaster over the intercom. Unable to raise a response he unbuckled, climbed out of his chair and made his way toward the door to the cargo hold. As he did, it opened and he found himself staring down the barrel of a pistol.

"G'day champ," said the gunman, his voice barely audible over the drone of the ancient Antonov. A larger man stood behind him, square-jawed with an ice-cold gaze.

The engineer raised hands. "Please don't kill me," he said with a heavy accent.

"You do exactly as you're told and no one's going to get hurt," said Bishop.

The engineer nodded.

"Where is Salim?" asked Bishop.

The engineer pointed over his shoulder. "In the nose."

He pushed past the man, stood between the pilots and showed them his weapon. "Keep flying and no one dies."

The pilots glanced at each other and nodded. Bishop climbed down the short ladder into the glass nose of the aircraft. Salim was sitting below in the navigator's chair.

"Move and I'll blow your brains all over their cockpit," Bishop said as he shoved the barrel of the pistol against the arms trafficker's head.

Salim froze.

"Didn't expect to see me here, did you?"

"I can get you money, lots of money."

"I don't want money," snapped Bishop. "I want to know who your boss is and then I want vengeance."

"Vengeance? I've never done anything to hurt you."

"It's not for me," said Bishop. "It's for a friend, a friend who works for a certain intelligence organization." He tossed plasticuffs in his lap. "Put your hands in and pull them tight with your teeth."

Salim complied. Bishop holstered his pistol and checked the cuffs. Satisfied his prisoner was secure he returned to the cockpit. "Do you have a satellite phone?" he asked the crew.

"Yes, in the communications bay," the engineer said pointing to the workstation behind his.

Bishop limped across and sat. "I've got a call to make." He turned to Ice. "Can you see if there are any parachutes in the back?"

"You're not jumping on that ankle."

He grinned. "It's not for us."

ABU DHABI, UAE

Frank sat at his terminal in the Sandpit with his eyes glued to the battle-tracking map. The icon denoting the *Charlotte* hovered fifteen nautical miles off the Libyan coast awaiting a call from Bishop and Ice. However, their iPRIMALs hadn't checked in since they hit the airfield.

He stood and walked into the room opposite where the intelligence team worked. Flash, flat brim cap reversed on his head, headphones on, was hunched over his laptop.

Frank waved to get his attention. "Hey, can we get a fix on the aircraft from the runway? It's possible Bishop and Ice are onboard."

The hacker shook his head. "Sorry bud, there's no radar out there and smugglers don't run GPS transponders."

"iPRIMAL?"

"If they're onboard, the aircraft will be moving too fast for the satellite chipset."

"Right–" Frank was interrupted by a loud ringtone in his cordless headset. "Hang on, I've got to get this." He dashed back into the operations room and sat at his terminal. The call was from an unknown number.

"Hello, this is Lascar Logistics, you're speaking with Francis," Frank said as he answered the call.

"Francis, is that what you're using now?"

He recognized Bishop's voice.

"Where the hell are you guys?"

There was a pause. "Thirteen thousand feet and climbing. Look, I've got a couple of things I want you to do. Have you got a pen and paper?"

"Yeah, send."

"OK, first things first; I've got a package I want to deliver. Flash will know how to contact the recipient."

Two minutes later the call ended and Frank took the list of tasks downstairs to the living area where Vance and Chua were making coffee. "Bishop and Ice have hijacked the smuggler's plane and captured Salim."

A broad grin split Vance's features. "Best news I've heard all day. Did you release Mitch and his team?"

"Yes, they're making headway for Crete with the girls. Bishop has asked us to make some arrangements." He handed the piece of paper to Vance who read it and passed it to Chua. He waited for his offsider to read it. "What do you think?"

Chua nodded. "Looks reasonable to me."

Vance turned back to Frank. "You heard the man. Let's make it happen."

Chapter Thirty-Two

UBUD, INDONESIA

"SAME AS USUAL?" asked Wayan as Saneh entered the Yoga Monkey Juice Bar.

She shot him a vibrant smile. "Yes, thanks." Then she made her way to the computer in the corner, logged into her email account and read Bishop's message.

Her training, experience and intuition all kicked into overdrive as she deleted the message and logged off. Scanning the room her eyes fell on an attractive Eurasian working on a laptop. The woman locked eyes with Saneh then looked away.

Something about her put Saneh on edge. She rose from the computer, took her purse from her bag, fished out some money and left it on the bar.

"Miss Sarah, this is too much!" yelled Wayan as she stepped from the shack and started across the paddy fields.

"It's yours."

She broke into a trot making a beeline for town. She'd

stashed a grab bag in a massage parlor on the far side. When she reached the outskirts, she glanced back over her shoulder. Her fears were confirmed; the girl from the bar followed her. Ducking down a side alley she hid behind a stack of cardboard.

Her tail wore sneakers, which made it hard to hear her footsteps. Saneh coiled like a spring as she waited. Diving out from behind the boxes she aimed a blow at the woman's head.

The tail blocked and counter-punched, confirming she had training. Saneh ducked under her fist and unleashed a devastating sidekick that caught the girl in her midsection, knocking her backward. She lay immobilized on the ground gasping for air.

"Are you alone?" Saneh snarled.

The woman wiped spit from the corner of her mouth. Tires screeched at the end of the alley.

The door of a van slid open and two men leaped out. Saneh sprinted in the opposite direction. She slipped into a narrow walkway that led between vine and moss-coated buildings. Hurdling a stone wall she landed in a Hindu temple. A bald headed monk spotted her yoga pants and crop top and yelled out in indignation.

She clasped her hands and bobbed her head. "Sorry." Sprinting across the manicured lawns she ducked around a shrine and cleared another wall.

Tumbling a dozen feet through vines and bushes she slid down a muddy bank head first into an icy cold river. As she bobbed to the surface she spotted her pursuers on the bank above her. Swimming hard she made for the opposite bank.

Dragging herself clear of the water she slipped into the jungle and made for high ground. On the run she came up

PRIMAL Deception

with a new plan. She'd head to Bali's capital, Denpasar, where she had another grab bag with cash and a passport.

Crouching in the bushes at the side of the road she watched the traffic. Moments later a light blue cab appeared, and she stepped out flagging it down. The driver pulled over and she climbed into the back seat. "How much to take me to Denpasar?"

The cabbie glanced at her wet clothing. "Five hundred thousand."

She laughed. "I'll give you two fifty."

"OK."

They turned onto the main road and as they rounded a corner she spotted a police checkpoint ahead. "Go around it," she demanded.

The driver slowed. "I can't. It's the only way."

Saneh opened the door before they'd stopped moving and jumped clear.

"You there. STOP!" yelled a voice. "Get your hands up!"

She turned from the voice and sprinted along the sidewalk. As she ran something slapped into her thigh. Reaching for the wound her hand grasped a cold steel cylinder. She tugged the dart from her leg and suddenly felt light headed.

A blurry figure approached and she lurched onto the street, narrowly missing a passing motorbike. Strong arms grabbed her, tires screeched and she was thrown into a van. Her hands were bound as the dizziness and nausea became overwhelming. She felt the prick of a needle in her neck and then, as they bounced along a potholed road, she succumbed to a powerful sedative.

THE MEDITERRANEAN

Bishop finished inspecting the An-12's cargo before joining Ice at the communications station in the cockpit. "That's a shit load of ordnance. We're talking anti-tank missiles, mortar rounds, twenty-three mike mike's, dushkas and a couple hundred RPGs."

Ice stuffed a length of rope into a canvas bag. "Yeah, and none of it's going to make it into Syria."

"Hey, I've been thinking about that. We know some people that could put it to good use."

Ice raised an eyebrow as he clipped a makeshift pilot chute to the end of the rope. "Let's deal with Salim first."

Bishop gestured to the bag. "Is that going to work?"

The big man grinned. "I don't care if it doesn't."

"You're cold, man, Ice cold."

The Antonov's engineer tapped Bishop on the shoulder. Since he'd organized for the Turkish men to receive a sizeable amount of compensation their attitudes had changed considerably. "The pilot wanted me to tell you we're coming up on your drop zone."

"Excellent, what altitude are we at?"

"Twelve thousand feet."

Bishop gave him thumbs-up and turned back to Ice. "OK brother, we're on."

Ice gathered up the chute and bag.

The two PRIMAL operatives left the cockpit and climbed into the cargo hold. Skirting the boxes of ammunition they moved to the ramp. Bishop donned the communications headset reserved for the loadmaster. Ice bent over a body on the floor.

Salim stared at them with wide eyes, his hands and feet bound, mouth taped over. Ice had already fitted him with a

Russian parachute he'd found in the aircraft's emergency locker. He hooked the free end of his rope to the canopy release handle. Giving Salim a reassuring pat on the shoulder he hauled him to his feet. "We're ready."

"One minute," reported the pilot over the headset. Bishop activated the ramp controls; it lowered with a whine revealing a blue sky and thousands of feet below them, golden sands.

Ice tethered himself to the floor with a safety line and shoved Salim forward. A damp patch appeared on the front of the Syrian's pants. Bishop shook his head; Salim had pissed himself.

"On target," said the pilot.

Bishop grinned as he made a chopping motion with his hand.

Salim dropped to his knees as Ice gave him a shove with his boot. The man squirmed on the ramp in a futile attempt to stay in the aircraft. A sharp kick from Ice sent him sailing over the ramp, the line playing out.

Bishop threw a mock salute as Salim disappeared behind them followed by the pilot chute. "Have a nice vacation, fuck bag."

NAHAL LAVAN RESERVE, ISRAEL

Keila stood alongside the Toyota Prado and scanned the horizon through dark sunglasses. Her short hair danced in the wind, her jaw taut, determined.

One of the four-wheel drive's doors opened and Abel appeared. "Keila, we've been here for an hour. What exactly are we waiting for?" the lanky analyst asked.

"Redemption," she whispered as she checked her GPS again.

Another door opened and Fahim and Jacinta joined them followed by Dan, the only other uninjured member of her *Kidon* team.

"Are you going to tell us what this is all about?" asked Dan. The operative was technically on leave while the three analysts were supposed to be at work. All Keila had told them was she required them all to accompany her on the two hour drive to the desert.

She sighed. "I wanted to keep it a surprise." As she spoke the soft drone of an aircraft approached. "Where is that coming from?"

They scanned the sky in search of the plane.

Abel pointed to the west. "Over there."

In the distance an aircraft tracked across the cloudless sky. Keila followed it with hawk-like eyes. She was the first to spot the bundle dropping from the plane toward the desert floor. It fell hundreds of feet before a parachute bloomed, arresting its descent.

"Is that what we're here for?" asked Dan.

"Sure is. Everyone back in the truck."

She drove them across the dusty valley floor, toward the parachute. As they got closer they could see a figure dangling beneath it. The chute disappeared behind a rocky outcrop. Keila skidded the vehicle to a halt and leaped out. As she climbed the small hill she drew a Glock and clutched it in her hand. Dan was close behind, his pistol ready.

From the top of a boulder she spotted the collapsed chute beside an immobile body. As she clambered down the slope the wind inflated the parachute and dragged it a few yards.

Dan overtook her on the down slope. He ran to the

canopy, deflated it and rolled it into a ball. Keila made a beeline for the body.

It was a man, medium build with dark hair, a scraggly beard and a nasty lump over his right eye. Bound and gagged he was breathing but unconscious.

"Who is it?" asked Dan as he secured the chute under a rock.

"Salim."

"What!" His eyes shot skyward. "How the hell? Where did he come from?"

The others arrived and formed a semi-circle around the body.

"No way!" Fahim exclaimed. "You got him, you got Salim." He slapped her on the shoulder.

The figure on the ground gave a muffled moan, his eyes flickered open and focused on the barrel of Dan's pistol.

The *Kidon* operative knelt and ripped the tape off the man's mouth.

"Where am I?" he managed.

Keila smiled broadly. "Welcome to Israel, Salim. I trust you will have an enjoyable stay."

INDIAN OCEAN

A sharp pain in her forearm woke Saneh from her slumber. Her eyes flashed open and she found herself staring into a black hood. Another spasm of pain ran along her forearm and she grunted.

"She's awake," said a gravelly voice.

"Good, I'll dial the boss in," replied another. She

detected the faintest hint of an Israeli accent over the hum of jet engines.

She tried to move her arms and legs but they were firmly secured to the chair. Suddenly, the hood was torn from her head. She squinted in the bright light.

Once her eyes adjusted she determined that she sat in a Gulfstream business jet configured for VIP long haul. She'd heard rumors that Mossad had a number of these aircraft specifically for rendition.

Her chair looked to be specifically designed for detainee management. The restraints were permanent. To her side, a technician was loading vials of what had to be her blood into a cooler box.

To her front sat the man with the Israeli accent. "Afsaneh Ebadi; or should I call you the Mantis?" She recognized him from the van in Ubud. He had a square jaw with a cleft chin and slate gray eyes.

"My name is Sarah Carter and I'm an Australian citizen. Where am I and why have I been detained?"

The operative chuckled as he rose from his seat, walked around and crouched behind it. She could hear him opening the snaps on a case. Then he placed a tablet with a stand on the chair. He finished securing the device with the sash belt, activated it and turned back to Saneh. "I've got someone who wants to talk to you." He sat on the opposite side of the cabin and watched her intently.

She shot him a scowl and then turned her attention to the screen. It took a moment for the call to connect. A flashing red light told her the camera was active but the screen remained blank.

"Afsaneh Ebadi, you're supposed to be dead." The voice sounded robotic, transmitted through digitization software.

"Who is this?" she asked.

"Someone who's been looking for you… and now I've found you."

The screen blinked on and she found herself face-to-face with her former Mossad handler, Manfred Lisker.

Lisker stared at her from the high definition screen. "It's been a long time, Afsaneh."

"I finished my mission. You and I don't have business anymore."

He shook his head. "No, you were compromised and allegedly killed in the Ukraine."

"I stopped Qods Force from obtaining a chemical weapon of mass destruction. I did the job that you asked me to do."

"And you think that your obligation to us ended with that?"

She fell silent, her jaw clenched.

"You are personally responsible for the death of five Mossad officers. That's not a debt you ever repay."

"What do you want from me?"

His expression softened. "You're the last Tiberias operative remaining. The director has ordered your termination."

"Tiberias has been canceled?"

"Yes, my dear, times have changed. Mossad has changed."

"So what do you want?"

"You were one of my best agents. I want you back."

She glanced at the gray-eyed operative. He winked.

Focusing back on the screen she frowned. "What happens if I say no?"

"Then you'll exit that aircraft in the middle of the Indian Ocean. I've already told the director that you have been terminated." Lisker paused then looked directly through the screen at her. "I'll also personally see to it that

Tariq Ahmed, Aden Bishop and James Castle all end up on the kill list."

Saneh fought back her rage and managed a thin smile. "What choice do I have?"

Lisker smiled. "Excellent, Avi will manage the details. It's good to have you back on board." His face disappeared and the flashing red light blinked out.

She turned to Avi and wriggled her hands. "Is this how you treat your assets?"

He sighed, rose and undid her restraints. "Welcome back."

Reaching down, she massaged her calves. "Is there anything to eat?"

Avi sat back in his chair and nodded to the rear. "The galley's in the back. Help yourself."

She rose, rubbing at the needle marks on her forearm. "What's the blood for?"

"What?"

She gestured to the man who'd taken her blood. "The samples."

"Screening and biometric enrolment, I'll explain it later. There's a bag in the overhead locker above you. Inside are clothes, a new passport and ten thousand cash. You'll be leaving us in Mumbai so I've got," he checked his watch, "four hours to brief you."

She nodded, found the bag and took it into the galley where there was a bathroom. Removing jeans and a T-shirt from the bag she entered the bathroom and sat on the toilet. Cupping her head in her hands she sobbed quietly. She let the tears flow for half a minute before she dried her eyes and changed out of her sweaty clothing. Minutes later a different woman emerged from the bathroom. The lethal assassin who'd killed on behalf of both Iranian and Israeli intelligence was back.

"OK, first things first. Tell me how you found me?"

He smirked. "That information is on a need to know basis."

Her eyes narrowed. "If you want me to work with you then there's going to have to be an element of trust."

He considered the comment. "Your old employer, Tariq Ahmed."

"He gave me up?"

A nod confirmed the question.

"Why would he do that?"

Avi winked. "Because someone tried to kill him and I saved his life."

"Who?"

"Funny you should ask. It just so happens that the man responsible is your first target. His name is Sheikh Sayeed bin Khalifa Al-Hasher." He reached into his pocket and removed a memory stick. "Everything you need to know is on this."

She took the drive. "Target pack, surveillance reports, mission profiles?"

"Everything." He pulled a tablet from the pocket on the side of his chair and passed it to her. "Lots to study. But first I'm going to brief you into the program that replaced Tiberias. Quite a lot has changed since you left us."

JARJANAZ, SYRIA

The An-12's ramp lowered into the dust of the Jarjanaz airfield. It felt like yesterday that Bishop had been standing in the rear of the Priority Movements Airlift Hercules delivering aid to Salim. The ache in his ankle and the absence of the arms trafficker reminded him that it had been much longer.

He stumbled as he stepped off the ramp, gritting his teeth as pain shot up his leg.

"You OK?" asked Ice from behind him.

"Ankle's playing up."

"Yeah, I saw you popping pills on the flight."

"I'll get it checked out when we get back to Abu Dhabi."

They surveyed the barren airfield. There was no one in sight.

"So where's your man?" asked Ice.

Bishop sat on the end of the ramp. "He'll be here."

Ice took a seat alongside him. "I could crush a beer."

"Me too," said Bishop as he reached down and massaged his ankle.

"We've got visitors."

He spotted dust clouds on the horizon. Half a dozen technicals and a Russian-built truck drove onto the tarmac and circled the Antonov, their weapons facing outward.

Bishop rose as a group of armed men alighted and moved toward them. He recognized Mullah Masif among them. The elderly Syrian sported a smile a mile wide.

"My Angels," he declared, assaulting Ice with a mighty bear hug.

The PRIMAL operative grunted. "Good to see you again, Masif."

The FSA brigade commander turned to Bishop. "You are the robot man, yes?"

Bishop laughed as he extended his hand. "Yeah, I didn't get a chance to say hello last time."

Masif grasped his hand and pumped it with vigor as he

yelled over his shoulder. "This is the man who destroyed Mohammed's hospital!"

"Doesn't sound so great when you describe it like that."

The warlord's men raised their weapons in the air and cheered.

He waited for the cheering to abate and gestured inside the cargo hold of the aircraft. "Masif, we stumbled on this gear in Libya and wondered if you could put it to use."

The FSA commander peered inside.

"Go on, take a look."

Masif and two of his men moved inside as Bishop sat back on the ramp. The pain in his ankle was savage. Behind him he could hear the excited voices of the FSA soldiers.

A moment later Masif reappeared. "We will take it all. How much do you want?"

He shook his head. "No, you misunderstood. It's a gift. Courtesy of your friend, Salim."

Masif stepped off the ramp. "Salim is no friend of mine. Where is that dog?"

He grinned. "The Israelis have him, so I don't think you'll be seeing him anytime soon."

It took the warlord's men a little under fifteen minutes to unload eight tons of military-grade hardware. Then, with a final round of hugs, they drove off across the desert to continue their war of independence.

With their aircraft empty the Turkish aircrew was soon on their way. Bishop and Ice sat in the ruins of the airstrip's former service center, watching as the An-12 launched off the runway in a cloud of black smoke.

"How come Mitch and the team get a Mediterranean cruise and we get more sand and camel dung?" asked Ice as they waited.

"The luck of the draw."

As the Antonov climbed away he spotted a speck on the horizon. It grew and soon he could make out their Hercules.

"We clear for landing, boys?" asked Mike over the radio.

"All clear, bud."

The transporter banked, lined up for the approach then touched down with a screech.

Bishop grunted as he climbed to his feet.

Ice grabbed him around the waist. "You've been in the wars, old man," he said as they limped toward the transporter.

"I think I need a few robot parts like you."

Ice raised his mangled hand. "We both need some time in the shop."

The aircraft stopped opposite them, engines idling, side door open. The two men climbed inside and Ice slammed the door shut.

Bishop turned to his partner as he hobbled toward the cockpit. "You keen for some time off after this? I'm thinking somewhere cold."

Ice nodded. "The further from the Middle East the better. How about New Zealand; you ever been to Queenstown?"

TYMPANI, CRETE

Kurtz parked the hired van across the road from the police headquarters in Tympani, Crete. Saying his farewells to the rescued girls, minus Eshita, he crossed the street and climbed into a silver Peugeot parked at the curb. "Did you make the call?" he asked Mitch who sat in the driver's seat.

"Yes, shouldn't take long."

He watched in the wing mirror and sure enough two policemen appeared from the station and made a beeline for the van. When they reached it, Mitch started the engine and pulled onto the street.

The PRIMAL team had made landfall in Crete only a few hours earlier. They'd been met by two Lascar employees who'd hired cars, booked a villa and made all the travel arrangements they needed. Their equipment was now on the bottom the Mediterranean, the *Charlotte* sanitized and moored at a public wharf for the police to find.

"So what happens now?" asked Kurtz as they drove into the mountains.

"Job's done, mate. You and the boys go back to living your lives," answered Mitch.

"And you?"

"I've got some loose ends to tie up in the UK. Then I'm heading back to Abu Dhabi."

Kurtz frowned. "Do you think PRIMAL will ever go back to the way it was?"

"With the island and the whole team?" He referred to the organization's former base in the South West Pacific.

"Yes."

"No. Those days are over."

Kurtz nodded. "I was afraid of that."

They drove in silence until they reached the driveway for the villa. A taxi was driving out the gate and Mitch paused to let it exit.

"Are we expecting guests?" asked Kurtz.

Mitch nodded. "A special one."

The five-bedroom stone mansion perched on a dusty hilltop surrounded by olive trees. Beautifully renovated it had a swimming pool, modern amenities and views that stretched for miles.

Miklos greeted them in the foyer. The Czech had only been in the villa for a few hours and he'd already taken to wearing only floral board shorts. "Boys, how did it go?" he asked, beer in hand.

"The girls are safe with the authorities," replied Mitch as they entered the living area. He smiled as he spotted Sonia Jayaram sitting on the couch beside a battered and bruised Mirza. Pavel sat opposite.

Sonia got up and flashed him a vibrant smile. "Mitch, you did it. You found her, you found Eshita."

He bobbed his head. "No, Mirza found her. Then the team got her out."

She hugged him. "I can't thank you enough."

"Have you seen her?" he asked.

"Yes, she's upstairs resting. Tomorrow we'll fly back to England together, back to her father." There were tears in her eyes.

Mirza spoke from the couch, "Mitch and I will be coming with you. We need to finish some business."

She sat beside him. "What business?"

"A few loose ends, nothing serious."

Mitch saw the way she looked at Mirza and gestured for Pavel, Miklos and Kurtz to join him in the kitchen. "Let's leave those two to get reacquainted." He took a cold beer from the refrigerator and tossed it to Kurtz. Popping another he raised it in the air. "To the team."

The men echoed his toast.

"Right, so you're probably wondering what's happening next?"

Miklos shrugged. "I figured the job's done. We go home. That is, unless there is more work for us."

Mitch shook his head. "No, that's it for the time being.

The Sandpit's already wired payment to your accounts." He took a sip from his beer. "It's been great working with you lads. I look forward to the next one."

Kurtz sighed. "If there is a next one."

Pavel chuckled. "What's wrong my lanky German friend? Are you bored already?"

Kurtz glared at him. "You try living with my parents."

"Try living with Miklos."

Laughter filled the kitchen and the men drank.

"Seriously, if you're bored reach out to Kruger," Mitch said. "He's got a lot of work going in the anti-poaching business."

Kurtz sipped at his beer. "That sounds interesting. I might do that."

"Well, if we're flying out tomorrow I'm going to make the most of the swimming pool," announced Miklos.

"We can't go back in the living room so I may as well join you," said Kurtz.

"Let's fill a cooler with beers," added Mitch.

As the team relaxed outside in the sun, Mirza and Sonia sat on either end of the couch.

She leaned across to examine the stitches that Kurtz had put in his brow. "That looks like it hurts."

He shook his head. "It's fine. Occupational hazard."

"Mirza, I'm so sorry. I didn't know you would get hurt."

He shuffled across and took her hand. "I'm fine. Bruises, nothing that won't heal. What matters is that we got Eshita back."

"We? It was you and Mitch, you're amazing."

He dropped his eyes. "It was your persistence and compassion that brought us together. Not to mention you got me out of jail."

She reached across, lifted his chin and looked him in the

eye. "You're brave, humble and utterly desirable." Leaning in she kissed him softly on the lips.

It took Mirza a moment to respond. When he did it was to passionately embrace the woman he'd loved since he'd saved her life in New Delhi.

They kissed for a full minute before she pulled away. "You know I love you. I've loved you since Delhi."

He blushed. "Me too."

"So what are you going to do about it?"

His brow furrowed. "I'm not sure what you mean?"

"This isn't India, Mirza. We're not constrained by caste, religion or money. We're two people with similar interests who love each other."

"I know." He locked eyes with her and smiled. "When we get back to London can I take you on a date?"

It was her turn to smile. "I'd like that. I'd like that a lot."

Chapter Thirty-Three

ABU DHABI, UAE

THREE BEERS and a handful of painkillers had taken the edge off Bishop's throbbing ankle. He limped down the Hercules' ramp and out onto the tarmac toward the PRIMAL hangar.

"You need a hand?" asked Ice as he caught up.

Bishop laughed. "I thought it was broken?"

As they entered through the security door Bishop spotted a pair of SUVs parked inside next to the shipping containers and transportable buildings that were PRIMAL's temporary home. They made their way to the planning room where Vance and Chua were waiting.

"Looking a little rough around the edges boys," Vance said.

Bishop lowered himself into a chair. "You should see the other guy."

"We won't keep you for long, just wanted to congratulate you on a job well done. Mitch and the team are safe in

Crete and the girls have been handed over to local authorities."

"And Mossad?"

Chua answered, "We've heard nothing. I'm hoping that your special delivery has bought us a little grace, at least as far as Keila and her team are concerned."

"Do you think Saneh is safe?" Bishop made a mental note to check his emails.

"I know she's safe," said Chua.

He sat up. "She's been in touch?"

"You could say that." Vance nodded toward the room's windows.

Bishop's heart raced when he spotted the figure standing outside, a silhouette that was etched in his mind and engraved on his heart. Stumbling to his feet he limped to the door and pushed it open. Tears filled his eyes as he hobbled slowly toward Saneh.

"Hello, soldier," she said in a soft voice.

"Saneh," he managed hoarsely.

"Yeah, that's what they call me."

He swallowed. "I was worried."

"I know." She took a step toward him.

Bishop suddenly became very aware of his miserable state. His T-shirt was sweat-stained, his face covered in grime and he had tape lashed around his boot.

"You've been in the wars again."

He shrugged. "You know me."

She reached out and brushed something from the side of his face. "Yeah, I do."

He wrapped his arms around her and buried his face in her hair. The smell of her triggered emotions that he had suppressed since she left. He never, ever wanted to let her go again. "I love you," he murmured.

She broke away from him. "I love you too, Aden, but things aren't the same. You've got to give me space and time."

He nodded. "Yeah, I get it."

She glanced down at his feet and spotted the makeshift strapping on his boot. "What have you done to yourself?"

"I twisted my ankle," he said sheepishly.

She sighed. "I guess I should be grateful you survived without me."

Back in the briefing room Ice, Vance and Chua turned away from the reacquainting lovers.

"I'm so glad she's back. I couldn't deal with any more of his moping," said Ice as he took a beer from the fridge. "So boss, what's next?"

Vance shrugged. "We're cease-ops until Tariq decides to share the identity of Salim's benefactor."

Ice returned to his chair. "You think he knows who it is?"

Vance shot Chua a glance.

"We believe that it's someone with significant influence. Tariq's balancing justice against the need to protect his empire."

Ice took a long pull from the beer. "You think he's afraid?"

Vance and Chua looked at each other and nodded.

"Shit, that's not good."

"No, but until he lets us in there's nothing we can do," said Vance.

"What's the go with team Mitch?"

"He and Mirza are flying back to London to put a few things to bed. Kurtz, Pavel and Miklos are back on stand down."

Ice finished his beer and went to crush it with his mechanical hand. Remembering it was damaged he reverted to his organic hand and still crushed it with ease. "What about us?" He nodded toward Bishop and Saneh.

"Those two are going to want some down time together. You're more than welcome to help us out in the Sandpit. It'd be nice to have a gym buddy who's not into that pansy ass CrossFit shit."

Chua scowled and Ice laughed. "Sounds good, boss. Sounds good."

LONDON, ENGLAND

Mirza watched from a café at Heathrow airport as Sonia and Eshita emerged from the arrivals gate. He and Mitch had gone ahead to make sure that none of Imam Rahman's people were tailing the Pakistani teenager's father.

Padak Mozaz had been easy to spot. He stood at the gate frantically scanning the crowd for his daughter. Mirza couldn't even begin to imagine the torture the man had been through. The thought of it made him furious and he imagined beating Imam Rahman's face to a bloody pulp.

Mitch returned from the counter with two takeaway coffees. "Mirza, look." He nodded toward the gate.

Sonia and Eshita had arrived. They paused, the teenager searching the crowd. Mirza's heart lurched as she finally spotted her father. She ran through the bystanders, arms outstretched. The joy on the face of Padak Mozaz was all the reward Mirza needed. At that moment the fear, the pain and uncertainty of his undercover mission were swept away.

He locked gazes with Sonia. The lawyer's eyes were

filled with tears but she wore a broad smile. "Thank you," she mouthed.

"I'm tearing up," mumbled Mitch.

Mirza turned to the Brit, his own eyes shining with emotion. "We did a good thing, my friend."

Mitch grasped his shoulder. "We did, but it's not over till that prick Rahman sings." He handed Mirza his coffee. "Come on, let's get going."

Mirza rose and gave Padak and his daughter one last glance. Sonia was with them now and Padak held his daughter tight. She shot him a smile and he thought his heart would stop beating.

"Come on, lover boy. There's work to be done."

Mirza followed him from the airport to the cab rank. Moments later they were in a taxi, leaving the terminal.

"Where too, champ?" the cabbie asked in a thick Geordie accent.

"Birmingham," said Mitch.

ABU DHABI, UAE

Tariq stood gazing at the Arabian Gulf through the floor-to-ceiling windows of his office. He hadn't left the safety of his fortress since returning from the ordeal in Bahrain. Not for fear of his own safety but because if Sheik Al-Hasher managed to kill him nothing would stand between PRIMAL and Mossad. The last thing he wanted was for his father's legacy to become a puppet of the Israeli Intelligence apparatus.

Guilt assailed him; he had already betrayed one of his friends. He knew that Mossad would find and neutralize

Saneh; she had been an Iranian assassin long before joining PRIMAL. Everyone paid for their sins, eventually.

The telephone behind him buzzed. "Sir, you've got a call on line one from Sheik Al-Hasher," said his assistant.

"Put it through." He walked over and picked up the cordless phone from its cradle.

"Tariq, it's good to hear your voice," the Sheik said icily. "When you left early from my function in Bahrain I was afraid something might have happened to you."

"I had some car trouble. Nothing I wasn't able to handle. Please thank your people for the offer of assistance, though."

There was a pause at the other end of the phone. "I'm going to destroy you, Jew-lover. You can hide in that tower of yours but I'm going to tear it down around you. First, I'm going to destroy your reputation and then I'm going to tear your empire apart, piece-by-piece. You picked the wrong enemy."

Before Tariq could respond the Sheik terminated the call. His blood boiled as he stood clutching the phone in his hand. It took every inch of his discipline not to call Vance and unleash PRIMAL on the arrogant Prince. The thought of Bishop and Ice kicking in his door brought a smile to his face. But that wasn't the solution to this problem. He needed to keep PRIMAL away from both Al-Hasher and Mossad and find a solution without them. He also needed to leave the tower and show Al-Hasher that he was not intimidated by his threats.

Activating the intercom he waited for his assistant to pick up. "Emily, can you find out when Al-Hasher is next racing at Yas Marina?"

"Yes sir, if you give me a few seconds I'll check his Facebook page."

Facebook? He shook his head; what sort of fundamentalist used social media?

"Sir, according to his page he's racing tomorrow."

"Excellent, is our corporate booth available?"

"Yes, sir. Would you like me to make arrangements for catering? Will you be taking any guests?"

"No, arrange for my security detail to meet me here at eleven hundred."

"Excellent, sir."

He ended the call and slumped into his chair. His last security detail had been brutally murdered by Al-Hasher's cronies. Both men had been friends, comrades from his time in Special Tasks Branch. He walked across to a wall and placed his hand on a panel. It hummed, clicked and the panel slid aside revealing a safe. Inside was an assortment of firearms. He took out a Glock 26, inserted a magazine and slid the compact pistol into his pocket. This time he wasn't taking any chances.

Chapter Thirty-Four

ABU DHABI, UAE

SANEH FELT Bishop's arms around her waist as she finished steaming the milk and poured it over each of their double-shot espressos.

"Did you sleep OK?" he asked as he nuzzled her neck.

They had spent the night in his apartment but Saneh didn't have the heart to tell him she'd barely slept. Hence the double shot latte. She had lain awake next to a man she loved dearly, unable to tell him her darkest secret.

"Not too bad." She turned and kissed him. The touch of his hands and lips felt like home and for a moment she forgot about Mossad and lost herself in him.

"What do you want to do today?" he asked when they parted.

She glanced down at the cast on his injured ankle. "You need to rest. I'm going to head over to my apartment and sort a few things out."

He wore an expression like a whipped puppy.

She kissed him again. "When I get back I thought we could order in and watch cheesy action movies all afternoon."

"You know how to push my buttons."

They finished their coffees before Saneh left him propped up on the couch cuddling Daisy, the border collie. Bishop had purchased the explosive-detection dog for PRIMAL but she suspected that it was actually for her.

She caught a cab across town to the gated resort where she rented a villa. The place was exactly how she left it. She found her motorcycle leathers in a wardrobe and slid them over her athletic frame. They fit snug over muscles toned by hours of yoga.

Her Ducati Panigale R rumbled to life with a twist of the key, its throaty exhaust note reverberating off the walls of the garage. She'd purchased the superbike a week before discovering she was pregnant. It had sat here ever since. Her eyes misted as she dropped her visor. That was a lifetime ago.

Minutes later she blasted along the highway toward the Yas Marina Circuit, V-twin engine howling at high-revs. Presenting a member's pass at the track entrance she parked the bike next to a row of supercars alongside the pit lane. Removing her helmet she tossed her long brown hair in full view of the crews working on the cars.

Unzipping her leathers to reveal a hint of cleavage she strode along the line of vehicles, stopping to inspect those that caught her eye. A silver Porsche 918 Spyder sat in prime position at the end of pit lane. The mid-engine hypercar's liquid metal paint shone in the sun.

"What a beautiful car," she said to the technician who was crouched beside one of the rear wheels.

He glanced at her and his eyebrows rose. "Yes, it is. A

lot of people believe it is the best car Porsche has ever built."

She pouted. "How fast does it go?"

He rose, wiping his hands on a rag. "Quarter mile in nine-point-eight seconds."

She gave a whistle. "That's faster than my bike."

"Oh really, and what do you ride?"

"A Ducati Panigale R."

It was his turn to look impressed. "That's a lot of power for a little lady."

She smiled. "I can handle it." Striding around the car in her heeled boots she stopped at the driver's door. "Can I sit inside?"

He glanced around. "I don't think my boss would like that."

"Oh please." She squeezed her shoulders back causing her breasts to strain against the leather.

He let out a sigh. "OK, but only for a second."

She slid her slender legs into the cockpit, relaxed in the bucket seat and placed her hands on the steering wheel. The car fit her like a glove.

The mechanic smiled. "Looks good on you."

"Most things do." She winked. "How many gears does it have?"

He gestured to the paddles either side of the wheel. "It's a seven speed automatic. But that's not what makes it unique. Along with the V8 it's got two electric motors that generate an additional two hundred and eighty horses."

As he spoke she reached down into her boot and slipped out a device the size of a packet of mints. Feeling under the dashboard she found the car's OBD-II port and clipped in the drive.

"Right, little lady. I need to get this beast track-ready. You're going to have to get out."

Saneh needed to give the device at least twenty seconds to do its work. "Where is the stereo?"

He laughed. "This is a high-performance vehicle. It's got a soundtrack of its own."

She clapped her hands. "Let's start it."

He swallowed, shaking his head.

She fluttered her eyelids. "Please."

"OK, fine." He reached across and checked the car was in neutral. Then he pressed the start button.

Behind the seat, the engine burbled to life and Saneh let out a sensual moan. "It sounds so good." She gave the accelerator a tentative poke and the engine growled louder. "It's almost sexual."

He rolled his eyes and killed the ignition.

Saneh slipped the electronic device back into her boot and climbed out of the cockpit. Leaning close she gave the mechanic a kiss on the cheek. "Thanks." Then she strode back toward her bike.

"Wait. Can I have your number?"

"Sure, 1299," she said quoting the capacity of the Ducati's engine.

He shook his head as he watched her don her helmet and turn over the superbike. She waved and gunned the throttle, racing toward the access gate.

"God damn," he murmured as she disappeared.

BIRMINGHAM, ENGLAND

Imam Rahman stood at the front of the room with a Koran clutched in his hand. Before him a congregation of young men and women knelt on the floor, hanging on his every word.

His eyes were wide and spit flew from his mouth as he ranted. "The *kafir* oppress us and they deny us the right to live our lives the way the Koran decrees. They deny us Sharia law, and they deny us our basic human rights. It is for this reason that we must fight back. Brave lions fight them in the Levant but we must also fight them here." Pausing he sipped from a glass of water. "You all remember Saifan." He spoke softer now. "He and his brother, Mubarez, fought back. They fought here on the streets and now Mubarez fights in Syria. Do not let them fight alone." He folded his hands and dipped his head. "Now let us pray."

Once his sermon was complete the Imam moved to the steps outside the mosque to thank his congregation as they departed. Alongside him his bodyguard held a donation bowl.

A bearded young man hugged the cleric. "You have inspired me, Imam. I want to do more."

Rahman smiled as he gripped the youth's hands in his own. "Excellent, come to the study group tomorrow night. We can talk then."

The youth took coins from his pocket and dropped them into the bowl. Then another, equally keen to support the cause, replaced him. The process continued as everyone made their way outside.

Rahman stood diligently in the afternoon sun thanking each and every member as they left. As the minutes ticked by the amount of money in the bowl grew.

Neither he nor his bodyguard noticed the tiny insect-like drone as it flew toward him. With a flight time limited to mere minutes it had limited utility for surveillance. Originally designed to stick to a target and track it, this particular model had been modified.

He registered a faint buzz before the insect darted into his neck. Feeling a sharp sting Rahman slapped his skin. The blow mortally wounded the tiny aircraft and it fell into the garden bed in front of the mosque.

"Imam, are you OK?" his bodyguard asked.

Rahman rubbed his neck. "Yes, it was just a bug." Farewelling the last of the worshipers he moved back inside the mosque.

"A sizeable donation today," said the bodyguard as he joined Rahman in the main hall of the mosque.

"The Caliphate doesn't need money. It needs fighters," he said. "Every day the Americans and the Russians kill more of our brothers." He suddenly felt dizzy and braced himself against the wall.

"Are you sure you are OK, Imam?"

His face felt flushed and clammy. "I need a drink of water." As he took a step forward he lost control of his legs and slumped to the ground. He felt his heart race and his body convulse. Then he screamed in agony as every nerve in his body fired simultaneously. Froth spat from his mouth and he spasmed on the floor for a full thirty seconds before his heart literally exploded in his chest.

His bodyguard bellowed and others came running. An ambulance was called but it came too late; Imam Rahman died an agonizing death.

Mirza watched from the opposite side of the street as

the paramedics loaded the body into an ambulance. Then he turned and walked until he came to a cab parked at the curb. Climbing in he took a seat alongside Mitch.

"Everything alright then?" Mitch asked. "I saw an ambulance. I hope it wasn't for your mother," he said for the benefit of the taxi driver.

Mirza shook his head. "No, she's fine. Someone at the mosque had a heart attack."

The cabbie glanced at them in the mirror. "Where to now, lads?"

"London," said Mitch. "The Ritz."

He glanced at Mirza's battered face in the mirror. "You sure? That's a swanky hotel."

Mitch leaned forward and passed him a fifty pound bill. "Yeah, I've heard the cocktail lounge is first class. And this guy has a hot date with a lawyer."

ABU DHABI, UAE

Sheik Al-Hasher strode through pit lane dressed in a fire-retardant suit with a helmet under his arm. Racing was the only time he didn't wear traditional robes. He walked across to where his Porsche 918 waited, idling with a low rumble. His mechanic climbed from the car and removed a seat cover.

"She's running pretty sweet, boss. The tires are warm but you might want to take it easy on the first lap."

Al-Hasher scowled at the man. "I will assess the conditions myself. He slid into the cockpit and wiggled into the seat. As he adjusted his racing harness he thought he smelled perfume. Then a waft of gasoline overpowered the scent and he donned his helmet.

Clenching his hands on the steering wheel he checked the settings were in race mode and readied himself for the coming exhilaration. Then he flicked the car in gear and drove it smoothly into pit lane.

The car felt like a wild animal straining to break free from a leash. Accelerating out of the pits he eased on the throttle, grinning as the g-forces shoved him back in the seat. As he approached the first corner he braked heavily, enjoying the rapid deceleration. Reaching the next bend he stomped on the throttle and rocketed around the apex.

He knew every twist and turn of the Yas Marina Circuit and worked the car through his first lap in a respectable time of two minutes fifteen seconds. Pulling into pit lane he slowed to a halt alongside his mechanic.

"The brakes are pulling slightly to the left," he snapped through the window. The man made to respond but he accelerated away. As he cruised down pit lane he spotted a Lascar Logistics banner painted on one of the crash barriers. His lip turned up in a scowl. He was going to enjoy destroying the *kafir*-loving Tariq and his rancid empire.

As he exited he channeled his anger into his driving; this would be his fastest lap ever. He turned onto the main straight and felt the car oversteer ever so slightly. The stability system corrected sending the Porsche blasting down the straight.

The V8 howled at 8,000 rpm with the digital speedometer touching one hundred and eighty miles an hour before he backed off the throttle. Panic assailed him as he realized the car continued to accelerate. He stomped on the brake pedal but nothing happened.

The 918 Spyder reached two hundred miles an hour a

millisecond before it hit the edge of the track, bounced and slammed into the crash barrier. At that speed the car detonated into a fireball as it crumpled into the concrete wall.

Tariq Ahmed saw the explosion as he stood watching from his corporate box. For a split second he felt sorry for the Sheik and then elation replaced any grief. With one lapse in judgment Sheikh Sayeed bin Khalifa Al-Hasher had removed his threat to Tariq, PRIMAL and his Lascar Logistics empire. Now he just needed to work out how he was going to keep the Israeli intelligence services at bay.

AL-BAB, SYRIA

The mortar bombs fell like rain around Mohammed 'Al-Bab' Yassin's position. Shrapnel sliced through the air decimating his fighters and destroying their vehicles. He hunkered down behind the smoldering wreck of his armored Humvee and snarled into his radio, "Bring more reinforcements. We have to hold this position."

The response was curt. "We don't have any more men. You need to fall back or you will be overrun."

He screamed in frustration, smashing the radio against the Humvee. Usually his brigade overwhelmed with superior firepower but this time the FSA had annihilated his forces. It was all Salim's fault, he fumed, the weaselly arms trafficker had failed to resupply him following the debacle with the Jewish spies.

The rattle of tank tracks caught his attention and he scooted across to the wall of the compound his men were defending. His last operational T-55 had pushed up to provide them with fire support.

"Al-Bab!" one of his men yelled. "The tank is going to cover us as we fall back."

The compound they occupied was an isolated outpost surrounded by open ground. It was the final defensive position stopping the FSA from advancing on his hometown and cutting off the ISIS supply lines to Aleppo.

Another mortar round exploded close by showering Mohammed in dust. Bullets smacked into the compound and cracked overhead. His half a dozen remaining men fired back with assault rifles and RPGs.

"Al-Bab, we're nearly out of ammunition. We need to go now." The man wore a terrified expression. He knew that if his commander ordered him to stay then he would most likely die here.

Mohammed gritted his teeth. "Get the men ready. We will withdraw and reestablish our defenses in the town." Gripping his AK he sprinted to the side of the compound where the tank waited. The remaining fighters of what had been a fifty-man company joined him. When they were ready one of the men radioed the commander of the tank and it reversed slowly away from the shattered building.

Bullets and shrapnel clanged off the armored vehicle as his men used it as cover. The rate of fire slowed as they put their former outpost between them and the advancing FSA. When they were three hundred yards clear the tank stopped.

"Al-Bab, the commander says we should ride on top now," said the fighter with the radio. "It will be faster."

Mohammed nodded and climbed onboard with the others. The tank shuddered, its engine roared and then it took off across the fields toward the outskirts of the town. It hadn't made it more than another hundred yards when a powerful explosion tossed Mohammed through the air. The last thing he saw before he passed out was the tank burning fiercely.

When he came-to his situation had changed considerably. His hands were tied behind his back and a fierce looking soldier sat watching him with an AK-47 across his knees. "He's awake," the guard yelled.

Strong hands pulled him to his knees, sending jolts of pain through his shoulder. His chin was lifted roughly and he found himself staring into the face of a man who should have been dead.

Mullah Masif, the leader of the Wolf Brigade, wore a stern expression. "It seems the tables have turned."

"Fuck you," spat Mohammed. "I should have killed you myself."

"That's probably true but now I'm going to kill you." Masif took a pistol from the holster on his hip and aimed it at the ISIS commander. "Rot in hell, Daesh pig."

The bullet punched a neat hole in Mohammed's forehead and sprayed his brains across the ground. His body remained upright for a second before falling facedown in the field.

"What do you want done with the body?" asked one of Masif's men.

"Leave it. The dogs can eat that piece of shit."

Epilogue

NEGEV DESERT, ISRAEL

MANFRED LISKER SAT in the back of an SUV as it raced along a highway through the Negev desert. He flicked through a report on Sakkin Industries, a company established by an ex-Mossad colleague a decade earlier.

According to their website Sakkin Industries specialized in genetic research with an emphasis on the early detection and cure of defects in unborn children. That was what they told the public. The reality of what went on inside their razor wire protected research facility was a little more ominous.

Lisker glanced up from the report and saw that he'd passed the Negev Nuclear Research Center. He slipped the document into his attaché case and fastened the clasp as his driver turned off the main highway and stopped at a security checkpoint. A uniformed guard inspected their passes and the underside of the vehicle and they were permitted to enter.

The facility was at the end of a long drive. Nestled between two hills the building looked small but, as Lisker knew, most of Sakkin's workshops and laboratories were hidden deep beneath the yellow and red sands of the Negev desert.

The head of the Proteus Project, Dr. Marnisha Copeland, met him at the reception area. Tall, with auburn hair that she wore high in a bun, Lisker thought that Copeland looked like she would be more at home in an ancient forest than a sterile lab. Her delicate features had an almost elfin presence, like something from the pages of a Tolkien novel.

"Did you get the additional samples?" he asked as they descended in an elevator.

She nodded. "Yes, I had the DNA extracted and added to the library."

"Good, the donor is one of the most effective and lethal operatives we've ever had. Although, a little unpredictable."

Copeland took a tablet from her pocket and made a note. "I've read her file. Unpredictability is an indicator of intelligence."

The elevator halted and the doors opened with a hiss. Copland swiped them through a security door and into a long corridor marked **OBSERVATION**. On either side large windows let them view the workings of a state-of-the-art laboratory.

"So, explain to me what exactly you have been spending my money on," he said as they paused in front of a window. Inside white-coated scientists were working with blood and tissue samples.

"We've managed to separate the DNA strands and identify the genes' encoding for the attributes we want. This has allowed us to construct a new super strand and, in turn, a fertilized egg."

"Are you still limited to surrogate mothers?"

Copland nodded. "Yes, the artificial birthing project has not advanced as quickly as we would have hoped."

They walked to another window. It revealed a room filled with pens; inside each was a dog and a litter of puppies. The animals were all Belgian Malinois, a breed used extensively as military working dogs throughout the Israel Defense Force.

"They're clones?"

"Yes, but not from a parent source. They've been constructed from the best attributes sampled from over a hundred dogs."

The puppies looked healthy as they frolicked inside the pens. "What happens to the surrogate mothers?"

"After they have birthed and the pups have been weaned they return to active duty or are homed with families. You will be happy to know that our first litters have reached the end of their training."

"And the reports?"

"Excellent. All six dogs topped their class and have displayed all of the required attributes. In particular, their anxiety levels in a combat environment are remarkably low."

Lisker drummed his fingers on the window. "Good. Now, as much as I am thrilled that you are providing super dogs for the IDF, Mossad is not in the puppy breeding business. When do you anticipate commencing human trials?"

She glanced down at her tablet. "We have a surrogate mother identified and the DNA sequencing is complete. I anticipate we will be able to seed her within the next eight months."

"And the other aspects of the program?"

"We have made significant advancements with regards to identifying the process to control aging of the subjects. However, it could be decades before we're able to employ it effectively."

Lisker nodded. "We live in an age of instant gratification, Dr. Copeland. But you and I both know that Israel did not rise from the desert overnight. In time this project will reach fruition and when it does Israel will have the operatives it needs to keep it safe from any evil."

MOGADISHU, SOMALIA

The battered Nissan Patrol rattled its way from Mogadishu airport with a tall, square-jawed man at the wheel. Kruger, a former South African Recce operator, was currently on hiatus from PRIMAL. With the directors calling 'cease ops' he'd returned to Africa where he'd been working with an anti-poaching outfit based in Zambia. However, it wasn't protection of black rhinos that brought him to one of Africa's deadliest cities.

Barely three months earlier Kruger and Bishop had gone head to head with a poaching gang responsible for almost killing Saneh, causing the loss of her and Bishop's unborn child. It was Kruger's initiative that had saved Bishop from certain death, that and the help of one of Somalia's most notorious pirate kings, Al-Mumit.

As Kruger passed through an African Union checkpoint on the outskirts of Mogadishu he saw the smoldering remains of an armored car. Further down the road the shattered hulks of Al-Shabaab technicals had been shoved from the road. Spurred on by the success of their ISIS brethren the African Islamists had recently launched an offensive on the capital. They'd been defeated but not without taking a horrible toll on the local population.

In an industrial area of mostly abandoned and battle-scarred buildings he turned down a side street and approached a high-walled compound. As he drove closer he could see that the sandbagged fighting positions had been shot-up and the heavy-steel doors pockmarked by bullets. Al-Mumit's lair had not gone unscathed.

Identifying himself at the entrance he waited for the doors to swing open then parked his four-wheel drive next to a line of battered technicals. The last time he had visited the Pirate King the compound had been a hive of activity. Now the single-story cinder block building in the center of the compound looked abandoned, its doorway and windows dark and forbidding like the eyes and mouth of a skull.

Inside it wasn't any more inviting. His boot steps echoed as he made his way through the rabbit warren of rooms to the corridor that led to Al-Mumit's command center. The guard at the door held his AK with the casual confidence of a battle-weary veteran. He wore full combat rig including a helmet and body armor loaded with magazines.

"He's in here," the man grunted, pushing open the door.

The Pirate King's throne room was as empty as the rest of the compound. Gone were the scantily clad women who'd lounged on silver cushions before the throne. Gone were the throngs of hangers-on waiting for scraps. The only people who remained were two teenage boys perched behind modern computers. The youths didn't acknowledge his presence, continuing to stare at the screens as they gathered the intelligence required for piracy operations.

"Kruger!"

He recognized the toffy British accent but not the man speaking. Seated alongside one of the computer operators Al-Mumit wore filthy blood-stained fatigues. His face was drawn and haggard, his eyes bloodshot. The middle-aged Somali barely resembled the three-piece suit-wearing lord from three months earlier.

Al-Mumit rose and walked toward Kruger with an outstretched hand. "It's good to see you."

He shook the man's hand. "You look like you've been in the wars."

Al-Mumit nodded. "Yes, Al-Shabaab attacked us with little warning. I lost a lot of men."

"I'm sorry to hear that."

"It's not the worst of it, I'm afraid. They raided a village not far from here, Dinlaabe. Over forty girls were abducted from a school. That's why I've requested your services."

Kruger's eyes narrowed. "What's the link? You're not one for charity and I don't work for free."

Al-Mumit clenched his jaw. "My cousin was one of the girls taken. I want you to find them, Kruger. I will support you with all the resources you need. Find them, recover the girls and kill the kidnappers."

Kruger scratched his chin. "These people are ruthless. I'm going to need a team of the best and that's not going to be cheap."

"Money is no obstacle."

"I can't promise we'll get them all back alive."

Al-Mumit nodded slowly. "Make them pay for every life they take."

Kruger extended his hand and the Pirate King grasped it. "That will be my pleasure."

As he drove back through Mogadishu toward the

airport he already had a plan forming in his mind. He'd set up a base of operations at Al-Mumit's compound. His old friend Toppie would provide weapons and logistics.

What he needed now were competent men. He knew a couple of recce squadron boys that would be keen. However, he also needed a lieutenant. He didn't want to get PRIMAL involved, but that didn't mean he couldn't use one of the men on stand down. Kurtz had already contacted him, itching for some action. The lanky German was good in a gunfight, brutally efficient and smarter than his recce mates. Pulling to the side of the road he found the German's number in his iPRIMAL and dialed it on a satellite phone. Kurtz picked up within three rings.

"How's it, bro. It's Kruger."

"You got a job for me?"

"*Ja*, anti-kidnapping in Somalia. You in?"

"That depends," Kurtz said.

"On what?"

"Is it dangerous?"

He grinned. "Very."

"*Gut*. Send through the details."

"Will do, stand by." He ended the call. Just like that he had a second-in-command. He contemplated calling Bishop but dismissed the idea. The Australian needed some downtime after his last hit out in Africa. Anyway, Kruger knew he needed to keep PRIMAL involvement to the bare minimum. Hell, the organization was supposed to be on stand down. He laughed out loud. That wasn't likely to last.

Next in The PRIMAL Series

vinci-books.com/primal-exodus

**In the shadows, they fight. In the light, they fall.
PRIMAL Exodus: The reckoning begins.**

Turn the page for a free preview…

PRIMAL Exodus: Chapter One

LIFEBRIGHT FOUNDATION FACILITY, RWANDA

The truck came to a shuddering halt with a hiss of brakes and a belch of diesel fumes, slamming the twenty teenage girls crammed into the back against each other. Not a single one of the Somali schoolgirls cried out or complained. Shackled at the neck they sat quietly, dressed in filthy school uniforms as the tailgate dropped with a clang.

A girl, her friends called her Jamilah, turned as the canvas cover was lifted revealing the angry face of a white man dressed in a dark green uniform.

"Get out of the truck!" he bellowed.

As the girls filed from the vehicle Jamilah glanced sideways at another man who was standing with other Caucasian green-uniformed guards. He looked like a soldier, barrel-chested, thick-necked, with tattoos covering muscular forearms.

The girl in front of her stumbled. One of the guards caught her arm and effortlessly hoisted her upright. It was at that moment Jamilah noticed that these men didn't look at the girls like the rebel soldiers had. There was no lust on their faces, no leering or ogling as they shuffled across smooth concrete under powerful lights. No, these men paid scant attention to them. It sent a shiver up her spine as she recognized the look on the men's faces. She'd seen it before on the face of their village butcher as he selected cattle for slaughter.

As the girls shuffled under a roller door they were met by a team of masked medical staff and unshackled. From here Jamilah and the others were ordered to strip and forced to shower in open stalls. The water smelled of chemicals but at least it was warm. When they'd toweled themselves dry they were handed baggy blue smocks and pants.

Showered and clothed the confused teenagers were shepherded through double doors by the guards, into a rabbit warren of sterile corridors. Jamilah had lost all sense of direction when she was finally shoved into a tiny room with another girl and the door was locked.

Their cell was half the size of the hut where she lived with her mother and sister. It contained two hard-looking beds and a tiny alcove that housed a toilet and sink. As she inspected the amenities her cellmate, a girl from her class at school, slumped onto one of the beds and wept.

Jamilah sat alongside and wrapped an arm around her. "It's OK. Everything is going to be alright."

"How?" the girl blubbered. "We're miles from home and no one knows where we are."

"People will be looking for us, and they will find us."

"You don't know that," she said between gasps.

She was right. Jamilah had no way of knowing if anyone from their village was looking for them. A savage militia had taken her and her friends from their school.

Over a hundred of them, including her younger sister, had been snatched and transported to rebel camps across the border in Kenya. She'd last seen her sister in one of those squalid camps, before she'd been dragged away and loaded into a truck. Tears ran down her ebony cheeks as she remembered the fear on her sister's face and her terrified screams.

"Someone will come for us," she managed as she held her friend.

Little did Jamilah know that they were being watched. In his office Doctor Dennis Morrison was gazing at a screen that displayed the feed from hidden cameras in all fifteen of the facility's cells. Behind the elderly geneticist the head of security, Elias, stood with his muscled tattooed arms folded across his dark green uniform. Around his waist he wore a battle belt bristling with the tools of his trade: radio, pistol, magazines, a baton and handcuffs. Alongside him, dressed in a khaki shirt and slacks stood a middle-aged white man with a smooth bald head, Ross Krenich.

"How many more do you need?" asked Krenich, a Rhodesian-born smuggler.

Dr. Morrison turned from the monitors. "Quantity is not the issue. I'm concerned with the quality. Over half of the last shipment was diseased or infertile."

Krenich shrugged. "This is Africa, Doc. You get what the Lord intends."

"Then you're not going to get paid until all of the subjects have been screened."

"I've delivered twenty girls. I get paid for twenty girls," snapped Krenich.

"I'll pay double for healthy specimens."

"I selected the ones that looked good."

"Looks can be deceiving." The Doctor gestured to a low

table stacked with lunchbox-sized containers wrapped in shiny metal foil. "These are test kits. You can use them to check the girls' blood."

Krenich took one of the packages from the bench and examined it. "Easy to use?"

The Doctor nodded. "The instructions are simple. You take samples and then send them to me. My people will load them into your truck."

The smuggler tossed the kit back on the bench. "We test them and bring the healthy ones. Then you pay double?"

"Yes."

"Sounds like a deal. I'll see you in a week." Krenich gave the head of security a nod and departed the room.

The Doctor took a seat at his desk and unlocked his computer. "Are we going to have any problems disposing of the waste?" he asked as Elias made to leave.

"No, we'll incinerate them on site and ship the barrels out later. There will be no evidence."

"And the woman that's been sniffing around?"

"I'll take care of her."

"Good, now if you don't mind, I have a call to make."

The Doctor waited until his hulking head of security had left before he opened his Skype account. Checking the clock on the corner of the screen he confirmed it was time for his weekly update with the Proteus Program Director. On cue, a call request appeared from Marnisha Copeland, his boss. He accepted the call, and her elfin features appeared on the screen.

"Doctor Morrison, how are you this evening?" she asked.

"Very good, we've made some important progress this week."

PRIMAL Exodus: Chapter One

Marnisha's perfectly sculpted brow rose and she canted her head to one side. "Excellent."

Morrison swallowed, he found the senior geneticist's looks particularly disconcerting. Her long auburn hair, elegant neck and striking green eyes left him feeling flustered.

"Are you going to share the details?"

"Yes of course. We've had a breakthrough regarding the life-support system required to keep a womb alive outside of a body. I'm confident that within the next six months we will be able to birth one of your subjects without a host body."

Marnisha smiled, flashing near-perfect teeth. "That is exciting news. Well done, Dennis. Are you still having problems with the quality of your test subjects?"

"I'm confident that they will be improving in the short term."

"Excellent."

Doctor Morrison managed a nervous smile. "Is there any chance of an increase in funding? Acquiring optimal test specimens is getting expensive."

"With any luck. Now, talk me through the details of how you've managed to halt the deterioration of the host cells."

As the Doctor outlined the details of his procedure he gave the screen showing the cells a cursory glance. The medical staff had commenced testing of the new subjects. With any luck, one of them would provide the womb that would allow the next evolution in artificial birthing.

PRIMAL Exodus: Chapter One

NYAGATARE, RWANDA

Less than thirty miles from the facility where Jamilah was imprisoned, in the town of Nyagatare, Bianca Paquet strolled through the city's only upmarket hotel and positioned herself at the bar. The CityBlue hotel was a recent addition to the town; sleek, modern and utterly soulless. She had no intention of spending any more time there than required.

Athletic with short blonde hair and defined angular features, the thirty-two-year-old immediately drew the attention of every man in the venue, much to the chagrin of the hookers on the lookout for clients. Leaning over the polished bar she cocked one long tanned leg up from under her floral print summer dress revealing a Converse sneaker.

"What are you having?" the waist-jacketed bartender asked.

"What beer do you have?"

"Primus or Skol."

Bianca, a French Canadian, had been in Rwanda for over a month and was familiar with the local brews. "I'll have a Primus, please."

He took a beer from a fridge, flicked off the cap and slid it across the bar. She took a few greasy US dollars from in her bra and left them on the counter before turning and surveying the room. Her grey eyes swept from left to right evaluating everyone sitting at the low tables and then the few men standing at the black marble bar. The man she wanted to speak to was sitting alone at the corner, studying his phone. He was a security guard at a local medical facility.

Taking a swig from her beer she swept her hand through her short blonde hair and moved along the bar. A moment later the guard looked up from his phone and she flashed him a smile. He grinned back as he slipped the device into a pocket of his jacket and approached.

"Hello," he said with a South African accent. "I haven't seen you here before."

The man was tall with ebony skin and a chiseled jaw. Bianca guessed his age at early thirties, and probably, like her, ex-military. However, he'd taken a different path post-service, choosing to work for a corporation, whereas she was in Africa to teach children.

"I'm new in town."

His eyes narrowed. "Are you French?"

She shook her head and she sipped her beer. "No, I'm from Canada."

"Ah, yes. And what brings you to Nyagatare? No, let me guess. You're a doctor working with the WHO?"

"Close, I do work for the UN."

"So you are a doctor?"

"No, I work in logistics. I'm here to help non-profit organizations move more resources into the area." She paused. "What do you do?"

"Me, I'm in security. It's boring, but it pays the bills. By the way, my name is David."

"I'm Bianca, a pleasure to meet you, David."

"Are you staying here?" he asked.

"I should be so lucky. No, they've put me up in a dump across town. Where do you live?" Bianca continued the small talk, looking for any angle to pry into the guard's role at the medical facility and what he may have seen or heard. Twenty minutes and another drink later she'd made no progress and was doubtful about the rumors of kidnapped children. Politely excusing herself she left the bar.

Bianca sighed as she exited the hotel. The reality was

that her time in Rwanda was coming to an end. Her job teaching children had been satisfying but the non-profit had closed, funding drying up. Reluctant to return to Canada, she'd decided to investigate rumors of kidnapped children but that too seemed to be a dead end.

Flagging a cab she rode it through the dusty streets in the direction of her hotel. Nyagatare was a surprisingly clean township considering it was home to a population of fifty-two thousand Rwandans, most living well below the poverty line. The buildings were low slung and built primarily of mud brick with tin roofs that sweltered under the African sun.

She frowned as the cab slowed and the driver pulled over to the side of the road. "Why are you stopping?"

"I don't want any trouble," the driver said as he glanced up at the rearview mirror.

Bianca checked over her shoulder and saw a black four-wheel drive parked a distance behind them. "Keep driving."

"I don't want any trouble."

"I'll give you trouble," she hissed as she slid a thin fighting knife from a sheath fastened high on the inside of her thigh.

The driver took one look at the blade and jumped out of the vehicle.

"Son-of-a-bitch."

Bianca glanced over her shoulder and saw that two men had left the four-wheel drive and were approaching. She checked the front of the cab. The driver had taken the keys and she didn't have enough time to hotwire it. Instead, she chose to leave the cab and confront the men with her knife hidden behind her wrist.

"Can I help you?" she asked as the two men stopped a short distance from her. They were both black and dressed in cargo pants with khaki shirts worn loose over T-shirts. They had the same bearing as David, who'd no doubt tipped them off.

"Boss wants to talk to you."

Bianca smiled as she took a business card from her bra and flicked it at the man. "Well, then he can contact my office in Kigali."

The man opened his shirt enough that Bianca could see his pistol in its holster.

She grimaced. "Fine, lead the way."

They directed her to the rear seats of a black Toyota Landcruiser. One of them opened a door and she looked inside. A thick-necked white guy with tattooed forearms sat in the back.

"Get in."

"I'm good here."

One of the men placed a hand on her shoulder and she twisted out from under it and struck him in the throat with her palm. He doubled over, coughing. The other man pulled his pistol and aimed it at her head.

"You going to use that?" Bianca asked as she let her knife slide down into her hand.

The boss in the four-wheel drive shook his head and the man holstered his gun.

"So what's this about?" she asked.

"I was hoping you could tell me," said the guy inside.

Bianca shot him a look implying she had no idea what he was talking about.

"Rwanda isn't a safe place for a pretty blonde. Keep sticking your nose in where it's not wanted and you're going to find out first hand." He waved his men into their vehicle and drove away, leaving Bianca with the abandoned cab.

Intimidation was something that she had lived with her

entire life. She'd faced bullies throughout her childhood and into her military career, never being dissuaded her from her goals. Plus, whoever the guy was in the four-wheel drive, he'd just confirmed there was definitely something worth investigating at the medical facility.

She sheathed her knife as she strode back to the cab. As she reached the driver's door there was a shout from her left and the cabbie appeared from behind some bushes. "The meter is still running," he announced cheerfully.

"Only in Africa," she mumbled as she climbed into the back seat.

Grab your copy...
vinci-books.com/primal-exodus

About the Author

Jack Silkstone grew up on a steady diet of Tom Clancy, James Bond, Jason Bourne, Commando comics, and the original first-person shooters, Wolfenstein and Doom. His background includes a career in military intelligence and special operations, working alongside some of the world's most elite units. His love of action-adventure stories, his military background, and his real-world experiences combined to inspire the no-holds-barred PRIMAL series.